SPUN YARNS UNWOUND: VOL. 3

FANTASY FOR ALL

DEBBIE MUMFORD

DEB LOGAN

WDM Publishing

FANTASY FOR ALL

This volume of Spun Yarns Unwound contains fantasy stories written by WDM Publishing's authors.

Deb Logan loves to write contemporary fantasy for younger readers, and these eight tales provide an overview of her style. They start with tales for early readers, then move to middle grade fantasy, before ending with tales for teens.

Debbie Mumford has enjoyed reading fairy tales and fantasy since childhood and writes its short form as often as she can find the time.

So sit back, relax, and enjoy the magic our authors create!

COPYRIGHT

EIGHT STORIES BY DEB LOGAN

PART I
THE FOX AND THE FLEAS

DEB LOGAN

AUTHOR OF *THUNDERBIRD*

THE FOX AND THE FLEAS

A "READ-TO-ME" STORY

$\mathcal{R}$ ory Fox sat beside his den on the grassy hillside. He scratched his furry red ears. A moment later he nipped at his back leg. Then he nibbled his shoulder.

Mother Fox looked up from grooming her long, bushy tail. "What's wrong, Rory?" she asked. "Why are you nipping and scratching?"

"I have fleas, Mother." He looked at her and blinked back tears. "They're biting me all over. I can't catch them with my teeth. What can I do?"

Mother Fox stood and flicked her ears. "Come with me, my son. It's time you learned how a fox deals with fleas."

So Rory followed his mother to the edge of Farmer McNabb's field. Once there, Mother Fox sat down and curled her tail around her toes. Rory tried to copy her, but the biting fleas made it hard to sit still.

"Now, Rory," she said, "do you see Mrs. Sheep out there in the meadow?"

Rory used his keen eyes to peer across the field. "Yes, Mother. She has her twin lambs with her."

Mother Fox nodded. "You must go and ask Mrs. Sheep for a bit of her wool. When you have it, meet me at the pond by those trees." She pointed her long nose at a thicket across the meadow. "Be polite, my son."

"Yes, ma'am," said Rory, and he trotted over to Mrs. Sheep.

As he approached the family, Rory said, "Good day, Mrs. Sheep." He sat down in the sun-warmed grass and tried not to squirm as the fleas bit his rump.

Mrs. Sheep stepped between Rory and her twins. "Wha-a-at can I do-o-o for yo-o-ou, little fox?" she asked.

"My mother told me to ask if you could spare a little wool," Rory answered, politely bowing his head.

"Wha-a-at do yo-o-ou want with wo-o-ol?" asked Mrs. Sheep.

"I'm being bitten by fleas," he admitted. "Mother is going to teach me how a fox deals with fleas."

"Ah-h-h," said Mrs. Sheep.

"Ah-h-h," echoed her lambs.

"There's a patch of my wo-o-ol on that stump by the thicket," Mrs. Sheep said. "Yo-o-ou are welcome to use it."

"Thank you, Mrs. Sheep," Rory said, remembering his manners.

Rory retrieved the scrap of wool and bounded off to find his mother. The fleas were biting his front legs now. He was very tired of being itchy.

He found Mother Fox sitting serenely beside the pond. She nodded her head when she saw the scrap of wool in Rory's mouth.

"Well done, my son," she said. "Now listen carefully. If you follow my instructions, the fleas will soon be gone."

Rory cocked his ears forward to catch every word. He wanted to do this right. He wanted the fleas to go away.

"You must hold the wool by the very edge, so almost none is in your mouth."

Rory laid the scrap on the ground and carefully picked it up by the smallest corner.

Mother Fox nodded. "Now, walk over to the pond and dip the tip of your tail in the water."

Rory obeyed. He felt the fleas run from his tail and move toward his rump.

"Now," said his mother, "move slowly and steadily backwards into the water."

Rory began to move. As each piece of his body went under the water, he felt the fleas run up to dry skin.

"That's right," said Mother Fox. "Keep going back until only your nose is above the water."

Rory hesitated. He could swim, but he didn't like getting his face wet.

"Trust me, Rory," said Mother Fox. "When only your nose is left above water, let the wool float away."

Rory took a deep breath and followed his mother's advice. As his head sank below the water's surface, he felt the fleas run across his nose and onto the wool. When the last flea jumped from the tip of his nose, he let go of the wool and swam straight to the shore.

Mother Fox sat in the cool grass with her tail wrapped tightly around her paws. She smiled a foxy smile as Rory shook the water from his coat and raced around the meadow. At last he flopped down beside her, happy that the fleas were gone.

"Well done, my son," she said. "Now you know how a fox deals with fleas."

PART II
A TRICKSTER HALLOWEEN

A Trickster Halloween

A Prentiss Twins Story

Deb Logan

Author of *Thunderbird*

CHAPTER 1

*H*alloween in Bozeman, Montana can be brisk, to say the least. Not that Justin or Janine Prentiss intended to let a little cool weather stop them from trick-or-treating. The Prentiss twins had grown up in Bozeman, so cold weather just meant dressing appropriately, and this evening's forecast of 45 degrees barely even qualified as cold!

"Don't forget your neck gaiters," Dad called from the kitchen where he was getting the cauldron of candy ready to hand out to the neighborhood kids who would soon descend on the front door.

Janine rolled her eyes. "It's bad enough wearing a winter coat under this witch costume, but a neck gaiter too?"

Justin shrugged his shoulders. "You can always ditch it once we clear the driveway, but you know you won't get out of the house without it." He grinned, which looked really odd beneath his carefully applied zombie face paint. "Besides, if you grab Dad's black one instead of your usual hot pink and purple stripe, it'll make you look all mysterious if your pull it up so only your eyes are showing."

"Good point," Janny said, grabbing Dad's favorite black polar fleece gaiter. "What're you using?"

"I thought ahead and borrowed a bright red one from Kent. I figure it'll look like my neck's been slashed."

"Oooo... good thinking!"

Just then Coyote raced into the entry hall, claws clicking on the hardwood floor. "How do I look?" he demanded as he skidded to a stop at Justin's side.

Justin beamed at his spirit animal and bond mate. Coyote made being a shaman with magical powers worth all the dangers they sometimes faced. Justin had always considered the stories of the furry trickster his shaman grandfather's best, but to discover last summer that Coyote— not just any coyote, but *the* Coyote—had chosen him, Justin Prentiss, to be his shaman and bond mate, well, unbelievable didn't begin to scratch the surface!

"You look great," Justin said, scratching behind Coyote's ears in just the right spot and admiring the dirty white bandages that wound around Coyote's body and dripped from his tail. "You make an awesome mummy-dog. Did Dad help you?"

Coyote flopped onto the floor, his tongue lolling out happily. "Nope. Winona used her magic. The wrappings aren't real, but they'll fool all the people we see tonight."

Janine laughed and sent a thought of thanks winging into her spirit animal's mind.

Winona. The mighty thunderbird.

Janine was the luckiest girl in the world!

I'm glad you are pleased with my efforts, She Who Cares for Thunderbirds. Consider it my contribution to the evening's festivities.

Janine nodded, though Winona wasn't in the house to see. The thunderbird had grown too large to enter the residence, though she often rested on the back deck just outside the sliding patio door.

Invisible, of course.

It wouldn't do to start a panic in the neighborhood by having a thunderbird, who looked a lot like a giant pterosaur, visible to anyone who walked past the house.

I just wish you could come with us, Winona.

I will shadow you from the sky, my shaman. You will never be alone while I live.

I know, but sometimes I wish I could show you off the way Justin can Coyote!

Ahh, but your friends and neighbors will not see Coyote, Winona replied sensibly. *They will see a pet dog dressed as a mummy. Cute, but far from the powerful trickster we know him to be.*

Janine sighed. *You're right, of course. Justin and I are lucky that Dad and Grandpa know our secret.*

Indeed, your father and Steadfast Guide are unique among mortal men.

"All right," called Justin, breaking into Janine's silent communication with her thunderbird. "Let's get this show on the road."

Dad came around the corner from the kitchen carrying the large plastic cauldron of candy. He inspected their costumes, nodded his approval, and waved them out the door with a cheerful, "Have fun!"

*T*wo hours later the troops returned home with tired feet, faces and fingers chilled to the bone, and bags full of candy. Beat, but happy, Justin and Janine shrugged out of costumes and coats while Coyote released his mummy wrappings in a sparkle of magical dust. Winona, from her perch on the back deck, offered to whisk away the twins' face paint as well, but they declined, deciding to wait and wash it off later. The make-up made a cool reminder of the fun they'd just had.

Coyote flopped onto the carpeting in the family room beside Justin while the twins upended their bags of candy and began sorting it into piles. The doorbell still rang occasionally and they heard Dad's voice boom as he greeted late trick-or-treaters.

"Well," said Coyote. "This has certainly been an interested look into human psychology."

Justin snorted. "What's that supposed to mean?"

Coyote chewed on the pads of his front paw. "Only that I've heard of Halloween, and am aware of its ancient origins, but seeing its practice in modern day is enlightening."

"Enlightening?" Janine said, looking up from her treats, her voice puzzled. "How?"

"Humans have chosen to forget us," Coyote said after giving his paw a final lick. "They have relegated us to myth and legend, and yet, when it benefits them— for the gathering of sweet treats and the opportunity to play innocent tricks— they can still find us in the depths of their minds."

Coyote speaks the truth, agreed Winona. *We are not as forgotten as modern society would like to believe.*

"I suppose," said Justin, tossing a hard candy into the air and catching it in his mouth, "but I could care less about the reasons we celebrate Halloween." He grinned a ghastly face-painted smile at Coyote and Janine. "I just like the treats... and the chance to trick my friends without getting in trouble!"

Janine laughed, but Coyote snorted and rolled on the floor.

"Tricksters for the win!" he yipped happily.

PART III
THE TWELVE DAYS OF TRICKSTERS

The Twelve Days of Tricksters
A Prentiss Twins Story

Deb Logan
Author of *Thunderbird*

CHAPTER 1

*J*ake Prentiss woke with a start, sitting up in bed straight-backed and bleary-eyed. Blinking sleep from his eyes, he glanced around his bedroom wondering what could have roused him from a deep, sound sleep so suddenly? Nothing looked out of place. Early morning light was just filtering around the window blinds painting the room with dim, not yet distinct colors. The air was cool—he always turned the heat down overnight—but not cold. Especially not as cold as might be expected for Bozeman, Montana in mid-December.

Well, he was awake. He might as well get up and check the rest of the house, though he couldn't imagine anything or anyone entering his home unnoticed; not with the twins' bond animals on duty. Throwing back the covers, he swung his legs off the bed, stuffed his feet into sheepskin lined slippers, and pulled on the warm flannel robe Emilia had given him more than a decade ago. He fingered the well-worn shawl collar, remembering. The twins had just turned three that Christmas. They'd been a happy, busy, young family. A complete family. By the next Christmas, the twins had been motherless and he'd been a widower.

Sighing, he knotted the belt around his waist and moved to his bedroom door. This robe was getting old. He really needed to buy a new one. After all, the twins were thirteen now. Teenagers. Emilia's babies were teenagers now. He sure wished she could see them. She'd be so proud. Of course, he also wished she were here to help him navigate the suddenly turbulent waters of parenting. There was just so much he didn't understand. He really wished his wife were alive to help him with all the decisions, choices that could affect the rest of the twins' lives.

His reverie was broken by a high-pitched shriek. Not his daughter's—thank all that was holy—but not something that belonged in his home either. He yanked the bedroom door open and raced down the hall to the family room. Where he skidded to a halt.

Why was there a cherry tree growing from the middle of the family room floor? And was that a parakeet hopping between the branches and shrieking?

"On the first day of Christmas," laughing voices sang, "my tricksters gave to me a parakeet in a cherry tree!"

Jake stumbled to his favorite overstuffed chair and dropped into it. Except for the tree growing out of the plush beige carpeting, the room looked completely normal for this time of year. The Christmas tree sparkled in the corner, its many strings of multi-colored lights giving it a merry glow. A fire crackled in the hearth, lighting the five festive stockings hung from the mantle. Dawn light crept across the floor from the patio door at the far end of the room, where the family room opened into the kitchen, its sliding glass providing a view of the snow-covered deck.

Well, not completely snow-covered. The wide oblong where his daughter's thunderbird habitually rested (invisible to normal human eyes) was suspiciously snow-free. He frowned. If Winona was on the deck, then Janine must be... he scanned the room and found his daughter curled on the sofa, clearly enjoying his confusion.

But Janine wasn't a trickster. No, the voices that had sung had been her twin brother Justin and his spirit animal, Coyote...a trickster if ever there was one. A small, wry smile tugged at Jake's lips as he closed his eyes and massaged his temples.

Emilia would never believe what her babies had grown into. Especially since last summer.

"Really, Justin?" he asked. "A cherry tree in the family room? Besides, isn't it supposed to be a pear tree? With a partridge?"

Justin popped out from behind the couch where Janine sat curled, Coyote padding beside him. "I like cherries better than pears," he said with a mischievous grin, "and parakeets are more fun than partridges." He glanced at the small green and yellow bird. "Did you know parakeets can talk? Even without any magical prodding?"

Jake nodded, his eyes still closed. "I've never had one, but a friend did when I was a boy. It only had a few words, but it definitely talked."

Opening his eyes he studied his son. Justin and Janine were very alike in looks, except for the gender difference which was growing more pronounced every year. Both had straight black hair, copper skin, long straight noses, and high cheek bones. Both were athletic, a good thing considering the many adventures they'd had since Janine had discovered the egg that had hatched a thunderbird. His daughter hadn't wanted to go to field camp in the Absaroka Mountains last summer, but Jake had insisted. And look where *that* decision had led!

Jake drew a deep breath and exhaled slowly. Looked at in a particular light, everything that had happened to his kids was his fault. If he wasn't a paleontologist... if he didn't lead digs at field camps every summer... if he didn't insist that his children accompany him on those digs... but he was and he did and Janine had found what looked like a rock, but was really a living egg.

He shook himself. What was done was done and couldn't be changed. And truthfully, he wasn't sure he'd want it to—and he knew without a doubt that neither of his children would wish for the events of last summer to change.

He pushed his concerns away and resumed his study of Justin. The similarity between the twins ended with their looks. Much like her thunderbird, Janine was quiet and contemplative. But Justin? His son was anything but quiet. Justin was the proverbial man of action. Always in motion; had been since birth. Why even when Emilia had held him in her arms to nurse him, Justin's tiny feet had drummed against the arm of her chair.

And smart? Both the twins were too smart for their own good, but Justin.... Well, Jake had always known that scheming was Justin's super power. At least, he'd thought so until he'd discovered that his thirteen-year-old son was a shaman bonded to a trickster demi-god … and a powerful magic user to boot! For on his thirteenth birthday, Justin had discovered that he was a *skin walker*, able to shift from an adolescent boy to a coyote in the blink of an eye.

And Jake had thought being a single parent of twins was tough!

"Seriously though, Justin," Jake said with a sigh. "What's with the tree? Christmas isn't for another two weeks." He glanced at Janine. "Are you in on this too?"

His daughter raised her hands and shook her head, aiming a long-suffering glance at her twin brother. "Nope. This is all Justin, though I'm sure Coyote was lots of help."

Coyote didn't respond. He simply sat on his haunches with his bushy tail wrapped around his paws and stared at the cherry tree, pride and admiration shining in his canine eyes.

Justin cleared his throat. "Coyote and I know exactly what day it is, Dad. It's Friday, December 13th."

Jake suppressed a shiver. Friday the thirteenth… and he was sitting in a room with a couple of dedicated tricksters. He could hardly wait.

"We've decided to treat you to a *traditional* Christmas this year," Justin continued, gesturing to the cherry tree, "and this is our opening gift."

"Uhm, Justin," Janine said, her eyes sparkling with mirth, "don't you have your dates wrong? The twelve days of Christmas usually don't start until Christmas Day."

"Whatever," her twin brother replied, waving away her objection. "We're not *that* traditional. Coyote and I have everything worked out to perfection."

"Right," Janine said. "You two do know that starting on the thirteenth means your twelfth day will be on Christmas Eve, not Christmas Day, don't you?"

Justin glared at her. "Of course we know." His face relaxed into a mischievous grin. "Trust me, Janny. We have everything under control."

Janine rolled her eyes, and Jake dropped his head into his hands.

*T*he next few days were a nightmare as far as Jake Prentiss was concerned. He went to bed each night dreading the next morning and the revelation of Justin and Coyote's next *gift*, not to mention their goofy rendition of the traditional Christmas carol. The song got longer and sillier with each passing day.

On the second day of Christmas... Jake woke to a pair of crows flying around his bedroom and cawing loudly.

On Sunday, the third day, three fat mallard ducks waddled past his desk as he worked on his computer in his home office, quickly followed by his son and Coyote popping in—literally! one minute they weren't anywhere around, the next they stood beside the mallards—to sing for him.

Day four brought four western meadowlarks swooping through his office at The Museum of the Rockies, their song echoing off the ceiling.

Tuesday, the fifth day, was actually a relief. No birds to shoo out of house or office. Instead, Justin presented him with a protective amulet woven from hairs from the five members of his family: Justin, Coyote,

Janine, Thunderbird, and Jake's father, a shaman known to the spirit animals as *Steadfast Guide*. Hmmm. Maybe all of this wasn't Jake's fault after all. Maybe his dad's beliefs had set everything in motion.

The gifts went downhill from there.

On Wednesday, six dozen duck eggs were delivered to his home before breakfast.

Thursday night he found seven tiny swans swimming in his bathtub.

Eight milkweed plants were discovered in the museum's exhibit of fossilized dinosaur eggs on Friday.

A bouquet of nine pink and yellow lady's slipper flowers rested beside his plate of bacon and eggs on Saturday morning.

On Sunday, Jake's boss, Dr. Abernathy, called him in for a special meeting. Jake arrived only to find ten flyfishing lures decorating his desk… just as his boss stepped inside. That had been a true nightmare. Papers skewered by hooks in lures from black ghosts to woolly buggers, and Jake trying to explain to Dr. Abernathy that despite appearances Jake hadn't been spending his days tying lures instead of working on the important exhibit they were there to discuss. Fortunately, Justin and Coyote had waited until Jake returned home before serenading him with that blasted ever-lengthening song.

Yesterday had set Jake's last nerve on edge. Justin and Coyote had not only popped into his office themselves… they'd brought an eleven member pipe and drum corps with them. And every single member had been decked out in full regalia, including kilts! Jake still wasn't sure how his coworkers had missed that show since the corps had marched through the museum, bagpipes screeching.

Probably magic.

What was he thinking? Undoubtedly magic!

Today was the twelfth day. The tricksters' grand finale. Jake had been bracing himself all day, but his work day was at an end and nothing had happened. Yet.

As Jake trudged through the deepening snow to his car, he ticked off items on his to-do list. Today was Christmas Eve. The museum would be closed until next Monday, so he had a few days of peace. As if anything about life with his magical children could be called peaceful! But tomorrow was Christmas, and Jake had been so preoccupied with the aftermath of Justin's nonsense that he hadn't found time to wrap gifts and place them beneath the tree. Fortunately, he'd done his shopping early, so wrapping was all that he'd left to the last minute. That and filling the stockings, of course. He smiled thinking of the five stockings hanging on his mantle. This time last year he'd never have guessed that he'd need stockings for Thunderbird and Coyote! What a difference a year had made.

He drove home in a swirl of snow. Having a white Christmas was never a concern in Bozeman, but this year it looked like they might be in for an actual blizzard. Fortunately, once he got home, Jake and the twins would have no need to leave the house again for several days. They had plenty of food, a good supply of firewood should they lose power, and even several gallons of bottled water.

Not to mention magic.

He didn't know why he worried about things like food and shelter when Coyote and Thunderbird, not to mention his own children, could obtain anything they needed with magic. At least, he thought they could. But what did he know? He was just an ordinary guy with an extraordinary family.

Jake pulled the family Range Rover into the garage, parked, and headed for the door into the kitchen. Pausing, he braced himself. There was still the twelfth gift to endure, and it was bound to be a doozy. After all, the traditional song called for twelve drummers drumming. He winced. He'd already survived a pipe and drum corps, how many more drums could he take?

Taking a deep breath, he pasted a smile on his face and opened the door.

CHAPTER 3

*J*ustin fairly danced with excitement. He could hardly wait for Dad to get home. This was day twelve of Dad's Christmas gift, and he and Coyote had worked really hard to make sure this was a twelfth night Dad would never forget.

"Are you sure everything is ready?" he asked Coyote.

Coyote rolled over on the plush beige carpeting of the family room and wriggled, scratching his back. "Of course," he yipped. "Just like it was the last twenty or thirty times you asked."

Justin stuck his tongue out at his bond animal before turning to his twin sister. "You and Thunderbird are ready too. Right?"

Janine rolled her eyes. "Yes, Justin. Relax. Winona and I are ready to follow wherever you and Coyote go. The only one you should be worried about is Dad. Have you given him any warning? His last trip through the Spirit World wasn't all that great, you know."

Justin grimaced. "I remember." He'd been incredibly proud of how his dad and his grandpa both had handled the battle with Unktehi, the demi-god of Chaos. "But this isn't the same thing at all. We won't be staying in the Spirit World, just passing through."

Janine cocked her head and narrowed her eyes. "Passing through to where?"

Justin grinned. He loved knowing something Janny didn't. "You'll find out soon enough. Now, we just need Dad."

Coyote rolled over and sat up, ears pricked forward. "Is that the Range Rover I hear?"

Justin concentrated, but didn't hear anything beyond the howl of the wind. He considered changing skins, becoming a coyote, but rejected the idea. He didn't need his other form's enhanced hearing, Coyote would listen for him. Besides, he needed to be a human boy when Dad walked through that door. If he were wearing his coyote skin, Dad would freak. He'd seen Justin transform before, of course, but Dad was much more comfortable with his son as a boy, and Coyote and Justin were about to make Dad uncomfortable enough without starting him out freaked.

A few minutes later, everyone clearly heard the Range Rover pull into the garage and park. It was almost time...and Justin danced from one foot to the other in excitement. This was going to be so cool. Beyond cool. Absolutely frigid!

Dad stepped into the kitchen, shrugging out of his down coat, and Justin and Coyote burst into song.

"On the first day of Christmas," they sang, "my tricksters gave to me a parakeet in a cherry tree!" On and on they sang until they came to *twelve tricksters tricking*, at which point Coyote opened a portal to the Spirit World and Justin grabbed his dad's arm and yanked him through.

CHAPTER 4

*J*ake struggled to regain his balance as his son pulled him through what he recognized as a portal to the Spirit World. *Twelve tricksters tricking?* What in the world did that mean? Why the portal? Where was Justin taking him? Jake's mind reeled with questions, none of which had answers. He gulped, pushed the questions aside, and concentrated on steadying himself. He trusted Justin. Whatever this was, it was the culmination of a gift. Justin wouldn't design a gift that would harm his dad. At least, not on purpose.

Pushing his worries aside, Jake looked around. He stood in a wide meadow under a clear blue sky, with what could only be a banyan tree in front of him. A massive banyan tree.

"About time," Justin called, causing Jake to turn around in time to see Janine and her thunderbird step through the portal.

"We are here as requested," Thunderbird said. "Greetings, Dr. Prentiss."

Jake nodded his acknowledgement. Normally he couldn't even see Thunderbird, let alone hear her speak. At home, she communicated telepathically with Janine, who then told everyone else what her bond animal had said. Jake had seen her before of course, but her appearance always surprised him. She looked like one of the pterosaurs he studied as a paleontologist. The size of a small elephant, her wings were formed by a membrane of skin and muscle that stretched from her ankles to a dramatically lengthened fourth finger. When she walked, she folded her wings upward and carried her weight on her knuckles. Her nut brown hide was covered in short, cinnamon colored fur, and her long neck supported a slender crested head with brilliant green eyes and a long narrow beak.

"All righty," barked Coyote. "Let's get this party started."

"Uhm, party?" Jake asked. "Your song said *twelve tricksters tricking*. Nothing about a party," he paused and glanced around, "and there are only two of you. Tricksters, I mean."

"Astute as always, Dr. Prentiss," Coyote barked. "I just meant, let's keep moving."

"Right," Justin said, a huge grin spreading across his face. "We're not there yet."

"And where exactly is *there*?" Jake asked, planting his feet and distributing his weight to keep Justin from yanking him off balance again.

Justin huffed and fisted his hands on his hips. He glared at Dad before glancing at Coyote. Coyote cocked his head and flicked his tail, his version of a shrug. Justin deflated a bit and threw out his hands.

"Fine," he said. "I wanted it to be a surprise, but we're going to Monkey King's banyan tree on Victoria Peak."

"You're taking me to Hong Kong?" Jake asked, his eyes wide.

Justin grinned. "Yep. Surprised?"

Jake nodded, swallowed, and said, "And tricked."

Coyote chased his tail in a circle, then stopped and said, "Can we go now? The Trickster Tribe is waiting!"

Jake closed his eyes and massaged his temples. "The whole tribe?" he asked, his voice barely louder than a whisper.

Justin danced from one foot to the other. Excitement shown in his eyes. "As many as can manage to get there. Come on, Dad! They're waiting, and I can hardly wait for you to meet everyone!"

Jake nodded, and Coyote opened a portal in the base of the banyan tree. All five of them stepped through into a jungle teeming with creatures of legend. The first to catch and hold Jake's eye was a monkey dressed in red and gold silk. At least, Jake thought it was a monkey. The creature was as tall as Jake and could have been the missing link between tree-dwelling monkeys and human beings. He wore soft, baggy pants gathered at waist and ankle, and a short vest. A gold band circled his furry head, and a single ruby dangled between his eyebrows.

Justin grabbed Jake's arm and dragged him closer to the creature, who sat on a living throne woven of banyan roots and runners. Giving a slight bow, Justin said, "Monkey King, this is my father, Dr. Jake Prentiss." Turning to Jake, he continued, "Dad, this is Monkey King, trickster god of China and chief of the Trickster Tribe."

Monkey King inclined his head. "Welcome, Dr. Prentiss. The Trickster Tribe is very pleased to claim your son as one of our number." The creature leaned forward and said quietly, "He's worked very hard on this gift. You have raised a fine son."

Jake nodded. "Thank you, Monkey King. I'm honored to meet you. Justin is very proud of you and your friendship."

Monkey King clapped and leapt from his throne. "Come, let me introduce you to our twelve tricksters. Coyote and Justin you already know, so besides me, there are nine others for you to meet."

Jake's head reeled as he met each trickster god. So many legends all in one place. And all real. As a scientist, a paleontologist, Jake had always relegated the tales his shaman father told to the realm of fantasy, just as he had all the other myths of the world. Until his twin children brought him face to face with two creatures of legend: Thunderbird and Coyote. Now he met ten more and he fought to expand his understanding of his world.

Monkey King was as real as Thunderbird and Coyote. So were the other nine.

Puck, also known as Robin Goodfellow, was a trickster out of the lore of the British Isles.

Kitsune, a small red fox with several tails, told him of her fame in Japanese mythology.

Anansi was polite enough, but the giant spider well known to the Ashanti people of Ghana in West Africa made him nervous. Spiders, even normal sized ones, weren't his favorite creatures.

Jake was more at ease with Azeban, the trickster raccoon associated with the Abenaki and Penobscot people of New England.

Kutkh, a raven from Eastern Russia, reminded him of the crows who were the namesake of his own tribe of birth.

Loki, Hermes, and Maui all wore human form, which made them much easier for Jake to relate to though they represented far flung cultures. Loki was Norse, Hermes, Greek, and Maui, Polynesian.

Last came Kokopelli of the Native American tribes of the desert southwest. Jake liked the hump-backed flute player, but couldn't decide if the trickster reminded him more of a man or an insect.

When the introductions were complete, Monkey King clapped his hands and announced, "Now that everyone knows each other, let the celebration begin."

Immediately tables appeared laden with every kind of food imaginable. Trickster Tribe roared their approval and fell upon the feast. Each was quick to point out their favorite delicacies to Jake. Janine and Thunderbird seemed as at ease with the food as they were with the tricksters. Jake marveled as much at his daughter's calm acceptance as at his son's friends. His children truly were extraordinary.

And speaking of extraordinary, the food piled on the tables was unexpected and delicious. Jake sampled sushi rolls from Japan, sticky rice, fish, and crisp vegetables rolled in seaweed wrappers. From Africa, Anansi's home, came a delectable mixture of rice and beans he called *Waakye*. Maui insisted Jake try a drink called *Nectar of the Islands*. Whatever was in it, the drink refreshed Jake and calmed his nerves, helping him feel more at home among this amazing group.

At last Jake settled himself on a banyan root beside his son. Justin was happily devouring a bacon cheeseburger along with a side of fries smothered in chili-cheese sauce.

"Think that'll hold you until we get home?" Jake asked, nudging Justin's shoulder and grinning.

Justin wiped his mouth on his sleeve and laughed. "Probably. How about you? Did you find enough to eat?"

"Definitely," Jake said, patting his belly. "If I ate like this all the time I'd be as round as Santa Claus." He stopped and stared at Justin, eyes wide. "You don't suppose…"

Justin grinned and nodded. "Yep. He's real too. Janny and I haven't met him yet, but the stories Monkey King and Kutkh tell… well, let's just say they're very exciting!"

They sat in comfortable silence for a few minutes while Justin finished his meal. Finally, Jake turned to his son, a solemn expression on his face.

"Thank you, Justin. This twelve days gift has been, well, unique and memorable." He cleared his throat as his emotions tried to clog it. "I'll admit, some of it annoyed me, but this," he gestured around the clearing beneath the banyan tree, "this has been amazing. I'm honored that you would think to introduce me to these tricksters, and that they would take the time to meet me." He stopped, swallowed, and took a deep breath. "You're growing into a fine man, Justin, Your mother would be proud of you. I know I certainly am, and I'm even more proud to be your father."

Justin ducked his head, a blush staining his cheeks. "Thanks, Dad. I'm glad you're okay with all of this," he gestured to the members of Trickster Tribe, "and with what Janine and I… well, what we are." He looked up and met his father's gaze. "I know you could've been disappointed or angry or tried to force us to be normal. I'm glad you didn't."

Jake shook his head. "I couldn't have changed what you are, either of you, and I wouldn't have tried. You're growing into your destinies, and even if those destinies scare me half to death, I know you must be who you are intended to be."

Justin nodded and lowered his gaze.

Jake slapped his hands on his knees and said, "Now, hadn't we better be getting home? We wouldn't want Santa to think we weren't excited about his visit."

Justin grinned, but before he could say anything, Monkey King joined them.

"I overheard your last comment, Dr. Prentiss," the trickster chief said. "I was just thinking the same thing."

"Please, call me Jake, sir."

Monkey King grinned. "Jake it is. You are welcome at any time, Jake, but for now, take your family home for Christmas." With that, he clapped his hands and the clearing under the banyan tree disappeared and Jake found himself in his own family room surrounded by Janine and Justin and Coyote. He glanced at Janine with a raised eyebrow and she nodded. Thunderbird had returned safely as well.

Hugging his twins, they dropped onto the couch, happily exhausted after an awesome day.

CHAPTER 5

*J*ake groaned and dragged himself from bed. Dawn had barely broken, but he could hear Justin and Janine giggling in the family room along with Coyote's excited yips and even an occasional screeching laugh from Thunderbird. Jake hadn't had enough sleep. He'd been up way too late wrapping gifts and filling stockings. He was tempted to roll back over and catch a few more winks. The twins knew the routine. They were allowed to enjoy all the treats in their stockings, but wrapped gifts had to wait until after breakfast. They'd be fine if he slept in a bit.

He pulled the pillow over his head, but it was too late. His brain was awake and working, remembering all the effort Justin and Coyote had gone to over the last twelve days to make Jake's Christmas memorable. He needed to get up and enjoy his kids while he could. They were growing up even faster than he'd imagined was possible.

Stuffing his feet into his slippers, he reached for his flannel robe. Instead of shrugging into it, he held it to his face and breathed a little prayer to Emilia. *They're not who we expected, sweetheart, but our twins are wonderful, thoughtful, and downright magical.*

As he pulled the robe on and knotted the belt around his waist, he thought he heard an echo of her sigh, *I know, and I'm so proud. Of all of you.*

PART IV
FAERY BEAUTIFUL

DEB LOGAN

BESTSELLING AUTHOR OF *THUNDERBIRD*

Faery
Beautiful

THE FAERY SAGA BEGINS!

PROLOGUE

Family holidays are the best. Especially this year. Now that I know I'm a faery, destined to live out my exceedingly long life in the Faery Realm, I'm careful to enjoy my human family. While I have them.

Take today. I don't think I've ever fully appreciated how nice it is to celebrate Thanksgiving with family and friends. Even though she's a few months into an unexpected pregnancy, Mom decided to go all out this year. She invited my best friend Lexie's family—Lexie, her parents Mr. and Mrs. Davis, her twin brothers Nick and Doug, and her baby sister Candy—Brent Rodgers, Lexie's boyfriend and my confidant, and, of course, Roddy, my erstwhile dragon guardian and current faery prince of a boyfriend.

The day was wonderful! The house smelled of roast turkey, apple cider, cinnamon, and fresh baked apple pie. The twins raced around causing mayhem, and Candy toddled into everything, with Mom beaming at them all.

"I've forgotten what it's like to have little ones in the house," I heard her whisper to Dad. "Next year we'll have a new addition to be thankful for."

Dad pulled her into his arms, placed a hand over her tummy and said, "We have a lot to be thankful for this year."

I turned away, smiling. It's great to see your parents so obviously in love. Even if the baby they're expecting is a consolation prize from the King of Faery. My many-times-removed grandfather had expected to steal me away when Roddy presented me to the Faery Court at Halloween. Grandpa had expected me to arrive in Faery and never leave, so he'd used magic to ensure Mom conceived while the parental units were sunning in the south of France. He'd also expected to execute Roddy for his supposed crimes. Needless to say, things hadn't worked out exactly as Grandpa had planned. He hadn't expected me to be so, well, me!

But everything worked out well. Roddy was not only alive, but his curse had been lifted and he was now back to his true form, a faery prince instead of a dragon. Mom and Dad were happily expecting a new addition to the family, and I was the acknowledged heir to the throne of Faery ... while still attending Jefferson High and living at home with my parents.

And best of all? Grandpa allowed me to tell Mom and Dad and Lexie and Brent all about being a faery princess and having magic. He placed a geis on them, of course. They're only allowed to speak of Faery with others who already know my secret, but at least I no longer needed to lie to my family or my best friends.

Life was good.

I sighed contentedly and sipped my hot chocolate. The feast was over and everyone had gone home. Well, everyone but Roddy. My prince sat beside me on the worn dark leather sofa in our family room, one arm draped around my shoulders, his feet propped on the sturdy walnut coffee table.

"I'm very fond of this room," he said, gazing at the braided rug in front of the fire. One of the burning logs popped, sending a shower of sparks up the chimney. "I spent many happy evenings curled before that fire, watching you covertly, and listening to you and Deirdre talk."

I rested my head on his shoulder. "Gran and I both loved you as a dragon," I said, remembering the great golden beast he'd been when we first met, "but I'm so glad Grandpa lifted his curse." I snuggled a bit closer, and his arm tightened around my shoulders. "I love you even more in this form."

"He only released me because of you," he sighed. "He'd fully intended to have me executed."

"I know," I whispered. "I remember."

I took another sip of chocolate, then leaned forward and placed my mug on the coffee table. While I was sitting forward, out of his embrace, I turned to look at him.

"You've never told me how Grandpa came to curse you in the first place," I said, frowning slightly. "I mean, I know it was all tied up with his daughter marrying a mortal, but I've never understood why he blamed you for her choice."

Roddy sighed, pulled his feet off the coffee table and onto the floor, and sat forward with his elbows on his knees. "It's a long, sad story," he said. "Are you sure you want to hear it?"

I nodded and, scooting to the corner of the sofa to give him some space, curled up to listen. "Tell me the story of Princess Rhiannon and Eoin the Strong. I want to know how my family came to be and why I'm now a faery."

CHAPTER 1

*R*hiannon was my best friend. She and Blodwen and I did everything together. All of Faery rejoiced in our friendship, the High King's daughter, the heir to Winter, and a daughter of Summer. What tragedy could befall a kingdom where all three courts were so inextricably twined?

Granted, Liannan, the Summer Queen, would've preferred to have her son and heir, Prince Idris, in our ranks rather than Blodwen, but Idris was young and Rhiannon and Blodwen and I were of an age.

From the time we were in the nursery, the three of us were inseparable whenever the three courts came together for celebrations. As we grew, we found ways to play together even when we were in our separate demesnes. Magic is a wonderful aid to mischief … especially for royal children. After all, who but our parents could deny us?

Besides, who would want to separate us?

All of Faery was enchanted by our friendship. A young prince who was growing into a handsome young man, and two princesses, each more fair than any other lass in the kingdom. Rhiannon with hair as dark and midnight, eyes the color of emeralds, and the pink of spring roses in her cheeks. Blodwen, with her golden hair, violet eyes, and creamy complexion, was Rhiannon's best friend and confidant and her equal in every way.

I think many in Faery expected me to wed Rhiannon. They hoped she and I would ascend the throne of the High King, and my younger brother, Bran, would rule the Winter Court. But Rhiannon and Blodwen and I laughed at their expectations. As beautiful as the princesses were, I wasn't interested in either of them in a romantic way. Not even when we reached marriageable age. They were my best friends, as close as sisters. I loved them both, but not as potential mates.

And that's when our idyllic existence began to fall apart.

When King Alberic realized that Rhiannon and I were not inclined to marry, he began to search elsewhere for a suitable mate for his only daughter ... without consulting her.

And in so doing, he planted the seed of our mutual destruction.

CHAPTER 2

*R*hiannon's faery steed raced along the enchanted river that divided Faery from the mortal realm. She glanced over her shoulder and urged the stallion to greater speed with hands and heels. She knew I would catch her if she allowed her pace to slacken. My charger, heavier boned than Rhiannon's mount, couldn't match her mare's speed, but the charger's depth of chest meant he could maintain his pace far longer.

Rhiannon, stop this nonsense. I sent my thought winging to her mind.

She bent lower over her mount's neck and replied in kind. *It's my life, Rhydderich Drest Guerthenmach. I won't be auctioned like a prize heifer.*

You are a princess of Faery, I countered, layering my mind-voice with soothing overtones. *You've known all your life this day would come, especially once we made it clear that we didn't wish to marry.*

Her misery bled through our mind-link and I fought to stay calm, to keep from empathizing with the tears I felt stinging her eyes. Her will faltered, and the mare slowed her pace. I had won. Rhiannon acknowledged my argument.

My princess had been raised with every comfort: beautiful clothes, rich foods, precious jewels, faery folk to entertain or obey her slightest wish. Every indulgence had been granted my dear friend. Everything but the desire of her heart. More than anything, Rhiannon craved her father's love. The King of Faery had ensured his only child possessed every physical trinket a girl growing to womanhood could need or desire, but he had denied her his love.

King Alberic had loved Rhiannon's mother fiercely — and that love had killed her. Queen Morgana died giving Rhiannon life. Alberic never forgave the child for murdering his wife, or himself for desiring the heir that had cost him his love.

As I drew even with her, Rhiannon dashed the tears from her cheeks.

"Forgive me, Roddy. My tantrum has winded your charger."

"Gobhniu always needs exercise, my princess," I said, slapping the horse's neck as we slowed to a walk. "I only feared Danu might miss a step and break one of her dainty legs."

Rhiannon ran her fingers through Danu's golden mane. "You needn't have worried. She's far too sure-footed for that."

I bowed my head. "As her mistress is far too level-headed to flee to the mortal realm to escape her father's will."

A crimson blush suffused her face, but she held her head high. "It is my right. Every faery maiden is allowed a visit to the mortal realm before she weds."

"Yes, but not every faery maiden is the sole heir to the throne of Faery. You are unique among us, my princess."

"Still, I claim my right. Will you accompany me, Roddy? I cannot compel you."

I straightened in my saddle. "You have never needed to compel me," I said with dignity. "Even if your father had not charged me with your safety, you and Blodwen are my dearest friends. I would follow you to the end of the world."

Rhiannon smiled through her tears. "Thank you, Roddy. You are a true friend."

We urged Danu and Gobhniu to an easy canter and headed for the door in the rock that led to the land of men. I studied Rhiannon as we rode. She'd grown to womanhood in my company. We'd played together as young children and she had cheered me on when I entered the training lists at ten. I'd been knighted at fifteen, years earlier than was usual, but none of us, not Rhiannon nor Blodwen nor I, had ever been content with the usual. Once knighted, my princess had requested me as her guard. After all, if she had to have a faery knight following her every footstep, she'd prefer that knight be a trusted friend.

King Alberic agreed. After all, nothing in Faery threatened his daughter, the guard was merely a formality. A left-over tradition from a time when the faery people warred with the race of men. I think Alberic hoped that continued close association would lead us to declare our love and petition for permission to marry. A marriage between the High Court and Winter would save him the tedious process of marrying her off to a foreign prince, though if he had to arrange such a marriage, he would ensure it produced a profitable alliance.

I controlled my charger with practiced skill. The enormous horse responded to the slightest movement of hand or heel. I knew Rhiannon admired the man I'd become. She often teased me that I was strong of arm and lean of leg, epitomizing all a prince of Faery should be. But I knew her teasing was good-natured. Her way of letting me know she recognized my quality even if she didn't want to marry me.

She and Blodwen both found me handsome, commenting on my high forehead, strong chin, long straight nose, and deep green eyes.

Rhiannon especially liked my thick golden hair, often plaiting it when we were young. Now my hair was clubbed at the base of my neck, not flying in the wind as did her waist-length midnight curls.

A shimmer in the air announced our approach to the enchanted portal.

I reined in Gobhniu and patted his neck. "Are you certain you want to do this, my princess?"

Rhiannon's gaze flitted to the magical doorway.

Beyond that threshold lay the realm of men. Neither of us had ever seen a mortal man, but we imagined them to be uncivilized brutes, incapable of wit or compassion. And yet, faery maids clung to their ancient right to dally with the sons of man. There had to be something attractive about the mortal creatures. Why else would our immortal maidens insist on such a tradition?

"The king has decreed my marriage to the prince of the wood elves across the Eastern Sea. Once I am wed, I will lose my ability to cross the threshold. It's now or never, Roddy."

"Aye, it is, but you did not answer my question, Rhia. Do you *want* to cross the threshold, or are you simply baiting your sire?"

Her cheeks flamed again and she shook her heavy mane of hair, but her defiance melted when she met my gaze. She sighed. "You know me too well, my friend. I'm angry with father, it's true. No matter what I do, he refuses to see me as anything more than chattel to turn to his profit."

She swallowed and turned her attention to the shimmering gate. "He's never loved me, Roddy, and now he's auctioned me off to the highest bidder, for an alliance we don't even need." She straightened in her saddle and gazed squarely into my eyes. "I intend to experience the other world before I lock myself in yet another loveless cage."

I bowed my head and placed a hand over my heart. "I wish I could change your destiny, Rhia, but since I cannot, I will protect you from misadventure."

Rhiannon smiled, straightened in her saddle, and urged Danu toward the gate. "Do we take the horses, or step through on foot?"

"Afoot, I think," I answered. "I've heard our horses aren't fond of their mortal counterparts."

She nodded, flipped her heavily embroidered skirt aside and dismounted in a fluid motion. I joined her before the gate and we stepped over the threshold in perfect unison.

A cyclone met our booted feet, enveloped us in warm wildness, and separated us. I glimpsed Rhiannon's green skirt swirling around her slender body, her dark curls whipping upward in a mass of tangles, before the whirling madness forced me to close my eyes. The wind supported us into the mortal realm, but when I opened my eyes again, I found that it had deposited Rhiannon on a flat rock in the midst of gray-blue water, while I was dropped on an island … in front of the shimmering portal door.

"Rhia! Are you all right?"

She grinned and called back, "I'm fine, but why am I here and you there?"

"The whim of magic?" I asked with a shrug. "Be still, my princess, I'll see if there's a boat on the other side of the island." I clambered over the rocks and around the curve of the island, losing sight of my princess, my friend.

CHAPTER 3

"*B*e still, indeed," Rhiannon muttered as Roddy moved out of sight. "What else would I do on a rock in the middle of a lake!"

She pulled a comb from her pocket, sat down, and using the still water for a mirror attacked the snarls in her thick black hair. She'd nearly tamed the knots the cyclone had left in its wake when a prickle of unease raised the tiny hairs on the back of her neck and arms. Tucking the comb in her pocket, she glanced warily toward the shore. An enormous red-haired man stood watching her through narrowed eyes. He held the reins of a powerful roan horse while the animal drank of the lake's clear water.

So this was a human man. An unbleached linen shirt covered broad shoulders, while a red and green plaid kilt displayed strong legs and feet clad in supple leather boots. A huge sword hung in a scabbard at his waist and a hunting bow showed above his shoulder. Bright copper hair was clubbed at the back of his neck.

Rhiannon shivered at the intensity of his gaze, but remembered her station and rose to her feet, holding his gaze all the while.

"Why do you stare, mortal? Have you never seen a maiden before?"

"I've never seen beauty such as yours," he said, his baritone voice rich with admiration. "You astound me, lady."

And he astounded Rhiannon. His voice and words defied her expectations. A shiver ran down her spine and she wished faeries could swim.

"How came you to be on that rock, my lady? Do you require assistance?"

Silence enveloped her. What could she say? *A magical whirlwind deposited me here and I have no boat?* She smiled.

He leapt to his saddle with more grace than she had imagined possible for such a large human and urged his horse into the water.

Rhiannon's pulse pounded. What could she do? Precisely nothing. The rock offered no hiding place and no space to run.

The horse lost his footing, but the big man soothed him and urged him forward. The steed swam to Rhiannon's rock.

Before her addled mind thought to scream for Roddy, the man scooped Rhiannon from her perch and turned the horse back to shore. She clung to him like a burr on a saddle blanket until the horse stepped onto dry land. Once out of the water, she pushed his arms away and jumped to ground, whirling to stare up at the red-haired man.

"How dare you! How dare you lay hands on the Princess of Faery?"

He dismounted and stood before her. "Princess is it? You didn't answer; I took your smile for an invitation."

"Next time wait for the invitation to be explicit," she said, maintaining her dignity despite an unusual fluttering in her belly.

He inclined his head in acknowledgement of her words. "Forgive me, lady, but I couldn't mount and ride away leaving such a fair maiden stranded on a rock in a lake. It would have been churlish."

She relaxed, though the fluttering in her belly continued. "There is nothing to forgive. You did me a kindness. It was unnecessary, but you couldn't know that."

One of his eyebrows rose. "Unnecessary? You intended to fly from yon rock, perhaps?" He peered behind her, as though expecting to find wings.

She ignored the comment.

He shrugged, turned to the horse and rummaged in a saddle bag. His hand emerged with a loaf of brown bread. Taking a sgian dubh from a sheath on his calf, he cut a piece and offered it to her.

"Don't touch that, Rhia!"

The mortal whirled to face Roddy. The faery knight had glided to shore on a light coracle and now leapt to face the man.

"Be at ease, Roddy. He has offered me no harm."

"Still, my princess, you must not taste anything he offers or you will owe him a charm."

"I'm aware of the rules, Sir Rhydderich."

The man stepped back so that he no longer stood between Rhiannon and her guard. He studied Roddy, noted the sheathed sword, and glanced at Rhiannon. "So it is true. You are a faery princess."

"I am and in reward for your chivalry, I grant you one wish."

"Rhia!" scolded Roddy, but she quelled him with a glance.

The mortal knelt before her with lowered eyes. "I have only one request, Fair One," he tilted his head and caught her gaze. "that I might once again gaze upon your beauty. Will you meet me here again?"

Rhiannon's belly somersaulted over her heart. Her knees shook and her mind screamed of danger ... but her heart sang.

"What is your name, mortal?"

"I am called Eoin the Strong by my clan."

"Well, Eoin the Strong, I shall honor your request. Meet me here at the next full moon with a selection of the finest bread your realm has to offer. It may be that I will make an exchange."

Roddy sucked in a sharp breath, but her friend held his silence.

Eoin rose, took Rhiannon's hand and kissed it. "I will be here with bread fit for the Ard Ri himself. And should you choose to grant me a boon, I will treasure it, Fair One."

Rhiannon left her hand in his longer than was strictly required, relishing the rough texture of his palm and the restrained strength of his fingers. Her belly continued to shimmy and tumble, but she controlled her features. At last she withdrew her hand and nodded at the handsome mortal. "Until we meet again, Eoin the Strong."

She strolled to Roddy and allowed her friend and guard to hand her into the tiny coracle.

He turned to Eoin and said, "Have a care, mortal. My princess is fair and generous, but that doesn't mean we all are." The faery prince stepped into the boat and waved it into motion.

Eoin bowed low and then straightened and saluted the coracle. "Until we meet again, Fair One."

CHAPTER 4

"*A*nd where were you when my headstrong daughter made such a rash promise?" Alberic, King of Faery, skewered me with an angry gaze. "If she accepts food from that creature, she will bind herself to him and to his world."

"He was beside me, as was his duty," said Rhiannon with aplomb. "He held silence because I commanded his obedience. I am aware of the import of my promise. If you are angry, sire, direct your wrath at me, not my faithful friend."

Alberic spun to face his daughter. "I *am* angry and I *will* deal with you. Right now I'm speaking to a knight in my service. Hold your tongue, wench."

Blood drained from Rhiannon's face, but she stood her ground despite her father's insult. "I am not a wench. I am the Princess of Faery."

A sneer twisted her father's face and Rhiannon flinched as though expecting a blow, but he chose to wound her with words instead. "You are not worthy to be a princess. Despite every advantage, you throw yourself at a mortal like a common nymph. You disgust me. And to think your lady mother gave her life for you. I'm glad she didn't live to see you behave so ... so ... immodestly."

"And what about you, Father?" Rhiannon snapped, anger sizzling in her clipped tones. "Would Mother be proud of the bitter, nasty little man you've become?"

Alberic drew back his arm, but I threw myself between father and daughter and caught the king's wrist.

"Forgive me, sire," I said through clenched teeth, "but I cannot allow harm to come to my princess. Not even from you. Not while I have breath in my body."

"Take your hands off me, youngster, or you may find your breaths very limited indeed."

I released the king's wrist, but remained between Alberic and Rhiannon. "Rhiannon, my princess, please leave. Your father and I have much to discuss."

Rhiannon stiffened ... and then turned and strode from the room.

"Sire, you know I love Rhiannon as a sister," I said, lowering my eyes and bowing my head, "and I am your obedient servant, but knowing her as I do, I believe you would do well not to antagonize her about this."

Alberic's face turned crimson and his eyes narrowed. "*I* should not antagonize *her*?" he said, his voice seething with anger. "When she behaves with such wanton disregard for her station? When she plans to leave Faery to consort with a *mortal*?"

"My king," I said, trying to sooth him with my tone, "you know how headstrong she is. If you oppose her, she may do something we will all regret. Leave her to me. Ignore this assignation. Rhiannon knows her own worth. She won't do anything reckless."

As long as you don't goad her into it, I thought, miserably.

The king glared at me, but nodded. "Fine," he said. "I won't oppose her … for now. But be warned," he said, "prince or no, if you allow harm to come to my daughter, your life will be forfeit."

I bowed before my king. "I understand, sire. I shall see to it that no harm comes to my princess."

CHAPTER 5

*R*hiannon paced before the shimmering threshold gate, her richly embroidered blue skirt swishing past the close cropped grass. Her pulse raced at the thought of seeing the handsome mortal again and she fought to steady her breathing.

"Remember, my princess, don't eat anything he offers. Don't even touch the bread he brings," chided Roddy. "The enchantment against mortals tasting faery food or faeries partaking of mortal fare is binding, regardless of your station."

"I'm not a child, Roddy. I know the law."

A deeper, more commanding voice answered. "Yes, but will you obey, obstinate child?"

Rhiannon's face settled into a mask as she turned to face her father. "What are you doing here?"

"I've come to protect my interests and the interests of Faery. I will accompany you as you fulfill your oath to this mortal clod."

"I neither require nor desire your presence."

"What you desire is of no consequence."

Rhiannon turned away from her father to face the portal. "Such has always been the truth. Roddy! Attend me. The moon has risen, my destiny awaits."

Roddy strode forward to take Rhiannon's hand. "Don't let him goad you into foolish action, Rhia," he whispered. "Please, my princess, if you have any love for me, don't throw your life away. I couldn't bear it."

She met his gaze, smiled sadly, and squeezed his hand. "Whatever happens, Roddy, none of it will be your fault," she answered quietly. "You have been a true friend my whole life. I love you like the brother I never had."

Roddy nodded and looked away. Together, they stepped into the whirlwind.

This time, Rhiannon was ready. As the portal winds tore at her skirts and tangled her hair, she bent them to her will. Holding tight to Roddy's hand she stepped from the shimmering vortex onto the lake's sandy shore.

King Alberic landed on the rock.

A golden pavilion glowed in the moonlight a few paces down the beach from Rhiannon and Roddy's landing point. Rhiannon gazed at the inviting structure and released Roddy's hand. She shook out her skirts, smoothed her tangled locks, and took a deep breath to steady her nerves.

"Don't go inside, Rhia," Roddy pleaded in a gruff whisper. "The barbarian means to trap you."

"Nonsense, Roddy. Eoin has prepared this tent in my honor. Of course I will observe his efforts."

At that moment, the tent flap was thrown back and Eoin the Strong emerged. He strode to Rhiannon and made a courtly bow.

"Welcome, Fair One," he said, a smile lighting his handsome features. "I am honored that you came."

"I gave you my word, mortal. I am bound by the promises I speak."

"And glad I am that you are. Please, come inside and be comfortable. I have brought the bread you requested."

"Rhia, don't," warned Roddy.

She hesitated, but Alberic chose that moment to vanish from the rock and reappear at Rhiannon's side.

"Rhiannon! Stop this nonsense and return with me to Faery at once."

She turned away from her father and placed her hand on Eoin's outstretched arm. "I would love to see what you have prepared for me, Eoin the Strong." She awarded him a dazzling smile before throwing a look of contempt over her shoulder at her father.

Eoin glanced from Rhiannon to the two men, and placed his hand over hers where it rested on his arm. He smiled at her. "This way, Fair One," he said leading Rhiannon to the pavilion. As an afterthought, he called over his shoulder, "You gentlemen are welcome to join us, as well."

CHAPTER 6

I followed my princess, my closest friend, into the pavilion the mortal had prepared for her, and my heart sank. Rhiannon was clearly enchanted. She clapped her hands together and turned a slow circle in the center of the warmly lit room, her eyes sparkling with delight.

Loathe though I was to admit it even to myself, Eoin the Strong had prepared a shelter worthy of royalty. Canvas walls were hung with richly embroidered tapestries, some depicting woodland scenes of hounds and foxes, horses and deer, while others showed courtly halls peopled with knights and ladies. Beneath our feet lay the pelts of large animals, bears and wild cats as well as sheep and cattle. Flickering lamps hung from support poles, giving the structure a welcoming glow, and folding camp chairs cushioned with colorful pillows were scattered throughout. But the centerpiece was a large wooden table lavishly decorated with boughs of holly and liberally sprinkled with bright red berries and white mistletoe and bearing enough loaves of bread to feed a small village for a month.

There were round loaves, their golden brown crusts scored in cross-hatch patterns, long narrow loaves, oblong loaves so dark their crust seemed almost black, small bread of every shape imaginable — buns and rolls and scones—and in pride of place a large wreath that had been cut and twisted before baking to display the rich filling inside.

My mouth watered just looking at the display, and I could feel Rhiannon's delight washing against the edges of my mind. I glared at Eoin. This mortal was dangerous.

Eoin drew Rhiannon to the table and led her past, pointing out each type of bread in turn, describing its nature and telling of its creator.

"I am not a baker, myself," he said, giving her a shy smile. "Warriors have little time to develop such homey skills, but my mother and sister made the wreath for you, Fair One. They said to tell you each ingredient was added with love and honor, in the hope of meeting you one day."

He fell to one knee, holding her hand in both of his and gazing up into her lovely face. Adoration shone in his eyes. "Will you partake, Fair One?"

"Rhiannon! No!" shouted her father. "Don't even think of disobeying me in this!"

Rhiannon ignored him. She had eyes only for the mortal at her feet. She stretched out her hand and caressed Eoin's hair, his cheek, finally kneeling to face him, one hand in his, the other resting lightly on his shoulder.

"We come from different worlds, Eoin the Strong," she said, her voice soft, but calm and controlled. "Do you understand what you are asking when you offer me your food?"

He gazed into her eyes with clarity and purpose. "I understand, Fair One," he answered. "I am offering you a home. I am offering to protect and provide for you, to share your bed and your love, to father your children, to accept you into my clan and family. Forever."

She nodded, her expression solemn. "And if I accept, I am vowing to stay by your side, to forsake my title and inheritance in Faery, to live — and die — as a mortal."

King Alberic moaned, but said nothing more. Ancient magic was at play; her father had no authority over her in this matter ... and he knew it.

My own heart was breaking. With each word, I felt her resolve grow stronger. Rhiannon, my princess, my friend, as close as a sister, was about to choose this mortal over me. Over all of us.

"Rhia," I whispered, her name like a prayer on my lips. "Please don't do this, Rhia. Please don't leave us."

She glanced at me and smiled. Not a bright, happy smile, but a wistful one, tinged with sadness. "You have been my friend and brother, Roddy," she said, "but our childhood is at an end. We will be parted no matter which life I choose. If I remain in Faery, I will be sent across the Eastern Sea to the demesne of the wood elves."

She turned again to face the mortal and her expression softened, became more joyous. "I prefer to choose my own fate." Withdrawing her hand from Eoin's, she stood, leaned over the table, and broke off a piece of the filled wreath. Turning to face King Alberic and myself, she held out her free hand to Eoin, who rose and, accepting it, lifted it to his lips.

"I choose to live as a mortal with Eoin the Strong."

She bit into the piece of filled bread, chewed and swallowed.

A breeze wafted through the pavilion, dimming the lanterns and ruffling our hair. When it had passed and the lanterns once again glowed with steady flames, King Alberic strode to his daughter.

"It is done," he said, shaking his head. "Foolish child. I cannot undo what you have done, though I would if I could. The magic is ancient and beyond my skill."

He turned to the man to whom his only daughter had just pledged her life. "However, I can and will place a binding enchantment upon your union. If you ever raise a hand in anger to my daughter, she will be returned to me at once, whether she wills it or not. Do you understand this condition?"

Eoin straightened his shoulders and met my king's gaze steadily. "I do."

King Alberic nodded. "Furthermore, your line will continue unbroken until my daughter's true heir is born. A princess of your lineage will return to Faery and take Rhiannon's place as heir to the High King's throne."

Eoin and Rhiannon nodded in unison, though Rhiannon's cheeks reddened at the reference to children.

"Finally," the king continued, "as punishment for his failure to protect my daughter from her own idiocy, Prince Rhydderich Drest Guerthenmach, formerly heir to the throne of Winter is cursed to remain in the mortal world to guard my daughter ..."

"Father! No!" cried Rhiannon. "You cannot punish Roddy for my choice!"

Alberic shouted over her, his words drowning out hers. "...and her line until her true heir shall be delivered to me in Faery," he paused, turning his head to glare at me, "at which time he shall be executed for his crimes."

Rhiannon cast one miserable glance at me and burst into tears. Eoin gathered her into his arms and held her while she sobbed. Over her head, his eyes sought mine and I recognized his regret at having been party to my downfall.

"Rhydderich Drest Guerthenmach," King Alberic said, "you are no longer a citizen of Faery. I strip you of all semblance of your former life. Be a dragon until the end of your days."

I stared at him in horror as my body obeyed his command and ceased to be my own. Agony seared through me as my bones melted and reformed, muscles stretched beyond endurance, skin and hair morphed into scales and wings. I prayed to all the elder gods to end my suffering. *Let me die!* I screamed silently since I had no mouth or tongue to utter the words.

At last the excruciating pain receded. I lay panting at the entrance to the pavilion. I pushed myself upright and found I stood on four scaled legs ending in taloned claws. A huff of surprise escaped my lips … setting the pavilion aflame.

I retreated into the cool darkness and watched as Eoin carried Rhiannon to safety, Alberic striding out behind them. He smirked at me and said, "One final matter, Rhydderich. You are forbidden to show yourself to any being other than the daughter you currently guard, or those who know of your existence. To all others, you will appear as a child's toy, a plaything of no consequence."

He bowed to all of us as we huddled before the burning pavilion. "Enjoy your new life," he sneered, and disappeared.

The moment he was gone, Rhiannon disentangled herself from Eoin and ran to me. She stopped a few paces away, bowing her head and wringing her hands. "Can you ever forgive me, Roddy?" she whispered.

If I'd still had arms I would have wrapped her in a hug. As it was, I lowered my head, resting it on the ground between my front paws. "There is nothing to forgive, my princess," I said, my new voice sounding rough and gravelly to my ears. "Neither of us had any idea your father was capable of such malicious spite."

Eoin strode over to join us. "I am sorry for your banishment and this curse, Sir Rhydderich. I will do all in my power to make sure that your life with us is as pleasant as may be."

I closed my eyes. I really didn't want to look at the mortal who had caused all this mayhem. "I appreciate the thought, Sir Eoin, but the best thing you can do for me is to make my princess happy. Cherish her, and remember your promise to her father." I opened my eyes and glared at him. "Never raise your hand to her in anger or I will slay you before her father has the chance to spirit her home … and your children will be left parentless."

Eoin nodded and took Rhiannon's hand. "I swear to you, Rhydderich Drest Guerthenmach, I will give Rhiannon no further cause to rue this day."

I nodded and closed my eyes again, opening them immediately when I felt Rhiannon's arms encircle my neck. At least I would never be separated from her. We would be together forever.

EPILOGUE

"Oh, Roddy," I said, tears stinging my eyes. "I'm so sorry. Grandpa was just horrible."

"Yes," he said quietly, "he was."

"Were they happy? Rhiannon and Eoin?"

Roddy smiled. "Very. Considering how little they knew of each other when they made their choice, they built a good, full life together. They loved each other faithfully to the end of their days. Eoin was as good as his word, never giving Rhiannon cause for grief. And if my princess ever regretted her decision, I never knew it."

He closed his eyes, and I knew he was remembering my foremother.

"Watching Rhiannon, my closest friend, wither and die was the hardest thing I'd ever had to do," he whispered. "She was a princess of Faery. She should have lived forever. Instead, she died in a medieval manor attended only by her eldest granddaughter so that I could be present as a full-size dragon. Eoin had been dead for many years and she said that she was ready to join him, but I ... I was not ready to be left behind. To be cursed to live without her."

I scooted over to sit beside him and pulled him into a tight embrace. "Thank you," I whispered, and felt him start. "Thank you for waiting through all those centuries … for me."

He turned in my embrace and kissed my cheek. "You were worth the wait."

He pushed me away and stroked my hair. "I loved Rhiannon as a sister and I grieved to watch her die, but if she hadn't made her choice, if Alberic hadn't cursed me to guard her family, we wouldn't be here now." He raised my hand to his lips and kissed it. "And I'd endure it all again to gain your love, Claire."

He stood and pulled me into a full embrace, kissing me gently, but passionately.

"Evidently all of Faery was correct," he whispered. "The heir of Winter was destined to fall in love with the heir to the High King's throne, only her name wasn't Rhiannon … it's Claire!"

PART V
OF DRAGONS AND CENTAURS

DEB LOGAN

BESTSELLING AUTHOR OF *THUNDERBIRD*

of
DRAGONS
AND
CENTAURS

CHAPTER 1

I stumbled groggily to the kitchen wearing the frilly white nightgown Gran had insisted I sleep in the night before. Thank God it was Friday, and not just any Friday. Today was my fifteenth birthday! My parents might have deserted me, running off to the south of France and leaving me in the questionable care of my more-than-slightly dotty grandmother, but I intended to celebrate anyway. Just … later. After I was fully awake.

I found my way to my chair at the kitchen table. The smell of honey-cured bacon made my mouth water and the sound of its sizzle penetrated my sleep-fogged brain. I rubbed my eyes and commanded them to focus on our sunny yellow kitchen, snorting softly when I noticed the toy dragon abandoned on the rug by the sliding glass patio door. Gran never went anywhere without that silly toy, not even to the kitchen to fix breakfast.

Gran observed the spluttering bacon while she buttered toast at the island workspace. Her lime green bathrobe coupled with the short, wiry gray hair that sprang from her head with no discernible style or direction made me think of a demented dandelion. Between the yellow walls, bright white curtains and cabinets and Gran's less-than-subtle robe, the kitchen fairly pulsed with light.

I closed my eyes and wondered if I could skulk back to the dim safety of my bedroom without Gran noticing.

"Good morning, Sunshine!" Gran's cheerful bellow burst that particular hopeful bubble.

"Morning," I croaked.

She turned an unusually brilliant smile on me and the light level in the room clicked up a notch. I suppressed a groan. No one should be allowed to be so ... so chipper this early in the morning.

"Come on, girl. You can do better than that," she practically sang. "This is your fifteenth birthday; the day you come into your inheritance. Roddy and I had to work overtime to ensure we'd be here to share it with you."

My attention snagged on the word "inheritance" and I almost missed the rest of her comments.

"... you don't think it was their idea to leave you behind while they went to the south of France, do you?"

"What?" My brain finally clicked into gear and my eyes lost their pre-breakfast fuzziness. I stared at Gran in disbelief. "Are you telling me *you're* the reason I missed out on a trip to France? Gran! Are you nuts?"

I slumped back in my chair. Of course she was nuts. What else could explain her bizarre attachment to a toy dragon? Or the way she referred to it as a living person? Mom would be shocked, but I'd just have to suck it up and tell her that her mother had gone completely and totally around a possibly dangerous bend.

Gran's voice pulled me back from my dreary thoughts.

"Trust me, dearie," she said. "You'll have plenty of chances to visit France. Compared to the adventures you and Roddy are going to have, France is passé."

She'd mentioned Roddy twice now, her delusions were increasing. I eyed the plate of bacon and eggs she set before me. Was insanity infectious? Should I be eating eggs she'd fried? The glass of orange juice sparkled ominously as she patted my back and told me to eat up.

"Uhmm, by 'Roddy' do you mean your toy dragon, or are you referring to some new friend you're planning to introduce me to?" I asked, pushing bits of egg around my plate while my stomach tied itself in an unhappy knot.

Gran's sunburst smile lit her face as she slid into the chair across from me.

"I can't wait another minute," she said, her blue eyes sparkling like crazed sapphires. "I should wait 'til after school, so you'll have time to adapt, but I'm just too excited." She pulled a small jewelry box from her bathrobe pocket and slid it across the table. "Happy birthday, Claire. Your adventure is about to begin!"

I glanced from the little black velvet box to Gran's glowing face and thought, What the hell! You only live once.

My fingers caressed the box's soft surface before slowly and carefully lifting the lid. A pungent but sweet perfume teased my nostrils and a glimpse of silver encouraged me to continue. Soon the little box stood open in the palm of my hand, its contents shining in the streaming September sunlight.

An intricately worked silver medallion rested on a cloud of midnight velvet. The design showed a dragon in flight. His wings stretched from edge to edge of the two-inch silver circle, and his tiny emerald eyes stared directly into mine. My own eyes — a vivid green so intense people who didn't know me assumed I wore colored contacts to heighten the color — were a pale reflection of those brilliant gems.

They mesmerized me and before I realized what I'd done, the medallion rested in the palm of my hand.

Gran exhaled a long, contented sigh and the kitchen shrank as another presence filled the room. Compelled by the new aura, I turned toward the patio door and froze. A dragon crouched where Gran's toy had been.

I screamed, closed my eyes and prayed I was having a nightmare. I counted to a hundred, waited for my heart to stop beating a heavy-metal drum solo in my chest, and opened my eyes.

The hallucination remained. It ... she ... he stretched to fill the space from floor to ceiling with molten gold magnificence. Wings folded tightly against his back, he settled on his haunches, head bowed to accommodate the ceiling tiles. Razor-sharp claws tipped his massive feet (paws?), but his eyes captured my attention and held it hostage. Blazing green emeralds defied my desire to look away. The faceted gems of the medallion seemed like bits of colored wax in comparison. I gasped, surrendering to the hypnotic effect while merriment swirled up from their fathomless depths.

"Happy birthday, my lady," said a deep, rumbling voice that pushed against my mind like a storm-laden wind. "I've waited fifteen long years to address you directly." He closed those brilliant eyes and bowed his head until his snout touched the linoleum floor.

Time snagged, awaiting my response. An urgent premonition weighted my soul: the entire course of my future life hinged on my next words. The realization was a millstone drowning me in a well of despair. What should I say? Which words would be right, and how was I, a barely fifteen-year-old high school girl, supposed to know what they were? What could I say to a mythical creature who couldn't possibly be groveling on my clean kitchen floor?

I heard Gran's shallow breathing behind me and sank deeper into despair. She'd managed to infect me with her lunacy. I'd been worried about tainted eggs, but the damage was already done. She'd stolen my sanity.

Just when I thought my mind would shatter from terror and confusion, the dragon opened one gleaming eye and a bubble of laughter formed in my chest. I hiccoughed in an attempt to dispel the inappropriate sound, but failed. A soft giggle escaped my lips, followed by peals of wild laughter that quickly dissolved into a maniacal cackle.

"Claire!"

The shocked outrage in Gran's voice stifled me momentarily. I turned to face her, wiped my streaming eyes on the sleeve of my ridiculous nightgown, took a deep, shuddering breath, and avoided thoughts of the dragon behind me. Maybe if I ignored him, he'd go away.

"You're being very disrespectful," Gran said, her words clipped and tight. "I'm so sorry, Roddy. I don't know what's gotten into her."

"Shock," said the dragon, shattering my illusion of his nonexistence. "Feed her. I can wait for my lady's attention."

Gran glared at me. So I sat, picked up my fork and tried not to hear the rumblings and rustlings of a dragon curling up on the floor behind me. I ate my breakfast in stony silence, no longer concerned with infection.

"I know this is a shock," Gran said, picking up her coffee cup and sipping the fragrant brew, "but Roddy is part of your heritage. He's our family dragon, you see."

I dropped my fork and glared at her. "No, I don't see. I mean, yes, I see there's a dragon in the kitchen, but I don't see how and I don't understand what it has to do with me."

"Not it, dear," said Gran. "He. Roddy is a male dragon. And he has everything to do with us. Roddy is our guardian. He passes from grandmother to granddaughter in our family. He's been in our family for generations, haven't you, Roddy?"

The massive golden beast shifted behind me and answered in a soft, almost purring voice, "It has been my honor to serve the women of your family for over two thousand years, my lady. I am yours to command."

A frown crossed Gran's face. "Why are you calling her lady, Roddy? You've never called me lady."

"My relationship with each of Rhiannon's daughters is unique, Deirdre," he said. "Claire is my lady."

Gran stiffened. "What do you mean?" she demanded. "Why is Claire a lady, when I wasn't?"

Roddy tilted his huge head and gave Gran the dragon equivalent of a serene smile. At least, I hoped that was what his expression meant. "Do not trouble yourself, Deirdre. What is, is."

"I don't know what either of you are talking about," I said, standing up and edging toward the kitchen door, "but if we don't get moving, I'm going to be late for school."

Gran gasped, jumped to her feet, snatched plates from the table and raced for the sink. "Of course. I nearly forgot. Roddy, reduce. Claire, get dressed. We can talk about this later."

"You forget yourself, Deirdre," growled Roddy. "I am no longer yours to command."

Gran scowled, but turned to me. "Claire, pack up Roddy and get moving."

My mouth dropped open, but no words came out. The woman expected me to pack a dragon? Not knowing what else to do, I parroted Gran's words.

"Roddy, reduce."

"As you command, my lady," he said, and immediately the toy dragon lay at my feet.

"Well, don't just stand there," Gran said above the rattle of dishes and cutlery, "pick him up and get ready for school."

CHAPTER 2

I awakened the next morning to a delicious sense of reprieve. Saturday — no school. No need to worry about whispers and giggles and my nonexistent reputation. No significant homework either, since the school year was barely under way. A day of freedom to enjoy my newly attained status of fifteen-year-old high school student.

I met Gran at the front door as I came down to breakfast. I rounded the bottom step and nearly ran over her.

"Whoa," I exclaimed. "Where are you off to so early in the morning?"

Gran had donned her cheese orange poncho and lime green boots and car keys dangled from gloved fingers. Her short gray hair was tucked securely under a felted red hat. No one would ever accuse Gran of being inconspicuous.

"I'm off to the library," she said, pulling the front door open. "There's a poetry reading this morning. You and Roddy need a little time to get acquainted." She smiled and patted my cheek. "Have a nice day, dear."

I grabbed her arm. "Wait a minute. Aren't you supposed to be taking care of me?"

Genuine shock lit her eyes. "Darling Claire, you'll never need anyone to look after you again. Roddy is the most capable guardian imaginable." Her fingers caressed my cheek and she said, "You'll be perfectly safe with him."

"But Gran..."

"Trust me, Claire," she called, stepping through the door. "You're going to love Roddy." She closed the door behind herself, leaving me alone in the house .... If you didn't count the dragon.

I stared at the closed door and considered my options. I could follow her out and beg, but I still wore my PJs. I could run back upstairs, dress quickly and make a run for my best friend Lexie's apartment, but that would only delay the inevitable. I sighed, squared my shoulders and followed the path of courage; facing the dragon in his lair. Or in this case, my own kitchen.

A full-size Roddy reclined on the kitchen floor between the work-surface island and the sliding patio door. He raised his head at my approach.

"Good morning, Roddy. Gran seems to have deserted us for the time being."

He inclined his head and blinked. "Deirdre is a wise woman," he said in his deep, gravelly voice. "Do you have plans for breakfast, my lady?"

The mundane question caught me off-guard. "Uh...no, not really. I suppose I'll have a bowl of cereal."

"Would you like to break your fast with a centaur? I have a friend who would be delighted to meet you."

I snorted a laugh, but immediately regretted the rude noise. "You're serious, aren't you? A centaur? They exist?"

He showed his teeth in what I could only hope was a dragon grin. "I exist," he said in a reasonable tone. "Why shouldn't a centaur?"

His logic was undeniable.

"Well, sure," I said. "I mean, what good is having a dragon if I never do anything weird? Just wait a minute while I get dressed."

I bolted to the stairs, stopped, frowned and ran back.

"What should I wear?"

"Whatever makes you feel good, my lady," he said with a low rumble of laughter. "And don't worry about a coat. You will never be cold or wet with me to guard you."

Ten minutes later I joined him in the kitchen wearing my favorite faded jeans, a pink Juicy Couture T-shirt and a denim jacket. I'd considered wearing my sneakers, but had opted for hiking boots … just in case.

"Okay," I said, my voice fairly steady. "Let's go have breakfast with a centaur."

Roddy extended a front leg and said, "Climb aboard, my lady. You'll fit nicely between my neck ridges. Tuck your knees just behind my wing joints."

My jaw dropped. I tried to speak, but incoherent squeaks were all I could manage. Finally, I closed my eyes, licked my lips and spoke without looking at the huge golden beast.

"Are you serious? You want me to climb on your back and, and … well, ride a dragon? I don't even know how to ride a horse!"

I peered at him through the barest slits of eyelids.

"Come, my lady. You needn't fear falling. I will never allow you to come to harm."

Taking a huge gulp of air, I stepped up onto his extended paw. Trying to think light thoughts. I leaned forward and placed both hands on his shoulder, amazed to find the hide warm and supple. Not hard and scaly at all.

He raised his paw and I grabbed a neck ridge and pulled myself over his shoulder while he continued to lift. I scrambled around and found the spot he'd described. My knees wedged behind the wing joint and my butt slipped into a comfortable depression between spiky ridges. I leaned forward and hugged the ridge in front of me, which wasn't sharp or jagged, but smoothly cone shaped.

"Relax, Lady Claire. All will be well."

"Wait," I cried, tightening my grip on his ridge. "How are you going to get out of the house? None of the doors are big enough for you!"

"Magic, my lady," he replied, sounding happier than I'd yet heard. "Magic!"

The word resonated in my bones. I felt it, heard it, experienced it. A warmth like the heavy, bone-deep heat of a summer day spent sunbathing by the pool at Lexie's apartment complex spread through my limbs and I melted against Roddy's neck ridge. My eyelids drifted closed, too heavy to resist. Peace flowed through my soul and I smelled lavender and roses and the too-sweet bubblegum fragrance of Mom's heritage iris. My tastebuds tingled and the taste of honey-sweet nectar burst across my tongue.

Raw power licked my spine and flowed out my fingertips and I returned to consciousness. But I hadn't been unconscious, had I?

I opened my eyes and squared my shoulders, only to hunch forward with a scream. Wind whistled past my ears and brought tears to my eyes. Roddy flew through the cloudless sky with me clinging to his back like a lamprey on a whale.

Be at ease, my lady.

I squeezed my eyes shut and tried to pretend I couldn't hear Roddy inside my skull.

You are safe with me.

You're in my mind, I whimpered, feeling both terrified by the invasion and disgusted at my cringing weakness.

We are connected during flight, he said, his voice soft and reassuring. *When the magic recedes, all will return to normal.*

Magic?

A dry snort of laughter whispered through my brain. *Do these wings really look capable of keeping my bulk aloft? Aerodynamically speaking, dragonflight is impossible.*

Gee, thanks, I said, regaining my sense of self. *You certainly know how to reassure a girl.*

His laughter zinged along my spine and I relaxed my death grip on his neck ridge. After all, I hadn't died yet. I might as well enjoy the ride.

I leaned carefully to the side and peered down. Clouds scudded beneath us with an occasional break revealing a glint of water far below.

The whoosh of wind rang in my ears and I squinted in an effort to protect my eyes. Too bad I didn't have goggles.

Roddy roared and a bright purple ski mask dangled from my fingers. I almost dropped it in shocked reaction to its sudden appearance, but tightened my grip and pulled it into place. I sighed in exquisite relief.

Thank you, Roddy. That's much better.

You're very welcome, my lady.

By the way, where are we going?

I didn't want to seem rude or ungrateful, but my stomach rumbled in sullen dissatisfaction with its continued state of emptiness.

Ogham lives in Ireland. We'll be there in a few more minutes.

Ireland? I leaned over and peered through the clouds. *We can't possibly have come that far so fast.*

Magic doesn't answer to the possible, my lady, he said. *The rules you've learned in school don't apply here.*

A few moments later, Roddy arrowed to earth in a dive so steep I refused to open my eyes, and then, all motion ceased. I peeked past his neck ridge. He hovered in mid-air a few feet from the ground in the center of a circle of standing stones.

"Ogham," he called. "I've brought Lady Claire to meet you. Have we permission to land?"

"Roddy? Is that you? It's been a hundred years if it's been a day!"

A man's head and torso appeared at the edge of the tallest stone. He sported a neatly trimmed beard and mustache, copper as the setting sun and a long braid of equally red hair hung over one shoulder. He stepped slowly forward, revealing the splendid body of a sorrel stallion.

"Don't exaggerate, centaur," said Roddy. "It can't have been more than fifty years since I brought Deirdre by for a visit."

"Perhaps so," said Ogham. "You'd know the flow of human time better than I." He looked up and shaded his eyes with a calloused hand. "Why are you still aloft? Land so I can meet this newest charge of yours."

Roddy snorted and flame charred the nearest stone. "By the Old Ones, Ogham. I thought you'd never get around to issuing the invitation." He settled to the grass in the center of the circle and I loosened my grip on his ridge and pulled the ski mask from my face.

Ogham cantered over and held up his arms. "Allow me, milady."

Strong hands grasped my waist and pulled me from Roddy's back. He set me on the ground, but kept a hand on my arm.

My knees buckled and I fought to stay upright.

"I thought as much," he said with a nod. "Your first flight? Have no fear, milady, it's a common reaction."

Roddy snuffled behind me, and then said, "I promised her breakfast, Ogham."

The centaur neighed his laughter. "Of course you did. You always arrive at mealtime, you scoundrel."

Ogham escorted me to the tallest stone and through a nonexistent doorway into a comfortable dwelling. It was a cave, except it wasn't. The walls were rock and the floor packed dirt, but the room was light and airy rather than dank and musty. A hearth filled the far end and a scarred worktable stood before it.

"Come in and be comfortable," the centaur said.

Roddy followed me inside and I swear the room expanded to accommodate his bulk. He folded his wings tightly against his golden sides, sat back on his haunches and curled his tail around his toes like a gigantic cat.

I glanced around, but didn't see anything even vaguely resembling a chair. I'd just made up my mind to settle on the hard packed floor when Roddy spoke.

"Here, my lady. Ogham keeps this stone slab for company." He moved aside to reveal a bench of intricately carved marble.

"Stone slab, indeed," I said quietly. "It's absolutely beautiful." I traced the interlocking designs with a finger, delighting in the smooth, cool perfection of the seat. "Did you make this, Ogham?"

"I did, milady, long ago ... before Roddy left to guard your family."

At that moment Roddy erupted in a sneezing fit showering the room in a flare of sparks. Ogham and I raced to stomp out myriad small embers before they could emerge into full flame.

Once the emergency had passed, Roddy bellowed, "Breakfast, Ogham. Feed my lady now!"

Ogham scowled at the dragon, but clapped his hands and danced a complicated jig reminding me of a video I'd seen in school of the Lipizzaner Stallions.

A table appeared before us covered in crisp white linen and bearing steaming platters of fragrant food. I recognized oatmeal drizzled with honey, baked yams dripping butter and brown sugar, and loaves of dark-crusted bread, but many of the platters contained mysterious concoctions whose ingredients I couldn't even begin to guess.

"Wow," I said, "this looks wonderful, but where're the bacon and eggs?"

Ogham froze and then slowly turned his head to stare at me in astonishment. "You would eat the young of a bird, or, or," he grimaced and swallowed convulsively, "the flesh of a mammal?"

"She is human, Ogham. Her ways are different." Roddy turned his brilliant green gaze on me. "Ogham is an herbivore, Claire," he explained quietly. "There'll be no meat at his table."

"I'm sorry, Ogham," I said lowering my eyes and bowing my head. "I meant no disrespect."

"Of course, milady," he replied, his voice less strained. "Forgive my overreaction."

"Wonderful," said Roddy. "Now that we're all friends again, let's eat!"

My belly rumbled its agreement and we all laughed.

That breakfast in the centaur's cave may well go down in my personal history as the best meal of my life. I sampled unknown but savory foods, giggled and swapped stories with mythological creatures and discovered friends I'd treasure for the rest of my life.

Ogham proved his bardic heritage by telling me faery tales such as I'd never heard before with an authority born of first-hand knowledge.

"Oh, yes," he said when I looked askance. "The original bards were all centaurs. We are the originators of the Gaelic gift for gab. The Blarney stone was ours long before the Celts arrived on this magnificent island. The druids co-opted our title when the faery folk retreated underhill, but they were a pale imitation of the great centaur bards."

"It's true," yawned Roddy, resting his chin on his forepaws. "A centaur can talk his way out of anything. Not even a dragon will flame a being who is in the midst of an astounding tale … and centaurs never run out of words."

"Well, outwitting dragons isn't much to boast of," said Ogham, his brow furrowed and somber. "After all, intelligence must be near equal to make a fair game of wits."

Roddy thumped the dirt floor with his tail barb and the tremor nearly knocked the centaur off his feet.

"Care to rethink your position, horse? I'm not above flaming you in mid-sentence."

Ogham chortled his high, whinnying laugh and swished his tail in Roddy's face.

Roddy rose, and for a heart-stopping moment I thought he meant to carry out his threat … but then he glanced at me and said, "I'm sorry to end our visit, Ogham, but I must return Lady Claire to her home."

With a clatter of hooves and a flick of his tail, Ogham danced the table and its contents away. He knelt before me and bowed over my hand.

"I'm honored to have met you, Lady Claire. I wish you long life and great happiness in your association with Roddy."

"Thank you, Ogham," I said, bowing my head before meeting his gaze again. "I'm sure I'll get used to meeting mythological creatures … eventually."

"Good-bye, Ogham," Roddy said, offering me his paw. "Come, my lady. Climb onto my back and we will return the way we came."

On impulse, I threw my arms around Ogham's neck and hugged him tightly. Then I scrambled to secure myself behind Roddy's neck ridge. "Good-bye," I cried. "Thank you for breakfast!" and Ogham's standing stones dissolved in a glorious shiver of sensory delights.

Maybe inheriting a dragon wouldn't turn out to be such a bad thing after all.

PART VI
FAERY UNPREDICTABLE

DEB LOGAN

BESTSELLING AUTHOR OF THUNDERBIRD

Faery
Unpredictable

CLAIRE'S 1ST CHRISTMAS IN FAERY!

CHAPTER 1

I remember when my worst problem was that my parents were headed to the French Riviera without me. Boy, those were the good old days!

Back then — we're talking three months ago! — I had a mother and father who loved me, a decidedly weird grandmother who told tall tales, and Lexie, my very best friend who stood beside me as we started high school. So what if the parental units took a super fabulous vacation without me? We were a perfectly normal American family.

At least, I thought so at the time.

Turns out, we were as far from normal as it was possible to get, and now it was time to put on my big girl panties and walk straight into the lion's den of what I'd discovered was the other side of my heritage.

Because I'm definitely not just a typical American teen. I'm not even human anymore.

Nope, I'm a faery princess.

Truly.

For real.

My transformation began on my fifteenth birthday when Gran introduced me to our family's guardian dragon, Roddy, and ended with my presentation to the King of Faery, Alberic, my too-many-greats-to-count grandpa on Halloween, or Samhain as the faery folk call it.

Yep. It's been a weird few months, but I'm adjusting … I think.

The doorbell rang, a five note fanfare that Dad had programmed when we bought this house. I took a deep breath, grabbed my powder blue fleece jacket from the back of the couch, and stepped to answer the summons. Roddy stood on the other side, his dark blond hair shining gold even in the dim winter sun that filtered through the shade of our wide front porch. Who knew jeans, hiking boots and a black leather jacket could look so sexy on a guy?

The sight of him warmed my heart and made me smile. Only six weeks ago he'd been a dragon, exiled from Faery since Rhiannon, the Faery king's daughter, had chosen to marry a mortal. King Alberic blamed Roddy for his daughter's defection. He cursed Roddy to life as a dragon and forced him to guard Rhiannon's family until her true heir should appear.

And who was that true heir? Why me, of course.

I'll never understand why fate chose me, or why it took as many centuries as it did for this heir-thing to materialize. I just know that I'm her heir and it's a genetic reality, not simply a political title I can decline.

On my fifteenth birthday, Roddy transferred his allegiance from my grandmother to me, and I discovered the truth about my heritage, that I was destined to not only take Rhiannon's place as Princess of Faery, but to become a full faery myself. Once I was presented to the royal court, I would no longer be human.

Great. Just what I always wanted: to lose my humanity and become part of a species I knew nothing about.

Roddy, in his guise of dragon, tried to prepare me for my presentation to the king, but he failed to mention that once I arrived in Faery, the king never intended for me to return to the mortal world. Of course, he also failed to mention that he, Roddy, was under a death sentence. Once I took my place in the royal court, his duty would be complete and the execution that had been deferred while the king awaited my arrival would be carried out.

It looked like King Alberic held all the power, but he hadn't reckoned on me.

I wasn't raised as a good citizen of Faery. I didn't know I was supposed to instantly obey the king's every whim. No sir! I grew up as a 21st century American woman. No king was going to dictate my life … or my dragon's death. I rebelled, and my rebellion nearly cost my life.

Incredibly, my bond with Roddy saved me, and Alberic, having nearly lost me before he'd even met me, released Roddy from his curse.

You can't begin to imagine my surprise when I discovered that my erstwhile dragon was actually a faery prince … and a really handsome one at that. Unbelievable!

And now the prince who had guarded my family as a dragon for generations stood on my front porch, ready to escort me to Faery. Christmas break had arrived and, according to the pact I'd negotiated with my many-times-removed grandfather, it was time for my first extended visit to Faery. The time had come for me to begin to learn my role as rightful heir to the High King's throne.

CHAPTER 2

*R*oddy and I stood at the center of a ring of enchanted roses, the air thick with their fragrance. Beyond the beautiful, if thorny, circle stood a castle, its windows shining in the morning light.

He held out his hand and smiled at me. I grabbed on like his fingers were a life preserver that would rescue me from certain death.

"Relax, Claire," he said, amusement coloring his words. "You've been to court before, you know what to expect. Besides, King Alberic loves you. He'll never admit it, of course, but he was thrilled with the way you stood up to him and demanded your right to return to your family. It proved you have the strength of will to rule."

I stared at him, eyes wide. "Really? I thought he was just humoring me because I nearly died."

"Well, there is that," he admitted with a shrug. "Come on. Alban Arthan is less than a week away and you have a lot to learn before the ceremony."

I sighed. "Great. I finally get a break from high school only to be forced into protocol school in Faery."

Roddy laughed and squeezed my hand. "Poor baby! Just think of all the little girls who dream of being fairy princesses. You owe it to them to enjoy this."

"Right," I grumbled. "Like any of them has a clue what they're wishing for. I think that falls under the category of 'the blessing of unanswered prayer.'"

"This is why I love you, Claire," he said, drawing me into bear hug. "You're such an optimist!"

He kissed me, and I forgot all my worries. If I had to give up my family and move to Faery to have Roddy in my life, the sacrifice would be worth it. I could grumble all I liked, but he was alive and well and back in his natural form because I was who and what I was.

Roddy lived. Everything else was secondary.

I broke our kiss and smiled up at him. "As long as you're with me, I can face anything. Even Grandpa Alberic. Come on. Let's go be royal."

At our approach, one of the roses bushes leapt aside and we stepped out of the threshold circle. An ornate black carriage pulled by silver stallions waited for us. Roddy handed me in and I settled beside a window, remembering my first carriage ride in Faery. Grandpa Alberic and his aide, Cadmar, had been with us on that journey. Well, I'd see them both soon enough.

Roddy bowed to the stallions, said, "To the castle," and joined me in the carriage. As soon as we were settled, the carriage moved forward.

"Seriously? No one's driving?"

"The horses know where they're going," Roddy said, his eyes twinkling. "Remember, Claire, you're in Faery now. This isn't Big Vista, Washington."

Well, duh! Can anyone say *understatement?*

It might be the middle of winter in my world, but in Faery the sun shone in a bright blue sky while perfect puffy white clouds scudded by. The grass in the meadow was an unbelievably vivid emerald green and littered with wildflowers of every color imaginable. If I'd expected a white Christmas, it looked like I was in for a disappointment.

As the carriage moved across the drawbridge and under the arch of the massive stone gate, I rubbed my hands down the denim of my jeans. Maybe I should have dressed the part, but I didn't own anything that I imagined a princess would wear. What did I know about being royal?

"Relax, Claire," Roddy said, noticing my nervous gesture. "You look fine. If Alberic wants you to dress in a certain way, he'll let you know … and he'll provide the wardrobe."

I nodded, licked my dry lips, and said, "I know. I just hope he doesn't expect me to suddenly become someone I'm not."

"Don't worry," he said, squeezing my hand. "I'm pretty sure you gave him a good idea of who you are and aren't at your last meeting. You're going to be fine, Claire. You were born to be Princess of Faery."

The carriage pulled to a stop before the wide steps leading to the main entrance. To each side of the huge carved wooden doors stood a knight in shining armor. Literally. Their armor gleamed in the morning sun like they'd just finished polishing it. The doors behind them opened and liveried footmen appeared, ran down the stairs, and opened the carriage doors. Before I could do more than blink, I'd been handed out of the carriage and escorted through the entry hall, down a wide corridor, and into Grandpa Alberic's study. Roddy strode beside me every step of the way.

Grandpa sat behind a large mahogany desk, its surface littered with important looking documents, maps, quills, and ink bottles. He looked up when Roddy and I entered the room, a wide smile softening his stern features. I grinned back at him, marveling again at just how deeply our family resemblance was written in our genes. His blue-black hair, fine boned face and clear, pale skin were the mirror image of my own. Even our eyes were the same shade of green, though his carried a depth of knowledge that I doubted I'd ever achieve. Looking at his unlined face and lithe body, it was difficult to imagine that he was old beyond my comprehension. How old? I had no idea, and I wasn't about to ask, but I knew he'd waited over a thousand years for his daughter's true heir to be born ... and here I stood.

"Claire!" Grandpa exclaimed as he stood and came to meet me, arms open wide for a hug. "I'm so glad you're back. I can't tell you how dull life has been without our verbal battles."

Forgetting everything I'd learned about court protocol, I rushed to meet Grandpa and was immediately enfolded in a warm embrace.

"I'm glad to see you too, Grandpa," I said, my words muffled against the fawn colored velvet of his doublet. I stepped back and looked up into his oh-so-familiar face. I'd only known him a short time, but he really did feel as much like family as Gran, who'd been part of my life forever. Maybe it was magic, or maybe blood really does tell.

Whatever! Grandpa was definitely part of my life now, and we were both anxious to make up for lost time.

"Prince Rhydderich," Grandpa said, nodding to Roddy while keeping one arm around my waist. "Thank you for escorting Claire home to Faery."

"It was my honor, sire," Roddy replied, executing a flawless bow with precisely the right amount of depth. I sighed inwardly wondering if I'd ever be as confident in my courtesies as Roddy.

Grandpa inclined his head in acknowledgement of Roddy's bow, then smiled. "You're dismissed, Roddy. Your mother is in residence for the festival; go and find your family. I'm sure they're anxious to see you."

"Thank you, sire." Roddy glanced at me and grinned. "I'll see you later, my princess."

"Counting on it," I replied. "Say 'hi' to your mom and Bran for me."

"Of course," he said before turning and leaving the room.

Grandpa shook his head and held me at arms' length. "Really, Claire. We must work on your manners. 'Say 'hi' to your mom'? You were speaking of the Winter Queen!"

I shrugged. "Yeah, but I was also talking to my friend about his mother. Roddy knew what I meant, and he would've thought something was seriously wrong with me if I'd gone all formal on him."

Grandpa led me over to the hearth where a grouping of well-padded intricately carved wooden chairs stood before a blazing fire. I chose one with deep red velvet cushions and carvings of roses and vines. Grandpa settled in one carved with stags and hounds and sporting rich brown cushions,.

"I suppose," he said, "but do try to limit your casual comments to family time. You can be familiar with Roddy when you are alone or the two of you are with me, but in front of courtiers, try to maintain a sense of dignity. There's been quite enough gossip about my heir and the heir of Winter already."

My eyes widened and I was glad I didn't have a drink to choke on. "People are gossiping about me and Roddy? Why?"

Grandpa narrowed his eyes, but seemed to decide I'd asked an honest question. "Because of who you are," he said, his tone suggesting he was explaining the obvious … which he probably was, "and the fact that Roddy has resumed his true form and walks the corridors of my castle."

I frowned. "Why does that lead to gossip about him and me?"

Grandpa sighed. "Claire, my entire kingdom knew that Roddy was under a sentence of death. Everyone knew that as soon as Rhiannon's true heir was returned to Faery, Roddy would die. But you're here and he's not only alive, he's been restored as Winter's heir. Obviously you did something to change my mind … for you're the only person in Faery who could have brought his redemption about. So just as obviously, he must be very special to you."

"Oh." Not my most brilliant come-back, but my brain was busy processing. I mean, I knew all of that, but …, "I guess I just never thought anyone would care enough to put those pieces together," I finally said, "or be interested enough to gossip about it."

Grandpa laughed out loud, a delighted sound that cheered my soul. "My darling, Claire! You are the most interesting thing to happen in Faery for centuries of your time. Everything you do, everything you say, even your smallest gesture will be of infinite interest to my subjects. To *your* subjects."

I startled, my mouth dropping open. I closed it with a snap, swallowed, and said, "Seriously? I'll be watched that closely?"

"What is the contraption the mortals use? Oh, yes. A microscope. Consider your life to be the focus of a microscope, Claire. Your people are curious about you. Everything about you. That is why you need to pay attention to your lessons with Ogham and Cadmar. Learn as quickly as you can. The sooner your actions are predictable and consistent with court etiquette, the sooner the intense scrutiny will abate."

"As long as you're an unpredictable faery," he continued, "the kingdom will watch your every move, wondering what you'll do next. Why, you've already saved Roddy's life and changed my plans for you. Both of those are things our people considered impossible. You're a full faery now, and yet I allow you to return to the mortal realm. Why? Because you bullied me into it. Of course people are curious about you!"

"I did not bully you," I said hotly, then more primly, "we negotiated."

He laughed again. "Of course we did! But no one else has ever forced me to *negotiate* something I'd already decided upon. You are a wonder in their eyes … and frankly, in mine as well."

Huh. Who knew that standing up for myself was such a novelty in Faery? Of course, these people were far older than they looked and had been dealing with each other for longer than I could imagine, so maybe my youth and inexperience would've made me unpredictable even if I hadn't been determined to save Roddy and live my life on my own terms.

At any rate, I'd pay attention to my lessons because I needed to understand this new world I was destined to live in, but I wasn't in a hurry to become predictable. I had the feeling that unpredictability might just turn out to be one of my most valuable tools. I just had to learn what was expected, so I'd recognize what wasn't.

Evidently, the first expectation I'd smashed to smithereens was that the High King never changed his mind. Good to know. And good to know that I could make the impossible happen.

CHAPTER 3

A routine established itself over the next few days. My faery maid, Elya, woke me each morning and helped me dress in one of the gorgeous gowns Grandpa had provided. As soon as I was presentable, which took remarkably little time considering I'd never have been able to figure out how arrange all those layers of cloth without Elya's help, I joined Grandpa for breakfast, a cheery way to start my day.

Next, I joined my friend Ogham, a handsome sorrel centaur who tutored me in magic, in his classroom. I'd come a long way in the few months he'd been teaching me and could now handle most basic spells and incantations.

When Ogham released me from class, I retired to my solar for lunch. I'd never heard of a solar until I visited Faery, but it turned out to be a pleasant sun-filled chamber that reminded me of a drawing room from a Regency romance novel. My own private reception room, with lots of large windows set in walls of some warm wood, like maybe cherry. The tile floors were covered with intricately woven rugs featuring Celtic knots and maze patterns, and the furniture seemed to change with the time of day. At lunch a large, a highly polished cherry dining table surrounded by beautifully carved chairs filled the space. At other times of day it featured comfy overstuffed chairs and couches artfully arranged in several conversation areas. I loved it. Especially when it was filled with people I was beginning to think of as friends: Roddy, Ogham, Bran, and various other faery folk I met on my visits to the Summer and Winter Courts before I was officially presented to Grandpa at Samhain.

The afternoons were my least favorite part of the day: protocol lessons with Cadmar. Grandpa's chief advisor was a tall, lean faery without an ounce of fun in his psychological make-up. He got off on the wrong foot with me early on by disrespecting Roddy, before I understood who Roddy truly was. Now that Grandpa had reinstated Roddy, Cadmar was a bit easier to take, but I still resented the way he'd acted in our first few meetings, which made our lessons a bit tense, and that was without even taking the subject matter into account.

So, cheerful breakfasts, fun mornings, entertaining lunches, and boring afternoons. No biggie; I could live with that. After all, I was a high school student. Especially since my evenings were reserved for Grandpa and Roddy.

The trouble began on the day before the festival of Alban Arthan.

I was enjoying lunch in my solar with Lady Meredith and Prince Bran and wishing Roddy could've joined us, when Cadmar entered the room. I knew immediately that something was up because the protocol master looked like a storm cloud had settled on his face.

Now, Cadmar's never been my favorite person and he always looks like someone stuffed a metal rod down his jacket, but we'd been getting along pretty well the last few days. Wondering what I could possibly have done wrong before I even got to his class, I stifled a sigh and controlled the urge to roll my eyes.

"Good afternoon, Cadmar," I said, trying to remember to phrase my comments appropriately. "Would you care to join us for lunch?"

Cadmar stopped across the table from me, bowed with a dignity I wasn't sure I'd ever learn, and said, "Thank you, Princess, but no. I've come to deliver a summons. Your grandsire, King Alberic, requires your presence in his study." He met my gaze straight on and added, "Immediately."

I swallowed, though my mouth was suddenly as dry as the Sahara. My heart drummed so loudly I could barely hear myself think, and my fingers froze to my silverware. What could I have possibly done? Grandpa had been fine last night. He and Roddy and I had played *Bows and Axes*, a board game that reminded me of a cross between chess and Battleship, and I'd lost spectacularly. A condition that always pleased Grandpa.

Forcing a calm I didn't feel, I placed my silverware neatly across my plate, wiped my fingers on my linen napkin, and rose. Nodding to Meredith and Bran, I said, "I'm sorry to leave in the middle of our meal, but duty calls."

As they murmured polite understanding, I walked around the table to join Cadmar who offered me his arm. I declined his support and swept from my solar ahead of him. I knew the way to Grandpa's study; I didn't need a guide. The ringing of his booted feet on the stone floor told me Cadmar followed at the requisite distance, but the additional tramp of soldiers' boots failed to reassure me.

Why did I need an armed escort in the corridors of Grandpa's castle?

Something was seriously wrong, and I doubted I was the cause. I couldn't imagine doing anything to warrant such precautions.

When we reached the door to Grandpa's study, I paused to close my eyes, take a deep breath, and pull my thoughts under tight control. Cadmar took that opportunity to move past me to the door. I opened my eyes, exhaled quietly, and nodded to him. He opened the door. I stepped inside, and Cadmar closed the door behind me, leaving me alone with Grandpa.

King Alberic stood before the hearth, facing the merrily dancing flames. When the door closed, he turned to face me. If I hadn't already known something was wrong, I would've known it now. Grandpa's face was serious and drawn. For the first time since I'd known him, he looked old.

"Claire," he said, his voice quiet and somber. "Please, come and sit with me."

I didn't say a word. There are times to be boisterous and rowdy, or even sarcastic and flip. This was so not one of those times. Instead I walked across the room and settled in my favorite chair, the one with the red cushion and the rose and vine carvings. Grandpa perched on the edge of his seat, elbows on knees, hands clasped.

"I don't know how much Cadmar has told you about the upcoming festival, Alban Arthan," he said, then paused as if waiting for me to supply information. I took the hint.

"Alban Arthan, or midwinter, takes place tomorrow night. In my world it's known as the winter solstice, the shortest day of the year. After midwinter, the days begin to lengthen until we reach the spring equinox when day and night are of equal length. The days continue to get longer until midsummer, or the summer solstice, which is the longest day of the year. Right?"

He nodded. "From a human perspective, that's correct."

I frowned. "There's a difference between the human perspective and the faery perspective?" I asked. "I mean, the shortest day of the year is the shortest day of the year. It shouldn't matter which realm I'm in."

"Perhaps," he said, staring at his clasped hands, "but it does."

Silence reigned. Only the crackling of burning wood dared to break Grandpa's moody stillness. At last he looked up, sighed, and picked up the thread of our conversation.

"In Faery, magic is everything. Even the seasons change as a result of magic. I know that in the human realm where you were raised, people believe that science explains all, that the movement of the planets, the ebb and flow of the tides, the timing of light and dark are all based on scientific principles. Immutable principles."

He sighed again. "They're wrong. Their scientific knowledge explains their world only so long as Faery magic maintains its proper balance." He leaned forward and extended his hands to me. I laid mine in his and he grasp them tightly. "Something has happened that will disturb that balance. Something so catastrophic that both realms could find themselves locked in eternal winter."

I gasped and tried to pull away, but he held on tightly.

"This concerns you personally as well, Claire. Let me say it outright, then I'll explain as well as I can." He gazed into my eyes, and I saw sorrow and concern and steely determination reflected there. "The Wyrd Stone has been stolen and Roddy has been arrested. He is in the dungeon and you will not see him again. Do you understand what I'm saying?"

I yanked my hands from his, jumped up and moved behind my chair. I wanted a barrier between him and me. I gripped the carved wood of its back and glared at the King of Faery.

"No!" I shouted. "I don't understand and I don't believe you. You're just looking for a way out of the deal you made with me. You want Roddy dead! You've always wanted him dead. I ruined your original plans and now you've found a new reason to persecute him."

I raced to the door, had my hand on the knob before I turned to throw my final barb. "If it's a choice between you and Roddy. I choose Roddy. Always."

I wanted to storm from the room, but Alberic was too fast for me.

"Stop!" he commanded and I froze. He pointed at the door. "Lock."

A current of magic ruffled my hair like a summer breeze. I was trapped and I knew it. He released his hold on me, and I slumped against the door that was now useless to me until he chose to allow me to leave.

"Come and sit down, Claire." The king's voice was gentle, the words carried no command.

I stayed beside the door.

"Why do you think I commanded Cadmar to bring you here?" he asked quietly. When I didn't respond, he answered his own question. "Because I knew you would react this way. I know how close you are to Roddy, but you must believe me, Claire. I'm not trying to frame Roddy as your human friends would phrase it. He has been arrested because he is the only one with sufficient reason to do this foul thing."

"Yeah. Right. He's also the only faery who has lived after you decreed that he should die," I snarled. "You're just looking for a way to fix that little problem." I stepped away from the door and folded my arms across my chest. "What's your evidence? Why should I believe you, and why can't I see Roddy and hear his side of the story?"

"Think, Claire! We've held this ceremony for thousands of years ... and the first time Roddy is back in Faery, the Wyrd Stone goes missing?"

"So? It's also the first time *I've* been in Faery for Alban Arthan, why haven't you thrown *me* in the dungeon?"

He sat down in his favorite chair, the one carved with stags and hounds, and scrubbed his hands across this face. "Because you have no idea what or where the Wyrd Stone is," he said in a resigned voice, "and you don't have an ancient score to settle with me."

I huffed. "And Roddy does?"

"Of course he does, Claire! I transformed him into a dragon and forced him to guard your bloodline for more of your centuries than I like to count. Because of me, he had to watch his best friend grow old and die in the mortal world. Because of me, he believed he would be executed the moment he presented you to me."

"Prince Rhydderich has more than sufficient reason to hate me, Claire," he said quietly, once again staring at his hands. When he glanced up, he motioned me to my chair, and this time I moved. Once I was seated, he continued, "There's one final mark against Roddy," he said gruffly, as if determined to get all the nastiness out in the open. "He is Winter's heir, and without the Wyrd Stone, Winter will remain ascendant forever."

I slumped against the back of my chair. "Okay," I said. "I can see your reasoning," I held up my hand to stop the comment he was about to make, "but you're wrong. Your evidence is circumstantial. You have no proof, only suppositions based on his title and your presumptions about his feelings. Just because *you'd* want revenge, doesn't mean Roddy does. I know Roddy, a lot better than you do now. Probably better than you ever did. He's innocent."

A horrible thought floated to the surface of my mind. I glared at Grandpa and growled, "Don't even think about torturing him to force him to give you information he doesn't have."

An expression flitted across his face and I knew I'd guessed the real reason Roddy was in the dungeon and the king had forbidden me to see him.

Putting all the steel I could manage in my voice, I said, "If you harm him, if you so much as touch him, I will go back to Big Vista and refuse to ever set foot in Faery again."

His face went stern and cold. "What makes you think I would allow that to happen?"

"Rhiannon accomplished it," I said, making my expression mirror his. "If she could escape you, so can I."

We stared at each other, both determined not to flinch from the confrontation.

Grandpa looked away first. I think I won because I was fighting for Roddy's life again, while he was just defending his right to rule. I had the greater stake in our conflict.

Grandpa turned, pointed at the door, and said, "Open!"

The door flew open, revealing Cadmar on the other side.

"Cadmar," the king commanded. "Hear and obey."

Cadmar went to one knee on the threshold. "Always, my king."

"Release Prince Rhydderich from the dungeon. Escort him to his chambers and seal him inside. None may enter his chamber except you, me, Princess Claire, and one knight of your choosing who will see to the Prince's needs while he is under suspicion."

Throwing a scowl at me, Cadmar rose, inclined his head to the king, and said, "It shall be done immediately, my king."

Grandpa flicked his fingers at the door and it closed behind the courtier.

"Does that satisfy you, Princess?" His voice was still cold, his expression grim.

"Thank you, Grandpa," I said, vowing to myself not to cross him again for anything short of a life and death situation. "Roddy and I will figure this out."

His frown deepened until I thought his face might crack. "Did you not hear..."

"I'm sorry," I interrupted. "I know Roddy is in prison. I just meant I'd tell him everything I learn and he'll help me figure it out. How much time do I have? Will you be looking for other suspects too?"

Relief lightened his features. "You … we all have until midnight of the Festival of Alban Arthan — that's tomorrow night — and yes, I will instruct Cadmar to search for others who might have done this terrible deed."

"Thank you, Grandpa," I said. I stood, moved to his side, and kissed his forehead. "We'll find the Wyrd Stone … and I'll prove Roddy is innocent. He doesn't hate you, Grandpa. He's not like that."

Grandpa caught my hand and kissed it. "I hope you're right, Claire," he said, his voice rough with emotion. "For all our sakes."

CHAPTER 4

*R*oddy turned when I stepped across the threshold of his chamber. An expression of joy and wonder lit his features and he rushed to hug me. I relaxed into his embrace, soothed by the strength of his arms and the steady beat of his heart. No way would I allow anyone — not the king, not some unknown thief — to separate me from Roddy.

"Claire! How did you do this?" he asked, but before I could say anything he hurried on as though he'd been waiting to talk, and perhaps he had. "I know it had to have been you. Cadmar was livid when he released me from the dungeon and brought me up here. You're the only one I know who can upset him that much."

He pushed me to arms' length, but held onto my shoulders, his expression serious. "I didn't do it, Claire. I need you to know, to believe, that I'm not guilty."

"Of course you're innocent," I said, my eyes widening. "You didn't really think I'd believe them, did you?"

He relaxed slightly and hugged me again. When we broke apart, he kissed the top of my head and scrubbed his eyes. "No," he said. "Not really. But I worried. I was afraid I'd never see you again. Never get to tell you…"

"I know," I murmured. "Grandpa tried to forbid me to see you, but that didn't work out as he expected." I grinned. "He's got to get over thinking I'm just going to do what he says. Not going to happen," I said, shaking my head. "Not when I disagree with his command."

We walked over to the hearth where a grouping of three hunter green overstuffed chairs waited. Like my own chambers, Roddy's consisted of two rooms — a sitting room and a bedroom. A large fireplace occupied the wall between the rooms, opening into each so that one fire blazed in both. Besides the chairs before the hearth, the sitting room contained a walnut desk situated between two long, narrow windows, and a small dining table just big enough to accommodate two straight-back chairs. The stone floors were strewn with shorn sheepskin rugs.

I curled into one of the overstuffed chairs, while Roddy sat opposite me.

"Okay," I said. "We both know you didn't steal the Wyrd Stone, but we've got to figure out who did and get it back before it's needed for the ceremony."

"Yes," Roddy agreed. "Unless I want to spend the rest of my life in these rooms, we've got to clear my name."

I nodded. "So, tell me about this Wyrd Stone. I was so worried about getting you out of the dungeon that I didn't think to ask Grandpa."

"I appreciate that," Roddy said with a quick grin.

"You can skip the part about Alban Arthan and the length of days stuff. I've got all that. Just tell me about the stone. What is it … what does it look like … and why is it so important?"

A slight frown creased his forehead as he concentrated on my questions. "The Wyrd Stone is a magic artifact from our ancient history. It contains immense power and is used to control the turning of the seasons. Twice a year we unveil it in a sun ceremony. At Alban Arthan it turns the tide of days so that they begin to lengthen in preparation for the Summer Court's ascendance at Beltane. When it's used at Litha, midsummer, the days begin to shorten."

I shook my head. This all sounded like superstitious nonsense to me. "I don't know," I said. "I always thought the length was daylight was determined by the earth's position in relation to the sun. You know, as the planet orbits the sun ... it's not a perfect circle. The ellipsoid pattern causes the daylight to vary."

"That's right," he agreed, "as far as it goes. What science doesn't understand is that the earth's orbit is controlled by the Wyrd Stone."

"Seriously?" I gaped at him. "You're telling me that some little rock in Faery makes the earth circle the sun? Roddy! That makes absolutely no sense."

He smiled and leaned back in his chair, steepling his fingers under his chin. "Think of it like this, Claire. If you had a radio-controlled plane, it would fly, but you'd control it from the ground with a radio transmitter. The plane would receive the signals and respond accordingly. If you stopped sending orders, the plane would fly in a straight line until it crashed into something, right?"

I nodded. I'd never flown an RC plane, but I understood what he was saying.

"The earth's orbit around the sun is like that. The Wyrd Stone is the transmitter, the earth's core the receiver. Twice a year, we adjust the earth's orbit with the stone. If the adjustment isn't made, the earth maintains its position relative to the sun and the length of days remains static."

He sighed. "I suppose the king thinks I did it because I'm heir to Winter and if the Wyrd Stone isn't found, the days won't lengthen and Winter will be eternal."

"Something like that," I agreed. "Of course he also thinks you want revenge against him for all those centuries you spent as a dragon in the human world guarding my family."

His eyes widened and he sat forward. "Really? He said that?"

"Yep."

"Well," he said, leaning back again. "If I ever get the chance to talk to him, I'll have to ease his mind." Roddy smiled at me. "After all, if I hadn't been a dragon assigned to your family, I'd never have known you ... and you were worth the wait, Claire."

My cheeks warmed with a blush and a happy, shivery feeling spread from my belly to the tips of my fingers and toes. Roddy certainly knew how to make a girl feel special!

The heady moment was broken when the door to Roddy's chambers opened and a faery knight stepped over the threshold.

"Excuse me, Princess," he said, standing rigidly at attention, "but Prince Rhydderich's evening meal has arrived. Will you be joining him?"

I glanced at Roddy and quirked an eyebrow. He grinned.

"Yes, I believe I will," I told the knight. "And you are?"

"Javan, your highness. Cadmar assigned me to assist Prince Rhydderich during his ... uh ... incarceration."

"Thank you, Javan. Please continue with your duties."

Roddy and I sat quietly while Javan arranged our meal on the small walnut dining table across the room. I noticed several pixies hovering outside the open door. They'd undoubtedly prepared and delivered our dinner, but were prevented from entering the room by Grandpa's geis.

The small, nut-brown creatures scrutinized Javan's every move, their large, dark eyes filled with concern as he arranged the dishes. One in particular seemed to be in charge. He twisted the hem of his apron in his long-fingered hands and hissed loudly whenever Javan set a plate or a spoon in the wrong position.

Javan, for his part, was sensitive to the pixies' instructions, glancing at them frequently for cues as to where items belonged.

At last the table was set and Javan, obviously relieved, stepped to the door, bowed, and left, shooing the pixies from the threshold as he closed the door.

Roddy rose from his overstuffed chair and held out his hand to me. "Shall we dine, my princess?"

I grinned, jumped to my feet, and took his hand, enjoying the warmth of his fingers on my own. "Let's eat," I said. "I'm starved."

The pixies had outdone themselves, and my mouth watered as Roddy seated me at the small dining table. Grilled trout on a bed of lemon and parsley, wild rice in mushroom sauce, a beautifully arranged platter of fresh fruit — including some I'd never seen before — and a tureen of a hearty vegetable soup. Not to mention the most lavishly decorated cake I could've imagined, if baking and cake decorating was my thing, which it most definitely was not.

The frosting looked like it was spun from moonbeams with tiny stars twinkling in its sugary depths. Delicate rosebuds shimmered against a heavenly blue background while the whole confection seemed to hover above the raised dais of its plate. I couldn't begin to guess the flavors I'd taste when I had my first bite … and I really didn't want to wait until I'd finished the main course!

"Wow!" I exclaimed. "I don't think prisoners eat like this in the human realm. You must really rate with the kitchen staff."

Roddy laughed, and I smiled, pleased to have elicited that carefree sound.

"Well, I am a prince," he said, filling his plate with trout, rice, and fruit, "and the heir to the reigning monarch. Everyone wants to please royalty … at least until I'm proven guilty and banished from Faery."

"Which you won't be, because you're not," I said quickly, dismayed to see his light mood vanishing. I dipped a cup of soup from the tureen, inhaling a savory fragrance that sang of fresh, growing things, and turned our discussion to another topic. "You haven't told me what the Wyrd Stone looks like. How will I recognize it when I find it?"

He paused, a bite of flaky fish almost to his lips. "It's a brilliant blue stone about the size of your fist," he said, popping his fork into his mouth. He chewed, swallowed, and continued, "But you won't have to worry about recognizing it. If you get close, you'll know it."

I swallowed a spoonful of the delicious soup and frowned. "How?"

"It'll call to you, especially this close to midwinter. You'll hear its song and you'll be drawn to it. It's irresistible when it's ready to work its magic."

I nodded, set my soup aside, and filled my plate with tender fish, savory rice, and succulent fruit. I definitely needed to make friends with the pixies. After all, I was royalty too, and this was a better meal than they'd been feeding me. Of course, I wasn't in prison. Maybe they felt sorry for Roddy and were making an extra effort to please him.

"So, since we know you're innocent," I said between bites, "who would you suspect?"

He laid down his fork, wiped his fingers on a napkin of such fine linen it seemed a shame to soil it, and frowned. "Part of the reason I'm a suspect is because I'm Winter's heir. Since winter would continue if the Wyrd Stone couldn't perform its function, we'd benefit. But I can't believe that any of my family, or anyone under Mother's influence, would do such a thing. I also don't believe that anyone connected to Winter would leave me to take the blame for their actions. I've been gone so long, and everyone seems genuinely glad to have me home and free."

I pushed a piece of something that might have been pineapple except for its purple color around my plate, avoiding Roddy's gaze. "What about Bran?" I asked quietly. "He was heir in your absence ... your return has pushed him back into second son status."

Peeking at him through my lashes, I saw him lean back in his chair and steeple his fingers beneath his chin.

"If he's upset, he's been doing a really good job of hiding it," he said. "I don't want to believe anyone in Winter has done this, but I suppose Bran would have the strongest motive ... after me, of course."

I nodded. Bran was on my short list of suspects to investigate. I hoped for Roddy's sake that his brother was as innocent as I knew Roddy to be.

"Okay, leaving Winter aside, who else might benefit?"

"Well, there aren't all that many courtiers who are tied solely to the High King's court and I can't think of any reason one of them would do this. Your grandfather reigns regardless of whether Winter or Summer is in ascendance. His court is above the changing of the seasons."

"So that leaves the Summer Court, right?"

"Yes."

We'd finished our meal by that time, and I watched with an unseemly anticipation as Roddy sliced the amazing cake. The frosting sparkled like sunlight on water or starlight in a clear midnight sky, its color shimmered through the visible spectrum, and very likely beyond. I could hardly wait to taste the airy confection that spectacular frosting contained.

I held my breath as Roddy lifted a slice of layered cake, deposited it on a gold plate, and presented it to me.

"Is this your first slice of celestial cake, my princess?"

I lifted my gaze from the enchanting cake to his face. "Is that what this is?"

He smiled. "It is. The kitchen pixies know it's my favorite."

I nodded, scarcely hearing his words. Celestial cake. Beneath the frosting, the cake was startlingly white. A white so pristine it would make the purest snowfall seem dingy and grey. Its aroma was intoxicating. A delightful mixture of nature's best: chocolate, honey, a garden full of blooms warmed by sunlight and a fresh spring breeze. My mouth watered in anticipation of the taste that would accompany that fragrance.

With trembling fingers, I lifted my first bite to my lips. A starburst of flavor exploded across my tongue, arousing a sensory experience in my whole body. The taste tickled my nose and tingled in my fingertips and toes. It warmed my belly and elicited a sensation of comfort and safety and … love. How extraordinary! A cake that tasted like love.

Faery was an amazing place.

"It's good isn't it?" asked Roddy, enjoying a bite of his own piece of cake.

"Good?" I gasped, barely able to speak. "How can you call this cake good? It's so far beyond good, it's … it's …" my words stumbled to a stop. I had no words. I was incapable of rational thought. I closed my eyes and savored every delicate sensation of that indescribable dessert.

When the last crumb had disappeared, and I felt capable of speech again, I opened my eyes to find Roddy smiling at me.

"That was incredible," I said, as content as a purring cat.

"I'll be sure to have Javan tell the pixies how much you enjoyed your meal."

"Do that," I said, eying the remainder of the cake. "Honestly though, I'm not sure that cake should be legal. I mean, talk about addictive."

"Not to worry," he said. "The pixies are under strict orders not to make it too often."

With that, he opened the door to let Javan know we'd finished our meal. While the faery knight cleared the table, Roddy escorted me back to our comfortable overstuffed chairs. After that amazing meal, I felt a deep kinship for their stuffed status.

When all evidence of our meal had been removed and the door closed behind Javan, we returned to our earlier conversation.

"So," I said, "who do you suspect in the Summer Court?"

Roddy leaned back, elbows resting on the upholstered arms of the chair. "I don't know. It doesn't make any sense for anyone in the Summer Court to steal the Wyrd Stone during Winter's reign. If the stone doesn't exert its power, Summer won't return to ascendance. They have no motive."

His fingers drummed a tattoo against the chair, and then suddenly stopped.

"Unless…"

"Unless, what?" I asked, leaning toward him.

"Unless you were the motive."

"Me?" I yelped. "How could I be a motive for someone in Summer stealing the Wyrd Stone? I didn't even know it existed until today."

"Well," he said, a bit hesitantly. "It's just that it suddenly occurred to me that Idris might have a motive. I mean, everyone knows that you and I are close." He stopped, swallowed, glanced at me and then studied the floor.

"And?" I prompted.

"And, well, all the courts are gossiping about us and ..."

I threw up my hands in exasperation. "I don't see how people gossiping about us could be a motive for Idris to steal the Wyrd Stone."

"Fine," he said. "Here it is. He's a prince, too. If he's jealous of your feelings for me, he might steal the stone to frame me. That way he'd get rid of me and be able to make a play for you himself. You know he was interested at the Samhain Ball."

"Interested in dancing," I countered, my face blazing.

"No, Claire. Interested in marrying you, the heir to the High King."

"Then he's not interested in me, he doesn't know me. He's interested in the throne. Not the same thing at all."

"People could say the same thing about me," he said quietly.

The warmth of my blush died and I leaned forward to take his hands. "Then they don't know either of us," I said. "I fell for you while you were still a dragon, and you ... well you know me better than anyone. Sometimes I think you know me better than I know myself."

I squeezed his hands. "Look at me, Roddy."

He lifted his eyes and gazed into mine.

"I know you care for me, not just my position as heir to the throne. You know how I know?"

"I think so, but I'd like to hear you say it."

"Because you cared for me when you didn't expect to live. You were my guardian and friend even though you expected Grandpa to kill you as soon as you presented me to him. But most of all, I know that you love me because your kiss, our bond, pulled me back into my body when I should have died."

I leaned closer and kissed his cheek. "Never doubt our love, Roddy. I don't."

Our lips were a centimeter from a passionate kiss when the door opened and Cadmar strode in.

Roddy and I jerked apart, but not before Cadmar noticed our proximity.

"Princess, your grandsire asked me to escort you to your chambers. You've spent far too much time in this miscreant's company."

"Watch it, Cadmar," I said, with a distinct growl in my voice. "You're on shaky ground."

"I'm only concerned for your reputation, Princess. I told your grandsire that you shouldn't be allowed to spend unchaperoned time with this … this …"

"Don't finish that sentence, Cadmar. Not if you value your position at court."

He drew himself up to his full height, his silver hair sparkling in the light.

"As for the unchaperoned part, Roddy and I have been together for months in Big Vista. No one's been watching over us there."

Cadmar sniffed. "That was different. He was a dragon at the time. Now, however, it's highly irregular for you to be spending time in a man's chambers without proper…"

"He's under arrest," I yelled. "Where else am I supposed to see him when he can't leave these rooms?"

"I've offered my services as chaperone."

"No way," I cried, jumping to my feet and advancing on him. "You just want to spy on us. You don't want me to find the real thief. You just want Grandpa to have an excuse to execute Roddy after all."

I stepped close to him and poked him in the chest with my index finger. "Tell me, Cadmar. Did you steal the stone to frame Roddy? Did you take it so Grandpa would do him in and you wouldn't have to deal with him anymore? Did you?"

Cadmar's pale face whitened, but his eyes blazed. "How dare you?"

"Claire."

Roddy's quiet voice broke through my rage. I turned to find him standing beside his chair. He held out a hand to me and I strode to his side and grasped it.

"It's all right, Claire," he said, soothingly. "It's getting late. Perhaps it's time we said good-night. Come see me tomorrow?"

"Of course," I said. "Wild horses couldn't keep me away." I glared at Cadmar. "Or even obnoxious courtiers." I squeezed Roddy's fingers and stretched to kiss his cheek, then swept from the room without another word to Cadmar.

CHAPTER 5

The next morning I sent Billow, a storm sprite I'd met at the Winter Court, to Cadmar to inform him that our lessons were at an end. At least until Roddy's name was cleared.

With that task accomplished, I almost ran to Ogham's classroom. The centaur who mentored me in the use of magic had been friends with Roddy for centuries. I knew he'd help me solve the mystery of the disappearing Wyrd Stone.

For being inside the High King's castle, Ogham's classroom was remarkably like the cave he'd been living in when I first met him. Rock walls, packed earth floor, huge fireplace, and a scarred work-table. Even the carved marble bench I'd rested on during that first meeting was the same.

I settled on the bench while Ogham chopped herbs at the table.

"So our friend is in trouble again," he said, somberly. "Tell me everything, Claire."

So I did. I told him how Grandpa had started by forbidding me to see Roddy right through to all our suspicions and suppositions.

"Not much real evidence to work with," he said when I finished my recitation, "and not much time to figure it out. Where do you plan to start?"

"I'm going to start with Bran," I said. "Figure out where he stands. If he's with us, he'll be able to help. If he's not … well, if he's not, he goes to the top of my list of likely suspects."

Ogham nodded. "I'll make a tour of the castle today. See if I can detect where the stone might be hidden. Finding it won't clear Roddy, but it will certainly ease the tension."

"Good plan. Meet me in my solar for lunch and we'll compare notes."

"Good hunting, Princess."

I nodded and left him to his work.

Where to find, Bran? I knew he was somewhere in the castle, both the Winter and Summer courts were in attendance for the celebration, but the High King's castle was enormous. Especially now with magical spells laid upon it, expanding it to fit all the dignitaries. If I wasn't so angry with Cadmar, I'd be really impressed with his managerial skills. As it was, well, I was better off not thinking about him at all.

I could wander these corridors for a week and still not run across Prince Bran. I stopped, leaned against the cool stone wall and gazed out a nearby window at the endlessly fascinating landscape that was Faery. Magical castle … magical landscape that bloomed in midwinter … missing magical stone. Everything here was magical.

Including me!

I rolled my eyes and slapped my forehead with the palm of my hand. Of course! I didn't need to search the castle for Bran. I needed to remember who I was — a magical being, and royalty at that!

Closing my eyes, I reached within myself to the well of magical energy that pooled at my core, tapped it, and set my intention. *I need to see*

Prince Bran at his earliest convenience. Preferably now. Releasing the magic, I sent my summons winging to Queen Maeve's youngest son.

A moment later, Prince Bran shimmered into existence a few feet from where I stood. Dressed casually in a leather vest over a snowy linen shirt and dark breeches, he was still unbelievably handsome. My heart flip-flopped as he sketched a courtly bow and then cocked a questioning silver eyebrow at me.

Silver and gold, that described Maeve's sons. I'd first known Roddy as a dragon, a magnificent molten gold beast with mesmerizing emerald eyes. Now, in his natural form as a faery prince, my friend was golden haired, his skin tanned to perfection.

Bran, on the other hand, was silver. His hair wasn't blond and it wasn't grey, it flowed around his face and shoulders like a stream of liquid silver, highlighting his grey-blue eyes and accenting his pale, porcelain skin. Bran was every inch the handsome faery prince.

"How can I be of service, Princess Claire?" he asked, his tone friendly, but a bit puzzled. Faery royalty rarely summoned each other with magic. Grandpa always sent a courtier to find me.

My cheeks heated under his quizzical gaze, while my heart thundered like a herd of galloping horses. I reached within, sought calm, and found it. I hadn't summoned Bran to admire his admittedly handsome face. I needed to determine his guilt … or innocence … in the matter of the missing Wyrd Stone.

"Thank you for coming so quickly, Prince Bran," I said, pleased by how calm and steady my voice sounded. "Will you walk with me? I have something I'd like to discuss."

"Of course, milady." He smiled, offered me his arm, and led me to a set of wide French doors that opened onto a stunningly beautiful formal garden. Flowers of every size and shape lined a maze of white-stoned walkways, a riot of color in what should have been the gloom of winter.

We stepped onto the path and I was immediately aware of hundreds of flower faeries watching us from beneath petals and leaves. I hesitated. This wouldn't do. I wanted my conversation with Bran to be private.

Bran felt my hesitance, glanced around, breathed a sigh of understanding, and whispered to me. "You can dismiss them, Princess Claire. This is your domain."

"Oh," I said, an interesting mixture of embarrassment and relief warming my cheeks. "Of course. Thank you, Prince Bran."

He laid his free hand over mine where it rested near his elbow. "Please, call me Bran. We're practically family."

"Okay, if you call me Claire."

He inclined his head. "Agreed, Claire."

I smiled, took a deep breath, and surveyed the faeries in the garden. "Thank you all so much for making this garden such a pleasant place," I said, hoping my voice would carry to all the tiny creatures. "Another time I'd love to get to know you all, but today I need to have a private conversation with Prince Bran. Please leave and don't return until I go back into the castle."

A sigh of breeze wafted through the garden and when it stilled, Bran and I were alone.

"Nicely done, Claire," he said. "Not everyone treats the little folk with such courtesy."

I glanced at him in surprise. "Seriously? Well, shame on them. I'm very fond of the flower faeries. Especially the ones who inhabit our garden at home."

He nodded and led me to a marble bench beside a stunning rhododendron overflowing with the palest of pink blossoms. Once we were seated, he turned to me, his expression serious. "Now, how can I assist you, Claire? I doubt you summoned me just for a walk in the garden."

"No," I said. "I wanted to discuss Roddy's current, ah, situation. You know what's going on, don't you?"

His jaw tightened and he turned his gaze from me to his hands, clasped tightly in his lap. "I do," he said, his voice rough with … what? Suppressed anger? "I know that his association with you has once again led him into peril."

My breath caught and my heart constricted. I stared at him, open-mouthed. "What?" I cried. "You're blaming *me* for this?"

His hands relaxed and his shoulders slumped. He leaned forward, bracing his forearms on his knees. "No," he said with a sigh. "Of course not. Not really."

My pulse settled and I breathed a little easier.

"It's just that it's hard to see Mother so upset again," he continued. "She's been closed off, stoic, for centuries. Worried and frightened and afraid to love anyone, even me, for fear her loved one would be snatched away." He looked at me and I saw deep pain reflected in his eyes. "She'd just begun to recover; having Roddy home whole and healthy allowed her to relax and be happy again. But now…" He stopped, too emotional to continue.

"I'm so sorry, Bran," I whispered. "You know I'd never do anything to hurt Roddy."

He nodded, returning his gaze to the grass at his feet. "I know," he said, quietly. "I've been a bit jealous since he's been back. Everything has seemed to go his way. He's Mother's heir again. He has King Alberic's favor. And," he gazed into my eyes, "he's got this amazing bond with you. I envy him your regard."

My pulse jumped and then settled as I saw the truth in this silver-haired faery's eyes. He admired me, but he loved his brother. Bran was not the villain of this mystery.

"But then I remembered," he continued, "the price he paid for what he was enjoying, and all envy fled. My brother has endured so much hardship in his life. He deserves all the happiness he can find."

"Thank you for your honesty, Bran," I said quietly, placing my hand on his arm. "I had to know the truth."

He startled and stared at me, wide-eyed. "Wait," he cried. "You thought … you couldn't have … you suspected *me* of stealing the Wyrd Stone and framing Roddy?"

I shrugged. "It was a possibility. I had to investigate."

His jaw dropped. When he closed it, a pallor of pain settled on his already pale features. "Does Roddy think so?"

"No," I said, shaking my head so hard my short curls bounced. "He agreed I should question you, but he knew you wouldn't do such a thing."

He breathed deeply, closing his eyes. "Good," he said. "I wouldn't want him to think me so disloyal."

I sat quietly, giving Bran a moment to compose himself. When he opened his eyes, he nodded to me. "How can I help?"

A warm glow settled in my middle. I had help. Roddy might be under house arrest, but Ogham and Bran were ready to help me clear his name. I might be a stranger in a strange land trying to understand the incomprehensible, but I had people who understood the rules to guide me.

I jumped to my feet and paced back and forth in front of the bench where Bran continued to sit. "Okay. We know Roddy didn't steal it and neither did you." I stopped in front of him, frowning. "So, who do you think it might have been?"

He leaned back, flicking away a rhododendron blossom that brushed his cheek. "No one in Winter," he said. "I know our court must look guilty, but everyone is so relieved to see Mother happy again that they'd never risk exposing either Roddy or me to harm. My people love Mother. They'd never do anything to cause her pain."

I nodded and started pacing again. What can I say? I think better on the move. "That leaves Grandpa's court and Summer. Neither of which would seem to have a motive." I plopped onto the bench beside Bran. "What am I missing?"

He shrugged. "Whatever it is, I'm missing it too. I can't see why anyone would steal the stone. It doesn't benefit Summer, and while you could argue that Winter would win, its theft is causing our queen pain, and the high king's court has no reason at all to steal it." His eyes met mine. "This makes no sense."

I breathed deeply, inhaling the sweet floral scent of the sun-warmed garden. Magic was in the air. I studied the flowers and the impressive structure of the High King's castle. I was heir to all of this. Castle, kingdom, and the magic that flowed through all of it.

"Fine. I've investigated you," I smiled at Bran, "and you passed with flying colors. Now I need to talk to Idris. Roddy thinks I might be a motive for Idris to misbehave."

Bran raised an eyebrow, and I felt an embarrassed flush heat my neck and cheeks.

"Yes," he said. "I can see my brother's point. If I may make a suggestion, Princess?"

"Of course."

"Don't summon Idris with magic — he's not likely to be as understanding as I — send a messenger instead."

"Oh," I said. "Did I do something wrong? I'm so sorry, Bran."

"Don't be concerned, Claire," he said. "I didn't take offense, but it is considered rude to summon as you did. Especially since your royal summons has a compulsion attached. Courtiers don't like being compelled."

Shame flooded my system. "Of course they don't. Most of my fights with Grandpa are about him trying to force me to do or not do something. I had no idea my summons had a compulsion attached. Thank you for telling me."

He nodded. "I thought as much. Let's go inside, that will let the flower faeries return. Once they're back, you can ask one to request that Idris join us for lunch."

We strolled back to the castle door and stepped inside. I watched as a breeze swept gently through the garden. When the leaves and blossoms stilled, I felt the gaze of hundreds of eyes settle on me.

"They're back," I whispered, and stepped over the threshold into the garden once more. "Is Una here?" I asked, holding out my right hand.

A tiny flower faery fluttered to me and hovered above my outstretched fingers. She was perfectly proportioned and about the size of my fist, with curly red hair and wearing a bright yellow Tinker Bell dress.

I smiled at her. "Thank you for coming, Una. Would you please find Prince Idris and ask him to join me for lunch in my solar?"

She bobbed a curtsy in mid-air. "Of course, Princess Claire. It is my honor to assist." She fluttered away on gossamer wings, and I returned to the castle corridor where Bran waited.

CHAPTER 6

*L*unch with Ogham, Bran and Idris was a complete disaster.

Summer's heir had never joined me for lunch before. His sisters had come a time or two, but I think Idris had been waiting for an invitation, and now that he had one, he seemed a bit miffed to find Bran there as well. The dark-haired prince's expression was surly when he nodded to me and he fairly glared at Bran. Ogham he ignored completely.

He was accompanied by a courtier, a young man named Keldan who I'd met once or twice. The faery knight was Idris's opposite in looks. Where the prince's hair was blue-black and his eyes a gorgeous sapphire blue, Keldan's hair was such a pale blond, it appeared white and his brown eyes were touched with gold. Following his prince's lead, he held his silence in a cool and aloof manner.

The pixies had outdone themselves, presenting us with an excellent meal of creamy potato soup with leeks and garlic, fresh crusty bread with real, melt-in-your–mouth butter, and a selection of every kind of cheese imaginable. But our conversation was stilted, even before I got around to asking about the Wyrd Stone.

"Excuse me," said Idris, his voice dripping with sarcasm. "Am I to understand that in addition to having my birthright stolen — for if the Wyrd Stone is lost, Summer will never come to power again — you're actually accusing me of the stone's theft? Why would I steal the stone? And if you think it would be because I wish to blame Rhydderich, my next question is why would I wish to harm that miscreant you have chosen to befriend?"

Bran saved me from answering a potentially embarrassing question.

"Because my brother stands between you and the High King's throne," Bran said calmly, though his voice was deadly serious. "Roddy has Princess Claire's favor, and while he lives, you don't stand a chance of gaining her hand."

Keldan gasped, and Idris rose so quickly his chair toppled over. He didn't bother righting it, but strode around the cherry dining table headed for the door, Keldan hurrying to keep up. The prince stopped part way there, and turning to face me, said in a glacial voice, "I'm sure you're very charming, Princess Claire, but you are allowing your association with Winter to blind you more effectively than if you were lost in a blizzard. I am content to be heir to my own kingdom, poor thought that they may be in comparison to your own brilliant prospects."

He bowed to me, started to turn toward the door, then cocked his head and said, "See that you discover the whereabouts of the Wyrd Stone, for without it, my own prospects are bleak. Look to Winter, milady, for they are the only faeries who profit by the stone's loss."

With that pronouncement, Idris and Keldan left my solar.

"Well," said Ogham. "I don't know whether to take that as righteous indignation or bluster designed to disguise guilt. What do you think, Bran."

Roddy's brother gazed thoughtfully at the door where Idris and Keldan had disappeared. "I've never liked Idris," he said. "We've been rivals over one thing or another since childhood, but I can't see him stooping to something like this."

"But," I broke in, "he didn't answer the question. He just deflected by asking his own, and did you see Keldan's face? He was paler than death. Doesn't that make the pair of them seem guilty?"

"Perhaps," said Bran, "or perhaps we simply caught Idris off-guard and he didn't know how to react other than to push the blame back at us. As for Keldan, he's probably never heard anyone talk back to Idris before. His pallor was undoubtedly shock."

"Bran is right," said Ogham. "I think Idris is an unlikely thief. However, if he wanted the stone stolen, all he'd have to do would be whisper the idea in the right ear … or ask Keldan to suggest the theft."

"Great," I said. "We're back to suspecting everyone in two courts. We'll never find the stone in time for the festival."

"Take heart, Princess," Ogham continued with a nod. "I believe you've hit on our direction. Forget the culprit. Find the stone."

"Yes," agreed Bran. "Once we have the stone in hand, the High King can discover the thief through his own arts. For now, we must search the castle for an enchantment powerful enough to mask the stone's signature."

"But what if it's not here?" I cried. "What if the thief has already sent it somewhere else, or worse yet, destroyed it?"

Ogham shook his chestnut head. "Unlikely, Claire. Bran is right, we need to be looking for a masking spell. The Wyrd Stone is too powerful to be destroyed by any but the High King himself, and most faeries would find it difficult even to move it from its appointed place." He nodded to Bran. "I salute you, Prince Bran. I hadn't considered a masking spell during my morning's fruitless search. I should have."

"Your words are gratifying, Ogham," Bran said, inclining his head toward the centaur. "Now, we need to organize this search, and we need more faeries."

He strode to the windows which overlooked the gardens where we'd talked that morning. After gazing out for a moment, he nodded and turned to me. "Claire, speak to the flower faeries. Ask them to join us in the search. Ogham, assist the princess in describing what the faeries should search for. We don't need to hear about every scrap of magical energy they detect."

"Excellent suggestion," said Ogham, joining him at the window. "What will your task be?"

"I'll return to Winter's quarters, assemble the storm sprites, and give them the same task. Between the sprites and the faeries, we'll find the stone."

His confidence was infectious. I felt more light-hearted than I had since Grandpa told me he'd imprisoned Roddy.

Ogham and I trotted off to the gardens, with him lecturing me about the proper way to explain the task to the flower faeries.

The tiny fae were as excited as Una had been to be of service to the royal line, and me in particular. Don't ask me how, but it seemed that I had become a favorite with the little people of the castle. One of the kitchen pixies approached as Ogham and I finished instructing the flower faeries and cautiously touched the hem of my gown.

"Yes?" I said, giving her my full attention once the flower faeries had flown.

"Your pardon, Princess," she said dropping into a deep curtsy, "but I heard your instructions, may we help as well?"

"We?" I said, looking around, for she was quite alone.

"The kitchen pixies, milady. We're very fond of Prince Rhydderich and would love to find some way to help him. May we search as well?"

Ogham answered for me. "Of course you may," he said, "but don't neglect your duties to the king to do so. Did you understand the instructions well enough to tell your fellows?"

"I did, sir," she said, bobbing happily in place. "We'll search in shifts so no meals will be delayed. Thank you, sir, milady." With that she disappeared down the corridor.

"Wow," I said, staring after her. "That was a great idea of Bran's. We've got even more help than I dared to dream of."

Ogham nodded. "And very effective help. The pixies and flower faeries in particular know the castle and grounds better than any courtiers ever could. And storm sprites," he shook his head, though he was grinning, "they're born trouble-makers. If there's mischief afoot, they know how to find it … and join in. Fortunately, this time they're on the side of sanity."

"You really think this will work?"

"I do, Claire. It won't free Roddy, but finding the stone will allow the king to use other methods to determine the guilty party."

"Like what?" I asked. "Will he be able to see fingerprints or something."

Ogham laughed. "Psychic fingerprints, maybe. I don't know what method he'll choose, I just know that our king has ways of detecting such things."

"Gotcha. I'm going to go tell Roddy. I promised I'd visit him today, but I wanted to have something encouraging to tell him. I think this development qualifies."

"I do too. I wish I could accompany you, but I'm not included in the lucky few who can visit him."

Impulsively, I threw my arms around his waist and hugged my mentor. "Thank you for all your help, Ogham. I'll tell Roddy 'hi' for you."

CHAPTER 7

The search team came through for us. I was in Roddy's chambers telling him everything that had happened when Javan burst in.

"Princess," he said, bowing to me, then turned to Roddy. "Prince Rhydderich, I am commanded to escort you and Princess Claire to the king's audience hall."

"What's happened, Javan?" I asked, my heart beating a loud tattoo in my ears.

"I don't know, Princess," he said, his eyes darting from me to Roddy and back again. "I only know I'm ordered to escort you … now."

We hurried through the corridors to the Grandpa's audience hall. When we stepped inside, I marveled again at the majesty of the chamber. Tapestries depicting Fae creatures, dragons, and griffins adorned walls of polished stone. Warm wood floors inlaid with parquetry of every tree species and sprinkled with bits of gemstone and faery dust supported the courtier's feet. For the hall was rapidly filling with the denizens of Summer, Winter, and the High King's court. Javan escorted us to the far end of the hall where a raised dais supported two thrones. Grandpa sat upon the larger, an intricately carved seat with plush red cushions. When he spotted me, he gestured me to the smaller, a finely chiseled onyx chair padded in velvet of midnight blue.

I ascended the steps and took my place on the onyx throne. Javan and Roddy remained at the foot of the steps until Grandpa spoke.

"Prince Rhydderich, please take your place at my granddaughter's side. Sir Javan, you may take up your post at the door of the hall. Once all have entered, no one is to leave without my permission."

"Sire," said Javan. "I hear and obey."

Roddy looked bemused, but climbed the steps to the dais and took his place beside and just behind my throne. I caught his eye and smiled encouragingly. He wasn't in chains and he was standing near the king. Whatever was happening, it couldn't be too bad.

When all the courtiers had taken their places, a herald appeared in the entry, tapped his staff on the parquet floor, and announced, "Her Royal Highness, Queen of the Summerlands, Liannan, accompanied by her heir, Prince Idris, and her daughters, Meredith, Lady of Water, and Blodwen, Lady of Flowers."

Summer's royalty processed down the aisle to a raised seating area to our left. Each curtsied or bowed to us before taking their seats. Queen Liannan was resplendent in spring green, her red hair flowing down her back in artful cascades, but her iridescent eyes were hooded and cautious. She didn't know what was going on any more than I did.

Idris and Meredith both wore shimmering blue garb that accented their dark-haired good looks, but Blodwen fairly shone in a watermelon pink gown, her golden hair dressed in a riot of curls. She smiled at Roddy, and I remembered they had been childhood friends.

The herald tapped his staff again and all eyes turned to him. "Her Royal Highness, Queen of Winter, Maeve, accompanied by her son, Prince Bran."

Roddy's family walked solemnly down the aisle. When they reached the foot of the dais, Maeve dropped a careful curtsy before lifting her gaze, her expression sorrowful. Her eyes widened in surprise when she saw Roddy standing beside me, and a small gasp escaped her lips. She nodded to Grandpa, and moved to her seat in the box to our right.

Prince Bran also bowed to the throne, but he smiled at me and at Roddy, his features relaxed.

As soon as Winter's royalty were seated, Grandpa stood, majestic in garb of black studded with sparkling silver and blood-red garnets.

"I have called you here today to discover the truth regarding the recent theft of the Wyrd Stone." He paused while the room rustled with shifting feet and quiet murmurs. When the assembled courtiers quieted, he continued. "You will be pleased to hear that the stone has been recovered. A kitchen pixie named Mela detected a masking signature and alerted the centaur Ogham, who informed me. The stone has been restored to its rightful position and its power will be revealed in the ceremony of Alban Arthan tonight as planned."

He walked past me and stood before Roddy, placing a hand on his shoulder. "Winter will be gratified to hear that I have already tested the stone and found no trace of Prince Rhydderich or his magical signature upon it." He turned his gaze on Roddy. "My apologies, Prince Rhydderich, for any inconvenience you have suffered due to this crisis."

Roddy lowered his eyes and inclined his head. "Thank you, sire. I am relieved that the stone has been found."

Grandpa nodded and returned to his throne, where he continued to stand. "Now that we know who did not steal the stone, it is time to discover who did." He turned and held out a hand to me. "Claire, accompany me, please."

"Me?" I squeaked.

Grandpa smiled. "Of course, you," he said quietly. "Consider this a lesson in how to rule."

I placed my hand in his and rose, lifting my skirts carefully to avoid tripping as we stepped down from the dais.

"The stone has provided me with the magical signature of the culprit, as well as leaving its own imprint upon the person foolish enough to touch it without permission," he said as we walked among the courtiers of Winter, Summer, and our own court. Faeries stepped aside to allow us passage as we wove our way through the crowd.

Grandpa held my hand lightly, but even so, I was aware of a pulse running through his fingers, warming and cooling as we progressed, reminding me of the children's game of 'hot and cold.'"

Grandpa's fingers steadily warmed as we approached a knot of courtiers standing near the box where Summer's royalty waited. We walked unerringly to this group, which parted until we found ourselves face-to-face with a pale and sweating faery knight. Keldan. The courtier who had accompanied Idris to lunch in my solar.

His eyes wide as saucers in a face the shade of curdled milk, Keldan fell to his knees before his king.

"Keldan, no," said Idris, shock apparent in every syllable. "I trusted you! How could you do such a thing?"

Keldan licked his lips and glanced at Idris, then focused on Grandpa. "Mercy, sire," he cried. "I meant no harm to you or your court. I would've returned it in time for tonight's ceremony."

"No harm?" Grandpa roared. "You caused an innocent faery, a prince of royal blood, to be thrown into a dungeon!" He paused as two faery knights approached and stood on either side of the disgraced faery. The other courtiers had moved away from Keldan, so that Grandpa and I now stood in an open space beside Summer's royalty, with Keldan on the floor at our feet.

At a gesture from Grandpa, the knights hauled Keldan to his feet and held him securely, one on either side.

"No harm," Grandpa shook his head and then turned to Queen Liannan. "This faery is your subject, Liannan, do you wish to take charge of his punishment, or will you leave him to me?"

Liannan turned cold eyes on her son's friend. "He has brought shame to Summer and put the entire kingdom in peril," she said. "I renounce him and leave his fate in your hands, my king."

Grandpa nodded, a satisfied expression on his face. "As you wish, milady. Come, Princess Claire."

Continuing to hold my hand, he led me back to dais, where we took our seats once more upon the ornate thrones. The faery knights — I noticed now that Javan was one of them — pulled Keldan into place before us. Roddy, who had waited on the dais, placed a comforting hand on my shoulder.

"Keldan," Grandpa said, "for your crime, you are forever banished from Faery. You will wander the mortal realm from winter to summer until the end of time."

The disgraced knight cast one beseeching glance in my direction, but I thought of Roddy in prison and turned away. However, the punishment Grandpa had pronounced worried me. I leaned toward the king and, shielding my mouth with my hand, whispered, "Grandpa, I really don't think it's a good idea to turn this guy loose on the mortal world. I have friends and family there, remember?"

Grandpa looked thoughtful, nodded, and returned his attention to Keldan.

"Is there anything you wish to say before I send you from this court?" Grandpa asked. "Any explanation you wish to make?"

Keldan slumped in the guards' grip and lowered his eyes. "I have no excuse, sire. I meant no harm to Prince Rhydderich. I only wanted to disgrace him. To separate him from the princess so that she might take note of my prince's sterling qualities. I ... I ... did not think my actions through."

He straightened and met my gaze. "When I accompanied Prince Idris to your luncheon, Princess, I finally understood the pain I had caused."

He turned to Roddy. "My deepest apologies, Prince Rhydderich. I am shamed that I did not confess at the lady's table as I should have done."

Roddy said nothing, but nodded to the disgraced knight.

Grandpa cleared his throat and we all looked at him. "I'm pleased that you show remorse and accept responsibility for your actions, Keldan. I am moved to amend your sentence."

I breathed a sigh of relief, and Roddy's fingers tightened on my shoulder.

"You are banished to the mortal realm, however, if you live an exemplary life there I will review your case in a hundred of their years. You may live in hope of returning to Faery."

Keldan's expression lightened and he inclined his head. "You are merciful, my king."

"I am," agreed Grandpa. "See that you deserve it." He waved his hand and a surge of magic swept Keldan from the room ... and from Faery.

CHAPTER 8

The Festival of Alban Arthan was an especially joyous occasion. Even Idris seemed to enjoy the celebration, though he was devastated by his friend's treachery.

He approached Roddy and Bran and me as we stood at one end of the ballroom talking. "It seems I owe you an apology," he said, nodding to me and Bran. "Your suspicions were correct."

"Not quite," said Bran. "If you'll remember, we suspected *you*, not your knight."

Idris scowled. "Yes, well, it comes to the same thing, doesn't it?"

"No," I said, resting a hand on his arm. "It doesn't. He may have done it to advance your cause, but you didn't ask him to. You were as innocent as Roddy. I hope you'll forgive my suspicion."

His eyes widened and his expression cleared. "Of course, Princess," he said, then more quietly, "I hope we can be friends someday."

I grinned. "Please, call me Claire, and I think being friends is a great idea."

He grinned right back and turned to Roddy. "And you, Prince Rhydderich? Will you and your brother forgive me as well?"

Bran slapped him on the back. "If Claire calls you friend, I will too. Just try not to get in my way when the games begin next summer."

Idris looked annoyed for an instant, then smiled and shook Bran's hand. He glanced at Roddy and cocked an eyebrow, waiting.

"As Claire said, there's nothing to forgive, Idris," Roddy said and held out his hand. "I'd be honored to call you friend."

The two princes clasped hands and grinned.

Bran motioned me to join him and we laid our hands across theirs. "This Midwinter got off to a rocky start," Bran said, his voice full of laughter, "but it's turning into the best one ever."

Idris grinned. "Indeed. The heirs to Summer and Winter have found friendship. That bodes well for Faery."

"Yes it does," I agreed. "I can't wait to see what happens next."

Roddy laughed. "Whatever it is, Claire, if you're involved it's sure to be unpredictable!"

PART VII
LEXIE'S CHOICE

DEB LOGAN

BESTSELLING AUTHOR OF THUNDERBIRD

LEXIE'S CHOICE

PROM IS JUST AROUND THE CORNER!

CHAPTER 1

*M*y best friend is a faery princess. No. Really. Claire is the descendent of a long-ago faery princess who defied her father and married a mortal. And Claire, lucky girl, is the end of the line, so to speak. Hard as it is to believe, on her fifteenth birthday, she inherited a dragon and began her transformation. It took a couple of months and a lot of drama, but when it was over, she was a real, live faery princess...with an attitude.

Claire has never been a pushover, and the mere fact that her blood had betrayed her didn't mean she was going to meekly accept the king of Faery's authority over her. Just because the guy was a king and her many-times-removed-great-grandfather did not mean she would be an obedient little princess. No sir. Not my best bud, Claire!

Since she's not a docile little faery, she worked a deal to stay in the mortal realm during the school year and broke the unexpected news to me and her parents. Can you believe that king guy's nerve? He actually thought he could just steal Claire away with no explanation and give her parents a booby prize in return ... twins!

I've already got twin brothers. I can tell you, they're no prize.

But, this story isn't about Claire. Not really. It's about me. The Best Friend. The Sidekick. Yeah. Sidekicks have lives too, and I like mine just fine, thank you very much. At least, most of the time...

I leaned my forehead against the cool metal of my locker and sighed. "I still can't believe Brent asked me to prom." Brent Rodgers, my boyfriend, was so much more in Claire's league than mine, but early on he'd chosen me. After we discovered Claire's faery princess status, he'd been relieved, but I still wondered from time to time if Claire's erstwhile dragon, Roddy, hadn't put a hex on him. I mean seriously, who in their right mind would choose me over Claire? Especially a hunky, captain-of-the-football team, straight-A kinda guy like Brent?

Claire slammed her locker shut and rolled her eyes at me. "Like he was going to ask anyone else. Honestly, Lexie. You two have been an item forever!"

She grabbed my arm and pulled me toward the front door and freedom from high school drudgery. "This is so cool. You and Brent. Me and Roddy. The four of us going to prom together." She squeezed my arm and beamed an angelic smile. "Just like we dreamed when we were kids!"

I smiled back at her; I couldn't help it. Her excitement was infectious. But that didn't cure the gnawing in the pit of my stomach. We'd almost reached her car before she noticed my silent brooding.

"What?" she asked. "You're not seriously worried about Brent. The guy's been crazy about you for years. So spill. Why so depressed?"

I leaned against her cherry red Mustang convertible and expelled a long sigh. "It's the same old story. I can't afford a nice dress. Boring, I know."

The economy, in general, sucked in our little southwest Washington town, but my family's finances were in the crapper. Dad had been laid off two years ago and hadn't found another job. Mom had snagged a part-time secretarial position, but it paid peanuts. By some miracle,

Dad was still collecting unemployment and since he was home, my preschool sister, Candy, had managed to avoid day-care. My fifteen-year-old twin brothers and I all had after-school jobs to help with clothes and food money, but there was no way our limited budget would stretch to pay for the kind of prom dress I drooled over.

Claire unlocked the car doors and motioned me inside. I slid onto the leather seat of the immaculately clean car and sighed again. I loved Claire, and I wouldn't trade places with her for all the coffee in Seattle, but ... well, let's just say money was the least of her worries.

Once we were both settled inside, Claire turned to me. "Don't worry about it. I'll take care of the dresses."

I gave her my best I-don't-think-so glare. I did *not* like charity, not even from my best bud. Besides, who wants to wear a hand-me-down to prom?

"Don't give me that look," she said. "It's not my fault I can ask the flower faeries to make prom dresses for us. I didn't ask to be a faery princess!"

My glare faltered and my breath caught. "Flower faeries? For real?" The flower faeries only made the most delectable fashions in the world — far superior to anything made by mortal designers.

Claire grinned, delight dancing in her clear green eyes. "Lexie! This is prom! The culmination of our high school career. Of course we're calling in the flower faeries. And don't worry about your folks," she added, answering my next concern. "Mom and I will think of something to justify the gift."

I released the breath I'd been holding and allowed a small smile to light my face. Maybe lack of money wouldn't make prom a disaster after all.

CHAPTER 2

I'd glimpsed flower faeries around Claire's yard from time to time ever since she'd granted me the ability to see the other side, but I'd never actually met one. The dream of a faery-made prom dress sustained me through my shift at the coffee shop, though it did make me jittery.

"What is with you today, Lexie?" my manager asked. Terry was a nice woman, but she ran a tight ship, and I'd just overflowed my fourth cup of espresso in a row. "You're not usually so careless. Is everything all right at home?"

My face must have matched the red of Claire's Mustang. It certainly felt hot enough to set off a fire alarm. "Sorry, Terry." I wiped up the mess and transferred the black liquid to a clean cup. "Brent asked me to prom and..."

"Say no more," she interrupted. "Believe it or not, I was young once. I know how important prom is. Make sure you put it on the schedule. You're not working that day. You'd be useless anyway."

I grinned, rinsed out the dishrag, and ran to the back to sign myself out of work for the afternoon of prom. When I returned to the counter, a seriously dreamy guy was accepting a cup from Terry. He thanked her with quiet courtesy and then glanced at me.

Our gazes locked, just for a second, but that second stretched into eternity. His grey-eyed gaze raked my soul and left me quivering. I didn't doubt my reaction after he broke our connection and left the shop, what I wasn't sure of was whether it had been fear or anticipation that caused the flutter.

I pressed my hands to my belly to stop the rampaging butterflies and gulped. Terry scowled, so I pushed the incident to the back of my mind and concentrated on serving my customers. The shop was busy and before I knew it I glanced up to find Claire smiling at me.

"Hey, girl," she said, a mischievous gleam in her eye. "Isn't your shift about over?"

I checked the clock and grinned. "Five minutes. Just enough time to run through my log-out routine. Meet you out front in a few."

She waved me off, and I cleaned the counter, said good-bye to Terry and gathered my belongings. Flower faeries! I was about to meet some flower faeries in the flesh and have a dream dress made. Sometimes having a faery princess for a best friend absolutely rocked!

A few minutes later, Claire and I climbed the steps to her porch and slipped inside the front door. We tiptoed through the entry and peered into the living room.

Yep. Nap time at Camp Twins-Run-Amok. A small red pop-up tent stood in the middle of the room surrounded by toy cars, trains, trucks, and fire engines, with a liberal sprinkling of stuffed animals. Inside the tent, two little boys slept, their expressions relaxed and angelic.

I snorted quietly at the thought. These little hooligans might be only three, but they were no more angels than my own twin brothers. Who would've thought all those years ago when Claire was an only child, and I was fighting to stay ahead of the demon spawn who were my brothers, that both of us would end up as elder siblings to twin boys? Sure as heck not me.

Claire nudged me, and we moved with practiced stealth to the kitchen where Mrs. Murray sat with a steaming cup of coffee. "Welcome home, girls. Thanks for coming in so quietly."

"No problem, Mrs. M. 'Let sleeping twins lie,' that's always been my motto."

Mrs. Murray smiled, while Claire rolled her eyes.

"We're going to be upstairs, Mom. I've got some flower faeries coming in to help us with our prom dresses, so don't be surprised if you feel a bit of magic in the air."

Mrs. Murray waved us toward the stairs. "Have fun, but remember your father and I have final say as to the appropriateness of the dresses. Faeries have no sense when it comes to teenage girls." She narrowed her eyes. "That goes for you too, Lexie. I don't want your mother thinking I've let you run wild at the mall."

Claire and I exchanged looks and replied in unison. "Understood."

I hesitated a second before asking, "What are we going to tell my parents?"

"I've already spoken to your mother." Mrs. Murray's gaze softened. "You've been so helpful to us with the twins, and your mother has given me such wonderful tips and moral support...I just asked her if she would allow us to give you this small 'thank you' gift. She argued a bit, said it wasn't necessary, but in the end she agreed."

Mrs. Murray stood, crossed the room, and gathered me into a hug. "It's the least we could do. Thank you so much for supporting Claire and helping her adjust to all this...well, to everything." She kissed my cheek and studied my face for an instant before waving us off. "Go on, now. Go have fun with Claire's flower faeries."

I glanced back as we left the kitchen. Mrs. Murray was wiping her eyes.

CHAPTER 3

"Oh. My. God, Claire! I must be dreaming." I shook my head, as if the motion would clear my vision. Her bedroom was, well, not her bedroom. All the normal furniture had vanished to be replaced with low tables around the edges. More like benches really. Of course, flower faeries are on a whole different scale from human beings. The diminutive creatures resemble the traditional image of fairies: large butterflies with humanoid bodies. In the center of the room was a round dais in front of a silvery waterfall of light.

I nodded to the delicate beings who floated and flitted around the room and edged closer to Claire. "What is that thing?" I whispered.

She shrugged, busy greeting each of the tiny faeries. "Think of it as a mirror. It'd take too long to explain it properly."

"Mirror. Gotcha." I stood perfectly still, not sure what I should be doing.

Claire turned to me. Her eyes widened, but then she giggled. "You look like a deer caught in headlights."

"Well, I feel kind of like one. What am I supposed to do? Where should I stand? There's no place to sit."

Claire clapped her hands, and the flower faeries assembled before her. A squadron of gossamer-winged girls in rainbow hued dresses floated before us at shoulder height.

"Thank you for coming, fair ones. This is my friend, Lexie. She is a mortal, but she has been gifted with the Sight by King Alberic. If you are willing, I would like you to make a gown for each of us."

The faeries buzzed with excitement. I tried to listen, to really hear what they were saying, but I couldn't distinguish words. All I got was an impression — a breeze rustling flower petals, or water trickling over small stones — but they seemed happy and excited. At least, I hoped none of them were offended to be asked to dress a mortal.

Claire turned to me with a dazzling smile. My breath caught. Most of the time, I didn't see a faery princess when I looked at Claire. Most of the time, I just saw my best friend. The girl I'd known since preschool. The one who'd always been there for me, and who I'd been loyal to in return. Claire was, well, just Claire.

But at that moment, standing within the familiar four walls of her now unfamiliar room, I suddenly knew I was in the presence of royalty. I saw Claire as the flower faeries saw her: incomprehensibly beautiful, the embodiment of grace and honor and nobility, and powerful beyond my understanding.

I stumbled back from her, my eyes wide.

A small frown creased her brow and she stepped toward me, concern coloring her light green eyes...and suddenly she was my Claire again. My best friend in all the world. The girl who knew my secrets and loved me anyway.

"What's wrong, Lexie? Are you sick? I can make all this go away if it's freaking you out."

I smiled, a bit on the wobbly side, and reached for her hand. "Are you kidding? Miss the chance to see your friends at work? Not on your life!"

She grinned, and my world righted itself. Who cared that Claire was immortal, and I would age and die? Best buds are best buds. Besides, how else would I get a flower faery gown for prom?

We spent the afternoon taking turns on the dais, gazing into the waterfall mirror while the flower faeries worked their enchantment. Visions of me in gorgeous dresses with my hair styled in impossible coifs flashed before my eyes. A few of the designs would've made Brent's eyes pop right out of his head, but I knew those gowns would never make it past Mrs. M's censorship. What a shame. I mean, who knew I had boobs that could look that glamorous?

I've got to admit, my own eyes popped at some of the fashions the faeries dressed Claire in. Wow! No way would Roddy want her to be seen in public wearing that little number. The fabric resembled moonlight sparkling on water...and little else! I mean, she was covered ... kinda ... but the gown left nothing to the imagination, and Claire had a lot to display!

"Good thing your mom's not here for that one," I said when I finally found my voice.

Claire giggled and winked at me. "Now you know how I felt when they put that sunshine number on you!"

"Any chance we could get pictures, you know, just to dream on?"

"Oooo ... good idea."

Two tiny 3-D replicas appeared on the bench beside me. There we stood in all our glory, me and Claire. Sunshine and moonbeams. Mortal and Fae. Two hotties in gowns that would never be made.

"Wow. What a cool souvenir. Maybe someday, after we've been married for ten years, I'll be brave enough it to show Brent."

"Yeah. I know what you mean. Maybe I'll have it made for my wedding night. What do you think? Would it work as a nightgown?"

I laughed so hard I couldn't breathe. When I finally had control, I said, "Sure, as long as you don't plan on wearing it very long!"

Claire's cheeks flamed scarlet, but laughter danced in her eyes. "Well, isn't that the point?"

"Beats me. Whoever's first has to promise to tell."

"Deal!"

We both grinned like maniacs and tried to swallow our giggles while the flower faeries flitted past, presenting Claire with yet another vision of loveliness.

Claire decided on a pale iris-blue strapless gown, which made her alabaster pale complexion and short, curly black hair shine like moonlight on dark water. The bodice hugged her tightly with intriguing folds pleated and held in place by tiny stars. Okay, they weren't really stars, but they winked and shone like pinpoints of light in a brightening morning sky. At the waist, the gauzy fabric released to flow over her hips in a cascade, ending in a tumble of lace at mid-calf. The flower faeries assured us the cobbler elves would produce a pair of high-heeled strappy sandals in exactly the right shade.

My gown, well, all I can say is, "Dream. Come. True." I stood on the dais and stared open-mouthed at the vision in the waterfall mirror. "Can they truly make me look like that in real life?" I asked, pushing the words past a suddenly parched throat and unimaginably dry mouth. I licked my lips and drank in every detail, barely hearing Claire's reply.

"Oh, yes. They'll deliver the dress, and the fabric's enchantment will give you that glow without the need for make-up. You'll be just as stunning at prom as you are right now."

"Wow!"

The cobalt blue gown set off the natural tan of my skin and made the burnished highlights in my chestnut hair pop. I really did glow, but with a different aura than my best friend. Claire was all moonlight and magic, where mine was more healthy and vital, like sunlight on a field of spring flowers.

I said as much to Claire, but she scoffed at the idea. "The gown isn't giving you that glow. It's enhancing your inner beauty. That's part of the magic of the flower faeries. They find the beauty of each individual and set it off to perfection. Kind of like a jeweler setting a precious stone. What works for a diamond is all wrong for a ruby. You'll notice the faeries didn't put any of my designs on you. We're too different."

She was right. The pale gown they'd designed for her wouldn't suit me at all, and the bold color of my creation would overpower Claire's delicate features.

I couldn't take my eyes from the vision before me. My chestnut hair swept up in a froth of curls, and artfully escaping ringlets exposed the clean lines of a graceful neck. Wow. Who knew my neck could be sexy?

The cobalt blue gown was, I don't know, something classic ... maybe Grecian? The gown flowed from a heart-shaped neckline and wide-set shoulder straps. The fabric hugged my curves without revealing too much, while making it clear I wasn't a little girl anymore. The hem skimmed the floor, just allowing my toes to peek out. I'd be wearing strappy heels too, but mine wouldn't be seen.

I sighed in satisfaction. Claire might be a faery princess, but this gown made me look and feel like a Greek goddess.

"Okay, Lex. You're gorgeous. It's a fact, so stop admiring yourself and get down here. The flower faeries have work to do."

My cheeks burned, but I tore my eyes away from the enchanted promise and hopped off the dais. Instantly, Claire's room returned to normal. The dais, workbenches, and winged faeries winked out of existence, and Claire's usual bedroom furniture reappeared in all its comfortable solidity.

I turned in a swift circle. "How do you handle that? Doesn't that quick change drive you bonkers?"

She shrugged. "You get used to the magic. Una said we'd have our gowns by the weekend, unless there's some reason you need yours earlier?"

"Nope. That's still a week before prom. Whatever makes those little magicians happy." I grinned at Claire. "I can't believe I'm going to prom in the most gorgeous dress in the world! Brent is going to freak when he sees me!"

We broke into a spontaneous happy dance and then collapsed on her bed. Living a dream-come-true was just too cool for words.

CHAPTER 4

*T*wo nights later, Claire and I lounged in her room, pretending to work on our AP English essays, but neither of us was getting anywhere. I'd had a stressful shift at the coffee shop, and Claire had been stuck baby-sitting the twins all afternoon. We were bleary eyed and lethargic. That is, until Una popped into existence followed by a troupe of her friends carrying two neatly wrapped bundles.

Immediately, my heart pounded. A rush of energy propelled me to my feet. My prom gown! I wanted to rush the faeries and grab the promised gift, but I didn't. I'd heard enough of Claire's trials and tribulations as she learned the ways of Faery to know there would be protocol to be observed.

Sure enough, Claire had barely acknowledged the flower faeries before a stately looking male appeared. Tall, lean, and silver-haired, the male waited for Claire to notice him, though not with good grace. He radiated haughty irritation.

Now, I've known Claire forever, and I can read her like a book. She knew perfectly well the guy was in the room. In fact, I'd bet my right arm *and* my right leg she knew he was impatient and wanted her attention, but she kept right on praising the flower faeries for their quick work, and thanking Una in particular for bringing us the gowns. Finally, she cut the small talk and glanced at the silver-haired dude.

He stepped forward, took her extended hand, and bowed over it. "My princess," he said, his voice smooth and a little oily. "You're looking lovely today." His gaze slid toward me and then focused on Claire.

"Thank you, Cadmar. May I ask what brings you to the mortal realm?"

Once again, he gazed at me from the corner of his eye before concentrating on Claire. "I have accompanied the flower faeries at King Alberic's command. Is it true that you have commissioned a faery gown for a mortal?"

I held my breath. I knew this had been too good to be true. The king was going to hold back my prom dress.

"Yes." Claire narrowed her eyes, a wary tone in her voice. "Does my grandsire object to me giving my friend a gift?"

"Not at all, your highness. He simply wishes to be certain you understand the, shall we say, irregularity of the situation."

Something was going on, but I didn't get it. Worse, I'm not sure Claire got it either. Cadmar wasn't exactly smiling, but his attitude had changed. He seemed more relaxed; happier, somehow.

Claire must have sensed the same thing. "Is there something I'm missing, Cadmar? Am I breaking Faery law?"

He inclined his head, making it impossible to see his eyes. "I am not here to instruct you in our law, your highness. Do you accept these gifts from the flower faeries?"

Claire glanced from him to me, and back again. She hesitated, weighing her options. Studying the packages with a wary eye, she bit her lip for a moment. "I don't see why I shouldn't. I asked Una and her friends to make the gowns. They did so happily, and now they have delivered them. Yes. I accept the gowns."

Cadmar clapped, and the flower faeries disappeared. The packages plopped onto the floor at Claire's feet.

"Excellent." He inclined his head, a smug smile lifting his thin lips. "Princess, you will now accompany me to Faery. The High King commands your presence."

"What?" Claire exclaimed. "What's wrong? What did I do?"

"That is not for me to say, your highness. The High King requires your obedience. Now."

He clapped his hands again. He and Claire disappeared.

Alone in her bedroom, I stared at the packages. A couple of minutes ago, I'd been dying to get my hands on them. Now, I stepped around them and left the room. I had no idea what was going on, but I sure hoped my best friend hadn't gotten herself into too much trouble just so I could have an enchanted dress.

CHAPTER 5

*S*aturday dawned bright and beautiful, and I was up with the sun. I had the early shift at the coffee shop, and then I planned to meet Brent for lunch. I glanced at my cell phone as I dressed, wanting to call Claire and make sure everything was all right. I hadn't heard from her since Cadmar had whisked her away last night.

I squashed the impulse. One of two things was true: either Claire was home sleeping in her bed — in which case she wouldn't appreciate an early bird call, or she was still in Faery. My cell coverage didn't extend to the magical realm. She'd call when she got back. Or she wouldn't. If that happened, Brent and I would track her down through Roddy.

Even though I'd now known him for three years, I still had trouble believing Roddy wasn't just a normal guy. Of course, I had trouble believing my best friend was a faery princess some days. Magic changes everything, and yet it doesn't change how we see the people we love.

Roddy was the beginning and the end of Claire's adventures in Faery. She'd inherited him on her fifteenth birthday. Of course, he'd been a dragon at the time. A dragon she'd come to love and for whom she'd been willing to sacrifice her life. I still got the shivers every time I remembered how close Claire had come to dying that Halloween night.

Anyway, it turned out Roddy had been cursed into dragon form by the High King, Claire's many-times-removed-great-grandfather. Claire's sacrifice broke the enchantment, and Roddy turned into a really handsome faery hunk. He then returned the favor by waking Claire with true love's first kiss. Yep. My best friend lived through a real, live fairy tale! Technically, I guess she's still living one.

So Claire made a deal with her grandpa. He allowed them both to return to the mortal realm, so Claire could finish high school. I know. How lame is that? My friend has the chance to live in Faery for eternity and she chooses to come home for chemistry class! But, yeah, I'm glad she made that deal, 'cause I'd miss her terribly if she'd just disappeared.

But, returning to the current problem, if Claire didn't call soon, Roddy would know how to find her. Roddy and Claire were a unit. True love, indeed.

Just like me and Brent. Geeky science girl and hunky football star. The rest of the world might find us a strange combo, but we fit. Had since we were fifteen and Claire had a crush on him. I still couldn't believe Brent chose me over my gorgeous, feisty, and clever best friend, but he did.

I'd been nuts about him for years, but never expected to have a chance with him. I mean, hello! He could've chosen any girl in the school, and she would've fallen over with stars in her eyes. Seriously, I was the luckiest girl on earth.

I danced through my shift at work. Lunch with Brent. Prom in a week. Gorgeous dress. Oh yeah — slight falter — Claire might be in trouble. Roddy would take care of it — dancing resumed.

On my break, Terry drew me aside. "So, prom's next week?"

I grinned and nodded happily.

"You got everything covered? I mean, I can give you an advance if you need. Prom dresses aren't cheap."

My eyes teared up a bit, and I hugged her, which flustered her. Terry is not a huggy kinda gal.

"Thanks, Terry, but Claire and her mom are helping me with that."

She flapped her hands at me and wiped her own eyes. "Good." She straightened her apron and shifted back to business-as-usual. "Just so long as you've got everything worked out."

I reached for another hug, but she escaped to the front counter.

Didn't I tell you? Luckiest girl in the world!

Just before my shift ended, a new customer slid into a seat in my service area. I grabbed a menu and moved to greet him, but the words died on my lips.

The seriously good-looking guy from a few days before smiled at me. My world folded in on itself. Like a butterfly caught in a spider's web, I could struggle, but I couldn't escape the lure of his perfect smile, smoky grey eyes, exquisitely chiseled face, and you-know-you-want-to-run-your-fingers-through-me honey-brown hair.

"I hoped to meet you." His voice was as smoky as his eyes, but the words released me, and I blinked myself back to some semblance of normality. My pulse raced fast enough to qualify for Nascar, but I licked my lips and attempted to smile. "I'm Lexie. What can I get you?"

He smiled even more brightly, and quipped, "Oh, that's a loaded question, but I'll settle for a cup of coffee and a Danish."

My cheeks flamed. I hurried off to get his order. Too hurried. Flustered. I forced myself to slow down, to imagine what Claire would do if a good-looking guy was flirting with her. She wouldn't get all...

I stopped dead and almost overflowed yet another cup of coffee. Leveling the pot just in time, I considered the thought. Flirting. Was that too handsome guy actually flirting with me?

No one flirted with me. I belonged with Brent. Everyone knew about us. Sure, some of the older patrons of the coffee shop engaged in playful banter, but that wasn't flirting. That was just some old guys teasing a girl they'd watched grow up.

I stole another glance at the hunk. Definitely not an old guy, and definitely no one who'd known me since I was in diapers.

A warm bubble lodged just beneath my heart and slowly expanded. Someone besides Brent found me attractive. The warmth spread down my arms and tingled in my fingertips. I chose the very nicest Danish, plopped it onto a plate, and grabbed the coffee cup. I returned to the customer with a new assurance in my step.

"Here you go," I said with a smile. "If you need anything else, just let me know."

"I'll do that." His grey eyes held my gaze. "I'm new in town. I don't suppose you'd be available later to show me around?"

I giggled. "That would take about three minutes. Big Vista isn't exactly Seattle."

"True." His voice dipped into a husky baritone. "But I'm sure it has its...charms."

I might've melted into a puddle right then and there if the door hadn't chimed. I glanced up to check out the new arrival. Brent, framed in sunshine, searched the room. He spotted me, and a smile lit his face. I smiled in return, the stranger forgotten.

"So what do you say," the guy continued, "do we have a date?"

I broke eye contact with Brent and glanced back at the customer, who didn't look nearly as drop-dead gorgeous as he had a moment ago. "Sorry, but I already have a date. Have a nice day."

A flicker of irritation crossed his face, but I barely noticed. My shift was over, and Brent was here. Those were the important facts.

CHAPTER 6

*B*rent and I were just biting into thick, juicy burgers at BurgerTown, when Claire and Roddy slid into the booth beside us. I chewed as fast as I could and swallowed before asking, "Oh my gawd, Claire! Are you okay? What happened?"

She scowled and shrugged. "Just some administrative mumbo-jumbo. Evidently giving faery gifts to mortals is more complicated than I thought." She exchanged a meaningful glance with Roddy and sighed. "Don't worry about it. I'm sure I'll get to tell you the gory details eventually."

I frowned at my burger. "If it's going to get you in trouble, Claire, just give back the dress. I'm sure I can find something at the mall."

Claire's face blazed red, the most color I'd ever seen on my unusually pale-skinned friend. "Absolutely not. Look, Lex, we're already in this whether we give the dress back or not. If we're gonna pay the price, we might as well enjoy the reward."

I didn't like the sound of that. I'd heard too much about faery justice ... or lack thereof. "What price?"

Claire scowled, opened her mouth, closed it again, and glanced helplessly at Roddy.

Roddy studied Claire's face before turning to me. "I wasn't there, Lexie, but from what Claire has said, and more importantly, what she hasn't, I'm guessing the king laid a geas on her. Whatever it is, I'm sure we'll find out eventually."

I stabbed a fry into a puddle of ketchup and bit it viciously. Being poor sucked! All this trouble just because I couldn't afford to buy a nice dress for prom. I pushed my plate toward Claire. "Have a fry. They're really good if you imagine they're faery idiots."

Claire giggled, but worry flickered around her eyes.

After lunch, we went our separate ways. Brent needed to spend some time with his folks. Empty nest syndrome hit them hard when he headed to college in Seattle. I missed him too, of course, but we spent long hours on Skype while we both did our homework. Somehow, I doubt he called his mom as regularly.

Claire was busy for the afternoon too. She'd promised to watch the twins so her mom and dad could take in a matinee movie. And even though I wouldn't hang with Roddy without Claire, he had to return to Faery. Being a faery prince had its own set of responsibilities, quite apart from my best friend.

So, I was on my own with free time to spare. What would I do with a glorious spring afternoon? The mall? Nah. Too depressing. Filled with stuff I couldn't afford even if I wanted it. A movie? By myself? Please!

I could go home and help out with the laundry, but I'd worked hard all week, I deserved a break. Sunshine, flowers, time to smell them. That was what I wanted.

I grabbed my shoulder bag and headed to the used book store. I'd splurge on a second-hand novel and drive out to Big Vista Lake. I could sun, read, and enjoy the decadence of time alone. Yep. That was my plan, and I was sticking to it.

As I paid for my paperback, a romance novel with a kissing couple on the cover, a familiar figure approached the counter. I stared in disbelief at the gorgeous guy who'd flirted with me that morning.

"Are you following me?" I blurted before my brain engaged. My cheeks flamed at my audacity. Why in the world would a guy as heart-poundingly handsome as him be following me? I turned back to the cashier, accepted my change, and mumbled, "Sorry."

The guy laughed. "Of course I'm following you. You'd follow her, wouldn't you?" he asked the guy behind the counter.

The old guy gave a sallow smile and a quick nod.

I grabbed my book and escaped out the door, before the situation could get any more mortifying.

"Hey! Wait a minute," the guy called, following me into the bright spring sunshine. "I'm sorry. I didn't mean to embarrass you. I saw you through the window and decided to take a chance. Want to show me around now?"

His gray eyes begged me to say yes, and really, why shouldn't I? The day was glorious, and I had nothing better to do than read the romance novel clutched in my hand. A sudden desire to be reckless and spontaneous swept my soul, and I made my decision. Stuffing the book in my shoulder bag, I met his hopeful puppy gaze. "Sure. Why not?"

He grinned, and my heart fluttered. His thousand-watt smile was enchanting. The beauty of the day intensified, and anticipation spread through my body like warm honey. This was going to be the best day of my life!

"I'm Jeff, by the way, and you're Lexie, right?"

"Right. Nice to meet you, Jeff."

"Lexie."

A cascade of shivers raced down my spine. My name had never sounded so delicious before.

"That's an unusual name. I like the sound of it." He smiled again. Wow. The guy could power whole cities with that thing.

My brain kicked back in gear when he took my arm and said, "Where shall we go first?"

I laughed to cover my embarrassment. How long had I been standing there mesmerized by his smile? "Like I said earlier, there's not much to see in Big Vista."

"Then show me the parts that interest you. I know where you work. Where do you live? Go to school? Hang out? Who's your best friend, and where does she live?"

A tiny piece of my brain yelled, *Are you nuts? Those are too personal! This guy is dangerous.* But Jeff smiled again, and the dissenter was silenced. Bound and gagged and tossed into a deep, dark corner of my mind. If I'd been able to think straight, my reaction would've proved the dissenter's point. But I was enchanted by Jeff and his dazzling smile, which I returned with a sappy sigh.

We spent the afternoon touring my usual haunts. I showed him Claire's house and chattered about the coincidence of both of us having younger twin brothers. We drove past the grade school where Claire and I started kindergarten, the middle school where we'd been outcast dorks together, and the high school where we'd learned the truth. I maintained enough sanity not to spill Claire's secret identity, but that might have been the Faery King's geas more than any innate self-control on my part.

A single smile from Jeff, and words tumbled from my lips like a mountain stream over smooth stones. Every now and then, when his attention caught on something else, my dissenter surfaced enough to kick me in my metaphorical shins and I would blink and wonder what it was about this guy that made him so easy to talk to? But then he'd smile again, and I'd slip back into my bubble of happy brainlessness.

We ended the day at Big Vista Lake, sitting on a thick wool blanket, watching ducks paddle in the shallows.

"This has been a wonderful day, Lexie. Thank you for showing me your world."

"It has been fun," I replied. "Seeing it through your eyes has been, well, different. It's like you've never seen a small town before. You must be from a big city." I stared into his eyes and realized I'd been blathering on all day, telling him every detail of my life, but he hadn't told me a thing. The only facts I knew about Jeff were his name, and that his smile melted my defenses faster than butter in a frying pan.

"Wait right here," he said, giving me a ten percent blast of super-smile. "I've got a surprise in the car."

I frowned. A chill ran over me as he scrambled to his feet and headed toward the parking lot. My dissenter surfaced, freed at last by Jeff's absence.

You should run! What if he's a serial killer? What if he's going to get a chain-saw? I mean, really, what do you know about this guy? And this place—there's no one here. No one to help you. No one to hear you scream when he saws you into little pieces just for the fun of it.

I squirmed on the blanket, glancing around the park - deserted. I glanced over my shoulder. He pulled a picnic basket out of the trunk. Relief flooded my soul. I was being an absolute idiot. We'd had a great afternoon, and somehow in the midst of my chatter, he'd managed to plan a picnic at the lake. How sweet!

My dissenter gave one last gasp as Jeff walked back to our blanket, swinging the basket and grinning. *Don't eat anything. Trust me. DON'T EAT! Not even a taste* .... The voice dwindled to silence as Jeff knelt on the blanket and presented the basket to me.

"I thought I should at least feed you," he said with a shy smile, one that still managed to shoot lightning all the way to my toes, "after monopolizing your whole afternoon."

"How sweet," I exclaimed, pushing the dissenting voice firmly into a pit. "When did you manage to do this? You never left my side." I could hardly wait to open the basket and examine the contents, but I squashed the impulse, determined to maintain at least a tiny bit of dignity.

"Magic."

Alarm bells klaxoned through my brain like a tsunami warning at the coast, only to be silenced by one of his full-blown smiles.

"Aren't you going to open the basket?"

I grinned and reached for his gift, serenely happy Jeff had been so thoughtful. I unpacked a feast like no picnic I'd ever seen. When my family did picnic lunches, they usually consisted of peanut butter sandwiches, chips, apples or oranges, and ice cold pop. Jeff's idea of a picnic leaned toward the grand, and the basket appeared to be bottomless. Whoever packed it was a master of using every nook and cranny.

Sliced roast chicken garnished with dried cranberries, pickled asparagus and pearl onions, bite-sized bits of cheese, gourmet crackers, and, wonder of wonders, caviar! All served on translucent china, with snowy linens and crystal goblets. The final touch - a frosty bottle of fresh apple cider. Where he'd found fresh cider in May was beyond me, but the crisp smell of apples made my mouth water for a taste.

"Jeff, this is amazing." I arranged the food on the blanket between us.

"I'm glad you're pleased."

"Pleased? I'm totally blown away." I laughed, and filled two plates while he poured the cider. "You certainly know how to charm a girl."

His hand twitched, and a bit of cider splashed on the blanket, to be absorbed by the warm wool.

"Charm. What an interesting word choice."

I cocked my head and studied him as he topped off my goblet and handed it to me. In the dark recesses of my mind, the dissenter rattled his chains.

"Well, I am charmed," I said, not sure why the word had bothered him. "This whole afternoon has been, well, enchanting." I frowned. Charmed. Enchanting. Claire under a geas. Unease tightened my brow in a tiny frown.

Jeff grabbed his goblet and touched it to mine. "Let's drink to a long and happy friendship."

Instead of joining his toast, I lowered my goblet and turned my gaze and attention to the lake. Something was wrong, my dissenter was right. Oh, Jeff wasn't a serial killer, and I wasn't in danger of being chopped up by a chainsaw, but intuition told me a Faery connection was involved.

"Who are you?" I asked, continuing to stare at the ducks drifting on the lake's glassy surface. "Why are you here? What do you want with me?"

A long silence answered my question. I resisted the urge to glance at him, to see what he was doing.

Just when the quiet's pressure felt like it would crack my skull, he answered. At least, I assumed it was him since I was carefully not looking. The voice was deeper, more mature, with ages of self-knowledge supporting it and giving it strength.

"Who do you think I am, Lexie?"

I shivered, but stared steadfastly at the glistening water. "I have an idea, but I'm not allowed to speak it."

"Try."

Startled, I almost turned to him, but caught myself at the last instant. I ground my teeth and took several deep breaths. "You're a faery." I'd said the word. That sealed it. If he'd been human, the geas King Alberic had laid on me would've prevented me from speaking. I wrapped my arms around myself and rocked back and forth, just a bit. Just enough to gain my balance.

"Okay. You're a faery. Why are you here? What do you want from me?"

He sighed. A circle of tiny mushrooms popped up around our blanket. "You can look at me, Lexie. While the faery ring holds, I swear I will not use the glamour against you."

I had enough experience with Claire to know that faeries cannot lie. They are experts at twisting the truth, but they are incapable of outright deceit. I closed my eyes, asked my dissenter's forgiveness, and turned to face my fate.

When I opened my eyes, Jeff looked much as he had before. Still handsome, still youthful, but now an overlay of power provided a quiet magnificence.

"You haven't answered my questions," I said, meeting and holding his gaze.

He nodded. "For one so young, you are formidable. Our princess has chosen well."

A blush burned my cheeks, but I refused to be turned aside by his praise. "Please, don't avoid my questions. Why are you here? What do you want from me?" Another bit of lore popped into place - the magic of three. I'd just asked the same questions three times.

As if reading my feeble human mind, he sighed and shook his head. "I'm sorry, Lexie. Despite the power of three, I cannot be compelled to disobey my king."

I pounced on the thought. "So King Alberic sent you. Okay. That's a start."

I rummaged through my brain seeking an answer. Why would Claire's great-grandfather send a faery to bother me? I mean, he'd been aware of me for three years now. He'd laid a geas on me, preventing me from blabbing faery secrets to the human world, but other than that he'd ignored me. I wasn't part of his game plan, but I wasn't important enough to bother about. So why now? What had I done to annoy the King of Faery?

Claire and I hadn't done anything rebellious lately. We'd been too busy planning for prom to cause any trouble.

"Wait! Is this about my prom dress?" I cried, eyes wide with incredulity. "I mean, really! If the king doesn't want me to have a faery-made dress, why did he let Claire give it to me? That can't be what this is all about!"

Jeff's eyes widened and his face paled. He actually looked like he might break into a cold sweat. I glanced to be sure the mushroom circle still surrounded us. It did. I was safe.

"What? You didn't expect me to make the connection? Humans are short lived, we're not stupid."

His face went from frost white to lobster red. "I never implied you were stupid."

I rolled my eyes. "Right. You have complete faith in the equality of our intellects."

He regained his composure and smiled. "I am certain of your intelligence, Lexie. It's your experience that is lacking. Humans simply don't live long enough to gain enough experience to allow them to properly analyze any given situation."

"Oh, please..."

"However, your leaps of logic are impressive. Since you have already made the connection, there can be no harm in verifying the obvious. Faery gifts are dangerous in the hands of mortals. King Alberic charged me with ascertaining your worthiness of the gown in question."

"Look. It's no big deal. Claire was just trying to help because she knows money is tight for my family. But if the king is wigging out about it, I'll tell her to return it to the flower faeries. I can buy something at the mall." I closed my eyes and mourned the amazing gown I'd never get to wear. Maybe I could find something at the second-hand store. Something of quality, and not too worn.

My shoulders sank. I tried to straighten them, but a weight seemed to push me into the earth. Despair. Yeah. That was the weight. I couldn't even afford a prom dress. I'd never manage college. I'd be serving coffee at Terry's cafe for the rest of my life.

"You also jump to conclusions, Lexie," Jeff murmured. "Leaps of logic can give you brilliance, but never confuse the two. You have concluded wrongly."

I peeked at him through my lashes.

A mischievous smile lifted his lips and danced in his eyes.

The weight of despair lifted, and I straightened. "What?"

"I find you worthy of Princess Claire's gift. More than that, I find you worthy of the interest of Faery."

I frowned and bit my lip. "What does that mean?"

"It means you may keep the gown and wear it in good health."

Warmth flooded my face, and I stifled a scream. It was all I could do to keep from hugging the faery dude.

"But, and this is very important, never loan the gown to anyone. It is for you and you alone."

"Absolutely," I cried. "Thank you. Oh! This is just too cool. Thank you so much!"

"You are very welcome, Lexie. I am honored to have made your acquaintance."

And with that he disappeared, along with the faery ring, and the sumptuous feast I'd never so much as tasted.

Well, faeries were like that — here one minute, gone the next. I leaned back on the blanket and pulled my book out of my bag. As far as anyone else was concerned, my day had gone just as planned. I'd come to Big Vista Lake to sun and read a romance novel. The reality of the afternoon just wouldn't be believed.

CHAPTER 7

The day of prom arrived, and the Murrays treated Claire and me to the works. Appointments at a posh salon - hair styled, nails and toes polished, and cosmetics expertly applied. I relaxed in the massaging chair while my feet soaked in warm soapy water and thought, *Oh yeah. Humans do just fine in some things.*

Later, we unwrapped our gowns in Claire's room.

"By the way, I'm guessing your grandpa's geas about the dresses is over. I passed."

Claire slumped onto the bed, her dress a rumpled heap in her lap. "I'm so glad! I hated not being able to warn you. What happened?"

So I told her about my afternoon with the enchantingly handsome guy. "All in all, it worked out okay. Nothing bad happened. I got permission to wear the dress — and was duly warned about loaning it out. And I think I made a friend, though it's hard to tell with immortal faery types." I pulled the dress over my head and twirled experimentally in front of the mirror. Oh yeah. This dress was SO worth it!

"Wow." Claire slipped into her own gown. "He actually said you were worthy of the interest of Faery? Those exact words?"

I frowned, thinking back over the fateful conversation. "I think so. Why?"

"Well, it's just that those words are portentous, especially coming from an emissary of the king."

"Wait a minute. Jeff was an emissary of the king? I figured he was just some poor schmuck who got a lame assignment. I mean, checking up on *me*? How boring!"

Claire giggled. "You underestimate yourself, my friend ... and my grandpa's weirdness. Jeff, make that Sir Geoffrey, is a member of the High Court and an emissary of the king. If he's taken an interest in you, well, anything could happen."

A chill ran down my spine that had nothing to do with the temperature of Claire's bedroom.

"Good anything? Or do I need to be worried?"

"Oh, no. You already avoided the bad stuff by refusing to eat or drink anything he offered. At this point, if anything happens, it'll be good luck."

"Uhm, about the food and drink thing. What would've happened if I'd tasted the cider?"

"You would've been transported to Faery and held as Jeff's captive."

I gulped and sat down hard on the bed. My ears buzzed and my vision darkened.

Claire pushed my head between my knees and intoned, "Breathe. It's okay. It didn't happen."

"But it might have," I whispered past painfully dry lips.

"Yeah. But you're forgetting ... you've got me and Roddy. I knew you were being tested. If you'd disappeared, we would've found you."

I squeezed her hand and curled up on her bed, closing my eyes. Sometimes it's a good thing not to know how close you came to an abyss.

CHAPTER 8

*P*rom was perfect. Brent and I doubled with Claire and Roddy. The guys had made dinner reservations at a swank restaurant in Seattle, so we had some travel time to deal with, but Roddy had splurged for a limo so even the car time was cool.

Our faery-made gowns were worth the trouble. The look on Brent's face when I came down the stairs from Claire's bedroom is permanently engraved in my brain. Awesome doesn't begin to describe the combination of awe, amazement, and pride all wrapped up in thinly disguised lust. I am *so* asking for a flower faery negligee for our wedding night! But that's years away, so for now, I'll pull out the memory of Brent's expression whenever I need an ego boost.

Claire and I were the hit of the prom. All the girls wanted to know where we'd found our gowns, and what the luscious fabric was. Claire calmly told the truth, they were designer originals made possible by her wealthy grandfather. What did I tell you about faeries and lying? Claire is no exception.

The other guys at the dance were the weird part, they seemed irresistibly drawn to us. Scary, in a very flattering way. But Brent and

Roddy were up to the challenge, and after a few minutes the attraction seemed to wear thin. I like to think Roddy cast a protective spell over us. That's certainly more appealing than thinking that all those guys got bored with us so quickly. At any rate, the room returned to normal, and the guys paid proper attention to their own dates. A good thing really. I'd hate for my gown's magic to kill someone else's dream when I was having an absolutely perfect night!

Just before midnight, the weirdest thing happened. Everyone in the room froze, including the musicians. The last note of the song echoed through a suddenly silent room full of statues. Only Claire and Roddy and Brent and I were unaffected.

I moved closer into Brent's arms and glanced around for Claire. She and Roddy walked calmly toward us, hand in hand.

"Don't worry. Everyone's fine. We're in a time distortion. Evidently, someone wants to talk to us."

Brent's arms tightened around me, and I glanced up and caught his gaze. At least we were together for this faery encounter.

Roddy nodded to Brent. "She'll be safe, Brent. Just follow our lead."

Brent nodded and relaxed a bit, but didn't release me. Which was a good thing. I had no desire to leave the security of his embrace.

I looked around, wondering how long this distortion thing could last, when the air in front of us wavered and three faery males shimmered into existence.

Claire curtsied. Roddy bowed. And Brent and I untangled and silently followed suit.

"Your Royal Highness," Claire said, head still bowed. "I didn't expect you to attend my prom."

"Rise and be at ease," King Alberic commanded. Once we were all upright, he stepped forward and kissed Claire's cheek, before turning to nod to Roddy.

When he turned to me, I wanted to sink into the floor.

"I am pleased to see you again, friend of my granddaughter, and you also, young man."

"Thank you, sire." Brent sounded so calm. Like he spoke to faery kings every day. I mumbled something that I hoped would pass as pleasant.

"Sir Geoffrey has commended you to me, Miss Davis. He tells me you are a worthy human."

I glanced up and recognized the other two faeries. King Alberic's emissaries, Cadmar and Jeff.

"I was impressed with Lexie, sir. Her reasoning is sound and her intuition impeccable," Jeff said. "In addition to being dear to our princess, I believe she is a human of worth in her own right."

My face flamed. I'm not used to praise. I mean, I'm a good kid. I work hard, help my parents as much as I can, and get good grades, but I'm nothing special. Except for Claire and Brent. They're the ones who make me shine.

Brent squeezed my hand, and Claire beamed at me.

The Faery King nodded. "Miss Davis, because of the good report of my advisor, and because of your own good judgment in your recent test" — I could feel Brent's puzzled gaze — "I have decided to grant you a boon."

"A-a boon, your highness?" What in the world did that mean?

"Yes. A boon. A gift, if you will."

"What sort of gift, Grandpa?" Claire asked.

"Miss Davis, I believe you desire to attend college?"

"Y-yes, sir. I do." Like that was going to happen. I made good grades, but not good enough to earn a scholarship at the university of my dreams.

"Well. Apply carefully. You will be accepted at any institution you choose."

My jaw dropped.

"Further," he continued, "you will be offered a full scholarship. Your tuition, books, lodging - every expense will be covered."

The room started to spin, and I leaned heavily against Brent. His arm encircled my waist, giving me the support I desperately needed.

"This will be a financially free ride, I think you would say, but you will work for your grades. No magic will convey to your coursework. That must be accomplished completely on your own."

He paused and studied my face, which must have looked like a ghost's, all my blood having retreated to my core to keep my heart functioning.

"Do not abuse this privilege, Miss Davis. Choose wisely and work hard."

"Uh, of course, sir. I-I'm ..." Speechless was what I was. Too completely flustered to string words together in meaningful sentences.

Claire rescued me, stepping forward to hug her grandfather. "That is so totally awesome, Grandpa! Lexie's thrilled. She's just too stunned to talk right now. But she'll snap out of it, and I'll give you a full report when she does."

Roddy and Brent chimed in, "Thank you, sire."

"Yes. Thank you. This is too good for words."

Jeff moved to stand beside me as I clung to Brent like a drowning girl clutches a life preserver. Jeff placed a finger under my chin and lifted so that our gazes met. "You are worthy, Lexie. Make of your life what you will. Make your dreams come true."

And then they vanished, and we were once again in the midst of happily gyrating bodies.

Dude. Faeries can be dangerous, but they can also ROCK! They'd certainly made my prom experience totally unforgettable.

I turned in Brent's arms and grinned at him, envisioning a wonderful future where I'd be able to join him at college next year, and we'd live happily ever after. My own personal faery tale ... with an amazingly awesome ending.

PART VIII
BEAUTY OR BUTTERFACE?

DEB LOGAN

AUTHOR OF *FAERY UNEXPECTED*

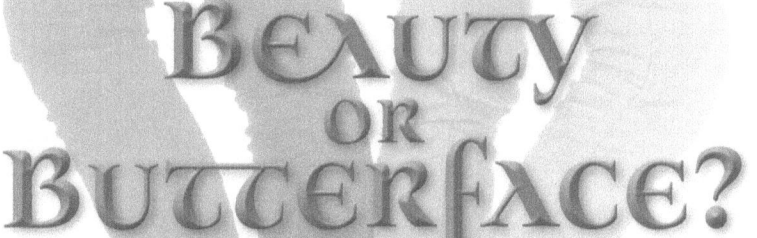

BEAUTY OR BUTTERFACE?

SPUN YARNS
A SHORT STORY

CHAPTER 1

athers! What can you do with them? Nothing. That's what. You just go along with their mad whims and hope to all the gods the universe holds that they don't screw up your entire life. At least, that's what happens when your father is king and you're his only son and heir.

It's not like the old days, when magic ruled and every royal family had a fairy godmother to help them out. I know the legends; I've heard Dad's stories. To hear him tell it, my mother's fairy godmother was instrumental in their lives, but that's probably just another of Dad's tall tales. I've certainly never seen a fairy, but if I had, you can bet I'd've wrangled a wish for some way to make Dad ease off on the life-altering expectations.

Don't get me wrong. I'm no pushover. I pull off the occasional small rebellion. Sometimes even manage to logic my way around a few of his crazier ideas. But when it comes right down to it, I obey or the castle guard will see to it that I'm grounded for life. And in my case, grounded means a private cell in a dank, dark dungeon that smells of mold and rat droppings. Possibly with chains — just to make sure I get the point.

Yeah. I know who's boss ... and someday, if I don't screw things up, it'll be me!

Dad's latest obsession is securing a line of succession, and since I'm his only son, that means I have to marry a princess and produce an heir. Pronto!

Great. The most important decision of my life and Dad wants me to make it in the next five seconds.

No pressure, son. Just make a choice. You'll only have to spend the rest of your life with her. Not to mention have sex with her on a regular basis so I can have a grandchild. Nope. No pressure at all. Just get on with it!

Thanks, Dad. Can't wait.

CHAPTER 2

"*P*hilip, my boy! How are you this morning?" Dad beamed at me from his seat at the breakfast table. Sunlight streamed through spotless windows and sparkled off gleaming cutlery and polished serving dishes. A sideboard groaned under the weight of every possible delicacy a king could desire first thing in the morning. Platters of eggs (scrambled, fried, deviled, and poached), rashers of crisp bacon, salvers of thinly sliced beef and savory fish, stacks of buttered toast, waffles, pancakes, bowls of colorful berries, and, of course, my least favorite food, steaming, gluey porridge.

You'd think we were expecting an army to join us for our morning meal.

Dad looked unusually chipper this morning, which put me on edge. "What's up, Dad?" I asked, eyeing his perfectly tailored suit complete with purple sash of state slashed across his rotund torso. Dad can manage a dignified appearance if he has to, but most of the time he looks like a short, round, balding Santa relaxing in the off-season. Thank all that's holy, I take after my maternal grandfather, tall, slim, with a full head of wavy chestnut hair. "You're awfully well-dressed for so early in the morning."

I waved the butler, Jennings, away and stepped to the sideboard. Dad was old-school. He preferred to sit in state while Jennings offered him dishes and then served the items Dad chose. Always seemed like a waste of time to me. Why sit there and wait when I was perfectly capable of scooping up my own scrambled eggs?

When my plate was enticingly loaded with fried eggs, bacon, toast and marmalade, and several slices of honeydew melon, I joined Dad at the table.

"Great news, Philip," Dad said, wiping a bit of yolk from his chin. "I'm finalizing a treaty with Lindesland this morning. A very advantageous one. I'm sending you to Stefan's kingdom. You're to marry his daughter, and when the two of us are gone, our kingdoms will be merged. You and, eh, uhm, what's her name will rule a new and vastly larger realm. Isn't that exciting?"

The blood drained from my face. My appetite fled, and a knot of molten lead formed in my belly. "You've chosen my wife? Without even asking me?"

Confused disappointment dimmed Dad's smile. He looked like I'd just refused the best gift in the world. Bewilderment glazed his eyes. He frowned momentarily before his gaze cleared and his smiled brightened.

"Not at all," he cried, slapping his palm on the table. "I've forgotten the best part. Stefan has *two* daughters. Identical twins! You'll have your choice of brides."

I groaned and buried my face in my hands. Why did I have to be born a prince?

CHAPTER 3

King Stefan's castle was much like our own: ancient in design but refurbished to include all the modern conveniences. My suite of rooms was suitable to my station. Luxurious bedroom complete with a king-sized (of course!) four-poster bed hung with velvet curtains in royal purple, a comfortable sitting room paneled in dark wood and overlooking a rose garden, and a private bath with Jacuzzi and sauna.

My royal guards and I arrived late in the afternoon. Dad referred to the guards as my retinue. I thought of them as jailers, there to make sure I didn't make a run for it. I mean, why in the world would I need four burly men to protect me from Stefan and his daughters? My best protection would be the destruction of that treaty, but that wasn't going to happen. I just had to resign myself to choosing between two identical girls.

I could hardly wait.

After being shown to our rooms, I was informed that dinner would be at seven, and that I would meet the family in the drawing room promptly at six-thirty. One of my men would accompany me, of course, but being a well-trained guard, he would fade into the background.

I had just finished adjusting my cuff links when a knock sounded on the door. David, my jailor for the evening, opened the door to a young man in Stefan's livery.

"Highness," he said with a precise bow, "I'm here to escort you to the drawing room."

I glanced out the window at the sunlight fading across the rose garden. Just like my freedom...rapidly disappearing.

"Highness?" said the footman.

"Yes," I said, turning to face my inevitable doom. "Of course."

We strode through carpeted hallways, down a sweeping staircase with a lavishly carved bannister, across a stone-flagged entry and paused at a richly polished mahogany door. The footman opened the door, stepped inside, and announced me.

"His royal highness, Prince Philip of Glencowrie."

Straightening my shoulders and inhaling deeply, I walked into the room. The tableau that met my eyes surprised me. King Stefan stood before the window, gazing out over the perfectly manicured lawns. His wife, Queen Isabelle, sat in a high-backed chair on the far side of the room. I'd expected two young women, but the king and queen were alone.

King Stefan turned when I entered and marched to meet me, hand outstretched. "Philip," he said. "I don't believe I've seen you since you were a small boy." He grasped my hand and shook it. "You've grown into a fine man."

"Thank you, sire," I said, gripping his hand, but not too firmly. No need to turn a hand shake into a duel. "I'm pleased to be here."

Stefan smiled and led me across the room to his queen. "Allow me to present my wife, Queen Isabelle."

I clicked my heels and bowed over the hand she graciously extended. "An honor, your majesty."

"You are welcome in our home, Prince Philip," she said. "I hope you will enjoy your stay."

Her words were courteous, but I thought I detected sadness in her eyes, a slight tightness at the edges of her mouth. Was something amiss? Had my arrival interrupted a disagreement? My own mother having died when I was still in diapers, I was unaccustomed to the nuances of a married couple, but something felt … odd.

I pushed the thought away and smiled. I was probably projecting my own unease onto Stefan's queen.

"I'm sure you're anxious to meet our daughters," Stefan said.

I nodded politely while trying to breathe past the sudden tightness in my chest.

Stefan gazed meaningfully at a door beside a large stone fireplace. A footman moved to open the it and called, "Their royal highnesses, Princess Dawn and Princess Aurora."

A rather plain young woman stepped into the room. Short dark hair curled around a face dominated by a bulbous, overlarge nose. Her lips were thin and uninteresting, but her eyes…her eyes were large and dark and surveyed me with wary intelligence. She wore a deep blue evening gown that failed to glamorize her angular, too-skinny frame.

I clicked my heels and bowed to her, my heart sinking. Identical twins. The next girl wouldn't be any more attractive.

When I straightened, I realized just how wrong a guy could be.

The second sister had entered the room and her radiance filled every shadowy crevice. The breath left my body and my lungs forgot how to function, until her gaze met mine and she smiled.

My heart pounded, the thrum of my own pulse drowning out every other sound in the room. I inhaled sharply, wondering what I'd done to deserve such a prize?

She was perfection personified. Hair so golden it looked like she'd captured the sun and pulled it into ringlets. Lips so full and red they made the roses in the garden look drab. Sapphire blue eyes twinkled mischievously in a face whose complexion was a glorious mix of peaches and cream.

Like her sister, she wore a gown of deep blue, but that was the only similarity. This gown clung to a lush bosom, flowed past a trim waist, and spilled over ripe, round hips. I burned to take her in my arms, run my hands over those curves, kiss those rose-red lips…

"Prince Philip?"

King Stefan's voice jolted me from thoughts rapidly descending into the lewd. I jerked my gaze from his luscious daughter and fought to focus on him.

"Forgive me, sire," I said, lowering my eyes and closing them for a brief moment. When I looked up again, my emotions, and my lust, were under control. Barely. "You were saying?"

Stefan smiled, a trace wanly. "If you will escort Princess Dawn," he said, glancing at the mousey sister, "we'll go in to dinner now."

I chanced a glance at Beauty, for that was how I thought of her, and saw her place a perfect hand on the stunned footman's arm to be escorted in to dinner. The young man looked like he'd been hit between the eyes with one of Cupid's arrows.

My own eyes narrowed with jealousy. I looked away quickly, caught my breath, and turned my attention to my assigned partner. A butterface, if ever I'd seen one. Crossing to her side, I held out my arm. "May I see you to the dining room, Bu … Princess?"

Good Lord! I'd almost said *Butterface* aloud! I was more addled than I'd realized.

Brown eyes sparkling good-naturedly, she rested a hand lightly on my forearm. "Of course, Prince Philip," she said. Her voice was soft and musical, a balm to my jangled nerves. "I look forward to getting to know you."

And suddenly, surprisingly, I found myself pleased to be her dinner partner.

Since there were only five of us, the grand dining table had been replaced with a small one. It sat rather forlornly at one end of the large room, looking as out of place in the grandeur of the dining hall as Butterface did beside Beauty. King Stefan took his place at the head of the table, Queen Isabelle on his right and Butterface, uhm, Princess Dawn on his left. Princess Aurora sat beside her mother, and I took my place beside Princess Dawn. Which placed me directly across the table from Beauty.

I couldn't have asked for better placement for that meal. I could gaze with besotted wonder at the stunning face and form of Beauty, while conversing quietly with her lovely-voiced and quick-witted sister.

For Dawn proved to be a delightful conversationalist, well-informed and not shy about sharing her opinions. Our topics ranged from racing — both cars and horses, to school experiences — we'd both attended prestigious boarding schools and were pleased to be finished with them, to the perils of royal birth.

I genuinely enjoyed listening to her speak, both for the musicality of her voice and the logical flow of her thoughts. As long as I didn't concentrate on her appearance, I found her lovely and engaging.

"So, tell me truthfully, Philip," she said as the butler served a lovely crème brûlée for dessert, "What do you think of this treaty our fathers have designed?"

"Well," I said, stalling as thoughts whirled through my head. Truthfully? How could I answer truthfully without giving offense?

"Come now," she whispered leaning toward me so that I breathed in a hint of lavender and roses. "You can't have been entirely pleased with this arrangement."

"No," I admitted. "Father's been after me for the last few months about choosing a wife and providing him an heir, but..." I hesitated, met her gaze and, recognizing a spark of irritation that matched my own, plunged ahead, "I never expected him to take the choice out of my hands."

She nodded. "I understand completely." A mischievous grin lit her face. "I suppose he tried to appease you by saying you still had a choice. Twins, after all."

I grinned. "Yes, he did pull that one out. Can't say that it made me feel a lot better." I stopped, held her gaze, my mood suddenly serious. "Of course, it's no help at all to you and Aurora. There's only one of me."

She sat perfectly still, an air of thoughtfulness wrapping around her like a cloak. Then she cocked her head and smiled at me, the playful expression making her features almost pretty. "You know, I think one might be all we need."

Her mother chose that moment to rise, ending the meal. So on that enigmatic statement my first encounter with Butterface came to a close.

CHAPTER 4

The next day Queen Isabelle suggested that Aurora show me the castle grounds. The princess smiled at me and said she'd be delighted.

I forgot how to breathe again.

Fortunately, before I could die of asphyxiation, she moved to my side, placed a hand on my arm, and guided me toward the French doors. Between her touch and my own faltering gait, the paralysis of my lungs subsided and I drew breath once more.

We strolled through the rose garden trailed by a maid and James, today's guard. I'd never really needed a chaperone to walk around a garden with a pretty girl before, but then that girl had never been Beauty...

I was hyper-aware of her hand on my shirtsleeve. The heat of her small fingers burned through the fabric, nearly scorching my skin. I glanced at my arm, convinced that the cotton must be smoldering, but all I saw was a small, neat hand tucked into the crook of my arm. Perfectly normal. Except that it wasn't. Normal, that is.

Her hair was loose on her shoulders today, spun gold glistening in the morning light. Her dove grey silk blouse and light blue cardigan clung to her curves. My mouth alternated between too dry to speak and practically drooling. And those trousers! Dark grey, neatly pleated, and so perfectly molded to her gorgeous … uhm … assets.

I closed my eyes, concentrated on not stumbling over my own feet, and let her guide me through the garden.

And that's when I discovered it. With my eyes closed, when I couldn't see the golden perfection of her, my world fell back into place. I heard the breeze sighing through the trees, caught the blend of delicate fragrances of the garden's flowers: roses, lilacs, lavender and violets. Without the sight of her to distract me, I felt the good solid earth beneath my feet, the crunch of gravel on the path. My mind cleared. I realized that we hadn't spoken a meaningful word in all the time we'd been walking.

My thoughts and attention had been completely mesmerized by her beauty, by my desire to touch her, hold her, do other, more intimate things to and with her. But when I closed my eyes, I was hardly even aware of her hand on my arm. I certainly had no awareness of her as a person.

Something was definitely wrong with this whole situation.

CHAPTER 5

Several days later, I still hadn't managed to figure out what was going on, but I had a wealth of experience with both Beauty and Butterface.

Beauty continued to dazzle my senses, but I had discovered ways to deal with the enchantment of her perfection. I'd learned to glance away, close my eyes, concentrate on a single thought. In short, my defense against Beauty's glamour was meditation.

Now there was a laugh. What red-blooded, healthy young male wants to meditate in the presence of a stunningly beautiful, perfectly proportioned female? Me ... because I also wanted to keep my sanity and be able to speak in complete sentences.

Butterface was a totally different story. She was charming and sweet, but with a deliciously wicked sense of humor. I loved spending time with her and thoroughly enjoyed our conversations. But I couldn't get past her unattractive exterior. Logical debate or game of trivia? I wanted her on my team. But hold her in my arms and kiss her? No thanks. Let's play chess instead.

On the last night of my scheduled visit, King Stefan sent word that I should join him in his study. Expecting a manly conversation complete with drinks and cigars, I was surprised to find all three of the ladies present. Stefan rose from behind his desk when I entered and motioned me to the sitting area to join his family.

I hesitated. The furniture was arranged in a cozy conversation square: two sofas faced each other across a low rectangular table. At each of the other ends stood an overstuffed leather chair. Queen Isabelle occupied one chair and King Stefan stood beside the second.

That left the sofas, each of which held a princess.

Which would it be? Would I choose to sit beside Beauty or Butterface?

I declined to choose. Instead I strode across the room and leaned against the edge of Stefan's desk. This placed me behind Beauty, but I had the feeling I was going to need my wits about me, so that wasn't necessarily a bad thing.

Stefan covered his mouth with his hand, but not before I saw the grin he was trying to hide.

We subsided into tense silence. Queen Isabelle stared at the table, her fingers nervously pleating and unpleating the edge of her sweater. Butterface sat straight as a board on the leather sofa, her unblinking gaze glued to the floor. King Stefan fidgeted, clasping and unclasping his hands or twisting his royal signet on his finger. Only Beauty appeared at ease. I couldn't see her face, but her shoulders were relaxed and she sat quietly.

Finally, Queen Isabelle cleared her throat and gave her husband a very pointed look.

"Right. Yes," he said. "Down to business. Philip, we've asked you here to this private room to finalize the treaty between Lindesland and Glencowrie. As you know, the agreement calls for you to marry my daughter. The time has come for you to make your choice."

My face felt like I'd stuck it in a fire, but I managed to nod. What to do? What to say? How was I supposed to meet my father's expectations without screwing up the rest of my life? If I'd been one of those lucky royals of old and had a fairy godmother, I knew what I'd wish for in that moment: I wanted nothing more (or less) than to merge Beauty and Butterface into one person! Too bad that wasn't an option.

My heart pounded so loudly I was sure everyone in the room could keep time with its rhythm. My palms were slick with sweat and my mouth was parched.

Rubbing my hands on my twill trousers, I straightened away from the desk and stepped to Queen Isabelle's side.

"Your majesty," I said, inclining my head to her. "Thank you for the honor of allowing me to get to know each of your daughters. Both of them are treasures." I focused my attention on the mother, knowing that a glance at one daughter would render me speechless, while catching sight of the other would weaken my resolve.

"Thank you, young prince," the queen said, her voice tight with strain, "but like my husband and daughters, I am anxious to hear your decision."

I nodded, closed my eyes and tried to think. *Don't look*, my heart whispered. *Just listen.*

Without looking, I leapt.

"I choose Butterface," I said. My eyes popped open in horror as I realized what I'd said. "I mean D-Dawn," I stammered. "I choose Dawn!"

To my utter bewilderment, everyone in the room burst out laughing.

The queen grasped my hand and cried, "Bless you, my boy!" while King Stefan staggered to his feet and raced to thump me on the back and pull me into a bear hug.

But most amazing of all? Beauty disappeared in a shimmer of sparkles and a glimmering woman appeared behind the sofa where she'd been seated. An ageless woman with wings and a wand.

"Wh-what's going on?" I cried, glancing to the one person in the room whose opinion I valued most, Butterface...who was a butterface no longer.

Dawn grinned at me with tears in her eyes. Her hair was still short, dark and curly, and her eyes were still deep brown and beautiful, but the rest of her facial proportions had changed. Her nose was no longer large and bulbous, but straight and just the right size for her face. Her lips were full, but not overblown, and her complexion was tanned and lovely with just the right blush of healthy pink. And the rest of her ... well, let's just say that my Butterface was no longer angular and stick thin. She was nicely curved in all the right places and filled out her jeans with perfectly proportioned ... assets.

I shook off her parents and stumbled to her side, feeling tongue-tied for the first time in her presence. "Wh-what's going on?" I asked taking her hands just to make sure she was real. "Who are you? What happened to you?"

She grinned even more widely and stepped into my embrace. She felt warm and soft and fit there absolutely ... perfectly.

After a moment, the winged woman coughed and suggested we all take a seat.

This time I had no trouble with the suggestion. I sank onto the sofa and pulled Dawn down beside me.

"Prince Philip, I am Merridee, Princess Dawn's fairy godmother," the winged woman said. "When the princess heard of her father's treaty with Glencowrie, she came to me and begged a boon. I deemed it a reasonable request, and granted her wish."

I waited for her to continue, but the silence, now more embarrassed than tense, stretched.

"And?" I prompted.

Merridee stared meaningfully at Dawn, who squirmed in my arms and moved away from me. She was blushing to the roots of her curly dark hair.

"Do you remember that first night at dinner," she began, "when I asked you how you felt when you heard about the terms of our fathers' treaty?"

I nodded and caught her hand. I still needed reassurance of her reality.

"Well, I felt like you did," she continued. "Angry that Father would bind me to you without even asking what I thought. So I called upon Merridee and she found a solution."

"You see, young prince," Merridee said, "Dawn wanted to be sure that the man she married would love her for herself and not just as a prize who came with a kingdom. So we devised a twin for her. Either choice would bring the kingdom, but only choosing the uhm … ugly … sister would show true understanding of Dawn's worth."

"But what if I'd chosen Aurora?" I asked, confused. "She didn't exist. How would that have won me the kingdom?"

"It wouldn't," admitted Stefan. "I would have found a way to break both the engagement and the treaty rather than leave my people in unworthy hands."

My head was spinning. Granted, my own wish had come true in this twisted revelation, but still, I'd been used, made a pawn.

"One of you should've told me," I said to the king and queen.

"They couldn't," said Dawn, very quietly. "Merridee laid a geas on them. Trust me," she said, looking full into my eyes, "neither of them was the least bit happy about this scheme. If you're angry, and you've every right to be, you must be angry only with me."

I stared into her dark brown eyes and recognized my heart's desire.

"I do feel used," I said, "but I'll get over it. The question is, will you ever get over being called Butterface? Because that's who you'll always be to me."

She smiled through tear-filled eyes. "I'll get used to it," she whispered. "And just so we're straight, by the time we finished dinner that first night, I knew this ruse was unnecessary, but I'd set it in motion and had to let it play out."

She sank back into my embrace. "Thank you for choosing me."

I stroked her hair and kissed the top of her head, reveling in her scent of lavender and roses. She challenged me and made me think, was my equal in every way, and she was lovely both inside and out. How could I be angry?

I closed my eyes, not as a defense mechanism, but in order to savor the magic of the moment. "Thank you," I whispered, for her ears alone, "for making all my dreams come true."

12 STORIES BY DEBBIE MUMFORD

PART I
EGG THIEF

DEBBIE MUMFORD

BESTSELLING AUTHOR OF *SORCHA'S HEART*

Egg Thief

SPUN YARNS
A Thrilling Short Story

EGG THIEF

a mixture of terror and elation spur me down the steep, rocky slope. The harsh, cold wind buffets me, making it had to keep my leather-booted feet beneath me.

I can't slow down. Can't fall. If I so much as pause...she might come back, might realize what I've done. If she catches me on this unprotected slope, she'll roast me alive.

The backpack bounces against my shoulders, its warm, reassuring weight throwing off my balance. I've done it! I slipped into her lair, stole an egg, and made it back to the cold, fresh air of the mountainside.

I've got to keep moving, got to make it to the forest. She won't be able to find me once I reach the trees' thick canopy.

I pant, cold air numbing nose and cheeks and making my lungs ache. But the precious egg in my pack, the one I risked everything to steal, is safe and warm, protected by a nest of soft woolen blankets.

The ground beneath my feet levels, turning from rock to coarse, low grass and sedge. Tree line is within sight, its stunted larch and fir trees twisted by the constant fierce, cold wind that whistles past my ears and makes my eyes water.

I'm going to make it. Those scraggly trees aren't much, but they're my only hope. The first cover on this wind-swept mountainside. Just a little way beyond the tree line, the proper forest begins. Tall spruce, firs, and aspen with sufficient canopy to shield a fleeing man from even a dragon's sharp vision.

The worst is behind me. Once I gain the forest, I'll be safe.

Terror loosens its grip on my heart and exultation bubbles through my core. A near-hysterical giggle forces its way past my chapped lips. Truly, I've done it. The jade-green egg with dark blue mottling is mine. A prize beyond measure. And not just because of the gold I will demand. My reputation will be made once I return to the city with a dragon egg in my pack.

I savor the fruits of my stealth. All that remains is to reach the safety of the forest.

A shadow passes overhead, and I stumble, my foot snagging on a tangled mass of sedge. I catch my balance and glance up at the clear blue, cloudless sky. My breath seizes and my heart plummets.

A dragon wheels in the sky.

She has returned, recognized her loss, and hunted me.

My pulse thunders, beating twice its normal tattoo. Blood sings in my veins, throbs at my temples, tingles in my fingertips. A burst of energy propels me down the slope. I must reach those trees.

With a screech of indignation, the dragon plummets to earth, landing between me and the trees. The backwash from her wings knocks me off my feet. I twist as I fall, keeping the packed egg safe, but sustaining a nasty jolt to my shoulder and wrenching a knee.

I gain my feet and crouch, ready to run, but where?

The dragon, a solid mass of muscle and anger, easily as big as my two-room hut, unfurls her wings and hisses. Her long, snake-like tongue lashes the air between us.

Dragon stink fills my nostrils, a noxious mix of sulfur, rotting meat and blood that solidifies the terror freezing my heart and paralyzing my thoughts. Pain throbs in shoulder and knee, darkening the edges of my vision. Bitter, poisonous bile gags me.

All is lost.

No way forward. Not past a hulking beast whose wings blot out the scraggly trees beyond.

No way back. Not across a barren slope of alpine tundra.

Death stares at me with malignant satisfaction.

The inevitability of my demise calms me, thawing my terror and freeing my mind. I still have a card to play. I still hold the egg.

She can't crush me for fear of harming the egg. Nor can she use flame against me.

While I hold her egg, we are at an impasse. I stare into her yellow, cat-slit eyes and know that she understands our stalemate as well.

I hunker down to think while the dragon studies me with narrowed eyes. She furls her wings and settles, the barbed tip of her tail tapping restlessly.

The elation of a few moments before has shriveled. I wish whole-heartedly I'd never imagined this foolhardy scheme. Why did I gamble my life on the insane possibility of stealing a dragon's egg?

For unimaginable wealth and everlasting glory.

To be the first man to climb the dragon's mountain and return with an unblemished egg.

To be the man who made it possible for the High King to take his place among the gods. To provide the key ingredient to the fabled elixir of immortality: the heart of an unborn dragon.

And all I have to do to make those dreams a reality is steal past a massive, angry dragon and make my way back to the city with my prize.

Before any scrap of a plan can present itself to my fevered mind, the dragon's tail ceases its tapping and a soft, low coo swirls upon the wind.

I frown. Do dragons coo?

The coo sounds again, soft, melodious, remarkably like the call of a mourning dove. The dragon closes her eyes and lowers her head.

Is this my moment? Can I steal past her while she's not looking? Could I reach the cover of the trees?

I lean forward, gathering my legs beneath me, ready to spring.

The egg in my pack jumps, pulling against the straps on my shoulders, ruining my balance. I stumble forward a step or two, catch myself and scramble back, away from the dragon's cruel talons.

Sweat beads my forehead and drips down my nose. The egg jumps again, hard enough to pull me onto my rump.

The dragon waits quietly, eyes closed, cooing, the sound oddly welcoming.

Another jump nearly unseats me.

I wriggle out of the pack, pull it into my lap, and swipe my shirtsleeve across my sweaty brow. Opening the pack, I shove layers of soft wool aside to expose the precious egg. A crack mars its perfection.

My heart sinks. I've waited too long. The egg is hatching.

Even if I survive the dragon, there will be no elixir of immortality. Not without the heart of an unborn dragon.

A louder coo burbles from the mother dragon. I glance up. Her eyes remain closed, her wings furled. If I didn't know better, I'd think she was asleep.

On a gut level, I understand: she is focused on the hatching egg.

Now is my moment. I must leave the pack with its now useless egg and run for cover. She won't follow. She's not interested in me. All she wants is to see her offspring safely hatched.

I glance back up the mountain. Are the other eggs hatching? Could I leave this one and grab another? If I did, would I be able to get it down the mountain before it hatched?

Slowly, carefully, I slide back from the nested egg.

The dragon ignores me, continuing to coo.

I stand, paralyzed with indecision. Escape past the dragon and return to the city, empty-handed, but alive, or seize this opportunity to return to the lair, grab another egg, and escape down a different path while she is focused on this hatchling's birth?

The voice of caution, my mother's voice, screams at me to run for the trees. To save myself. To live to scheme another day.

But another voice, a more daring voice speaks more convincingly. *When will you ever have such a chance again? You know where the dragon is and she doesn't care about you. A little peril could earn you riches and eternal glory. Seize the moment, or spend the rest of your life regretting its loss.*

I take a few cautious steps upslope, half expecting the dragon to pounce on me. She doesn't even open an eye. My injured knee aches, but does not give way. I turn and race full tilt back to the dragon's lair.

A few minutes later I step out of the howling wind, into the shelter of the cave. Leaning against cold rock, I stand on my good leg, resting my aching knee, and wait for my labored breathing to ease, for my eyes to become accustomed to the dark.

The air is fetid with dragon stink, the floor littered with broken bones and bits of moldering pelts, remnants of long-forgotten meals.

I push myself upright and limp into the gloom. At the rear of the cavern, the eggs huddle in a nest of stout limbs lined with the pelts of bears and wolves. Climbing into the nest was easier last time. Now my shoulder throbs with every heartbeat and my leg trembles with the strain of my injured knee. But I make it.

Exhausted, I collapse onto the warm, coarse furs and crawl to the mound of eggs. I only need one. One egg and fame and fortune will be mine.

I reach toward the mound of deeper darkness that is the pile of eggs, and encounter not a smooth, hard shell, but soft, leathery skin.

Disappointment floods my soul and I jerk my hand back. At least one of the eggs has hatched, but perhaps there is still hope. Perhaps a late bloomer languishes beneath its more advanced siblings.

I inch sideways and reach into the pile again.

Immediately glowing eyes pop open and soft, gurgling cries sound. Small bodies scurry in the dark, accompanied by snaps and cracks as shells are trodden upon. I soon find myself surrounded by blinking, luminous eyes.

By their pale light I see that all the eggs have hatched. Nothing remains on the furs but infant dragons and splintered shells.

My whole enterprise has been too late. I never had a chance of getting an unblemished egg back to the city.

My hopes dashed, I crawl back across the pelts. I still have to climb out of the nest and escape this accursed mountain. The task seems insurmountable now that no reward awaits me.

Disappointment makes me stupid. I've forgotten I'm in a dragon's lair. Forgotten that despite their small size, I am surrounded by dragons.

I am reminded forcibly when a hatchling bites into the calf of my injured leg and tears away both fabric and meat. I scream in agony, kick out with my good leg, my leather boot connecting firmly with a small body.

But it is too late. Blood pumps from my wound, exciting the hatchlings, turning their newborn hunger into a feeding frenzy.

I curl into a tight ball, hoping to protect my tender belly from sharp talons and teeth. My last sight before my vision darkens is of the mother dragon's arrival, bearing her final hatchling to the feast.

Her triumphant roar deafens me, and as oblivion descends, I think, *Mother was right. I should have run for my life...*

PART II
ASTROMANCER

DEBBIE MUMFORD

BESTSELLING AUTHOR OF *SORCHA'S HEART*

ASTROMANCER

SPUN YARNS
A Short Story

CHAPTER 1

yot wandered, awe-struck, through the serpentine halls of the Emerald Conclave. He'd dreamed of being invited into this building, into the prestigious gathering of Alchemists it housed, but he'd never expected his dreams to become reality. He was an astrologer of the third rank, possessed of nowhere near the innate magical talent required to join this august body.

He knew the way — when the Thrice Great called, he provided the knowledge — but Wyot took his time, absorbing every marvel as he walked. Who knew when he'd have such an opportunity again. The corridor sparkled, bathed in red-toned shafts of sunlight from the dwarf star of Rigil II. No matter where he looked, Wyot was dazzled. The walls were robed in gold, undoubtedly transmuted by members of the Conclave, while windows boasted crystalline panes from Luyten. Even the floor beneath his feet shone, consisting of highly polished marble from Barnard Prime. Priceless artwork lined the walls, showing scenes from every planet that was home to a Guild oracle...and since any planet without an oracle was isolated from the rest of the starfaring worlds, all were represented. And the statuary!

He didn't have words for the creative genius that graced the carefully crafted niches along his route.

"Astrologer Wyot!"

The whip-crack voice calling his name pulled Wyot from a reverential inspection of an exquisite rendition of his homeworld, Eridani. He snapped to attention before touching fingertips to brow in deference to an older member of the guild.

"How may I serve, elder brother?"

"You may follow me swiftly," replied the older man. Silver-haired and stern-faced, he wore his dignity like a cape over impressive robes of scarlet and midnight blue sashed with gold. "Your tardiness is delaying the business of the Emerald Conclave."

Wyot's heart hammered, unease zipped along his spine. The entire Emerald Conclave? What had he done? A meeting with the Thrice Great had been intimidating enough. "Apologies, elder brother," he said, striding to position himself a respectful pace behind the older man.

In silence, they moved through the remaining corridors, coming to a halt before a pair of ornately carved doors. Soaring sixteen feet from floor to lintel, the doors were covered in gold leaf, their carvings depicted Alchemical symbols, formulas, and stylized representations of the Guild's most famous accomplishments. Wyot stared open-mouthed at the gleaming surfaces, until his guide's voice snapped him back to attention.

"When I announce you, walk to the center of the room and salute," the man instructed. "Don't fidget and don't gawk. Whatever happens, don't speak unless spoken to, and even then use as few words as possible. Do you understand?"

Wyot nodded. "I do. Thank you."

His guide gave a gentle push, and the right-hand door swung silently open. He stepped through and called, "Astrologer Wyot, excellencies." He bowed, motioned Wyot inside, and then left, closing the door behind him.

As instructed, Wyot strode to the center of the room — easily identified by a sun surrounded by cleverly depicted orbiting planets, all inlaid in the marble floor. Once in position, he faced the conclave and raised fingertips to brow. Lowering his hands to his sides, he stilled mind and body and observed the leaders of the Alchemical Guild.

The conclave sat on a raised platform, behind a table spread with a snowy cloth; six men and five women. The Thrice Great sat in the center, a handsome man of indeterminate age — as befitted one who held complete control of the aging process. Dark hair, deep blue eyes, dressed in robes of saffron yellow trimmed with ocean blue. His fellows ranged on either side, men and women who appeared to be in the prime of their lives, dressed in rich fabrics, their eyes heavy with knowledge.

Silence reigned, became a palpable thing. Wyot fought not to fidget, to maintain calm, remain composed. Sweat tricked down his back as the effort not to so much as clear his throat became a burden.

After what felt like an eternity, the Thrice Great spoke. "We have heard good things of you, Astrologer Wyot, and have seen much in our meditations."

Wyot's heart rate surged. The Thrice Great, the most accomplished oracle in the universe, had seen Wyot in his meditations?

"What are your aspirations in the Guild, young astrologer?"

Sweat beaded Wyot's upper lip while his mouth felt as dry as the desert planet of the Canis system. He swallowed, raised his eyes and met the Thrice Great's gaze. "I would be an astromancer, excellency."

Several other conclave members shifted in their seats, but the Thrice Great held Wyot's gaze. "A lofty ambition," he said.

Wyot's cheeks heated. He longed to elaborate, to explain his audacity. Instead, he kept his gaze level, his mouth closed. He could almost feel the Thrice Great probing his mind, searching his heart, weighing his very soul. Nevertheless, he stood quietly and maintained eye-contact with the greatest Alchemist in the cosmos, the highest, most learned person in his order.

The Thrice Great broke their connection, sat forward and glanced at each member of the conclave in turn. "It is as I have foreseen. Astrologer Wyot will become our next astromancer."

Wyot's knees nearly buckled, but he remained upright by sheer force of will. His pulse throbbed so loudly against his ears, he almost missed his instructions.

"Return to your apartments. Pack what is necessary and report to the starfield. You will be met." The Thrice Great rose, as did the rest of the conclave. While his fellows filed from the room, the Thrice Great studied Wyot before nodding. "You have done well, Wyot. May you continue to be diligent in the next phase of your studies."

CHAPTER 2

*S*ub-Astromancer Wyot waited on the starfield, a small trunk at his feet. He glanced around, trying not to appear anxious, at the wide stretch of compacted and glazed earth. He'd passed the starfield everyday since his arrival on Rigil II — lovingly known as the Silent Egg by the younger alchemists-in-training, but had not set foot on it since the astromancer of the starship that had brought him here had transferred him from ship to starfield.

In the years since his arrival, he'd studied enthusiastically, had read extensively, but had never heard so much as a whisper regarding the magic the astromancers employed. He thrilled to think that he was about to become one of that elite branch of Alchemists who enabled faster-than-light travel. Without astromancers, the great starships would be useless, would be reduced to space junk doomed to orbit their native worlds.

The other branch of the Alchemical Guild that the general public was familiar with were the oracles. Wyot was familiar with their magic. While he couldn't claim a particular gift for divination, he could see as well as the next astrologer. He'd heard vague rumors that sight was also required for astromancy, but none of his instructors could, or would, confirm or deny. If the rumors were true, he hoped his small talent could be developed.

Of course, if the Thrice Great saw him as an astromancer, he must have the necessary talent and ability to become one.

His feet ached from standing on the hard ground. He shifted his weight slightly, wondering for whom he waited.

A shimmer of light appeared a few feet from him, and before he could step back in surprise, a man materialized. Wyot touched fingers to forehead before studying the man with frank curiosity. He stood nearly six feet in height, swarthy complected, broad chested, narrow hipped, hands cupped at chest level. He wore a uniform of sorts, which made him appear alien to Wyot's eyes, accustomed as he was to the flowing robes of the alchemists.

"You are Wyot?" the man asked, lowering his hands and pushing one into a pocket at his hip. "Recently promoted to Sub-Astromancer?"

"I am," replied Wyot.

The man touched fingertips to brow, and then met Wyot's gaze. "I am Astromancer Eadric. Thrice Great Kenelm has assigned your training to me."

Wyot bowed his head. "I am honored, elder brother. I shall study earnestly."

Eadric glanced at the trunk beside Wyot. "I see that you are ready. Good. Here is your first lesson: an astromancer manipulates the flux fields that surround every object, living or inanimate. He can move through space by choosing a field and grabbing hold. Whatever is attached to the astromancer moves with him. Do you understand?"

Wyot's mouth dropped open, while his mind raced to absorb the information. He shook his head. "No, Astromancer Eadric, I don't understand, but I accept that you do. I place myself in your hands."

Eadric nodded. "That is enough for now." He stepped forward and smiled. A genial expression that crinkled the skin around his eyes and displayed even white teeth. "Since we will work closely, let us dispense with titles. Call me Eadric, Wyot."

Wyot relaxed, he seemed to have passed the first test. "Thank you, eld … eh …Eadric."

"Very well. Let us return to my ship." He plunged one hand into his pocket and grasped Wyot's forearm with the other. "Pick up your trunk and hold it tightly."

Wyot reached down, grasped the handle of his trunk, and when he straightened, found himself standing in a small chamber with Eadric.

"Welcome to your new home."

"What…I didn't feel a thing," Wyot exclaimed. "When I arrived on Silent Egg, I felt the transfer, a kind of lurch, like I'd missed a step and nearly stumbled."

Eadric shrugged. "We each have our own style, and distance transfer is trickier. I assume the astromancer wasn't physically present for your transfer to the surface?"

Wyot frowned. "No. He wasn't." After a moment's thought he blurted, "I thought you just said whatever is attached to the astromancer gets transferred. How could he have sent me to the starfield without touching me?"

"Very good!" Eadric grinned. "You were listening." He clapped Wyot on the shoulder. "Don't let it trouble you. We'll get to the more advanced portions of our art in due time."

"Understood," Wyot said with a nod. He glanced around the small room, noted the brushed metal walls, curving slightly at floor and ceiling, a narrow bunk hung cantilevered from one wall, a desk and shelf attached to the opposite. A chair waited between the desk and a stack of built-in drawers.

"It's compact," agreed Eadric, "but you won't do much more than sleep in here. Come, I'll show you where you'll be training."

They walked a short way down a well-lit corridor and into another small chamber. This one boasted two sarcophagus shaped niches with an opposite wall as clear as glass, though Wyot knew glass was an unlikely component in a starship hull.

"The astromancer's compartment on any starship will always look something like this. Not all will have a transparent wall, but I prefer to see with my physical eyes as well as my third eye. I transmuted the chamber to fit my preferences."

"So this is where you work," Wyot said. "Where do you sleep?"

Eadric laughed. "I don't."

Wyot's jaw fell open and his eyes felt like they might burst from his head. What had he gotten himself into? He took a moment to calm himself before speaking. "I don't understand. How can you not sleep?"

"It's part of the enchantment, Wyot. Part of what makes us astromancers. We become one with the ship. Literally."

The words washed over Wyot. One with the ship? What did that mean?

"Come, let me show you the other areas of the ship you'll need to access. We'll stay in orbit around the Egg today and tomorrow while I instruct you in the basics. After that, your real lessons will begin. Astromancy is not something you can learn from books. You either have the gift, or you don't. Thrice Great Kenelm believes you do. We'll find out soon enough."

Wyot followed Eadric through the ship, memorizing passages, as well as the signs and symbols that would guide him. But all the time he marveled at the path he'd chosen. This path would take him to the stars, but at what cost?

CHAPTER 3

*H*aving unpacked his meager belongings and changed into the uniform Eadric had provided, Wyot returned to the astromancer's compartment.

Eadric had procured two chairs, which now sat before the transparent wall. "Join me. Once we're on our way, these will be unnecessary, but for now I thought we should be able to sit while we discuss the basics."

A wave of dizziness engulfed Wyot as he approached the invisible wall. He sat quickly, turning his gaze away from the yawning abyss and toward his instructor.

"Don't worry," Eadric said, kindly. "You'll get used to it. Besides, when we're in flight, you'll be safely across the room, bound to the ship."

Wyot nodded, but opted keep his mouth firmly shut.

"Now. Down to business. I'm about to reveal to you what is probably the most closely guarded secret of the Alchemical Guild. You may not discuss this with anyone who is not an astromancer or the current Thrice Great. Not even the other members of the Emerald Conclave are privy to this information. The penalty for passing this information to anyone outside our order is death. Do you understand?"

Wyot studied Eadric's face. Gone were all traces of humor or camaraderie. His dark face looked like chiseled stone, his eyes hard and serious. Wyot swallowed. "I understand."

"Do you accept these conditions? Do you vow silence?"

"I accept," Wyot said, his voice clear and strong. "I solemnly vow to speak of this to no one except as authorized by the Thrice Great."

Eadric nodded. "Well said." He put his hand in his pocket and drew something out. "This is the secret of star travel." He held out an egg-shaped stone.

Wyot stared at the stone, fascinated by the pulse of colors emanating from its core. Red. Orange. Yellow. Green. Blue. Indigo. Violet, and all the shades and tones between. The stone cycled through all the colors of the spectrum with a pulse as steady as the man's who held it.

"This is a star stone," Eadric said, his voice little more than a reverent whisper. "Every astromancer currently serving holds one. People think we power our starships, and they're right, after a fashion. But these stones power us."

Wyot longed to touch the stone, to hold it in his hand. Instead he clasped his hands in his lap and devoured it with his eyes. "What is it?" he asked. "Where did it come from?"

"The star stone is the highest achievement of the alchemical arts. Only a Thrice Great, a master of alchemy, astrology, and theurgy, can produce one. Even then, most Thrice Greats have only managed to produce one or two star stones during their long lives. Thrice Great Kenelm is the exception. He has produced one every ten years since he came to mastery. Fifty star stones to date."

"How does it work?"

Eadric nodded. "Good. You can focus beyond the light show." He pocketed the stone again. "We've had candidates become so mesmerized by the stone that they were incapable of conscious thought in its presence."

Wyot's head snapped up. "What happened to them? Did they recover?"

"Mostly." Eadric shrugged. "Obviously, they had to be reassigned. They're fine on Silent Egg. Able to work and study without trouble. But they're grounded for life. Can't be anywhere near a stone's influence."

"And no one thought to warn me?" Wyot frowned, heart racing with what might have been.

"You chose to try for astromancy. On some level you knew you might fail. It's part of the price."

Wyot swallowed his indignation, though it burned his belly. He hadn't thought his mind would be at risk. Never mind. Put it away. He'd passed another test. Concentrate on that.

"Fine. How does it work?"

Eadric nodded again, clearly pleased with his apprentice's discipline. "The stone allows us to see the flux fields. Allows us to use sight to push our vision out to our destination and manipulate fields across the galaxy. The stone enables star travel as long as it's paired with an astromancer who can guide the outcome."

He paused, stood, stared into the void of space. "Right now, I can see the fields around and within this ship. With the stone, I can follow those fields to infinity."

Turning to face the invisible wall, Wyot forced himself to look into the abyss, to see the utter blackness dotted with pinholes of light. Far distant stars winking through the void.

"I don't see flux fields," he murmured.

"You will," Eadric promised. "Once trained, you'll never be able to completely shut them out again." He turned back to Wyot. "Do you want to continue? Once you touch the stone, your perceptions will be altered forever. If you've changed your mind, now is the time to admit it."

Wyot drew a deep breath. There was more. He knew it. Eadric had yet to explain about becoming one with the ship, about not sleeping anymore. This was his chance to escape back to the surface. To become Astrologer third rank again. But if he did that, if he ran from this opportunity, he'd never know what he might have become.

"I'm ready to continue," he said

Eadric smiled. "I'm glad."

He drew the stone from his pocket and held it out. "Your choice. You can take the stone from me and experience the full jolt, or you can ease into it by stroking it once with one finger."

Wyot licked his lips and raised his eyes from the stone to Eadric's face. "Recommendation?"

"I took the full jolt. It's disorienting, but seemed easier to me. Of course, I don't ease into the water when I swim either. I dive right in."

"Good analogy. I'm a diver too," Wyot replied, but made no move to take the stone. "How much of a jolt? What should I expect?"

"Can't say, as it's different for everyone. What seems to be constant is the disorientation, so stay seated. When you're ready, tell me and I'll hand it over."

Wyot closed his eyes, took a deep, cleansing breath, and ordered his mind. This was his choice. His decision. His destiny. He opened his eyes and nodded. "I'm ready."

CHAPTER 4

*E*adric dropped the stone into Wyot's cupped hands. His first impression was of smooth warmth. The stone felt alive. The pulsations that varied the colors also throbbed against his skin. Like a holding a beating heart. The beating heart of living light...

And suddenly that light and life engulfed him. Images raced through his mind, past his physical eyes. Lights, colors, emotions. Knowledge, intuition, possibilities. All merged and flowed through his mind like a swift flowing river.

He gasped for breath. Tried to keep his head above the torrent. Failed. He would suffocate! Be buried in the avalanche his mind was in no way prepared to accept. He flailed, fought to stay conscious, to remain Wyot.

And then, when he knew he must die under the onslaught, he let go. Drifted. Floated on the crest of the wave. And in release, found his center.

Information eddied into corners of his corners of his subconscious. Found footholds in his thoughts. Filed itself where he would have ready access.

His breath shuddered out and he inhaled like a man deprived of oxygen to the point of death. Eyes he hadn't realized he'd closed flickered open and he saw the world with new dimensions.

Eadric smiled at him. "Welcome back." His mentor was now sheathed in an aura of soothing blue radiating out into fine lines of electric blue, which intersected and merged with lines radiating from every surface in the room. Connections. Everything was connected.

Wyot gazed out the window, into the depths of space. Lines radiated from each twinkling star, almost begging him to follow, to tug, to see where they led. Space was no longer abysmal. No longer void. Paths and routes and intriguing possibilities filled it to overflowing.

"Wyot," Eadric's soft voice pulled him back from imagined journeys and into the confines of the astromancer's compartment. "Can you hear me, Wyot?"

Smiling, Wyot stroked the stone, it's pulse now synchronized to his own hearbeat. "I hear you, Eadric, and I thank you for this gift. I am … more than I was."

"Yes. Yes, you are," Eadric said, and Wyot heard the relief in his mentor's voice. "You are now an astromancer. When you're ready, I'll guide your first steps."

"I'm ready."

Eadric rose, motioning Wyot to do likewise. "Think of the starfield where I met you this morning. Let the stone guide you to its flux field. Set your intention to be there, take my arm, and choose to experience it."

Wyot grasped Eadric's arm, saw his destination, sorted through the myriad fields that presented themselves, and made his choice. He and Eadric shimmered into existence on the starfield. Two men dressed in starship uniforms standing on the hard-packed earth of the Silent Egg.

"Well done," cried Eadric. "Astromancers usually have a few false starts, but that felt like you'd been doing it for years."

Wyot smiled. "I've always wanted to show this scene to my mother."

"What?" asked Eadric, a look of fear flitting across his face. "Wait. No. Wyot, you can't..."

Too late. Wyot reached into the recesses of his mind, plucked out the knowledge, and then applied it to the flux fields glimmering all around him. He found his mother's essence, grasped her tightly with intention and pulled her into his presence.

She shimmered into existence in front of him, confused and more than a little frightened.

Eadric stared, open-mouthed.

Wyot stepped forward, engulfed her in a hug, and whispered, "Hello, Mother. I've missed you."

"Wyot? Wh-where am I? How did I get here?"

He shrugged. "It's a new phase of magic, I'm learning, Mother. I just wanted to share it with you ... and to give you a hug."

She smiled and laid a hand on his cheek. "I'm so proud of you, my love, and I appreciate the thought, but you'd better send me back now."

"Yes. I think I had. I love you. Always."

"I know, dear. Come home for a visit when you can."

"I will. Good-bye." And he wrapped her carefully in intention and put her gently back where he'd found her.

Eadric stumbled forward a step or two and then sat down heavily. "You can't do that," he said. "It's not possible."

Wyot glanced down at his instructor. "Quite obviously, it is."

"We need to speak to the Thrice Great."

Wyot reached down, clasped Eadric's hand, and transported them to the chamber he had visited … only the day before?

Thrice Great Kenelm stood beside the inlaid sun. "I've been expecting you, Wyot. Eadric, I hope you are well."

"Just a little off-balance at the moment, excellency," Eadric replied.

"You knew," said Wyot, studying this grand master of his craft. "You were waiting for us."

Kenelm inclined his head and then met Wyot's gaze. "For you, yes. I wasn't sure whether or not you'd bring Eadric."

"Forgive me, excellency," interrupted Eadric, "but what the blue-white blazes is going on?"

"You have done well, Eadric. You have helped birth a new era in magic," he said, conjuring chairs from behind the table on the riser and motioning the men to be seated. "Wyot managed to absorb the vast array of knowledge the stone released in a way no one has done before. He now understands intricacies of the astromancer's art that have never before been plumbed. I suspect he has already demonstrated some of this to you, or you would not be here."

"He pulled his mother onto the starfield just now. I have no idea where from, but still, that's impossible."

Kenelm cocked his head. "It certainly has been before now." He turned his attention to Wyot. "Was it difficult?"

Wyot smiled, a self-satisfied cat smile. "Not in the least."

"You must explain the process to me sometime."

"With pleasure."

"But what does it mean, excellency?" cried Eadric.

"It means," said Kenelm, with a brilliant smile at Wyot, "That we have a new Thrice Great in our guild. Welcome, my son."

Wyot stared at him, and then smiled as another piece of information floated into place. He nodded.

Yes. He'd seen that possibility.

PART III
THE WHITE DRAGON AND THE RED

The

White

Dragon

and the

Red

CHAPTER 1

The floor of Edith's chamber was strewn with fresh, sweet-smelling rushes and a warm fire crackled on the hearth adding the scent of pine and a whiff of smoke to the air. Harold, her hand-fast husband of more than twenty years, sat before the fire wrapped in a soft woolen robe of royal purple. Edith had washed the battle grime from his limbs with her own hands, and now, as he leaned back in the sturdy wooden chair, she combed his long auburn hair.

Once his hair had shone like burnished copper, alive with golden lights, but now those lights had dimmed to pewter and the copper had faded and lost its sheen. Placing the carved wooden comb on a low side table, Edith dipped her fingers in a small silver bowl of mint-infused oil and began rubbing it into Harold's temples. She knew from long experience that the pressure and motion of her fingers combined with the soothing odor of the mint would ease a headache and help her lord find restful sleep.

How many times had she performed such ministrations for this man? After how many battles had she eased his pain and helped calm his mind? Too many to count, and yet, she treasured the memories, and the knowledge that she had been a good wife to this powerful man.

She had been so young when her father had given her in hand-fast marriage to the newly named Earl of East Anglia. Harold had been in his mid-twenties, tall and handsome and battle-tested. A warrior of renown. She hadn't been loath to marry, but neither had she known the man.

Fortunately, she had found joy in their union.

And now, twenty years and six healthy, well-grown children later, she still loved her husband… and knew that he cherished her as well.

But Harold was no longer simply an earl. He was now King of All England, and beset by many foes. He had need of all the support he could find, especially from the powerful church whose archbishop had placed the crown upon his head. The same church that refused to recognize Edith as his lawful wife, had instead named her harlot.

Harold had been forced by the Dead God's church to take another wife, the widow of the King of Wales. Edith knew that this new marriage was one of political convenience, but that knowledge did nothing to bank the fires of outrage that burned in her soul.

Twenty years.

Six fine children, including three sons.

But instead of being Harold's queen, she was known as his mistress. His whore.

Still, after his defeat of the Norwegian king, Harald Hardrada, at the Battle of Stamford Bridge, Harold had returned to her, his hand-fast wife, not his pretty little Welsh queen.

Edith would always be the one Harold turned to, no matter what the Dead God's church demanded.

CHAPTER 2

*E*dith woke to find Harold already dressed in a belted chainmail top over a rust colored tunic, his leggings and boots wrapped securely in place with leather thongs. A warm woolen cloak, pointed metal helmet and a sturdy, round shield of leather-covered linden wood waited beside the door.

"My lord," she exclaimed, "where are you going? You've only just returned from battle. You should be resting still."

He turned to face her, his expression grim. "Aye. 'Twas what I expected as well, but though I've defeated one foreign claimant to my throne, another threatens our shores. William the Bastard's ships have been sighted off Pevensey Bay. I must march south."

Edith swallowed her fear and forced her voice to calm. "But my lord, what of your men? Your housecarls and thegns sustained heavy damage against the Norsemen. Can they fight again so soon?"

Harold strode to the bed, took her face in his hands, and kissed her gently on the lips.

"They must," he said. "We must drive William back to Normandy." And turning, he strode from the room.

Edith sat alone in the large bed as fear curled in her belly and an ominous *knowing* bloomed in her mind.

He would die.

Her husband, her lord, her king.

Harold would die.

Closing her eyes and steeling her will, she made her choice. He would *not* die. She would protect him, and she would align herself with his pretty little Welsh queen to ensure that he did not meet his death in the coming battle.

What would it matter which of them was acknowledged Queen of England if the Bastard killed their King?

Ealdgyth, daughter of Aelfgar, widow of Gruffydd ap Llywelyn, wife of King Harold II would join Edith in the battle for their husband's life... or Edith would know the reason why.

CHAPTER 3

$\mathcal{E}$dith dressed quickly in her favorite deep blue tunic and fastened a rose mantle about her shoulders. She left the hood down, but braided her long dark hair and fastened the curling tendrils that escaped away from her face with a slender silver circlet. Her hair might no longer shine as it did in her youth, but it was still thick and dark.

When she was ready, she wrapped herself in a warm, fleece lined cloak and left the bower she had shared with Harold in the castle set aside for his use in York. Moving quietly through the unfamiliar passageways, she found her way up a stone staircase to a chilly tower. Heaving open a heavy wooden door, she stepped out onto the encircling walkway and leaned against the cold stone parapet.

Closing her eyes and opening her mind, she called to the White Dragon, the protector of the Midlands where she had grown to young womanhood. Never before had she sought the dragon's intervention in her husband's battles, but never before had he been threatened by a foreign duke when his own forces were weakened and battle-weary.

Great Wyrm, Wyvern of the low hills and gentle valleys of my birth, hear me now.

Edith poured all the belief and supplication of her early training into her prayer. Her mother, Matilda, had been a wise woman and an initiate into the mysteries before she had been given in marriage to Edith's father. Matilda had taught her daughters well, and though Edith had never had cause to call upon the White Dragon before, she knew with a certainty beyond mere faith, that the Great Wyrm would hear her.

Sure enough, a voice pealed through her mind. A sending so powerful she was forced to her knees and had to press her hands against her ears. The sound was within, to be sure, but she needed the outside pressure to keep the balance within her skull and forestall the faint that edged her vision with darkness.

Edith, daughter of Matilda, I hear your call and recognize your right of birth to petition my aid. What would you ask?

Even when he stopped speaking, his voice echoed like an avalanche of stones against her tender mind. When she felt sufficiently recovered, she responded, though she feared their conversation might cause her death.

If she died in this supplication, so be it. Harold must live.

Inhaling deeply she framed her request and sent it winging to the great White Dragon.

Harold, King of All England and the father of my sons and daughters, is in grave danger. He rides south to Pevensey Bay to fight against William the Bastard, Duke of Normandy. I ask that you protect Harold, Great One, and the men he leads into battle.

A strange prickling invaded her mind. Not painful, but unexpected and foreign. She braced for the pain his next words would bring.

What are the battles of men to me, little one? I care not which humans crawl along the earth in my domain.

Edith breathed a sigh of relief. He had moderated his sending. This time his voice soothed and warmed the edges of her mind, healing the hurts of his earlier message.

Her relief fled when his meaning registered.

But Great One, the Normans will not know you! They will not honor you as your deserve.

A soft, chiding sigh blew through her thoughts like a gentle breeze. *When have you honored me, daughter of Matilda? Have you thought of me even once since leaving your mother's domain?*

Shame overwhelmed her. The wyrm had the truth of it. What right did she have to ask his aid when she'd given him no thought, no honor, in the twenty years of her marriage. Only in her extreme need did she think of him now, and then only to seek his aid.

Forgive me, Great One.

A puff of solace touched her thoughts, followed quickly by a surge of ire.

You have betrayed me, daughter of Matilda, the dragon growled. *I see the shadow of another dragon in your mind. A great red beast with four legs as well as wings. Not a proper wyvern such as I!*

Edith shrank back against the stone parapet, her heart hammering in reaction to the dragon's clear wrath. What was he talking about? She'd had no thoughts of…

But she had. She had thought to seek Ealdgyth's aid in contacting the Red Dragon of Wales.

When her pulse rate slowed and she felt in control of herself again, she answered the White Dragon of the Midlands.

Nay, Great One. I know no other dragons, nor have I ever thought to seek congress with any save yourself. The red dragon you see in my thoughts belongs to Wales.

And what have you to do with Wales, little one?

Nothing, Great One, but my husband has another wife—do not ask me to explain, the ways of men are convoluted, especially where the Dead God's servants are concerned. This other wife was once married to the King of Wales, before he was killed in battle.

And what has that to do with me?

Edith closed her eyes and inhaled a deep, calming breath. *Since she and I are both bound to Harold, I hoped she might seek the aid of the Red Dragon of Wales.* She paused a moment before hurrying on, *Tell me, Great One, if she made this request, would you join Wales to protect England's king?*

A deep, rumbling grumble sounded in her mind and she made herself as small as possible as she huddled on the battlement. She had gone too far, suggesting that the mighty White Dragon might require the help of the Red Dragon of Wales. He would blast her mind to nothingness. Her children would find her crouched here, a drooling, helpless lump of flesh that had once housed their mother.

A shadow fell across Edith, and she opened her eyes to see a white dragon hanging suspended in the sky just beyond the parapet.

Come, little one. If you are so desperate for your lord's life that you would seek the aid of the woman who has supplanted you, I can hardly fail to grant your petition. Climb onto my back. I will carry you to your sister-wife.

Relief surged through Edith's heart and hope blossomed. Ealdgyth could hardly deny her if she arrived on the wings of a dragon!

CHAPTER 4

*E*dith sat astride the White Dragon of the Midlands, secure in her position between two pointed spines taller than her seated height. Her booted feet were tucked beneath the dragon's wing joints, and she was very glad of her fleece lined cloak. She hadn't thought to wear gloves when she'd left York a-dragonback, but Ealdgyth had gifted her a fine, fur-lined leather pair before the two women left the castle in London.

She glanced to the west across the early October sky to see her sister-wife firmly settled between the neck ridges of a great red dragon. Wales had not failed to answer Ealdgyth's call. If the White Dragon would fight for Harold and England, then the Red would not be left behind.

The two dragons and their riders circled the skies above Hastings, observing the battle that raged below. The dragons had promised Edith and Ealdgyth they would defend Harold and his men, but only in extreme need. If men could win the battle on their own, they should do so.

From high above, Edith watched as her husband commanded his men. His army had marched more than 240 miles to intercept William's forces on the Sussex coast. Nearly 7,000 Normans stood against the weary Englishmen, but Harold's men stood firm behind hastily erected earthworks and prepared to employ their well-practiced shield wall, unaware that supernatural aid circled in the sky above their heads.

The armies were well matched, despite the forced march Harold's troops had endured, and the battle raged from early morning until well into the evening. The White and Red dragons withheld their aid until William's forces feigned flight, causing Harold's shield wall to break formation. When the Norman's turned and loosed a hail of arrows against the English, the dragons joined the fray.

They swept the arrows from the sky before buffeting the combatants with the wind from their wings, leaving none on their feet, on either side of the battle. Landing between the armies with a great bellowing roar, the Red Dragon of Wales scorched a line of fire into the land before William's men, while the White Dragon of the Midlands hung in the sky above the red's head.

As agreed in advance, the White Dragon spoke, and his words echoed across the field causing all men to cower.

"Invaders from across the sea," he boomed, "leave this land. The throne of England is for those who have grown here and love this land. It is not for the likes of you. Be gone from our shores."

"Be gone!" echoed the Red Dragon with growling menace.

William's men dropped their weapons and scattered, too anxious to find their ships to worry about carrying swords or spears.

The White Dragon turned to Harold's army. "Fear not, the White Dragon of the Midlands and the Red Dragon of Wales have come to ensure King Harold's victory. Return to your homes and live in peace, knowing that should the need arise, we will fly to your aid once more."

"But only we are given proper honor," added the Red Dragon. "And only if called upon by those who hold the right by blood."

The two dragons cleared a space on the battlefield and deposited their riders gently on the blood-soaked ground. Before departing, they allowed each woman to place a hand on their heads and bestowed a benediction on the sister-wives.

When the dragons were mere specks in the sky, Harold stepped forward to stand before his wives. "How is this possible?" he asked as his men milled around gathering their belongings and slapping each other on their backs. "How came you to bring dragons to the battle?"

Ealdgyth smiled and, placing a hand on his cheek, kissed him gently. "Ask Edith, your first wife." Then she turned to Edith and curtsied. "The Dead God's priests do not rule me, sister-wife. I am honored to be second to you in Harold's household. If it pleases our lord, bring your children and join our household in London. I would learn from you, Edith the Fair."

Edith inclined her head and responded solemnly. "Thank you, Queen Ealdgyth. I will discuss our future and our lodging with our lord and king." Turning to Harold, she threw her arms about his neck and whispered, "You are safe!"

Harold kissed her soundly, then stepped back and said, "Come, Edith. Tell me the tale of how you and Ealdgyth brought the White Dragon and the Red to the Battle of Hastings."

"Gladly," she said, taking his hand, content to *know* that she and Ealdgyth and the Great Dragons had changed the course of English history.

PART IV
DEEP DREAMING

DEBBIE MUMFORD

BESTSELLING AUTHOR OF *SORCHA'S HEART*

DEEP DREAMING

SPUN YARNS
A Short Story

CHAPTER 1

*L*ast night I dreamed again of drowning. I floated in dark waters, the only light a shimmering reflection far above my head. I sank slowly, almost languorously, wisps of hair drifting past my face, veiling my vision and then wafting away again. Though I knew myself to be sinking into the depths, the folds of my favorite lawn nightdress continued to discreetly cover my nakedness. The gown billowed softly, silently, but the hem remained chastely around my ankles.

For some reason I cannot fathom, I felt no fear, only a relaxed peace.

Perhaps that unexpected peace came from the knowledge that I was already dead. My heart no longer beat within my chest, disquieting vapors no longer flooded my system. My earthly cares had been washed away by the deep water surrounding and suspending me.

When I became aware that I did not float alone, I turned, and seeing his face, awoke.

CHAPTER 2

*A*t breakfast that morning, I accepted a cup of tea from the serving maid. The delicate rose-patterned cup warmed my fingers, cold as the dark waters of a distant sea. I shivered, remembering my dream. Taking a careful sip of the hot liquid, I chastised myself. I was in no danger of drowning. The comfortable town house Father and I inhabited stood squarely in the middle of the most fashionable district of St. Louis. Hundreds of miles from even the Gulf of Mexico. Nowhere near the open ocean.

Certainly, the mighty Mississippi rolled past my city, but my daily tasks never took me near its muddy waters. Besides, I knew with a clarity beyond my understanding that my dream had nothing to do with rivers or lakes. Fresh water would not be my doom. No, the dark water in which my dream corpse floated tasted of salt.

Father hurried into the breakfast room, booted heels clicking on the polished oak floor. He was dressed for a warm summer day in a tan linen suit and burgundy cravat. His mustache was freshly waxed and his muttonchops neatly combed. His silvery gray hair glistened damply in the sunlight streaming through scrupulously clean window panes.

"Good morning, Meredith," he said, rounding the table and kissing me gently on the cheek. "How is my lovely daughter this morning?"

"I am well, Father," I replied before taking another sip of the hot, fragrant tea. "And you? Was your sleep undisturbed?"

He beamed at me as the serving maid offered him a platter of fried eggs, sausages, bacon, and crisp brown fried potatoes. "I slept splendidly well," he said, piling his plate with savory selections from the platter. The maid returned a moment later with a steaming cup of coffee.

Father took a large bite of egg, washed it down with coffee and fixed me with a twinkling gaze. "I've had the best news, Meredith."

"Oh?" I said, lifting my eyebrows and cocking my head, inviting him to tell me more.

"The message came late last night," he continued, "after you had retired for the night. I was so excited I nearly called your maid to wake you, but I contained myself."

"Well, I'm quite awake now. What is this exciting news?"

"My research proposal has been accepted. We take ship from New Orleans at the end of the month. By this time next month we'll be in residence at Fort St. Catherine, Bermuda!"

My breath caught and my hand trembled so violently I nearly dropped my teacup. I placed the cup in its saucer, pulled my hands into my lap, out of Father's sight lest he notice their trembling, and forced myself to calm. I managed a wan smile and murmured, "How nice."

Bile rose in my throat. My dream had suddenly become plausible.

CHAPTER 3

*B*ermuda was beautiful. Pink sand beaches, clear turquoise water, lush vegetation, a veritable paradise on earth. Father set up his research station in sturdy quarters in the rock fort that fronted the Atlantic Ocean on the northernmost point of Bermuda's St. George Island. I set up housekeeping in a quaint little cottage within sight of an idyllic beach.

Despite my proximity to the sea, I began to relax. The journey from New Orleans on the tall ship *Siren* had been hellish. While not given to seasickness, I was prone to the vapors, expecting nightly to be plucked from my bed and plunged into the dark water surrounding the vessel. My dream haunted me, and since my dream corpse was always clad in a nightdress, nights became times of ultimate terror.

By the time we made landfall in Bermuda, I was scarcely in better condition than my shipmates who had suffered from extreme seasickness. Safely on land again, I vowed never to venture into the water, no matter how delightful the natives assured me the experience might be.

We'd been in residence barely a month when Father invited a strange man to join us for dinner. I'd become accustomed to the relaxed life of the islands, dressing in loose fitting, light weight garments without benefit of corsets and hose, but when Father announced his intention of bringing a guest home for the evening, I bestirred myself to dress as a lady should.

Even with a ceiling fan stirring the air and the windows and door to the patio flung open to the night air, I felt stifled in the heavy green satin of my dinner gown. Perhaps my general discomfort could explain the odd feelings I experienced when Father introduced me to his guest.

I studied the man discreetly as Father ushered him into our small drawing room. A man in his prime, no longer youthful, but not yet subject to the deficiencies of middle age. Tall, well-made, with the breadth of chest that spoke of a certain athleticism. Certainly not one of Father's sallow-faced, near-sighted bookish friends. His wavy hair was carefully cut, black and full-bodied. His face was pleasant, but with a ruggedness of feature that would not allow the use of such a civilized term as *handsome*. No, this was not a pretty specimen, but I knew at once he had character.

"Meredith, my dear," Father exclaimed, "allow me to present my friend and colleague, Mr. Morgan Halloran. Morgan, my daughter, Meredith."

"Welcome to our home, Mr. Halloran," I said, lowering my eyes and giving him a small curtsy. "I'm so pleased to make your acquaintance."

"The pleasure is all mine, Miss Watkins," he said, bowing over my hand. "Your father has told me much of you. I've been anticipating our first meeting."

The moment his fingers touched mine, a shiver raced up my spine. The tiny hairs at the back of my neck rose, and my breath caught.

I raised my eyes and met his gaze. His eyes, grey as a storm-tossed sea, searched my own as though expecting to see ... I knew not what ... and then ....

I recognized him. The man from my dream. The unknown person who floated beside me in the depths of the sea. My partner in death!

I yanked my trembling hand from his grasp and turned away from him, but not before I saw his eyes light with satisfaction. He knew I recognized him. But how could he? How could he possibly know of my dream? I'd discussed it with no one, not even Father.

Dinner was a tedious affair. We spoke of trivialities, with me answering by rote. I longed to escape from Mr. Halloran's too knowing gaze, longed to strip off the constraints of heavy gown and corset, longed to bathe myself in the sea.

But, no, I could not bear the sea. Wanted nothing to do with that graveyard of all my hopes and dreams. I was confused. Morgan Halloran's presence addled my senses and brought dangerous thoughts to the fore.

"And you, Miss Watkins," the odious man was saying, "do you enjoy sailing?"

"I do not," I answered shortly. "I abhor everything to do with the sea."

"Surely not," he said. "The ocean is the womb of life, as your Father and I have been studying. You must allow me to take you out in my skiff, introduce you to some of the water's wonders."

"What a capital idea," said Father. "Meredith was not herself on our voyage here. I'm afraid she's allowed that experience to color her feelings for the sea. An outing in a small boat with an expert sailor such as yourself is just the ticket."

"Really, Father," I began, but my parent cut my protestation off with a wave of his hand.

"I shall be otherwise occupied all day tomorrow," he said. "Morgan, be a good fellow and call for Meredith after lunch. A few hours on the water on a fine day will do wonders for her."

"Delighted," replied Mr. Halloran. "Until tomorrow then, Miss Watkins."

I smiled, a very wan and vapid expression.

Was this to be the last night of my life?

CHAPTER 4

*M*r. Halloran called for me wearing a loose white linen shirt and lightweight khaki trousers. I wore only a simple skirt and blouse over my linen shift. I had determined the night before that costumes appropriate to St. Louis had no place on this island. I had no intention of keeling over due to heat prostration simply to maintain dignity of dress.

"Really, Mr. Halloran," I said as we strolled across our garden toward the pink sand beach that marked the threshold of the Atlantic, "you've no need to bother yourself with taking me out on your boat. I am content to watch the water from the shore."

He tucked my right hand into the crook of his arm. "It is no bother, Miss Watkins," he said. "I love the sea and would gladly share that love with you."

He stared straight ahead as he said these words, giving me no reason to read anything untoward into the statement.

"Besides," he said, "there is something I wish to discuss with you." He glanced at me through the corner of his eye. "Privately."

I pulled my hand from his arm and stopped just short of the beach, with sea grass tickling my ankles beneath my long skirt and the smell of salt alive on the breeze.

"We've only just met, Mr. Halloran. What could we possibly have to discuss, privately or otherwise?"

He turned to face me, eyes squinting against the sun's fierce glare. "Much," he said simply. His next words took me aback. "What do you know of your mother, Meredith?"

"My mother?" I breathed. "What can my mother possibly have to do with anything?"

He nodded. "As I suspected. You know little, if anything of she who gave you life."

I looked past him to the waves breaking on the beach. It was true. I knew little of my mother. She died giving me life, and Father rarely spoke of her.

"Her name was Maris," Morgan Halloran said. "Are you familiar with the meaning?" Without waiting for a reply, he continued, "It means 'of the sea,' and so she was." He caught my chin and turned my face to meet his gaze. "And so are you."

I stared deep into his storm-grey eyes and felt the truth of his words break and roll across my soul. "Who are you?" I whispered.

Without releasing my gaze, he answered. "I am he who has been sent to seek you. Your mother was stolen from our pod long ago. Land-locked, she suffered where we could not reach her. We felt her die, but felt also your life begin. Long have we ached to hold you. To ride the waves with you. To teach you the mysteries of the deeps, but we could not reach you."

I listened to his strange words, to the music of his voice, the ebb and flow of emotion. As though in a trance I gazed into the fluid depths of his grey eyes and felt the truth of his words swell within my heart.

"What am I?" I asked when he paused in his tale.

He smiled. "We are known by many names, depending on the seas where our pods dwell. Our pod, your mother's and mine and yours as well if you choose us, ply the deep waters near the coast of the place men call Ireland. We are known as selkies."

"Come with me," he said, holding out his hand and smiling. "Discover who you really are. Let me teach you to transform when we reach deep water."

"Am I a selkie?" I asked myself, rolling the name on my tongue … and testing it for truthfulness. I turned my gaze once more to the sea, observing the roll of the waves, noting the play of the breeze off the water. Could Morgan's tale be true? Could I be a selkie? If I was, would my kin bother to seek me out? Would my dead mother's kin truly be able to find me once I came within reach of their dark water? My thoughts raced, and then relaxed. My own name testified to the truthfulness of Morgan's words. The name my mother had insisted my father give me. Meredith. Lady of the Sea.

Just as I was ready to accept Morgan's tale, my dream swam to the surface of my thoughts. My body sinking in deep water. My death in the sea … with Morgan beside me.

"How can you know?" I cried, shaken and frightened. "How can you be sure that my mother's blood will overpower my father's? What if I am not enough of my mother's daughter to manage the transformation? I don't want to die in deep, dark water."

"Trust me," he said.

And I did.

EPILOGUE

I left my skirt and blouse, shoes and stockings on Bermuda's pink sand and waded with my kinsman into the Atlantic ocean wearing only a thin lawn shift. Wet sand squished between my bare toes. Warm water lapped my ankles, my calves. Wavelets played and foamed around my knees ... and my heart swelled with joy. Deep and dark or not, the sea held no fear for me. At last I understood the relaxed peace of my dream; it did not presage my death ... it foretold of my homecoming, and he who would lead me there.

We swam through gently rolling waves and when we reached deep water, Morgan taught me who — and what — I truly was.

PART V
NEEDLE-GREEN

DEBBIE MUMFORD

BESTSELLING AUTHOR OF *SORCHA'S HEART*

NEEDLE-GREEN

SPUN YARNS
A SHORT STORY

CHAPTER 1

I opened my eyes and stared into the leafy canopy so far above my head it might have been—What was the word? I searched my consciousness and delved into our collective memories. Ah. Yes. There it was—the sky. I pulled air into my tissues, refreshing the cambium layer running just beneath my bark. The air was crisp and clean and tasted of family. My grove.

I stood quietly, drawing strength and understanding from the life of the root system below me. I was Needle-Green, a redwood dryad. I had made the leap from growing sprout to sentient being.

Glancing around, I saw other dryads stirring. Hundreds of us littered the ground at the feet of our elders. Most were seedlings, tall stripling youths whose seeds had drifted to earth seasons earlier. They had germinated in the needle-strewn soil of our grove, sending rootlets down, questing for the life of our communal roots, while unsteady stems shot their cotyledons into the air.

A few, like myself, were sprouts. We had sprung up from boles of parent trees. Even fewer had leapt skyward from the decaying trunks of downed giants.

Whether seedling or sprout, we would carry the spark of redwood life into the future. And those of us who had successfully made the leap to sentience were now known as dryads. We had reached the second phase in the life-cycle of a redwood. We were conscious...and capable of movement.

Not all of us had succeeded. I closed my eyes and mourned the seedlings and sprouts who had failed to awaken. They would now shrivel and die, their remains enriching the soil of the grove. They would return to the circle of life as nutrients. Before I could follow that root too deeply, an elder spoke into our collective awareness.

Welcome to our grove, little dryads, whispered the ancient titan at the center of our grove. *We are pleased you have safely awakened. Pull in your rootlets and explore your world, but be careful to return to us before your small stores of energy run low. Only our root system will nourish you suffi-ciently to maintain your growth.*

Yesssss, sighed the surrounding giants. *Dryads who are too adventurous too soon have starved in the rootless expanse. Do not stray too far, little ones. Not yet.*

I shivered as though buffeted by a strong wind. Memories of dryads who had failed to return drifted through my thoughts and stuck there, like pollen collecting on cones. I nodded. Warning internalized.

Carefully, delicately, I experimented. Flexing my roots, I withdrew a filament. Nothing happened. I hardly noticed the decrease in water and nutrient flow. Emboldened, I pulled in all my filaments, sepa-rating myself from the life of the grove.

For a moment, I wobbled, my tender trunk unsteady, unbalanced, but then I divided the base of my trunk into twin stems capable of inde-pendent movement. I widened my stance, trying to compensate for my loss of anchorage. The exercise left me vaguely dizzy. Quickly I sank my roots back into the security of the grove's interconnected system. Peace flooded my cambium like sap.

Well done, little dryad, said my parent tree, the one from whose bole I had sprung. *I remember well my own dryad days,* the giant redwood sighed. *Dancing in the moonlight with my fellows, creeping through stands of aspen and big-leaf maple, searching for the perfect place to plant myself permanently. Heady days await you, Needle-Green. Enjoy your wanderings, but don't forget to come home for nourishment.*

I'll remember, elder, I replied, bowing my leafy head in respect. *I will explore with care; I will bend but not break.*

The elder sighed its approval, and I withdrew my root filaments once more. Separation anxiety pulsed through my cambium, but this time I knew I could reconnect whenever I chose, so I stood firm and endured. After a moment, the disorientation passed and I stepped cautiously from the bole that had supported me throughout my life as a sprout.

From deep within a chant pushed its way into my awareness, like a sprout pushing up from nutrient rich soil.

Seedling or sprout, mindless you grow.

Dryad, awaken! Withdraw and explore.

Cone-bearer, choose: new grove or old?

Elder, advise; teach and strengthen.

Fallen, be proud; decaying, you nourish.

The entire life-cycle of a redwood reverberating through my cambium, I marched from the grove on tender-barked stems, leafy head held high. The world was mine to explore. I would find my place in it.

———

CHAPTER 2

I drifted for several days. Sometimes walking freely, sometimes freezing in place and pretending to be a slumbering sprout. No longer connected to the collective consciousness of my grove, I couldn't delve into the depths of antiquity to find answers to all my questions. But I had absorbed enough knowledge into my own tissues to recognize potential dangers as well as possible delights.

On one particular starry night I joined several of my fellow dryads in a meadow adorned with wildflowers. A glorious full moon bathed the clearing with silvery light while a gentle breeze tickled our needles. We danced beneath the gaze of celestial beings, heard their music pulsing through our heartwood. The patterns we wove were ancient and intricate, binding the magic of moon and star to the soil beneath our stems.

During that dance, I discovered a new truth: dryads were not just a phase of redwood life. We were a necessary part of the earth itself. For what was soil but the protective bark of the earth mother? She needed us, the free-roving phase of an ancient race, to pull the magic from the spheres and push it past her soil into her cambium, into her very heartwood.

Dryads discovered the magic; the root systems of mature redwood groves kept it safe and secure and flowing freely beneath the soil's surface.

No wonder a moonlight dance was such a powerful memory for my parent tree!

I almost turned around in that moment to return. I had wisdom to impart to my grove. But I delayed. The dancing had tired me. I pushed my roots into the meadow's soil, a poor substitute for the root mass of my grove, drawing up what nourishment I could find, and slept.

I woke to find the meadow transformed. Sunlight streamed from a cloudless sky, warming a circle of redwood dryads. Ten of us had sunk our roots in the final pattern of our dance and fallen into exhausted sleep.

Wild flowers swayed in the breeze around us, a riot of color alien to our grove-trained eyes. We were accustomed to dim light filtered through the branches of our elders, soft greens, muddy browns, and the ochre of ancient bark.

I stretched and blinked in the blazing brightness of unfiltered day until I heard a new sound. Tromping and clattering and chatter, but not the chatter of magpies or squirrels. No this was too varied. Some sounded high and light, while other bits growled low and deep.

Searching my knowledge base, I stretched rootlets toward the dryads on either side. If we could touch, we could communicate. I peered at my fellows, saw panic on their leafy faces, and knew they were extending roots to me as well.

Alas, our circle was too wide. Too many of our fellow dancers had drifted on, leaving gaps we were too young to be able to bridge. So we stood, silent as unconscious saplings.

The tromping, clinking, chattering horde drew nearer, and I found my reference. Humans!

Those strange beings who roamed the surface of the earth like moving groves. Odd creatures who, my memories told me, were divided at the core. Some were female—the ones with high, light voices, and some were male—the deeper, growling variety. How bizarre. Why split a species when pollen and cone could be produced on different branches?

Thoughts and questions raced through my awareness while I maintained my impersonation of an unawakened sprout. Humans could be dangerous. Indeed, they were the only predator a redwood grove feared. Ancient giants had been felled before their time by these seemingly puny creatures. Caution was called for.

The tromping grove approached our circle and stopped. I held myself still and silent, urging them to move on with every fiber of my being.

"Will you look at that," growled one of the males. "Aren't those redwood saplings?"

One of them knelt beside Soft-Bark and fingered its needles.

"Definitely redwood," she said. "I'm getting a distinct lemony fragrance."

"What are redwood saplings doing in this meadow?" asked another. "We must be miles from the nearest grove."

"Probably wind-blown seeds," growled the first male. "Nothing unusual about that."

"But would wind-blown seeds germinate in a perfect circle?" asked the female. "It's like a fairy ring of redwoods."

"Aren't those called 'cathedral rings'?" asked another female voice.

"Nah," said a male. "Cathedral rings sprout around a decaying stump. There's no sign of a mature tree here."

"Let's dig one up and take it back to the institute," said the first male. "Maybe there's something unusual about the genetics of this ring."

"Good idea," said another male.

I watched in impotent horror as the humans shed parts of their bark and began to pull shiny objects from cavities within those bark bits.

Soft-Bark shivered as a female took hold of its trunk and steadied it while a male dug around its base with a metal tool.

"Wow," he muttered. "Really shallow roots. I'm amazed this one didn't blow over."

Wrapping a bit of colorless bark around Soft-Bark's quivering roots, the male shoved it into the bark-bit cavity before merging the bark-bit against his trunk.

The chattering horde of humans tromped away with Soft-Bark as their defenseless captive.

My fellow dryads and I stood silent in the meadow, all joy in our adventure vanished.

The day was moving toward dusk before any of us stirred. At last we roused from our stupor and collapsed our circle until our canopies touched. Sinking our roots into the poor soil, we reached for one another, connecting as a miniature grove.

What will happen to Soft-Bark? asked the dryad on my right.

If they don't release it, it will die, said the one standing directly across from me.

What if the humans discover Soft-Bark is aware? asked another.

A shudder passed around the circle, though no one answered. We stood in silence, mourning our departed kin.

Finally, I shook off my gloom and spoke. *We must return to the grove. The elders must know that Soft-Bark was taken by humans. They will know what we should do.*

Do? cried another dryad. *What can we do? Soft-Bark is gone. We must continue our quests, determine whether we will join to found new groves or return to the grove of our birth.* It shook its leafy head sadly. *There is nothing to be done for Soft-Bark.*

I stretched tall and sent a small current through the root circle. *Whether or not we can help Soft-Bark, we should return. The elders should know of its captivity, and we should replenish. This occurrence has sapped our energy.*

The others nodded, and one by one we pulled up our roots and began our long trudge home.

CHAPTER 3

*T*he elders were dismayed to learn of Soft-Bark's loss. The ancient trees murmured and creaked, their branches scraping together as if they sought to pull up their roots and walk the earth again as they had in their dryad days. Needles rained down on those of us huddled on the forest floor.

Another redwood fallen prey to humans, mourned the titan who was the heart of our grove. Two thousand years old and nearly 375 feet tall, the titan contributed not only its own long memory to our grove, but also the collective knowledge of the grove that had nourished it as a tiny seedling. The memory of our redwood grove stretched into the distant mists of time.

Throughout my long life, humans have passed through our grove, the titan said, its voice solemn and thick with grief. *But only within the last few centuries have they posed a threat to the lives of redwoods. First they felled our kindred with shining metal claws, then they built metal boxes that rolled and raced and fouled the air. They are a blight upon the earth mother's bark.*

Deep silence fell upon our grove as we contemplated the titan's memories of humans and their effect upon our species. Indeed, upon the very air that sustains us all.

At last, after every member of the grove had perused the memories, from youngest dryad to the titan itself, the grove relaxed once again into a state of peace and relative calm.

As I was drifting into secure and nourishing slumber, my parent tree nudged my thoughts.

Beware humans, it said, its voice muted and sad. *When you venture forth into the wide world again, seek an alluvial flat far from their habitat. Establish a new grove there, that redwoods may exist in peace.*

I will, I said, drifting into untroubled slumber and dreaming of a misty valley with a free-flowing stream and a comfortable, silty floodplain… far from the prying eyes of humans and their metal monsters.

CHAPTER 4

I was nearing sexual maturity, almost a cone-bearer, before I
found the valley I sought. Nearly twenty years had passed
since my awakening, since Soft-Bark was ripped from the earth. I
never forgot my fellow dryad's capture, though it was not the only
dryad to be lost. My generation had dwindled to half its original
number before I discovered the valley where I would found my new
grove.

During the long years of my quest, I grew strong, able to travel further
from the peace and plenty of the titan's grove without damage to my
cambium or heartwood. My parent tree had advised me to make a
choice, to plant myself in an established grove before my roots ossi-
fied in some far-flung meadow and I found myself unable to continue
my search.

You are wise, elder, I said. *I am nearing the end of my dryad phase. It is time
to choose.* I was now nearly twenty feet tall. I could stride long
distances in a single day, but it was becoming much more difficult to
elude the notice of humans. Time indeed to plant myself in a comfortable grove. Perhaps one of my seedlings or sprouts would succeed
where I had failed. Perhaps a dryad that I nourished and advised

would find a safe harbor for redwoods to grow into the future with fresh water and clean air.

Still, I wanted one last chance. One final season of walking free before I sank my roots deep into earth's soil and became a permanent part of a grove's root system.

I left our grove on a fine foggy spring morning, turned my back to the sea and allowed the misty breeze to blow me toward my future. Before I had gone more than a dozen strides I was joined by Blooming-Heartwood, a dryad a few seasons younger than myself, but well-grown and strong.

Bloom brushed its canopy against mine in the traditional request for communication.

I stopped, sank a few roots into the soil and reached toward it. Bloom did the same, and soon our mingled roots opened our awareness of each other.

I bowed my canopy in acknowledgement. *Blooming-Heartwood, how may I assist?*

Bloom raised its leafy head and met my gaze. *Your parent tree mentioned that you are embarking on one final quest. I would join you.*

It dropped its gaze while I considered. In all my long years of searching, I had always traveled alone. Often I had crossed paths with other dryads. Frequently we had danced together in moonlit meadows— though never had I allowed myself to tire to the point of exhaustion again. I never slept in meadows, nor did I allow any dryad I met to do so. I honored Soft-Bark's memory with my care.

Why would you wish to journey with me, Bloom?

Bloom's needles rustled as it shook back its canopy. *You are well known for strength and caution, Needle. I would learn from you in field and forest before you plant yourself in a grove.*

You could learn from my memories, I said.

Remembering is not doing. I would join you in your journey.

I raised my eyes and studied the fog rolling across our home grove. I had no wish for companionship, but neither did I have a reason to deny Bloom's request.

Nodding, I began to withdraw my roots, replying as the last filament released Bloom's. *I would be honored by your company, Bloom.*

Turning my back once more on my home, I strode into the morning mist, Bloom following in my shadow.

Bloom was a pleasant companion. We slipped through forests of hemlocks, spruces, and Douglas firs. Traversed wide meadows, dipped our tired trunks in fast moving streams. In the evenings, we planted ourselves in stands of big-leaf maples or scrub oak and enjoyed the rich fragrances of flowering shrubs in the undergrowth.

Spring had melted into summer, and summer was sliding toward autumn before I noticed a thin stream of water falling over a cliff and pooling in a rocky crevice. I stopped, sank my roots into the soil and waited for Bloom to join me.

How are you at climbing? I asked, nodding at the barely there waterfall.

Bloom studied the trickle of water and frowned. *That's not much of a stream. Do you truly think it's worth the effort?*

I rustled my needles. *I'll never know unless I look,* I said, gazing thoughtfully at the steep ascent. I shook myself and returned my attention to Bloom. *You needn't come, of course. You could wait here. The air is pleasantly damp and the soil has good flavor.*

And miss the opportunity to see what secrets that cliff holds? Bloom asked. *I will come. This is why I asked to accompany you.*

We spent the morning scaling the cliff. Dryads are not good climbers. Our feet are better suited to pushing roots into squishy mud than to clinging to rocks and scrabble. Our lowest branches can be used as arms with twiggy hands at their ends, but they are not nimble-fingered. We prefer to link our branches in dance, not grasp for hand-holds to steady us from a fall.

Fortunately, we found a ledge half-way up that was wide enough to provide a resting place and even had enough soil in its crevices to replenish our flagging energy. After a too-short nap, we persevered and crested the top of the ridge in late afternoon.

The scene at the top banished our fatigue. We had found my dream valley.

Steep rock walls surrounded a wide, lush alluvial plain. A stream meandered though the valley, spilling into a deep rock basin near the edge of the cliff. A tiny trickle of water escaped over the edge—the same trickle that had lured me to make the climb, but the pool's main outlet was a stream that lead around a bend of rock and into another canyon.

Bloom and I walked into the sheltered floodplain, relishing the soft earth after our rocky climb. Other, non-sentient trees grew in the valley, but their stands were small and scattered. Plenty of room to establish a grove of redwood giants.

We followed the stream further and heard a roar of water. At the back of the valley stood yet another steep rock wall over which a massive waterfall flung itself into my valley. Bloom and I approached, breathing in the welcome moisture as the water fell into the streambed, the violence of its descent creating a never-ending mist.

Bloom and I sank our roots into the soft, moist soil and congratulated each other on a successful conclusion to our quest.

EPILOGUE

*L*ong years have passed, many generations of dryads have awakened and explored since Bloom and I discovered our hidden grove. We have grown and prospered. I am now the titan of my family. Dryads have grown and gone. Some have returned to plant themselves in this fertile valley. Others have chosen to put down roots in an older grove, but always they have directed dryads they met on their journeys to this magical place.

I still remember Soft-Bark. And all who come to sentience in my grove know the warning of Bark's story. But in all the long years since its founding, never has a human found his way into our grove.

I am content.

PART VI
SOFT-BARK AWAKENS

DEBBIE MUMFORD

BESTSELLING AUTHOR OF SORCHA'S HEART

SOFT-BARK
AWAKENS

CHAPTER 1

I opened my eyes and stared into the leafy canopy so far above my head it might have been—What was the word? I searched my consciousness and delved into our collective memories. Ah. Yes. There it was—the sky. I pulled air into my tissues, refreshing the cambium layer running just beneath my bark. The air was crisp and clean and tasted of family. My grove.

I stood quietly, drawing strength and understanding from the life of the root system below me. I was Soft-Bark, a redwood dryad. I had made the leap from growing sprout to sentient being.

Glancing around, I saw other dryads stirring. Hundreds of us littered the ground at the feet of our elders. Tall stripling youths whose seeds had drifted to earth seasons earlier. We had germinated in the needle-strewn soil of our grove, sending rootlets down, questing for the life of our communal roots, while unsteady stems shot our cotyledons into the air.

We would carry the spark of redwood life into the future. And those of us who had successfully made the leap to sentience were now known as dryads. We had reached the second phase in the life-cycle of a redwood. We were conscious ... and capable of movement.

Welcome to our grove, little dryads, whispered the ancient titan at the center of our grove. *We are pleased you have safely awakened. Pull in your rootlets and explore your world.*

Yesssss, sighed the surrounding giants. *Explore the world, but beware of the rootless ones.*

I shivered as though buffeted by a strong wind. Memories of humans, the strange beings who roamed the surface of the earth like moving groves, drifted through my thoughts and stuck there, like pollen collecting on cones. I nodded, warning internalized.

Carefully, delicately, I experimented. Flexing my roots, I withdrew a filament. Nothing happened. I hardly noticed the decrease in water and nutrient flow. Emboldened, I pulled in all my filaments, separating myself from the life of the grove.

For a moment, I wobbled, my tender trunk unsteady, unbalanced, but then I divided the base of my trunk into twin stems capable of independent movement. I widened my stance, trying to compensate for my loss of anchorage. The exercise left me vaguely dizzy. Quickly I sank my roots back into the security of the grove's interconnected system. Peace flooded my cambium like sap.

Well done, little dryad, said my mentor tree, the one near whose bole I had sprouted. *I remember well my own dryad days,* the giant redwood sighed. *Dancing in the moonlight with my fellows, creeping through stands of aspen and big-leaf maple, searching for the perfect place to plant myself permanently. Heady days await you, Soft-Bark. Enjoy your wanderings.*

I will explore with care, elder, I replied, bowing my leafy head in respect. *I will bend, but not break.*

The elder sighed its approval, and I withdrew my root filaments once more. Separation anxiety pulsed through my cambium, but this time I knew I could reconnect whenever I chose, so I stood firm and endured. After a moment, the disorientation passed and I stepped cautiously from the bole that had supported me through my life thus far.

From deep within a chant pushed its way into my awareness, like a sprout pushing up from nutrient rich soil.

> *Seedling so small, mindless you grow.*
> *Dryad, awaken! Withdraw and explore.*
> *Cone-bearer, choose: new grove or old?*
> *Elder, advise; teach and strengthen.*
> *Fallen, be proud; decaying, you nourish.*

The entire life-cycle of a redwood reverberating through my cambium, I marched from the grove on tender-barked stems, leafy head held high. The world was mine to explore. It was time to find my place within it.

CHAPTER 2

PART VII
WITCHLING

DEBBIE MUMFORD

BESTSELLING AUTHOR OF *SORCHA'S HEART*

WITCHLING

SPUN YARNS
A Short Story

CHAPTER 1

*K*aitlyn cowered on the threshold of Aelfric's chamber. One look at his face told her reality wasn't going to match her glorious dreams. A crackling green nimbus flamed around his close-shorn scalp and his dark eyes blazed.

"You fool!" He grabbed her arm and jerked her into his workroom. "Get inside. Don't you realize the war has reached us? Even this castle is not safe; the enemy's black magic is too near."

The familiar disarray of Aelfric's jumbled belongings vied for Kaitlyn's attention, the soothing odors of dried herbs and creamy unguents wafted through the air around her, but she refused to succumb, chose to remain focused on her master's livid face.

"What were you thinking?" he asked once he'd secured the door with a powerful spell. "Or is your adolescent mind incapable of coherent thought?"

Irritation and bewilderment warred. She'd expected astounded excitement, a congratulatory hug, not this angry condescension. "I'm sorry, master, but I had to come."

"I can't think of a single reason sufficient to excuse your blatant disobedience." The magical nimbus calmed, but Aelfric continued to scowl. "Our enemy is skilled in black magic. If his spells had found you outside enchanted walls," he paused, shuddered, and the last vestiges of anger drained from his face. "Well, child, I wouldn't like to think of the uses to which he would put your nascent power."

Kaitlyn lowered her eyes and hung her head. Aelfric hadn't called her *child* since she began her training more than three years before. Her fingers closed around the lumpy object in her pocket, and her resolve strengthened.

"Master, you need this." She looked him squarely in the eye, pulled a large, gold- encrusted bauble from her pocket and dropped it into his gnarled hand.

As soon as the ring touched his flesh, Aelfric screamed, an agonizing, soul-rending shriek. The formidable wizard fell to his knees. Kaitlyn watched in horror as he flung her prize across the room and pulled his body into a tight fetal position.

She dropped to the floor beside him, tried to capture and soothe the frenzied strands of magic enveloping his body. Shock made her stiff-fingered, awkward, but she sketched a healing sigil in the air above his sweat-sheened head. His shoulders relaxed visibly and the sick, panicked knot in the pit of her stomach eased. He rolled onto his back, eyes still closed, and allowed her to pull his right hand away from his chest to examine the wound. The ring's outline seared his palm, an angry red weal surrounded by charred flesh. The pungent odor gagged her.

"Master! I'm so sorry. I didn't know ..." She choked back bile, wiped her tears with the back of her hand and tried again. "What can I do? How can I help?"

Aelfric gasped and snatched his hand back. "Help me into the sitting room, then fetch the willow bark salve."

They stumbled into the tiny anteroom that lay between his workroom and bedchamber. Kaitlyn helped him to his favorite chair and then ran back to the workroom for salve and bandages. The wound dressed, she pulled up a low stool and sat at her master's knee.

"Now, let me think," Aelfric said. "I don't believe you came here to murder me, so tell me, what *did* you come for?"

A hint of a twinkle lit his eyes and she breathed a sigh of relief. "I was meditating on the ancient runes you assigned me last week, trying to understand how they could bind the ley lines, when a … well … a *compulsion* came over me." She paused to check Aelfric's reaction to her well-rehearsed speech. His face was grave, but he nodded slightly.

"I saw a sigil in my mind," she continued. "It hovered just above the page of runes, and I knew I had to capture it before it faded."

"And did you succeed?" he asked.

"Yes," she whispered. "I traced it in the air."

She remembered how the sigil had hung, shimmering in perfection — one second, two — before a gaping hole had sundered the fabric of space and time. She had watched in horrified fascination as a ring peeled itself from the bone-white finger of a long dead hand. The hole had resealed itself with an audible crack and she'd been left with a ring, an opal set in gold filigree, resting on the palm of her outstretched hand.

Her gaze snapped back to Aelfric's face. She stared into his midnight eyes and announced with all the drama her fifteen-year-old soul possessed, "Master, it's the Firestone!"

Aelfric's uninjured hand, which had been stroking his chin, stilled. "What do you know of the Firestone?"

"I … uh … I read about it in your Gramarye." She flushed and glanced away.

"When did I give you permission to touch, much less read, my Gramarye?" His voice exuded quiet control, but Kaitlyn heard the edge of steel.

"You didn't, master." She met his gaze and faced his displeasure. "Forgive me. I was curious. I overstepped."

"Indeed." He looked away and sat motionless; his face unreadable.

"Very well," he sighed. "I'll deal with your disobedience later. Tell me what you learned of that fabled ring."

Kaitlyn swallowed and, keeping her eyes on the floor, said, "Well, the Firestone gives its wearer the ability to withstand evil. No black magic can touch him; he is invincible." She dared to glance at Aelfric's somber face. "That's right, isn't it, sir?"

He nodded. "Yes, but there is more. Tell me, witchling, what is the cost of this wondrous gift?"

"Cost?" Kaitlyn's voice quavered and she berated herself for her hurried examination of the ancient text.

Aelfric made an impatient gesture with his injured hand, winced and returned it gingerly to his lap. "Yes, cost. Come now, have your years of training taught you nothing? Power always carries a price — something you must consider before you take it up. What is the Firestone's price?"

She took a deep breath, steeled herself and met his gaze. "I'm sorry, sir. I was snooping. I didn't take the time to read carefully or fully. I don't know the cost."

"And yet you summoned the ring?"

"Yes, sir."

"You disappoint me, Kaitlyn. I didn't think you a fool." He closed his eyes, leaning his head against the back of the chair. "Bring me the Gramarye. Perhaps we can mitigate your folly."

She climbed to her feet, feeling the weight of his disappointment, and stumbled to his bedchamber. The massive book lay open on its own sturdy wooden table protected by a sigil-spell. She remembered her pride in unknotting that spell and flushed with shame. The sigil dissolved under her fingers and she gathered the heavy tome to her breast without invoking the magic that would have borne it effortlessly to Aelfric. She accepted aching arms as a small part of her penance.

Even left-handed, Aelfric's sigil worked flawlessly as he accepted the book's weight and balanced it in mid-air before his eyes. The pages flipped to the Firestone reference and he swiveled the book to face Kaitlyn.

"Read. Absorb. Tell me the cost."

Heat suffused her face, but she stood her ground and read the entry, pushing her shame and humiliation to the back of her mind and focusing on the words' meaning. Understanding bloomed and pride at her summoning withered. She closed her eyes and sank onto the stool at Aelfric's knee.

"Report." His voice shattered her black thoughts and brought her back to the current situation.

"The Firestone gives its wearer invulnerability, no black magic, no magic of any kind can touch that individual. In return, the stone demands unbreakable loyalty. The Firestone touches the wearer, but allows no other contact. The wearer is forever isolated from human touch."

She opened her eyes and saw him nodding, his expression unexpectedly compassionate. "Why did you summon the ring, child?"

She sighed. "I thought it would give you the power to defeat Darius. I wanted you to end this war. I wanted my brother, Gavin, to live." Tears filled her eyes and escaped down her cheeks. "Master, I'm so sorry. I just meant to bring the ring to you so you could make everything right."

"You didn't stop to consider that I could have summoned the ring myself? Didn't wonder why I chose not to?"

The need to sob threatened to choke her, but she whispered, "No, sir. I didn't think. I found that sigil and acted. I thought you'd be so pleased that you wouldn't question my story of miraculous revelation."

After what seemed an age, Aelfric muttered, "And yet, she can touch it, and I cannot." He waved the Gramarye closed, sent it back to its table, and issued a command. "Go ... find the ring. I need to examine it."

Kaitlyn struggled to her feet and plodded to Aelfric's workroom. She stopped where her master had stood when she dropped the ring into his hand and cleared the morning's shock and disappointment from her mind. With a focused effort she visualized the moment he'd flung the Firestone across the room.

There. He'd chucked it over there.

Moving slowly and deliberately, she searched the floor. When she reached the shelves — a jumble of crocks, jars of herbs, models of castles, desiccated rodents, and the odd skull or bone — she scrutinized the ley lines for the ring's peculiar signature as well as seeking the cold metal with her fingers. Satisfied that the ring wasn't among the shelves' detritus, she knelt to look beneath the burdened furniture. At the far back, well beyond the reach of her outstretched fingers, she detected a glint of fire in a distinctive knot of magical energy.

She sat up and looked for a broom, a stick, anything to extend her reach. Nothing presented itself. Aelfric's staff stood in a corner near the ensorcelled door, but Kaitlyn knew better than to touch that instrument of power.

Power ... of course. She chided herself for a brainless chit. The last thing she needed was to confirm Aelfric's low opinion of herself. He'd think her a fool indeed if he saw her searching for a stick when she could call the ring with magic.

Settling herself more comfortably on the stone floor, Kaitlyn closed her eyes, stretched her left hand toward the ring's hiding place and traced a summoning sigil with her right. Before the sigil's flare died, she felt the ring's cool weight settle on her palm. She grimaced and returned to her master's side.

Aelfric sighed as she knelt before him holding the ring. "I'd half hoped it might have returned to its former master's tomb," he said. "Too bad. Well, let's get to work. Examine the ring closely. Tell me everything you see."

He closed his eyes and leaned back in his chair, his expression peaceful. But Kaitlyn knew from experience that in magic, meditation often masked intense effort.

She rolled the ring around in her fingers, scrutinized it, and recited her observations.

"The stone is an opal, roughly the size of a mouse skull, smooth, but not perfectly round. It's been polished, but not cut. The setting is gold, but carries no jeweler's mark. I don't know the purity." She closed her eyes and let her mind follow the ley lines emanating from the gem. "The stone is of the highest quality, but the setting isn't simple filigree. It's sigil- worked gold, just as the Gramarye said."

Her voice died away with the embers of her hope that she'd called the wrong ring.

"Hold it up," he whispered, his voice soft and rasping. "Let me see the working."

She held the ring level while he studied the sigil-worked filigree. At last, he nodded. "You may put it away."

Aelfric scrubbed his face with his uninjured hand while Kaitlyn nestled the ring into her skirt pocket. When he spoke, she looked up.

"The setting is a focusing spell," he said. "It channels the stone's raw power, allowing the wearer to control tremendous energy." Aelfric's dark eyes flashed as they met Kaitlyn's. "And because you meddled without guidance or understanding, this weapon is bonded to you."

"Bonded to me?" Kaitlyn's voice squeaked. "You think it wants *me*? But I'm untrained, I'm not ready! You're supposed to use it. You're supposed to be the hero!" Her face flamed, then cooled as blood drained from her extremities to her core. Her vision blurred and narrowed, her world darkening.

Aelfric seized her by the neck and forced her head between her knees. "Breathe, child. Deep breaths. The dizziness will pass."

She obeyed, and gradually, the ocean-roar of her own blood quieted. Several more deep breaths allowed her to push Aelfric's hand away and sit up. She blinked repeatedly to clear her vision, and then stared at her master.

"What have I done?" she whispered. "I don't have enough control to use this kind of power! I don't know anything about war or politics or saving the world." Blinking back tears, she cried, "I'm too young to seal myself away from other people!"

Aelfric's fiery gaze singed her soul. "And yet you expected *me* to accept that burden." He stood and stalked into his workroom, his final comment trailing in his wake. "You should have counted the cost before you meddled in affairs beyond your training."

Kaitlyn lingered by his chair, stung by the truth. She had interfered, and now Aelfric couldn't touch the Firestone. Her people needed relief from Darius' evil magic; the Firestone could end the war.

But to give up her humanity!

It was true, she hadn't considered the cost, mainly because it hadn't occurred to her that she would be the one to pay it. She'd expected Aelfric to use the stone and absorb whatever consequences might ensue. So easy to discount sacrifice when she wasn't the one required to make it.

She shivered, remembering her brother's battle-weary face. Her beloved Gavin deserved aid, but he'd ridden to battle knowing what might be required. She'd acted without considering the consequences.

Eyes brimming with unshed tears, she pulled the ring from her pocket and clutched it close to her heart. For good or ill, this weapon belonged to her; she must find a way to use it. Find a way to save her people.

Perhaps she could find a way to escape its terrible price.

"Master," she called, following him to his workroom, "what if we call a peace council? Could we show Darius the Firestone? Threaten him without actually using it?"

Aelfric turned in a swirl of robes and fastened his dark-eyed gaze on her face. "We can try, Kaitlyn, but it will only work if he reads resolve in your face. He will have to know that you are ready and willing to accept your fate."

She rubbed clammy hands on her skirt. "You're more experienced. Couldn't you pretend you summoned it?"

His gaze softened for an instant before hardening again. "No. This is your summoning. You must own it, or we have no hope."

Her shoulders sagged. She felt boneless, incapable of independent movement. Despair rolled through her mind. Even with the ring's power, she couldn't imagine herself standing up to a black warlock.

She surprised herself by nodding and saying, "You're right. This is my destiny, not yours. Please, arrange the meeting."

CHAPTER 2

*K*aitlyn stood beneath an ancient oak on a hilltop beyond the castle gates. Aelfric and King Lorien sat in cushioned chairs at a large, ornately carved table a few paces away. Aelfric had arranged the truce and magicked the furniture to this neutral spot. He hoped the oak's earth magic would lend support against the blackness that followed Darius.

A company of Lorien's best knights ringed the hilltop, while Gavin stood guard behind his liege's chair. Kaitlyn drew strength from her brother's presence though they hadn't spoken.

She had taken time to bathe and anoint her body with fragrant oils. Her normally unruly hair was braided into a neat dark plait and she wore her best gown of midnight blue. The Firestone weighed on her heart more heavily than it did the pocket of her gown.

Give me strength, she prayed. *Show me what to do ... and when to do it.*

With a skirl of pipes, Darius appeared on the hilltop. He sat upon a white stallion, his foam-green robes flowing into the deep turquoise of his mount's trappings. Younger than Kaitlyn had expected from the evil tales she'd heard, his dark hair and beard showed no trace of gray, but his eyes were as cold as a winter sky. He dismounted with fluid grace and vanished his horse with a negligent gesture.

Aelfric stood and all eyes turned to him. "Thank you for coming, Lord Darius."

Darius nodded without breaking eye contact. "I'm always ready for a civilized chat, Aelfric." His gaze swept Lorien as he continued, "Shall we end this bloodshed? Will you yield to me, my lord?"

King Lorien stiffened, but remained silent.

Aelfric gestured toward an empty chair. "Be seated, sir. There has been a change, a shift in power. We wish to give you every opportunity to leave peacefully before we resort to its use."

Darius snorted as Aelfric motioned to Kaitlyn. For the first time the black warlock's gaze fell on her and she felt a questioning push at the edge of her mind. She strengthened her shields and approached the remaining chair.

"You bring a hedge witch to the table? Don't tell me you're resorting to kitchen magic to counter me." Darius laughed and returned his attention to Aelfric. "What is this supposed shift in power you mentioned?"

Kaitlyn slipped her hand into her pocket, grasped the cool metal and pulled the Firestone into the light of day. The opal gleamed, myriad colors dancing in its depths. She laid it on the table's polished surface.

A hungry expression flitted across Darius' face and he reached toward the stone.

"I wouldn't do that," said Aelfric. He gave a wry grin and held up his bandaged hand. "The Firestone is finicky about being touched."

"But, the girl ... she's only a witchling!"

"Yes, I know. Disturbing, isn't it?" A genuine smile lit Aelfric's face. "But then, we've always known magic is capricious."

Darius licked his lips. "What do you want?"

"Remove your troops from my land," said King Lorien. "Go, and never return."

Kaitlyn watched Darius' eyes. She saw calculation ripple across his features and knew that he would call their bluff.

"Lord Darius," she said, noticing his frown at being addressed by a half-grown girl, "I would rather not accept this ring, but I will." She heard Gavin gasp; saw him leave his post and move toward her. Ignoring him, she pleaded with Darius. "Please, leave us in peace. For your own sake."

"You're nothing but a child, an untrained witchling," Darius said, his voice filled with contempt. "Even if you put it on, you won't be able to control it."

He rose, his chair falling over at the sudden movement, and began to gather energy between his hands. Gavin lunged the last few feet to place himself between his sister and her would-be attacker.

Kaitlyn barely managed to thrust her finger into the ring's circling embrace and fling her arm in front of Gavin before Darius' flaming arrow seared the air. It shot unerringly toward her brother with a force that should have skewered him and sliced her as well. Instead, the arrow hit the Firestone's field and clattered to the ground, harmless.

"Katie, what have you done?" Gavin cried. He stared in wide-eyed horror as fine threads of liquid gold streamed from the filigree of the ring's setting and laced themselves around her wrist and forearm.

Kaitlyn pulled her arm back and glanced from the golden threads surrounding her right arm like a long, fingerless glove to Gavin's stricken face. The lacing didn't hurt, but she felt it penetrate her skin, sink into her flesh, and merge into her bone. She and the ring were one, would be one long after her flesh dissolved.

She felt as much as heard Aelfric's moan of despair and Lorien's sharp intake of breath. Darius remained silent, cold as ice, though mental calculations raced across his grim face.

"I'm all right, Gavin," she said quietly. She took a shuddering breath and tried to hug her brother. Her hands met gentle, but firm resistance.

She stumbled back, made her way to Aelfric's side and tried to squeeze his shoulder. Her hand stopped an inch from his flesh. She met his gaze with a rueful smile. "Don't blame yourself, master. This is my own doing." She closed her eyes, calmed her mind, and turned to face Darius.

"Your time has passed, Lord Darius," she said. "Mine is just beginning. I suggest you leave now, before the Firestone singes your beard."

He studied her. "Brave words for a little girl who should still be at school."

"Be warned," she said. "I am new to these powers, but the Firestone knows them well."

With the speed and grace of a striking snake, Darius hurled a killing spell at Kaitlyn's chest. It bounced from her protective barrier. He jumped aside as the spell rebounded and expended itself in the grass at his feet.

A stifled curse escaped Lorien as Aelfric surrounded the king in a protective envelope of magical energy.

Darius glanced at the withered grass before bringing his hands together. When he drew them apart, witchlight crackled between his palms.

Kaitlyn stood her ground as the warlock approached, pulsing his hands back and forth, building the witchlight's intensity. When he reached her side, he turned his palms toward her, pushing the frenzied light at her torso.

Kaitlyn disappeared behind a wall of flame.

Gavin screamed and shot toward her.

Through the white hot aura of fire, Kaitlyn shouted, "No! Gavin, go back!"

Kaitlyn doused the witchlight as Darius seized Gavin.

"Advantage to me," he cried, cutting off Gavin's breath with the flick of a careless finger. "Remove the Firestone, or this one dies."

Kaitlyn tore her gaze from her brother's blue-tinged face, licked her dry lips and said, "I cannot. It has fused to my bone." She flicked a sad smile at Gavin. "This is my destiny."

Darius flicked a finger in Gavin's direction and the young knight fell to the ground, gasping. "We seem to have reached an impasse. You can't give me what I want, and I won't give you what you want."

"Ah, but I think you will." She walked toward him with unconscious grace, an awkward teenager no more. "You will release your warriors from their enslavement."

She stepped closer to him; he held his ground.

"You will cease the practice of black magic."

His resolve broke; he stepped back.

"And," she said, "you will leave this kingdom and never return."

He forced a smile that didn't reach his eyes. "And if I refuse?"

"The Firestone will suck you dry."

"I don't think so." He pointed at Gavin, crooked his finger and raised her brother into the air.

Without hesitation, Kaitlyn threw her arms around Darius' neck and hugged him tightly. Witchlight blazed around them.

Aelfric ran forward. Lorien strained against his protective envelope, and Gavin crashed to the ground yet again.

The light died, and Kaitlyn released her enemy. Darius staggered for a moment before crumpling to the ground, unconscious.

Aelfric moved to support Kaitlyn, but couldn't touch her. He scrutinized his erstwhile apprentice, shook his head and turned to release the king.

Lorien and Gavin approached cautiously. Kaitlyn gave them a weary smile.

"Did you know that would happen?" Lorien asked.

She started to shake her head, but the motion made her temples throb. "No. I expected to repel him, as I did Gavin and Aelfric. But the Firestone wanted Darius."

"What happened?" asked Aelfric.

"The gem drained him," she said, looking deep into Aelfric's dark eyes. "It emptied him of power, sucked out his capacity to work magic. He won't trouble anyone again, at least not with magic."

"What about his army?" asked the king.

Aelfric answered for her. "They were ensorcelled, forced to fight his wars. Give them a chance; they'll find new lives."

"And you, my lady?" King Lorien asked.

"Me?" Kaitlyn's smile trembled. She longed to dissolve into someone's arms and be cradled while she indulged in a good, long cry, but such comfort was now lost to her forever. "I am a witchling no longer."

She curtsied to Aelfric. "Find a new apprentice, sir. From this point forward, the Firestone will be my mentor. I will master the power I so foolishly assumed … and learn to live with its price. Which I have only begun to pay."

PART VIII
THE SOLITARY SORCERESS

DEBBIE MUMFORD

BESTSELLING AUTHOR OF SORCHA'S HEART

THE SOLITARY SORCERESS

SPUN YARNS
A *Witchling* Short Story

CHAPTER 1

*K*aitlyn felt him die. Felt his spirit depart this world, though it had been years since she'd seen his beloved face.

She stumbled, though the path through the white-barked aspen trees was well known to her and the morning clear and bright.

Fear and grief assaulted her mind.

She felt his power return to the reservoir of ambient magic. Felt a cresting wave of urgent desire break against her will as the magic in the very air around her ebbed and flowed, seeking a new balance.

The Firestone awoke, scrabbling for energy as it tried to claim more magic, claim more of her life.

She collapsed to the bare ground, bracing herself against the rough trunk of an aspen. Dropping her gathering basket, she hugged her knees beneath scrunched and disheveled skirts and petticoats.

"No," she whispered through gritted teeth, sweat beading her forehead. "No. You will not advance. I refuse to allow it."

Closing her eyes, her brow furrowed in concentration, she weathered the magical spike, struggled against the fingerless golden glove that covered her right hand and forearm, against the slender tendrils that sought to extend toward her elbow. With gritted teeth and clenched fists she fought for control...and won.

The fine tendrils retreated, the golden glove quieted. The magical storm calmed.

Tears slid down her heated cheeks. Partly in relief that she'd once again mastered the Firestone, but mostly in mourning for her dead friend. Aelfric, the master sorcerer to whom she had once been a contrary and headstrong witchling.

She rested her head on her knees and reflected for a moment on her loss while her pulse slowed and her breathing quieted, becoming even again. Aelfric was gone, the master who had guided her through the turbulent adjustment after she'd so rashly used the Firestone to defeat the evil wizard, Darius. She'd won a war and saved her brother, but at a terrible personal cost.

King Lorien had hailed her a hero, but the common folk had the right of it—they named her the Solitary Sorceress.

For that was the price the Firestone had demanded of Kaitlyn, that headstrong fourteen-year-old witchling. She had dared to summon the powerful talisman from its resting place and it had come to her in its quiescent state, a simple gold ring. But when she had claimed its power to defeat Darius, when she had placed the ring on her finger, it had bonded with her flesh, sending tendrils into her very bones, wrapping her hand and wrist in a golden sheath that had extended to her forearm before the battle ended.

The Firestone made her invincible.

It also made her untouchable. Literally.

For once she was bonded to the talisman, no other human could lay so much as a finger on her, nor she on them.

Sighing, Kaitlyn wiped her eyes on her linen apron, and picked up her gathering basket. Time to put away memories and push grief to a remote corner of her mind. Ten years had passed since that fateful battle. Nearly nine since she'd left Aelfric's side and gone into seclusion. She would mourn the passing of her counselor and confidant, but not right now. Now there were preparations to be made.

CHAPTER 2

She'd expected King Lorien to summon her to court. She hadn't expected her brother, Gavin, to be the messenger.

"Katie! You look wonderful!" Gavin dismounted and handed the reins to his squire, a jug-eared youth with bowl-cut tawny hair and eyes that looked ready to pop from their sockets.

"And you as well, Gavin. How is Lydia? And little Kathryn?" Kaitlyn smiled at her older brother, amazed at the calm tone of her voice, when her heart was pounding and her pulse roared in her ears. She wanted nothing more than to throw herself into his arms and be hugged and petted. She loved Gavin more than life itself. It was for his sake that she'd committed the folly which had cost her the ability to touch him, or to hold his little daughter.

He reached toward her, remembered himself, and let his hand fall. "They're fine," he said, forcing a smile. "Katie … we call her Katie, after you … is thriving. She's walking now and starting to talk as well."

"I'm so happy for you, Gavin," she said. "Please come in. Your squire is welcome too."

Gavin nodded and turned to the jug-eared lad. "Jamie, water the horses and picket them in the meadow. Then you may join us in the house."

The boy sketched a quick bow. "Yes, m'lord."

Kaitlyn opened the door to her small cottage and ushered her brother inside. Unusually aware of her surroundings, she gazed at the familiar room. Light streamed through diamond-paned windows and shone on a scrubbed oak work table and sturdy wooden chairs. The hearth was clean-swept, wood neatly laid, ready to be kindled later that evening. Bunches of lavender and thyme hung from the rafters, scenting the air with spicy sweetness.

Gavin took a seat at the table while Kaitlyn poured mugs of cider. Placing one before her brother, she settled in her favorite chair and sipped from her own mug. The cool liquid was tart, sweet and refreshing.

"I suppose you're wondering why I've come," Gavin said. He tasted his cider and nodded his approval.

"Not really," she said. "I assume Lorien sent you to bring me to court. He'll need a new wizard now that Aelfric is gone."

Gavin's eyebrows shot up and his eyes widened. "You know about Aelfric? But how?"

She gave him a pitying glance. "I'm a sorceress, remember? He was my teacher. I felt him pass."

"Oh. I didn't ... I'm sorry." He took another drink of cider and stared at the well-used table, fingering an old scar left by a chopping knife. "I was dreading having to tell you."

"He was a good man," Kaitlyn said, resisting the urge to reach for his hand. "A far better master than I deserved. Too bad I didn't heed his teaching more closely."

Gavin glanced up and met her eyes. "I'm so sorry, Katie," he said quietly. "About everything."

She dropped her gaze, unable to bear the love and tenderness she saw in his eyes. "I know. So am I, but it's my own doing and I've learned to live with it." She held up her gold-encased hand. "It hasn't mastered me. I've learned to control it."

He nodded. "Will you come? To court, I mean."

Taking another sip of cider, she considered.

Gavin waited a moment, then continued, "King Lorien bade me say that he recognizes he has no ability to compel you, but if you're willing, he would greatly appreciate your counsel."

A wry smile twisted her lips. "My counsel? The woman who cursed herself to a solitary life?"

Gavin frowned. "The woman who sacrificed herself for the realm," he said. His expression softened. "Who sacrificed herself for love of her brother."

She shuddered and covered her face with her hands.

"Katie, you were brave beyond your years. You may not have understood exactly what the cost would be, but you knew one would have to be paid, and you acted anyway."

The door opened and Gavin's squire sidled in.

Gavin nodded to the jug of cider on the sideboard. "Pour yourself a mug and wait on the bench outside."

The boy did as he was bid and escaped their company.

"Besides," Gavin said when the door closed behind the boy, "you've had years of secluded study, and Aelfric was sure that in learning to control both yourself and the Firestone, you'd've learned many other lessons as well."

"He said that?"

Gavin nodded. "I was with him when he died, as was the king. He said that you were by far the wisest and most powerful magic user in the realm. That Lorien would be lucky to have your counsel — if he could persuade you to return to court."

"And the king sent you to plead his case."

He shrugged. "He figured I'd stand the best chance."

She sighed. "He was right." She stood and walked to the window. Looking out over the neat rows of vegetables and herbs in her kitchen garden, she pondered her life. She had indeed learned control, and many other bits of arcane lore in the years since she'd left Aelfric and the king's court. Her master had gifted her with his most treasured gramarye and she had studied it well. She knew her art and she knew herself. What she didn't know was how to handle the company of people she could never touch.

She was afraid.

This self-imposed isolation allowed her to forget her handicap. She didn't miss what wasn't available.

But if she returned to court, her isolation would be tangible. She'd constantly be reminded of that which she could never have ... the simple touch of a hand, a kiss, a hug. Physical intimacy was forever beyond her reach.

Could she endure being adrift in a sea of courtiers?

Was she a coward to be ruled by her fears?

Turning from the window, Kaitlyn met her brother's gaze.

"I will come."

CHAPTER 3

*K*aitlyn moved into Aelfric's quarters. Wistfulness accompanied her as she walked through the workroom where she'd toiled as a witchling. She examined the shelves, still a jumble of crocks, jars of herbs, models of castles, desiccated rodents, and the odd skull or bone. She stepped to the small sitting room that lay between the workroom and bedchamber and stroked the back of his favorite chair.

So many memories.

She smiled. The Firestone had robbed her of human touch, but she could enjoy these artifacts of Aelfric's life. She sat in his chair, hers now, and rested her hands on wood polished smooth by his hands.

She would make these rooms her own, but they would always retain Aelfric's aura. She was content.

Gavin acted as her guide at court. He introduced her to those who had gained prominence in her absence and reminded her of folk she had known as a witchling. Everyone regarded her with awe, avoiding her eyes, but gazing avidly at the golden glove encasing her right hand and forearm.

No one attempted to touch her, but bowed and curtsied from a safe distance.

Lydia, Gavin's wife, welcomed Kaitlyn to the quarters she and Gavin shared with their child.

Little Katie provided the cruelest test of Kaitlyn's composure. The tiny girl was adorable, with wide blue eyes and sweet blonde curls. She toddled unsteadily to Kaitlyn with pudgy arms upheld.

Gavin stepped forward and swooped the little one into his arms, holding her up for Kaitlyn's inspection.

"This is your Auntie Kaitlyn, Katie," he said. "She a very great sorceress, so you mustn't bother her. Don't be begging for sweets or kisses."

Kaitlyn's eyes brimmed with tears, but she laughed and smiled at the little girl. "Oh, she can ask for sweets anytime she likes, just not for hugs or kisses. Will that be all right, Katie?"

Producing the sugar plum she had brought for this purpose, Kaitlyn dropped it in Katie's outstretched hand.

The child smiled, and Kaitlyn breathed a sigh of relief.

After sharing a quiet meal with Gavin and his family, Kaitlyn strolled back to her quarters in the Wizard's Tower. She didn't feel as alone as she'd expected. Wasn't as miserable as anticipated. Living in Aelfric's old rooms gave her a sense of peace and she enjoyed seeing Gavin again. Even watching the sweet interplay of his family hadn't upset her as she'd feared. She relished her brother's happiness, treasured the memories of their shared childhood that his interactions with Lydia and little Katie had brought to the surface.

She'd always known that she was different. Magic had marked her for its own early in her life and Aelfric had cautioned her that choosing to pursue her gift would pull her from the homely joys her girlhood friends would find.

Her path had simply taken a more radical twist than even her mentor had imagined.

Now, as a full-fledged sorceress, she found she was comfortable at court. The king and his nobles treated her with respect. She had ample time to pursue her studies and experiment with new brews and potions to the betterment of her people, and if she had no one with whom to share her life, well, neither had Aelfric. At least not until he'd taken on a certain wayward young witchling.

She rounded a corner and was jolted from her reverie by the sight of a man she'd yet to meet standing a few feet down the corridor. He leaned against an embrasure, gazing out, eyes hooded with concentration. A dark-haired man in his prime, he was well-muscled and sleek. Not like the soft-bodied courtiers with which King Lorien surrounded himself. A warrior, then. Perhaps one of the castle guard? No. He looked too at ease to be an off-duty guard.

Kaitlyn frowned. Something about the shape of his face — wide brow, high cheekbones, narrow nose — something was familiar. But what?

He glanced up, noted her, his gaze moving past, and then he looked at her again, frowned, and straightened from the wall.

"Kaitlyn?" he asked, stepping toward her. "Katie? Is that you?"

And his voice pulled him sharply into focus. Conall. Gavin's best friend, the boy she'd idolized as a girl. Conall. A boy no longer, but a well-grown man.

She glanced away, drew a calming breath, then met his gaze and stepped forward to meet him in the center of the corridor.

"Conall! How good to see you again. Do you live nearby?"

A smile spread across his handsome face. "As I live and breath," he said, reaching for her hands. "It is you, Katie! How long has it been?"

Kaitlyn side-stepped, avoiding his grasp. If she were still the girl he remembered, nothing would have been more natural than to clasp his hands in welcome. But she was no longer simply Katie, Gavin's little sister. She was the Solitary Sorceress, and this moment brought that realization home with the force of a gut punch.

Clasping her hands behind her back, she turned to resume her walk, nodding her head to invite him to join her.

He frowned at her evasion, but put his own hands behind his back and walked beside her, sliding sidelong glances at her as they went.

"Are you staying with Gavin, Katie?" he asked, his tone curious, but mild. "Or perhaps you and your husband have chambers here?"

A small smile played around her lips and she glanced at the stone-flagged floor. "I've never married. Perhaps you didn't know that I was apprenticed to Aelfric, the King's wizard."

He nodded. "Yes, now I remember. Gavin did tell me you'd gone to court to study magic."

He stopped and turned to face her. "I understand Aelfric recently passed from this life." He inclined his head and lowered his eyes. "I am sorry for your loss."

Tears threatened, but she willed them away. "Thank you, Conall. He was a great man, but it had been many years since I'd seen him."

He looked up, startled. "Then why are you here, if you were no longer studying with Aelfric?"

"The king called me to replace Aelfric. I am the new King's Wizard."

"But…" He stopped abruptly, drew himself up to his full height and gave her a courtly bow. "Forgive me, my lady," he said, his voice suddenly stiff. "I didn't realize with whom I spoke."

Kaitlyn's mouth was suddenly as dry and cracked as a desert streambed in full summer. She'd been enjoying chatting with an old friend. Now, as though the man had been transformed by magic, a stiff and formal courtier stood before her.

"There is nothing to forgive, my lord," she said quietly, and gesturing forward with her right hand, she turned to continue their walk.

A strangled sound caused her to turn back to Conall.

His gaze was fixed on the golden glove encasing her right forearm. Her cheeks heated as he turned a wide-eyed stare upon her face.

"It's you?" he asked, his voice strained. "You're the Solitary Sorceress? The hero who saved my life?"

She blinked. "What? How could I have saved your life? I had no idea where you were!"

"But it was you?" he pressed.

"Yes," she sighed. "It was me. In a moment of total idiocy I claimed a magic that should have killed me. Instead, it turned me into who I am, the Solitary Sorceress."

He passed a hand over his eyes, and then turned to walk on. "I never dreamed it was you, Katie," he said quietly. "I heard the stories, of course, but it never occurred to me that I could know such a legendary sorceress."

She nodded and resumed walking at his side. "Believe me, I never intended to become the Solitary Sorceress. When I called the Fire-stone, I thought only to give it to Aelfric. I expected him to be the hero. Never myself. Even in my youthful arrogance, I understood that I lacked the knowledge to control such a powerful object." She lapsed into miserable silence.

After a moment, she roused herself. "But tell me, how did my actions save your life? I'm sure you must be attributing your skill at arms to my foolishness."

He smiled ruefully. "Skill at arms? You forget, ten years ago Gavin and I were rank amateurs. Neither of us would have lived to gain skill if not for your so-called foolishness."

He shook himself and made a warding gesture before continuing. "I was at the mercy of an enemy soldier, flat on my back, unarmed, my head ringing from the force of his last blow. He stood over me, his blade at my throat, ready to deliver the killing stroke."

"What happened?" Kaitlyn asked, wide-eyed, breathless with anticipation.

He grinned. "You happened. Whatever you did caused the warrior to … I don't know … it was like he woke up. He shuddered, looked around the battlefield, then lowered his weapon. He just stared at me. After a moment he offered me his hand and helped me to my feet. It was the strangest moment of my life."

She nodded. "After the Firestone defeated Darius…"

"After *you* defeated Darius," Conall interrupted with a fierce glare.

Frowning back at him, she said, "Fine. After *I* defeated Darius, Aelfric said that many, if not most, of his soldiers had been ensorcelled. That they would surrender without further violence."

Conall nodded. "Aelfric was a wise counselor. That's just what happened. The knight who nearly killed me surrendered immediately. The poor man didn't even know where he was or who he was fighting."

They walked on in silence for a few moments before Conall spoke again.

"Since the other things I've heard are true," he said, "is it also true that you are untouchable."

She cast him a sidelong glance, then schooled her features, stared straight ahead and nodded. "It was the Firestone's price."

He stopped. She walked on for a pace or two, then turned to face him.

"You'll think me impudent," he said, stepping closer to her, "but may I try?"

She gazed at him for a long moment. Conall. Her childhood friend. The boy whom she could have loved grown to manhood. Was it possible? Could he end the enchantment? Would the Firestone bend to their combined wills?

She held out her encased hand to him. "I'd like that … very much."

Their gazes locked and both of them held their breaths as Conall slowly reached for her hand …

… only to have his fingers stopped by an invisible barrier an inch from her flesh.

She read the outcome in his eyes, in the furrow of his brow, and exhaled her disappointment.

He looked away. "I'm sorry, Katie," he murmured. "It's just that …" he paused, then looking embarrassed turned to walk. "I hoped that perhaps the Firestone had spared me for this moment."

Tears welled in Kaitlyn's eyes, but she clasped her hands behind her back again, raised her chin, and strode forward.

"You've always been special to me, Conall, and I'm glad to know I had a part in your survival, but the Firestone will not be cheated of its due."

They'd arrived at the door to the Wizard's Tower. Kaitlyn turned to Conall and gave him a brave smile. "This is where I leave you, my lord. It's been a pleasure to see you again."

Conall gazed at her as intently as though he wanted to take up residence in her soul. With the suddenness of a striking viper, he unsheathed his sword and bent to one knee, the blade tip upright on the stone flag, his hands on the pommel.

"My life is yours, Lady Kaitlyn," he said, eyes on the floor at the sword's tip. "Will you accept my service?"

Kaitlyn glanced around the passageway where other courtiers were pausing to watch the scene Conall was creating. This wouldn't do. Her heart hammered, heating her cheeks. Kaitlyn had no desire to be party to even more court gossip.

Rubbing sweaty palms on regal velvet skirts, Kaitlyn whispered, "Get up, Conall. You're making a scene."

Conall remained as still as though he'd been turned to stone. "Answer the question, m'lady," he murmured without looking up.

"I don't need your life or your service," she cried in irritation.

He raised his gaze and their eyes locked. She saw sorrow, no, anguish in their depths and knew that she had wounded him.

Inspiration struck, and she smiled gently.

"Rise, Conall. I have no need of guardian, protector, or servant," she said, her voice gaining strength as her conviction deepened, "but I do have need of a friend. The Solitary Sorceress grows weary of seclusion. Will you be my friend, Conall?"

Relief and hope mingled in a sunburst of surprise, the light originating in his eyes and spreading across his handsome features. He grinned, climbed to his feet, and sheathed his sword. "It will be my honor, Lady Kaitlyn."

She grinned back. "Katie will do, Conall. I said *friend*, not *courtier*."

He nodded. "And you shall have one. Until tomorrow, Katie," he said, then giving her a small bow, he turned and strode away.

Kaitlyn watched him go, feeling lighter than she had in years.

A friend. What a gift he'd given her.

A friend. She hadn't known she'd needed one.

Opening the tower door, she fairly flew up the stairs to her quarters. A friend. Someone who knew her of old, someone she could talk to without worrying about the impression she gave. A confidant.

She had a friend, and that friend was Conall. A man she might have loved had the Firestone not existed. A man who would surely have died without the Firestone.

Touching the golden glove with her left hand, she acknowledged her gratitude. The first she'd ever felt.

Slender tendrils extended and crawled toward her elbow.

She laughed and clamped her iron will over the Firestone. "I may be grateful for his life," she said, "but not that grateful. You will not advance."

The Firestone re-absorbed the tendrils, exuding instead an aura of peace.

"Yes. Let us be at ease with each other." She stroked the warm surface of the living sheath encasing her forearm. "You have a mind and an arm to wield your power, and I … I have a friend. Let us agree to be content."

PART IX
TO PROTECT A PRINCESS

DEBBIE MUMFORD

TO PROTECT A PRINCESS

SPUN YARNS
A *Witchling* Short Story

CHAPTER 1

*K*aitlyn reveled in the fine spring day. Sunlight fell softly through the canopy of the old growth forest, illuminating individual leaves with an otherworldly glow and dappling the soft soil of the trail their horses trod. Hoofbeats were muffled by dirt and duff, allowing distant birdsong and the scurrying of small animals to be heard. She breathed deeply, savoring the smell of growing things: shade-loving flowers, wild herbs, and the fresh young leaves of deciduous trees. Even the strong odor of horseflesh was pleasant, reminding her of other rides in happier times.

For this was not a journey that pleased Kaitlyn, nor, she imagined, was it a happy time for her charge, the Princess Melisande.

Turning her attention from the fine weather, Kaitlyn observed her princess. King Lorien's eldest daughter was regal and self-possessed, everything a king's daughter should be. She sat her horse with confidence. Eschewing the side-saddle so popular among the women of the court, she sat astride her bay mare straight-backed, the rough leather reins held lightly in her gloved hands. Though her riding habit was plain, a drab brown split skirt, slightly darker brown corset laced over an unbleached linen shirt, the weave of the fabric was finer than anything the rest of the party could afford. With the possible exception of Kaitlyn herself.

As King's Wizard, Kaitlyn had access to the best of everything Breoria, King Lorien's realm, could provide. The heroine of the Wizard Wars and savior of her people, Kaitlyn was both honored and feared. Known throughout the kingdom as the Solitary Sorceress, Kaitlyn's fame isolated her from all but a few close companions, and the Firestone held her apart from even those few.

Kaitlyn had paid a terrible price to save her kingdom and the people she loved.

In her youthful arrogance — she had lived all of fourteen summers when the fateful events took place — she had called forth a powerful magical artifact, the Firestone, and in desperation to save her beloved brother, had used it. The Firestone had given her the strength and magical prowess to defeat Darius, the evil wizard who threatened her people, but the artifact had claimed its price. The Firestone had bonded to her very flesh, encasing her right hand and forearm in a golden sheath and protecting her from physical harm ... as well as from all other human contact. No living being could so much as touch her hand. Not even Conall, the childhood friend who had grown into a man she might have loved. No. Kaitlyn belonged to the Firestone.

Pulling her thoughts back to her princess, Kaitlyn realized that their fates were not so different. Kaitlyn would not have chosen to be the Solitary Sorceress. That reality had been thrust upon her. Admittedly her own rash decisions had played their part, but the larger circumstances of war had forced her to her fate.

Melisande had not chosen the role that awaited her either, and she wasn't all that much older than Kaitlyn had been. The King's Wizard escorted Princess Melisande to her wedding to the king of a distant realm. A man the sixteen-year-old princess had never met. Her privileged status as king's daughter carried a heavy price: she was a bargaining chip in a game of state. Her lithe young body and the children she would eventually bear bought her father's kingdom a favorable trade agreement and a powerful ally.

Kaitlyn could not be touched. Melisande would be touched intimately by a man she didn't know and hadn't chosen. Which was the more terrible fate?

Lowering her eyes to her own black gelding, Kaitlyn breathed a prayer to the Mother Goddess that King Theirn would prove to be a worthy man, a man Melisande could come to love. But whether he was or not, the marriage would take place. It was Kaitlyn's duty to ensure that nothing came between Melisande and her marriage bed.

CHAPTER 2

The people of King Theirn's court were unusually subdued. Kaitlyn and the princess had been courteously received, their escort of one hundred men-at-arms suitably housed, their honor guard allowed to accompany them when they were shown to adjoining rooms. But the people of Theirn's castle were too solemn, moving about their duties on quiet feet, their eyes downcast.

Kaitlyn frowned. Something was amiss in this place, but her knowledge was too scant to identify the source of the problem.

The chambers they were shown to were sumptuous, though, as was fitting, Melisande's was the more spacious of the two. Each featured a four-poster bed with thick hangings to hold in warmth while they slept, a hearth with a merrily crackling fire, and a tub of steaming water. The bath was a particularly welcome sight after their journey.

Once the Breorian ladies were refreshed and suitably attired in their finest garb, they were shown to an anteroom off the great hall, where they awaited presentation to the king.

Melisande stood tall and proud in a gown of leaf green silk. Delicately worked lace accented her bosom and wrists and a tiara of gold filigree and pearls rested upon her auburn curls. Only the shallowness of her breathing and the paleness of her face betrayed her anxiety.

In her role as King's Wizard and protector of the princess, Kaitlyn wore a simple dark blue gown embroidered at hem and cuffs with gold thread. Her only jewelry was the golden sheath of the Firestone. In Breoria, the Firestone was all the adornment she needed. Everyone knew it for what it was—a badge of ultimate power.

"Courage, Princess," Kaitlyn murmured. "In a few moments you'll know what manner of man your father has pledged you to."

Without glancing toward the sorceress, Melisande reached out as if to grasp her hand. The Firestone's interference stopped her. She glanced at their hands and a hint of color stained her cheeks. "I'm glad you're here, Lady Kaitlyn, even if you can't hold my hand," she whispered. "I don't think I'd have the courage to face this alone."

Kaitlyn smiled ruefully. "Nonsense. You are a royal princess. You were born to courage. If I could, I'd be proud to hold your hand, but separation is my fate, just as marriage is yours."

Melisande nodded and, turning her head slightly, met Kaitlyn's gaze. "Thank you. It is good to be reminded that I am not the only one whose destiny is not of their own choosing."

"Indeed not, milady," Kaitlyn said, her voice serious. "I believe you would find that everyone, whether pauper or king, labors under the burden of their own particular circumstances. The best of us learn to master our fates and thrive despite our limitations. Those who do not lead miserable lives."

Melisande closed her eyes and bowed her head. After a moment she straightened her shoulders, stood tall, and met Kaitlyn's gaze with determination. "I shall meet my betrothed with dignity and strive to find peace in my new role."

Kaitlyn inclined her head. "An admirable decision, my princess."

The door opened and a servant bowed them into the great hall of the castle. Princess Melisande stepped across the threshold, followed by Kaitlyn. They stopped beside the steward. The man struck the stone floor with his staff and announced, "Her Royal Highness, Princess Melisande of Breoria, accompanied by Lady Kaitlyn, the King's Wizard."

Kaitlyn glanced around the great hall. A large stone room, its walls softened by colorful hangings and tapestries illustrating the kingdom's history. The flagstone floor was well scrubbed, the rows of fluted columns supporting the ceiling showed no sign of crumbling. Unusually solemn courtiers moved quietly to the sides of the room, opening a path between the princess and the dais where the king sat on a magnificently carved throne. A single counselor stood at his shoulder, beside and just behind.

Despite the distance that separated them, Kaitlyn could see that King Theirn was young, not more than a few years older than Melisande. She breathed a sigh of relief. Being of similar ages and backgrounds boded well for their union.

Her gaze moved from the king to the counselor and her breath caught. Instantly, she shielded herself. The Firestone tingled against her arm. *Yes,* she thought. *You feel it, too. Power. Malignant power. The king is attended by a wizard, and not a benevolent one.*

The steward stepped forward, motioning the women to follow. Using the movement to disguise her action, Kaitlyn leaned forward and whispered in Melisande's ear. "Have a care, milady. All is not as it seems."

Melisande gave a barely perceptible nod and followed the steward to the base of the dais, where she dropped a shallow curtsy and stood, head held high. Just behind her, Kaitlyn curtsied low and waited to be released.

"Welcome to Thaelon, Princess," the king said, and added, almost as an afterthought, "You may rise, Lady Kaitlyn."

As she straightened, Kaitlyn chanced a glance at the young king. Calling upon her magical sight, she recognized lines of power twisting between the king and his wizard ... in sharp spikes, glistening with malignant energy. She glanced away immediately and kept her eyes downcast. She could not afford to give herself away. The young king's wizard must think her an incompetent. Melisande's very life could depend on Kaitlyn's power remaining concealed.

The subdued quality of the courtiers and servants suddenly became clear. These people were terrified. They went about their business as quietly as possible so as not to attract the attention of the wizard.

Kaitlyn could not leave Melisande unprotected in such a court. Yet Kaitlyn's sworn duty was to witness Melisande's marriage and inspect proof of its consummation. Accomplishing both would require patience, planning, and the Firestone's power.

"Allow me to introduce my most trusted advisor, Lord Kagan," the king continued. "Lady Kaitlyn, you and Lord Kagan will no doubt have much to discuss. He holds the office of King's Wizard in Thaelon."

Kaitlyn allowed a small trickle of power to escape her shields. Kagan would be suspicious if he detected no magical ability in King Lorien's wizard.

"I'm always anxious to learn the ways of my betters, your majesty," she said, and felt Melisande stiffen. Glancing at her princess, she smiled brightly. The girl appeared to relax, but Kaitlyn knew she had understood the warning.

All through the welcoming feast, Kaitlyn held her shields tightly in place, carefully allowing small amounts of power to bleed through. She chatted gaily about the excitement of royal weddings and how she specialized in herb lore, maintaining excellent health among King Lorien's courtiers and the citizenry of Glen Breor, the Breorian capital city. The ruse was exhausting, but Kagan's dismissive attitude and obvious condescension made it all worthwhile. He suspected her of nothing more devious than an ill-advised love potion.

Kaitlyn was on the verge of relaxing her rigid control, when the king called her name.

"Lady Kaitlyn," the young man called from his central position at the head table. "I can't help but notice the unusual band around your hand and forearm. Pray tell, what is it? I've never seen the like."

Kaitlyn froze in the act of lifting her goblet to her lips. Her gaze darted to Melisande; the princess's face looked bloodless, her eyes wide with fright. Noting Kaitlyn's eyes on her, she dropped her gaze, pulling her hands into her lap.

Setting her goblet down, Kaitlyn raised her right hand for the king's inspection. "This?" she asked in a girlish voice. "Why 'tis nothing but a pretty bauble my master gave me when I attained my full power. I wear it to remind myself of his wise ways." She pretended to pull at the sheath. "Would you like to see it more closely? I can remove it for you, if you like."

Her pulse pounded at the audacity of her offer and she fought the impulse to bite her lip. She could no more remove the Firestone than she could remove her heart. Both would be her death.

The king waved away her offer. "No need, my lady," he said. "I was merely curious why a courtier would display more wealth than her princess."

"Wealth? Oh, heavens, your majesty! The trinket has no true value. 'Tis nothing but fool's gold."

The young man nodded. "Of course. I should have realized." And the conversation turned to safer topics.

Breathing a sigh of relief, Kaitlyn picked up her goblet once more, and pretending to drink, leaned back in her chair to observe the room. As earlier in the great hall, the courtiers attending the feast were reserved. They ate and drank, but spoke little and only in whispers. Their glances were furtive, restive, as though they were anxious to leave. Only Kagan and the king seemed at ease, but judging by the flow of magical energy between them, the young king was not truly aware of anything. He was completely enthralled by the wizard.

How long must Kagan have controlled Theirn? For his mind to be so completely ensorcelled that Kagan could carry on a conversation with her and have no need to attend to his puppet's every movement spoke of a long and close association.

If she broke the connection, as she must if she were to ensure Melisande's safety and see the marriage consummated, how much of the king's personality would survive? She had killed one evil wizard, and was willing to do so again if it was the only way to protect her princess, but would she destroy Theirn in the process? And if he survived, what damage might be done to his mind? Would she be sentencing Melisande to life with an imbecile?

At last the feast came to an end and the Breorian women were allowed to return to their rooms. Once safely inside, with their own guards posted in the corridor, Melisande opened the connecting door and called Kaitlyn to her chamber.

"Tell me everything," the princess commanded. "You are no fool, Lady Kaitlyn, though you've certainly acted one since we first set foot in the great hall. What concerns you?"

How much to tell this young woman? She seemed hardly old enough to bear such a burden, and yet Kaitlyn had been younger still when she had become the hero of the Wizard's War. She wished her old master, Aelfric, was still alive, still here to counsel her. But since he wasn't, Melisande was her only possible confidante. The Mother Goddess knew, whatever Kaitlyn chose to do, Melisande's life would be impacted.

"How did you find King Theirn?" she asked.

Melisande frowned, confused by the question. "He's younger than I expected, thank the Mother! And certainly handsome enough, but ... well ... there's something not quite right." She hesitated, bit her lip in thought, and then continued. "I realize that not everyone is as astute as Father, but he seemed, well, a bit hazy. Sometimes our conversation was fine, and sometimes he seemed unable to follow the thread of talk. Almost as though he were simple," she said, and then added hurriedly, "but I don't believe that to be true."

"You are very astute, milady. The man you met today was not the king."

Melisande's eyes widened. "How can you say that? We were surrounded by his court. Surely someone would have protested if the king were missing."

"Did you not notice how subdued and frightened the courtiers were? They live in fear of Lord Kagan," Kaitlyn replied. "But I didn't mean to imply that the king's person wasn't present. No, it was his mind that was missing."

Melisande's frown deepened. "I don't understand."

"The king is ensorcelled by Lord Kagan. The King's Wizard has enslaved the king and only another magician will be able free him."

Princess Melisande slumped onto her bed, eyes wide, her mouth an 'O' of horror. "That is why you acted the fool," she said. "You didn't want Lord Kagan to know how powerful you are, that you might endanger him."

"Yes, and I thank you for playing along, for being quick-witted and trusting me."

"I couldn't imagine what you were doing, but Father always says you're brilliant, so I knew there must be a reason."

Kaitlyn looked up in surprise. King Lorien thought she was brilliant? That was a surprise. She always thought he tolerated her as a poor substitute for her late master, Aelfric.

"Yes, well, I think I've deceived Kagan for the moment, but we have some hard decisions to make."

"How so? Shouldn't we simply break the betrothal and return to Breoria?"

"That is an option, but it could be a dangerous one. If we don't give sufficient reason, Kagan might guess that we know and imprison or kill us. Remember, our guards believe we are on friendly soil. They were vigilant against thieves and cutthroats on our journey, but here? They are sorely outnumbered and could be disarmed and captured before they realized they were in danger."

Melisande nodded. "Very well. What are your thoughts?"

"First, we must alert our men. We'll start with our honor guard and instruct them to pass the word. Discreetly. Your father sent his finest men with us, so discretion shouldn't be a problem. Then we must all, you, me, our men, endeavor to discover how deep this treachery goes."

"Yes," interrupted the princess. "I can see that if Kagan is our only enemy, you can likely defeat him, but if he has a cadre of men working for him willingly, that is another matter entirely."

Kaitlyn nodded. "Spoken like a true queen. Your father would be proud."

"Queen?"

"You will be Thaelon's queen when you marry Theirn. He will be lucky to have you by his side."

Kaitlyn paused. This would be the unpleasant part. Melisande had handled the situation well to this point, but ...

"But Kaitlyn, what about Theirn?"

Surprised, Kaitlyn glanced up to see Melisande's somber eyes gazing at her. "What about him?" she prompted.

Melisande shuddered, dropped her gaze, and asked quietly, "When Kagan falls, will Theirn's mind be whole?"

Kaitlyn breathed out a long sigh. "I don't know, milady," she answered. "There are too many unknowns. I don't know the specific enchantment Kagan has used, or how long the king has been enthralled. I don't know whether the young man was strong or weak-willed to begin with.

"I do know that when I killed Darius, the men under his enchantment were freed. Some of them emerged from the experience horrified, but whole. Others couldn't live with what had been done to them. Some, very few, but some, were raving lunatics and had to be locked away."

She reached out to the young woman, wishing she could touch her. "I'm sorry, Melisande, but I can't say what will become of Theirn, or this realm. If you were already wed, well, then Thaelon would have a queen to help it recover. But if you had wed him without discovering the truth, then Kagan would surely have ensnared you as well and none would be the wiser. I can't allow that to happen."

CHAPTER 3

The next few days were busy and stressful for the Breorians. Word was passed among the men and all were diligent in discovering information about Thaelon and its government. The guards posted at the ladies' doors acted as go-betweens, faithfully reporting findings every evening.

Melisande took pains to spend time with her betrothed in out of the way places, feigning a desire to see more of his kingdom and capital city. She was always attended by her father's guards, but tried to avoid Lord Kagan's presence. Slowly she began to see glimpses of Theirn's true personality behind Kagan's thrall and she dared to hope that the young king might be strong enough to survive when Kaitlyn destroyed Kagan.

For Melisande's confidence in Kaitlyn was absolute. Which worried Kaitlyn unendingly.

What if she couldn't do it? What if Kagan were too strong for her? If so, Kaitlyn wouldn't have concerns, Kaitlyn would be dead. But what of Melisande? What of their men? Their expectations, and their safety, weighed on her.

When she had defeated Darius, she had been young and naive. She hadn't known what she was doing. Hadn't even known the price of her decision.

Now she knew. She understood too well what the Firestone could do. Knew with complete assurance that it could defeat Kagan. But would it? She hadn't exactly been an ideal host to the relic, refusing to let it advance, to let it consume more of her than her hand and forearm. What if it decided Kagan would be a more amenable host? Could it transfer allegiance mid-battle?

She felt certain it could. The question was, would it?

So many lives hung on the trustworthiness of a potentially fickle artifact.

At last the time came to act. The conspirators gathered their information and the ladies of Breoria rode out to gather herbs in a nearby forest, attended by four of their faithful guards.

The men led them to a clearing they had scouted and picketed the horses while Kaitlyn and Melisande laid out their plans. The six sat down in the late spring sunshine, among the sweet grass and clover, to discuss their war upon the wizard. For they had determined that much like Darius before him, Kagan was the sole source of Thaelon's woes.

Princess Melisande began their council. "We are in agreement Kagan's usurpation of Theirn's throne constitutes treason against the Thaelon royal family and is punishable by death."

Heads nodded all around. Kaitlyn agreed, though she found it odd that not a single citizen of Thaelon was party to the agreement. Her own decision was more basic. Kagan had perverted the use of magic when he co-opted the lives of other men. She would destroy him for his misuse of the art she loved.

"We will strike day after tomorrow when the mid-day bell tolls. Captain Jains, you will assign four men to ride out with King Theirn and myself mid-morning. We will get as far from the castle as possible before we stop for a picnic. Hopefully distance will help to insulate Theirn from Kagan's control … and from any backlash at his demise."

"Yes, milady. I'll make sure Davin is one of the guards. He is skilled in healing as well as fighting."

Kaitlyn nodded. "That's a good thought, Captain." She cleared her throat and took up the narrative. "I will invite Kagan to a private luncheon in the castle gardens. I'd rather not do battle with him inside stone walls. There's no guessing the damage we might do."

Captain Jains spoke next. "I'll assign our remaining men to the steward and the various counselors we've determined most likely to be enthralled. I myself will be in the gardens watching over Lady Kaitlyn."

"No," Kaitlyn said, her temper flaring. "You will attend the princess. The gardens must be empty. There must be no witnesses. No one for Kagan to pull into his snare to distract me. If you must do something for me, Captain, station men at every entrance to the garden to keep everyone away. Themselves included."

"As you wish, milady."

"Excellent," said Melisande, clapping her hands. "Now that that's settled, we can enjoy our lunch."

Kaitlyn held out her hand to stay the princess. "There is one more thing. Captain, you must promise me that should I fail, you will spirit the princess away. You won't be able to help Theirn, but do not allow Melisande to remain in this wretched kingdom to become Kagan's pawn."

"No!" shouted Melisande. "I won't leave you here alone, at Kagan's mercy!"

"Melisande, you won't have a choice. I will be dead before you realize I have failed. Do not waste your life and the lives of your guards trying to rescue my corpse."

Melisande's eyes filled with tears and she turned away from Kaitlyn.

"But that's not going to happen, is it Lady Kaitlyn?" she asked, her voice choked with unshed tears.

"I sincerely hope not, Princess, but the future is never clear." Kaitlyn turned to Captain Jains. "Do I have you word?"

"Of course, milady. Princess Melisande's safety will be my first concern."

CHAPTER 4

*T*he fateful day arrived, and as Kaitlyn finished dressing, Melisande appeared at her side. The younger woman was dressed in a pale pink morning dress that brought out the roses in her cheeks, but her eyes were solemn.

"Lady Kaitlyn," she said, lowering her gaze, "I just wanted you to know how much I appreciate what you're about to do for my future husband and his realm. If all goes as planned, you will be honored above all other heroes. If not …" Her voice broke, and her words failed.

"If not, milady, you must make every effort to escape," Kaitlyn finished for her. "If you make it safely back to your father's court, I will not have died in vain. Warn your father. Prepare for attack … and pray it does not come!"

Melisande nodded and raised her head, blinking back tears. She gave Kaitlyn a rueful grin and whispered, "I truly wish I could hug you, Kaitlyn."

"No more than I, my princess. No more than I."

They gazed into each other's eyes for a moment, as though each was memorizing the other's soul. Then Kaitlyn roused.

"Go, milady," she said. "I have preparations to make and you must get your king as far away as possible." She paused a moment, then held up her hand in a sign of benediction. "May the Mother Goddess bless you, Melisande. Until we meet again, in this life or the next."

Melisande's eyes filled to overflowing and she turned and ran to her own chamber.

Kaitlyn stood quietly, reviewing their plans and hoping she had done all she could to ensure Melisande's safety. A tingling in her right forearm broke her reverie.

"Yes," she said to the Firestone sheathing her wrist. "You're right, as always. Too late now. The plan is in play and we must act our part."

The tingling intensified, and she smiled. The artifact was excited, knowing it was about to be used to its full capacity once more. She hoped it intended to use its magic to aid her ... not her adversary.

Too late to worry about that now. The Firestone would act as it had been created to act, and she would do what her conscience required.

CHAPTER 5

*K*aitlyn fussed with the table setting the kitchen staff had prepared in the garden. The noon sun beat down from a clear blue sky studded with perfect white puffy clouds, but the table rested in a shaded pavilion surrounded by flowering bushes and looking out on a meticulously tended lake. A swan and several ducks glided on the glassy surface of the sapphire water, while emerald green grass provided a perfect setting for the gem of the lake.

The cook had provided an excellent luncheon — cold chicken, potato salad, a green salad, and fresh strawberries — which Kaitlyn had no intention of eating. All was in readiness. The plan lacked only Lord Kagan's presence.

She felt him before she saw or heard him. A slight oiliness coating an otherwise perfect day. Her shields held as a magical tendril probed the surface of her mind. Only the small stream of energy she permitted to leak met his investigation. The Firestone vibrated in anticipation, a shiver she felt to the bone.

Patience, she thought. *We're almost there.*

The wizard strolled toward her and she moved to meet him at the edge of the lake. "To what do I owe the pleasure of this invitation, Lady Kaitlyn?" he asked with amused courtesy.

Kaitlyn smiled and met his gaze directly. "Our respective kingdoms are about to be related through marriage. I thought it was time we had a candid discussion of our magical … agendas."

Kagan's eyes widened as his eyebrows rose. He took a step away from her and placed a hand on his chest. "Magical agendas? I'm afraid I don't understand your meaning. What magical agenda could either of us have? You're an herbalist, and I … why I'm a simple advisor to my king who happens to have certain talents in the magical sphere."

"I am no hedge-witch, Lord Kagan," Kaitlyn said, moving to within arm's length of the man, "and you are no simple counselor. You are the real power in Thaelon. You have ensorcelled Theirn and are controlling his very thoughts."

As she spoke, Kaitlyn lowered her shields, allowing Kagan to glimpse her true potential. His eyes widened again, but not with the feigned innocence of a moment before. Now his face showed real shock. He lifted a hand as if in defense and then slowly lowered it as he regained his composure.

"You surprise me, Lady Kaitlyn," he said quietly, in a calm, self-assured voice. "You are not at all who you led me to believe you were."

She nodded, never allowing her gaze to leave his eyes. "And this kingdom and its king are not as they were represented to King Lorien. There are decisions to be made, Kagan."

"Decisions?" He gestured toward the shaded arbor and its table set for the noon meal. "Why don't we sit down and discuss these decisions you think need to be made over lunch?"

He turned and walked to the pavilion. Kaitlyn hesitated, decided she could do what needed to be done there as well as here at the edge of the lake, and followed.

Kagan held a chair out for her. She motioned him aside.

"I'm perfectly capable of seating myself," she said, and waited until he pulled out his own chair and sat before joining him at the table.

"Now," he said, reaching for the platter of cold chicken, "what are these decisions that we need to make?"

Kaitlyn declined the platter when he offered it and watched as he filled his plate with the cook's undoubtedly delicious meal. "I suppose our first decision is whether or not I break the betrothal and return to Breoria with Princess Melisande."

He nodded. "And what will determine your course of action?"

She leaned back and steepled her fingers under her chin. "Why your decision, of course. Will you release King Theirn and leave Thaelon, vowing never to return on pain of death?"

He choked and brought his napkin to his mouth, staring at her over its edge. When he had recovered, he asked, "And why would I do that, milady?"

Kaitlyn smiled a cold smile and held up her right hand. "Because if you don't, I will use the Firestone to destroy you as I did Darius," she paused before adding, "when I was but an untrained girl."

Kagan's gaze locked on the golden sheath covering her hand and forearm. "I thought you said that was a mere bauble."

"I lied."

His gaze flicked from the Firestone to her eyes and back. "That is the real Firestone?" he asked. "And you are its possessor? The legendary Solitary Sorceress?"

"It is, and I am," she replied. "Though if you are half the wizard I believe you to be, you already knew the answer. You would have read the ley lines surrounding us from the moment I released my shields."

He nodded solemnly. "Yes. Of course." He took a deep breath, held it for a moment, then asked, "May I be so bold? May I … touch it?"

Kaitlyn extended her hand. "You may try."

Kagan's fingers trembled as he reached for her hand.

Kaitlyn felt calm, though alert. She knew the Firestone would stop him an inch from her skin. So it was that the pressure of his fingers on the warm metal of the sheath broke her concentration, causing her to jerk away. But not before his fingers closed around her wrist.

"What?" she cried, gazing at him in horror. "How…"

Then she was too engaged to question the unexpected development further. Kagan had taken advantage of her momentary shock to attack her unshielded mind. Tendrils of magic blazed from his consciousness to hers, blinding her physical sight as well as her magical vision. She felt his oily presence sliding through her thoughts, seeking the core of her being.

Clamping down on the panic that threatened to engulf her, Kaitlyn marshaled her forces. She pushed all unproductive emotion, all fear, love, discouragement, and uncertainty into a corner of her mind and locked it down. Even her rage at this intimate invasion was set aside. She became the embodiment of drive and determination. Courage was secondary. Courage was only the mask, the face the world understood. Drive, the will to succeed, and determination to endure, to achieve her aim, to protect and defend Melisande and Breoria subsumed her being.

Kagan's oily attack presented a challenge. Whenever she tried to push him from her mind, his tendril simply slid sideways, into a new section of herself. He was slippery. Impossible to grasp or push. She was exhausting herself and her resources, while he slid inexorably toward her core.

She retreated. Took stock. Remembered her many battles against the Firestone. Her determination to hold it in place, to not allow it to move further up her arm. If she could withstand the Firestone, she could withstand Kagan.

But she continued to lose ground, continued to flail against the slippery oily ooze of his magic.

From what sounded like a great distance, she heard him chuckle. "You grow weary, little sorceress. Why not give in? Life will be so much easier when you don't have to think and worry and care about outcomes. Let go, and I will give you peace."

His words rolled across her mind, feeding the slime that sought to drown her. Was it possible? Were her drive and determination alone not enough? What more did she have? What additional resources could she bring to bear in this battle?

The Firestone burned with battle lust on her forearm, tendrils stretching from its edges into the air around itself.

Not now! she screamed at it. *I can't fight both of you!*

And the answer blazed across her mind. *Don't fight! Join!*

And Kaitlyn understood.

Without further argument, without thought to the cost, of what she might be required to sacrifice, she surrendered herself to the Firestone. Her duty was to Melisande and Breoria, and she could do little for either as Kagan's puppet.

Good!

Battle lust flamed from the artifact, its tendrils enveloping Kagan's hand where he still held Kaitlyn's wrist. The wizard writhed in horror, but the artifact held him fast, and together the Firestone and Kaitlyn burned Kagan from her mind.

He fought for freedom, both physically and magically, clutching his head with his free hand, but Kaitlyn didn't relent. The Firestone's Solitary Sorceress followed Kagan's magical retreat, purifying his passage with fire. They burned all the ley lines the evil wizard had built, cauterizing every connection he'd made to other living souls. Charring the remnants of magic from his being.

When they were finished, the Firestone released him and he collapsed at Kaitlyn's feet. No magical potential was detectable in the pulp of what remained of his decimated mind.

Kaitlyn stumbled to a chair, lowered her shaking body into it, and closed her eyes. The battle had been too close. She'd come too near defeat. She'd been arrogant. She hadn't really thought Kagan would prove a threat. She certainly hadn't expected his physical touch. But that touch had been the trigger for his attack. It had opened a conduit allowing him access to her mind. If it hadn't been for the Firestone ...

The Firestone!

She had fully surrendered to the artifact. What had it demanded in payment this time?

Trembling with fear at what she would see, Kaitlyn opened her eyes and glanced at her right arm. The Firestone lay quiescent against her hand and forearm. Exactly as it had been before the battle. Its tendrils had been reabsorbed. It had not advanced any further up her arm.

Thank all that is holy! she thought fervently.

Welcome, came a cryptic reply.

What? Who...?

Firestone. You stopped fighting. Communicate.

Kaitlyn swallowed. Had she been fighting the artifact all this time for no reason? No matter. She owed the artifact her life, and very possibly Melisande's as well.

Thank you.

Strong will. Worthy possessor. Proved self over time.

Aha! So her resistance had not been for naught. *I look forward to working with you ... and learning from you.*

Good.

Kaitlyn relaxed and ate a strawberry. All would be well. Melisande would return with her young king, now free from ensorcellment. Kaitlyn had felt Theirn's relief when she and the Firestone burned Kagan's entrapping lines from his mind and knew that the king had emerged whole. The marriage would take place, and after their shared experiences, Kaitlyn felt sure that the young couple would forge a much stronger bond than a mere marriage of state.

But why had the Firestone failed to protect her from Kagan's touch?

Remember.

Remember? What was there to remember? No one had been able to touch her since she bonded with the Firestone when she was fourteen. Not her brother. Not her master, Aelfric. Not even Conall, the man she might have loved.

A frown creased her brow as she remembered the fateful day she had bonded with the Firestone in order to defeat Darius. Surely not! But it was true. She had been touched twice since the bonding. Once today by Kagan ... and once more than ten years ago by Darius. Both had been defeated by the artifact's fires.

Her lips shaped a rueful smile as she reached for another strawberry. So, the only people she could touch were evil wizards whose power she wished to destroy? She could live with that.

But what if there was another possibility?

What if ... dared she even dream it? Perhaps now that she could actually communicate with the artifact, the Firestone would make an exception to its policy of no physical contact. Perhaps she and Conall might have a future.

Perhaps.

Kaitlyn smiled. The possibility existed. That was enough for now.

PART X
RED'S MISCHIEF REVEALED

DEBBIE MUMFORD

BESTSELLING AUTHOR OF *SORCHA'S CHILDREN*

Red's Magick

SPUN YARNS

A Sexy Short Story Collection

PROLOGUE

$\mathcal{R}$ ed reclined in the interstices of the ancient Irish glass that imprisoned him and watched as his proudest achieve-ments enjoyed a relaxing breakfast on the deck just beyond his windowpane. Maureen and Sean; Ray and Kathleen. Four hearts; two happy couples ... who would never have found each other without his interference. Granted, they hadn't appreciated his lecherous pranks at the time, but both couples had eventually admitted he'd done them a favor.

He smiled at the memories of the many couples whose romance he'd enlivened since Sean and Maureen had installed his window in the most prestigious suite in their Bed and Breakfast. He'd always been a voyeur; he could admit it. In fact, those voyeuristic tendencies were what had landed him in his current predicament.

Red's eyes drifted closed as he remembered Lysette. Everything began with Lysette — and a naughty plot to win her favors, which had gone so terribly awry.

He squirmed a bit in his glass prison as the delicious decadence of that long-ago escapade heated his loins. True, the consequences of his

CHAPTER 1

*L*ysette.

The comely faery lass danced among the poppies unaware of Red's careful observation. He drank in the grace of her slender body as she pirouetted from one side of the meadow to the other. Her black hair shone with the iridescence of a raven's wing, a perfect contrast to the moonbeam shimmer of her creamy complexion. The leaf-green fabric of her gown flowed and swirled around the firm, lithe curves of her breasts and buttocks, drawing his eye to their promise while modestly concealing her secrets.

Lysette.

Handmaiden to Titania, the Summer Queen of Tuatha de Danaan. Red ached to possess the dark-haired maiden, but he hesitated to approach her again. His ego still smarted from their last encounter.

"Take you to my bed?" she'd laughed when he'd offered for her at the Beltane fire. "Not if you were the last male fae in the kingdom!"

But as he watched her dance among the red-gold blossoms, a daring thought occurred. What if he rescued her? What if the fair Lysette found herself besieged, and Red valiantly fought for her honor and her freedom? Would she still withhold her glorious treasure from the hero who swept her from danger and returned her to safety underhill? Red's heart raced and his eyelids drooped as he imagined running his hands over her soft curves, kissing her berry-stained lips, sinking into her warm, welcoming depths ...

"Attend me, Red!" Titania's sharp voice slapped him back to reality, and Red whirled to face his liege.

The Summer Queen was a vision of perfection — from her flowing platinum tresses, emerald green eyes, and porcelain complexion, to her reed-slim body with its delectable curves. Red dropped into a courtly bow before his over-stimulated imagination could carry those thoughts further. The Summer Queen, a formidable power in her own right, was accompanied by her husband. Oberon's blue-black hair and hazel eyes made him the perfect foil to Titania's pale glory. In unity, the Fae's royal couple dazzled the eye; at odds, their temper disrupted the order of the natural world. Fortunately, today the atmosphere was charged with nothing more sinister than bored condescension.

"My lady," Red said, not daring to raise his eyes. "How may I be of service to my queen?"

Amusement colored her voice when she answered, "Still coveting the fair Lysette, I see. Methinks you need a quest, young fae, to occupy your thoughts and give outlet to your energies."

Red straightened, his face hot with embarrassment. Titania glanced at Oberon, and her green eyes flashed in response to his indulgent nod.

"Go forth into the human realm and find me a knight. He must be courageous and bold and skilled with weapons of war. Tuatha de Danaan requires a mortal champion, and you will bring him to the glade beneath the Guardian Oak three days hence. I will meet you there to inspect your choice." She leveled a stare at him that froze his bones. "Go, and do not return underhill until I have accepted your knight."

Titania extended her bejeweled hand and Red bowed to kiss it. He straightened, saluted Oberon and said, "I shall not fail, my lady. Until we meet beneath the Guardian Oak."

He turned on his heel, stole a final glimpse of Lysette and vanished into the mortal realm.

CHAPTER 2

*R*ed rested in the crook of an apple tree whose branches overhung the training field just beyond the castle's stagnant moat. He'd been watching the men-at-arms train for the better part of the day and despaired of finding a knight of any quality here. However, as this was the best fortified castle he knew of, he continued his vigil ... though his mind often wandered back to Lysette. Perhaps he could think of a way to combine his quest for a knight with his conquest of that raven-haired temptress. A clever fae could always find a way, and Red prided himself on his wit.

A trumpet fanfare sounded, and Red straightened, his interest piqued. A knight in armor rode forth from the castle, across the drawbridge and cantered to the field. Unable to hear what was being said, Red grabbed a ripening apple and bit into its tart flesh while he leaned forward to watch the knight's actions.

The mortal raised his visor and gestured to the men-at-arms. They gathered to one side and watched as the knight demonstrated various weapons.

Red chewed thoughtfully. This fellow just might do. He certainly met the requirement of skill with weapons and the dents in his armor spoke of courage in battle, but how was Red to determine his boldness?

He handed the apple core off to an inquisitive squirrel and drew his knees up under his chin without a thought to the precariousness of his perch. Schemes chased themselves across his mind until finally one took root and grew. Yes. That just might work. Better still, he might be able to twist it to serve his pursuit of the fair Lysette.

The knight finished instructing the men-at-arms, and the training session broke up. Red dropped lightly from the tree, wrapped himself in the invisibility of a summer breeze, and followed the knight back to the castle. Once in his quarters, the mortal removed his armor to reveal a powerfully built physique — especially through the chest, shoulders and arms — a face that remained handsome despite a nose that had been broken more than once, and sweat-soaked auburn hair clubbed at the base of his neck.

Red nodded in satisfaction. Physically, this mortal would do nicely; now to test his character.

The evening entertainments of a mortal castle bored Red, but he stayed close to the knight and amused himself by stealing tidbits of food from the plates of the prettiest maidens. He toyed with the idea of stealing other, more intimate delicacies from them, but resisted temptation. He could always return when he wasn't on a quest for the Summer Queen.

At last, the mortal knight retired to his chamber and freed Red to complete his scheme. As the young man closed his eyes, Red worked an intricate enchantment, capturing the warrior's will and summoning Lysette from Tuatha de Danaan in the same spell.

When the faery maiden appeared, Red melted into the shadows and waited for the final element of his enchantment to come into play. Lysette turned in a graceful circle, clearly seeking the wizard who had successfully called her to the mortal realm. She frowned and approached the sleeping knight.

Red forgot to breathe, so intense was his desire not to disturb the working. *Yes, my lovely, he thought. Just a little closer. Touch his shoulder; you know you want to ...*

Lysette leaned over the knight's sleeping form and trailed her fingers across his bare arm. Her sharp intake of breath caused Red to grin. Caught! He'd done it! He loosed his hold upon the mortal's will and leaned against the wall, prepared to enjoy the show.

The maiden touched the sleeping man again, more boldly this time, massaging the firm muscles of his upper arm before sliding her hand up over his shoulder and down onto his chest. Just as her hand reached the auburn curls that covered his powerful chest, the mortal's eyes sprang open and he captured her hand in a snake-swift strike of his own.

"Who are you?" he growled, pulling the dark-haired faery close. "Why are you in my chamber?"

"I don't know, my lord," she said, her voice a whisper of confusion. "I was summoned here, but I don't know by whom."

Against the far wall, Red bit his lip to keep from laughing aloud. The proud Lysette, in the grip of a half-naked mortal man. Oh, this was rich revenge, indeed. He hoped the knight would push his advantage, at least a bit. After all, if Red was to rescue his fair maiden, he just as well have the benefit of exposed flesh to accidentally fondle in the process. She could hardly blame *Red* if that barbaric mortal tore off her gown!

He kept silent, wrapped in his glamour of invisibility and watched in avid delight as the knight registered the stunning loveliness of the woman he held captive.

"Give me your name, fair maiden," the knight said, "and I'll release you."

"I cannot," said Lysette. "I ... I cannot speak my name in this realm."

The man straightened into a sitting position and pulled Lysette onto the bed beside him. His eyes narrowed as he studied her face. "What treachery is this? If you are not from this realm, whose kingdom do you claim?"

"The Lord Oberon is my king," said Lysette, modestly lowering her eyes from the man's naked chest.

"Oberon?" questioned the knight. "I know of no king named Oberon. Who has sent you to test my loyalty, wench?"

Lysette's lip trembled, and she tugged at her hand in an attempt to free herself from the knight's grip. His reaction pulled her onto his lap so that his free arm encircled her waist while the hand that held hers released her.

Yes, thought Red. *Take her now! Remove her gown, free her firm round breasts. Let me see her rosy nipples before I rescue her from your savage advances.*

Lysette held herself aloof, touching the knight as little as possible. He turned his head toward her, and their eyes met. Red watched in heart-pounding excitement as the couple leaned together into a kiss that scorched the very air concealing his presence. A shudder of wicked delight ran through his loins when the mortal raised his hand to toy with the ribbons holding Lysette's gown closed across her bosom. The strings loosed almost of their own accord, and Red lunged forward anxious to feel those perfect globes with his own heated fingers.

A whisper of power stirred his concealment, and Red whirled to find himself face to face with an indignant Lysette. Confusion befuddled his brain, and he froze in mid-stride.

"What ... "

"Red! What have you done?" He glanced from the angry faery maiden before him to the couple rapidly disrobing on the bed. Angry Lysette.

426

Aroused Lysette. How had he mangled his spell? How could she be in two places at once? He knew which he preferred, but he also knew which he had to deal with, and quickly.

"Lysette, my sweet," he said. "You are Lysette, are you not?"

"I am, you idiot," she cried, her eyes blazing, "but she is not!"

Red turned to watch the lustful pair tussle playfully on the bed. A wistful sigh escaped his lips. Regretfully, he turned to face the storm brewing in the dark beauty's eyes.

"If you are here," he asked in as innocent a voice as he could command in his excited state, "who is there?"

"That, you monumental idiot, is Titania, and I suggest you get that unwashed mortal off of her royal ass before his majesty the king comes in search of his wife!"

"Titania!" Red's stomach heaved, and all thought, lewd or otherwise, fled his mind. "Why would Titania answer a summoning for you and in your guise?"

"Because she wanted to see the knight you'd chosen for her," sighed Lysette. "She wanted to check on your progress without alerting you to her presence."

Red closed his eyes and tried not to think what this little prank was about to cost him. He'd intended to rescue Lysette before anything happened, but now Lysette wasn't Lysette, and Lysette had interrupted him and he didn't know what the smartest move would be ...

"Red! Do something!"

The panic in Lysette's voice startled Red. "What?"

"The queen is about to be mounted by that mortal! Stop him!"

Red whirled to face the panting couple and saw a tangle of arms and legs — completely naked arms and legs — not to mention a very shapely ass. An ass that even now positioned itself to allow its owner to slide onto a very engorged male member. Red strode toward the bed only to rush headlong into a very solid obstacle. The King of all Tuatha de Danaan, Oberon, Titania's husband, shimmered into existence between Red and the lusty couple, with his back to the bed.

"Attend me, Red," bellowed the king. "Where is my wife?"

Red skidded to a halt and sketched a very shaky bow. "Your wife, my lord? I have not seen the Summer Queen." He lowered his eyes before Oberon could read the lie beneath the literal truth of Red's words.

Oberon frowned, nodded to Lysette, and said, "I was told Titania came to inspect your knight."

Sweat trickled down Red's brow, and he tasted bile as he watched the queen inspecting the knight's anatomy in intimate detail behind Oberon's back.

A squeal of pleasure from the bed caused the King of Tuatha de Danaan to swing around and face the couple mating in oblivious fervor. "Lysette?"

Oberon turned back to the handmaid who cowered against the wall. "Are you Lysette, or is that Lysette? And if that's not Lysette, who is it? And why in the name of all that's magic are the two of you standing here watching this couple ... couple?"

Lysette sank to the floor, her hand clamped to her mouth. Oberon turned from her and glared at Red.

"I can explain, Sire," he said feebly, knowing his doom loomed over him.

"Cease!" roared the king, and the fornicating couple fell away from each other and lay quietly on the bed, to all appearances, sleeping peacefully.

CHAPTER 3

*R*ed knelt on a plush carpet of wood sorrel before the throne of the Summer Queen. Oberon stood a few paces away, his face swathed in a storm of violent emotion. Lysette waited behind Titania, ready to answer her smallest request.

Titania, resplendent in a gown woven of summer sunlight, gazed at Red with detached disinterest. The mischievous fae shivered in the midsummer heat. Soon the axe would fall and this misadventure would end. It had to end. He couldn't endure much more of the court's cold silence.

No one spoke of what had befallen the Summer Queen, but everyone knew. The Queen's silent misery froze her folk, while the King's white-hot anger singed any unwary enough to venture near. And everyone knew that Red stood firmly in the eye of both storms.

"Be done with it, wife," growled Oberon as he strode to take his place on the throne at her side. "Condemn this miserable wretch, or I will!"

"No," she said, her words glacial and slow. "The violation is mine, as is the humiliation. Vengeance shall be mine as well. No one shall so much as speak to this creature without my leave."

Oberon glowered at Red, his fingers tightening to white on the arms of the throne, but his voice was clear and calm when he said, "As you wish, my love."

"Lysette," she called and waited while her handmaid stepped forward and curtsied.

"His scheme was meant for you. Do you wish to advise me on his punishment?"

"Forgive me, lady," said Lysette. "He is rude and mischievous. He is unbelievably thoughtless and fickle, but I don't believe he meant me harm." She cast a sideways glance at Red and shame stabbed his heart at her words. "Please, lady, if you can find it in your heart, be merciful."

Titania sighed, straightened on her cushioned seat, and stared directly at Red. "Lysette makes a good point. You are thoughtless, Red. I would be within my rights to order your execution, but I bear some responsibility for this fiasco as well. You did not realize with whom you toyed."

The Summer Queen rose, glided across the deep green leaves to stand over the kneeling fae. "I sentence you to a hundred years' imprisonment," she said. With a wave of her hand she conjured a pane of glistening glass. "Use the time to consider your crimes. Learn to think before you return underhill."

Another wave lifted Red and slammed him into the glass. It liquefied around him, swallowed him, and digested him. He came to rest in the interstices within the crystalline structure.

Lysette.

At least he could still see Lysette. Perhaps she would take pity on him and place him in her chambers ...

The Summer Queen clapped her hands and the human knight knelt in Red's place on the sorrel. "Take this glass into the mortal realm," she commanded. "Place it carefully, somewhere quiet, that my errant subject's thinking may not be disturbed as he awaits his release."

The knight rose, picked up Red's prison and prepared to leave. The Queen stopped him with a gesture. She stepped forward, placed her fingertips on Red's glass and whispered, "Remember, master trickster, time runs differently in the mortal realm. A hundred years in Tuatha de Danaan will be an eternity there."

"Lysette," cried Red, but his voice was swallowed in the magic of the glass.

EPILOGUE

*R*eturning to the present, Red stretched and glanced at his favorite humans. Ah well, if he couldn't have Lysette, at least he could enjoy a good romp with Sean and Maureen, or Ray and Kathleen. A new mischief tempted him and he rubbed his chin in contemplation. Would the humans object to becoming a foursome? Now that could provide some interesting fare for the discriminating palate of a seasoned voyeur!

He'd definitely have stories to share when his incarceration ended and he returned to Lysette. She'd find he'd aged well, like fine wine. No longer a thoughtless and fickle youth, but a smooth and vigorous male. Ready for an eternity of endless love.

PART XI
TO DREAM OF FLYING

DEBBIE MUMFORD

BESTSELLING AUTHOR OF *SORCHA'S HEART*

To Dream
OF
FLYING

SPUN YARNS
A Short Story

CHAPTER 1

*A*melia Penfield poured tea from a pretty rose patterned teapot, handed her father a cup, and then took a dainty sip from her own. Keeping her eyes downcast, she felt her cheeks warm, but not from the heat of the tea.

"I'm concerned, Father," she said quietly. "I've been having very unusual dreams." She paused, took another sip of tea before returning her cup to the table. Knotting her hands in her lap, she raised her eyes to meet her father's gaze. "Of flying."

Professor Herbert Penfield's face drained of color, as she'd known it would. She knew the tales of her birth. Knew the circumstances that had led to her mother's untimely death.

"Flying?" he asked, his voice choked. He cleared his throat, put aside his teacup, and leaned forward to study her. "Tell me."

Her heart raced, throbbed in her ears as she'd heard the vast sea pound the shore in her dreams. A sound she'd never heard in life, hers having consisted of the sights and sounds of the booming—and very land-locked—city of Denver, Colorado. Closing her eyes, she sought calm. When she opened them again, she focused on her father, the solid rock of her life.

"In the dream," she began, her voice barely more than a whisper, "I'm sitting on a cliff overlooking the ocean. At least, I suppose it to be an ocean—it's a vast expanse of water, stretching to the horizon, with white-capped waves breaking against a sandy shore." She paused, it was easier to puzzle about this vision of an ocean she'd never seen than to contemplate what came next. She picked up her cup, took another fortifying sip of lemon scented tea, felt the warmth slide down her throat and radiate through her body.

Replacing the cup, she continued. "Next, I rise," she did so, "place my hands, palms together, over my head," she fit action to words, "and then swing my arms down so that they're straight out from my shoulders." Acting it out, she faltered, her cheeks heating with embarrassment. She sank back to her seat on the pretty blue velvet divan.

"Yes," encouraged her father. "Then what?" His cheeks remained pale, but excitement lit his eyes. Intellectual excitement tempered with concern.

"Why, then the inexplicable happens. I transform. Suddenly, I'm not a girl, but an enormous bird. I feel the wind pushing against my outstretched wings and I launch myself off that cliff to soar over the vastness of the ocean." Her breath caught and she licked her lips. "You can't imagine, Father. It's the most amazing feeling. The freedom. The joy. The power." She glanced at him and their gazes caught. "It's breath-taking...and totally addictive." She closed her eyes before whispering the final, terrifying words. "I want nothing more than to ascend the highest building and throw myself into the wind."

Which was, of course, exactly what her poor mother had done.

CHAPTER 2

*H*erbert Penfield paced from chair to window and back again. His daughter waited patiently on the blue velvet divan her mother had chosen for this room. Amelia. Dear, sweet Amelia. As far as Herbert was concerned, his dark-haired daughter was lovely beyond compare. Her complexion glowed with the copper lights of her mother's native heritage. She wore her straight black hair pinned in a demure knot at the nape of the neck, and was possessed of a lean and tidy physique. She was the picture of health, with the exception of the odd glitter in her gray-eyed gaze.

What could he do? How could he prevent a repetition of the horror that had nearly derailed his life sixteen years ago? He couldn't lose Amelia as he'd lost her mother. He would find a way to protect her from her own imaginings.

He dragged his hands through his hair, fingers snarling in the too-long tresses. This time he was forewarned; Amelia had come to him. He prayed it was in time. He paused in his restless stalking and studied her. Still able to sit quietly. Yes, her eyes glittered with a wildness he'd never noted before, but her demeanor remained calm. They still had time.

He moved to her, knelt before her. "Amelia, my dear," he began. "You know how precious you are to me, how much I love you." It wasn't a question. Didn't require an answer. Amelia had always known she was cherished. She nodded anyway.

"My darling, I don't want to upset or demean you, but I'd like you to ask Philomena to move your belongings into the guest room here on the main floor."

He waited for her to protest, to tell him he was over-reacting. She did neither, merely lowered her gaze and nodded. He sucked in a breath. Perhaps they hadn't as much time as he'd thought.

"I'd also like Philomena to prepare a cot in your room. She'll be sleeping there as well for the next few days. Just until I have time to think what's best to be done."

Again she nodded, but this time she raised haunted eyes to his. "I'm sorry, Father," she whispered and threw her arms around his neck. "I'm so sorry." Her slender body shivered, and hot tears soaked his collar.

"There, there, darling girl," he said, hugging her tightly. When she released her hold on him and sat back, he took her hand and patted it before standing. "I have no intention of losing you as I did your mother."

He stepped to the fireplace and leaned against the carved oak mantle. "We will find a solution. This time I understand the danger. I will not fail you as I failed your mother."

Amelia wiped her eyes with a lace trimmed handkerchief and rose gracefully. "If anyone can decipher this mystery, it will be you, Father. I'll give Philomena her instructions and we'll move into the guest room." She moved to the door, paused, and spoke over her shoulder. "I shan't fight you on anything, Father. I know you will do everything in your power to protect me. Even if it is from myself."

When she had gone, the room felt very empty. Herbert dropped into a wingback chair and leaned forward, head in hands. When Amelia's mother, Winifred, had come to him with a similar confidence, he had not taken the matter seriously. She was a new mother, after all, and everyone knew young women were given to blue moods after childbirth. He had dismissed her concerns as nothing more serious than flights of fancy brought on by the stresses of childbirth.

After her death, he would have given anything to go back in time, to explore her dreams, her fears, her odd pains with the sensitivity he hadn't realized was necessary. Winifred had dreamed of flight, had imagined herself a bird trapped in a woman's body, had believed if she could only achieve sufficient height she would transform and fly.

She had died in the attempt, leaving Amelia motherless and Herbert bereft.

Amelia would not follow in her mother's footsteps. Not if Professor Herbert Penfield could prevent it. He hadn't understood the severity of Winifred's delusions. He wouldn't make the same mistake with Amelia. He was a scientist, by Jove. He understood the physics, the mechanics of his world. He didn't pretend to understand the mind, but he knew other scientists who did.

He would call upon Dr. Fredrick Gottschein that very afternoon.

CHAPTER 3

*A*melia reclined on a chaise lounge in the office of her father's friend. Dr. Gottschein sat on a straight-backed chair, angled so that he was directly in her line of sight. Her father hovered behind him, wringing his hands and looking miserable.

"Are you certain, Fred? Are you absolutely convinced of the safety of this course of action? I will not risk her sanity."

Dr. Gottschein waved his concerns away. "Sit down, Herbert. You'll make Amelia nervous." He smiled at Amelia. "Are you comfortable, my dear? Despite your father's words, you have nothing to fear."

"Thank you, sir," she said with a tremulous smile. "I'm not frightened."

Her father paced across the room before racing back. "Truly, Fred? You're sure?"

Dr. Gottschein patted Amelia's hand, then turned face her father. "Herbert, sit down. Do I tell you how to build your airship engines? Do I question the mechanicals you bring to me for testing? Please provide me with the same respect. The mind is my field of study. Amelia is safe with me."

"Yes. Yes. Of course," Herbert Penfield said, perching on a chair well back from his friend. "Forgive me, old man. Nerves. You understand."

"Indeed, I do," Dr. Gottschein said, turning back to Amelia. "Now, are you ready to begin, my dear?"

"I suppose so, sir. I've never been hypnotized before. I'm not sure what to expect."

"You should expect to be safe and secure," he said, patting her hand once more before reaching into his pocket and withdrawing a golden orb. He dangled the shining pendant from a chain so that it swung in a smooth arc between them. "You need only watch this miniature astrolabe and listen to my voice. I'm sure you recognize it. Exquisite workmanship. Your father's, of course."

"Yes," she said, watching the small pendant swing back and forth, its tiny gears whirring, every surface gleaming as if in bright sunshine. "Father always does such precise work. It's really quite beauti…" Her words trailed off as her mind relaxed. She felt safe, utterly secure, and so very comfortable. As if she floated on a cloud without a care in the world. She was aware of her father, wringing his hands and fighting not to fidget, but she had no idea why he should be nervous. Everything was peaceful and calm.

She observed the good doctor as he replaced the astrolabe in his pocket and leaned forward to place his fingers on the pulse point of her right wrist. What a a very odd thing to do!

"Amelia." The doctor's voice floated to her as if through miles of muffling mist. "Can you hear me, Amelia?"

What an idiotic question! Her ears worked perfectly fine.

"Amelia, if you can hear me, please respond."

"I hear you."

"Excellent. Now, Amelia, I'd like you to tell me about your dreams of flying."

"Flying is the most amazing experience," she said. In her mind, she imagined raising her arms above her head, clapping once, and then lowering them to shoulder height. Only, they were no longer arms. Great, feathered wings stretched to either side of a body covered in fine golden feathers. She raced forward and flung herself off the precipice, catching the morning wind beneath her wings and rising to greet the sun.

"Tell me, Amelia. How is it that you can fly?"

"I can fly because I have wings. Great lovely wings with red and blue feathers. I can outfly the wind!"

"But, Amelia, you're a young woman. Men and women don't possess wings."

At his words, Amelia's wings disappeared and she plummeted to earth. A shrill scream wailed against her ears until she recognized it as her own. She heard the doctor shouting, commanding her to awaken, but she couldn't respond. All she could do was fall and shriek, until Thunderbird caught her.

Rest now, my child. I will not let you fall. You are safe. Cease your struggles. You may listen, but remain silent until I release you.

She didn't respond; had no need. Thunderbird knew her intimately. She relaxed in his talons and listened as he used her physical body to communicate with the human males who had summoned him.

"Amelia! Wake up," Dr. Gottschein commanded, sweat beading his brow. His fingers remained on her wrist. Her pulse had raced wildly while she screamed, but now it had slowed, regulated. He didn't understand why. Couldn't imagine what had so frightened her, didn't understand why she had failed to awaken when commanded.

"She will not wake until I release her."

The voice that issued from the young woman's body was harsh and guttural. Like nothing Herbert Penfield or Fred Gottschein had ever experienced. The professor leapt to his feet. The doctor would have done the same, but was loathe to relinquish hold of her wrist.

"Who is that?" asked Herbert. "That's not my daughter's voice."

"I am Thunderbird. Sit and I will explain how you may save our daughter's life."

Herbert drew his chair closer to Amelia and sank into it. "Our daughter?"

"Amelia's mother's mother belonged to my clan. She left our tribal lands for love of a trader. Winona knew her heart and her heritage. She left with our blessing."

"What has that to do with Amelia?"

"Be silent or I shall leave. If I leave before you understand what must be done, our daughter will die as did her mother before her."

Herbert bit back his retort and bowed his head in acquiescence.

"Winona flew from this life before she could explain our ways to her daughter, Winifred. Because she was ignorant, Winifred was doomed. Amelia also would have died had you not called me forth in this ritual."

"Ritual?" blustered Dr. Gottschein. "This is no magic ritual. This is a scientific procedure."

"Science and magic are the same. You are too ignorant to grasp this truth. What matters is that you did call me, and so Amelia has a chance at life."

"What must we do?" asked Herbert, his breathing shallow. He felt dizzy, confused, and frightened by this unexpected turn.

"You must return to our tribal lands, where the big river meets the western sea. Amelia must drink the water of life and undergo the ritual that will fully awaken her senses, allow her to be whom and what she must. I will calm her spirit to give you time to make the journey. But be warned, if she does not transform before the next full moon, she will die."

As the echoes of Thunderbird's words faded, Amelia opened her eyes. "Well, I must say, that was unexpected," she said, and swinging her feet from the chaise lounge, stood and ran into her father's arms.

CHAPTER 4

*A*melia stared open-mouthed at the airship her father had hired to transport them from Denver to the lands of her mother's people. She had seen airships before, of course, but never at close range, and never with the intent of boarding and journeying beyond the Rocky Mountains. The sleek little craft was secured to the top of a towering derrick, which served the dual purpose of mooring the vehicle and housing the lift that would carry her to the gangplank. She smiled, a genuine expression of pleasure; the first she'd managed in days. Who would've guessed that she would leave Denver for the first time, not in a coach and four, but in an airship?

She had sat in on Father's discussions with the captain yesterday, had listened quietly to their talk of engines and lift and airspeed. Had marveled at the captain's pride that his small craft gained its buoyancy not from flammable hydrogen, but from the more stable, but infinitely more rare helium. Her eyes had glazed at the minutiae of her father's technical questions.

Bored, she had concentrated on the map Father had spread across his desk. Beige parchment covered with sepia ink illustrated the topography of half the continent. Mountain ranges, river valleys, wide plateaus, and lakes, all were drawn to scale and with as much detail as could be rendered in two dimensions. The immensity of their undertaking frightened her. Their destination lay so very far away.

To ascertain that destination, Father and Dr. Gottschein had consulted as many of Denver's scientific community as might have knowledge of the terrain or cartography of the western shore of the United States. They were in little doubt as to the identity of the *western sea*; that was undoubtedly the Pacific Ocean. But the west coast was extensive, with many rivers emptying into the Pacific. Exactly which one was the *big river* to which Thunderbird had referred? Dr. Gottschein had even gone so far as to hypnotize Father in order to delve into his memories of Mother, to see if she had ever revealed the location of the lands of her people. Unfortunately, Father had nothing to contribute on that score.

At length a consensus was reached. Everyone agreed that the most likely candidate for the term *big river* would be the mighty waterway discovered by Meriwether Lewis and William Clark: the Columbia.

"I wish I could accompany you on this adventure."

Dr. Gottschein's comment pulled Amelia from her reverie. She glanced at the rotund little psychologist who had come to see them off.

"You are welcome to join us, Fred," her father stated. "I'm sure the captain could find you quarters, and just think of the case study you could write."

"Yes. Yes. Very generous. However, I am not constitutionally prepared for the rigors of travel, and you have no idea what awaits you when you descend from that ship to the shores of the Pacific."

Father clapped Dr. Gottschein on the shoulder before taking Amelia's arm. "I shall endeavor to take good notes," he said, "but I can't guarantee my observations will be unbiased."

"I understand completely." The good doctor turned to Amelia. "I do hope this all turns out well, and that you return to us freed from this dreadful delusion. I can only pray that the information your alter-ego provided will lead you to a successful outcome."

"Thank you, sir," Amelia replied, biting back a retort that she had no alter-ego. Such a comment would be pointless, since neither could prove their theory.

The Penfields took their leave of Dr. Gottschein and entered the lift at the base of the derrick. Though the day was bright and clear as only a morning in June can be, the steel railings were cold to her touch. The metal framework encasing the small platform seemed to absorb the day's light and heat, giving off a chill that soaked to her very soul. She stood in the center, one hand clutching her father's arm, the other the support railing.

The lift began its ascent with a lurch. She squeezed her eyes tightly shut and concentrated on maintaining balance while the world jumped and shivered around her. Good that breakfast had been light since her stomach couldn't decide whether it belonged in her throat or near her toes. She clamped her lips shut, breathed in and out through her nose, and was relieved when the lift ground to a halt.

Opening her eyes, she enjoyed a commanding view of the surrounding countryside. To the left she saw Denver's skyline, painted wooden edifices with glass windows gleaming in the sun. To the right, a long sweep of prairie stretched to the horizon, dotted with grazing cattle and wide-set farmsteads. Straight ahead loomed the majesty of the Rocky Mountains, great jagged peaks clothed in tall timber, armored with flat rock facets and snow-white glaciers.

"Welcome aboard the *Laura Lee*, Professor Penfield. Miss Penfield."

The captain's deep voice startled her, rapt as she had been in the stunning vistas. Releasing her father's arm, she turned to greet the man who would enable her to reach her destination within Thunderbird's timeframe. Tall, swarthy, bearded, he exuded an aura of competent command, reminding her of the swashbuckling pirate heroes of her favorite dime novels.

She stepped forward, aware of her father's careful scrutiny. "Thank you, Captain Markham. I'm looking forward to seeing your remarkable vessel."

Captain Markham touched his fingers to the bill of his cap and extended his hand to steady her as she stepped from lift to gangplank.

"Keep a careful hold on her," Father exclaimed as Amelia walked across to the ship. He said nothing more, but Amelia heard the unspoken fear that she would be tempted by this height and leap to her death.

"All is well, Father," she reassured him. "The captain's grip is firm and these guide ropes will prevent a fall." Even so, she heard his relieved exhalation when she stepped inside the airship's gondola.

He needn't have been concerned. Thunderbird had been true to his word. Her odd dreams had stopped, and while she was mesmerized by the incredible views from their lofty height, she felt no compulsion to fly...other than aboard the airship.

When both father and daughter were settled with their trunks safely stowed, Captain Markham gave them a tour of the *Laura Lee*.

"She's a fine, trim vessel," he said with pride. "We've an engine room which houses both the main solar-powered engine and the coal-fired back-up system, and a bridge where my co-pilot, Mr. Jenkins, and I plot and maintain our course."

He ushered them into both rooms, answering Professor Penfield's technical questions with relish. Amelia found the engine room interesting, with its polished surfaces, calibrated gauges, and bins of coal, but the bridge delighted her. Crystal panes of glass covered three walls, giving the pilot excellent views of the terrain. She would enjoy flight, she thought, and wondered if any reputable pilots would consider taking a young woman on as an apprentice?

Perhaps when her current adventure was completed, she'd speak to her father of such a possible future. For now, she kept her questions to herself.

They discovered that the *Laura Lee* not only had four passenger berths, a galley where they would take their meals, and a small observation deck, but also boasted a neat cargo bay. Indeed, Captain Markham's vessel appeared sturdy, well designed, and quite functional.

The Penfields returned to their berths as the *Laura Lee* departed her tower moorings. Captain Markham had informed them of the bell system that would alert them when they were free to wander the passenger areas.

Amelia sat on the edge of the bunk in her tiny berth. She had just enough room to open her trunk, which sat on the floor perpendicular to the head of her bed. Dressing would be tight, but then their estimated flight time was less than two days.

She leaned back against her pillow and closed her eyes. In just a few days, if all went well, she'd meet the native tribe to which she belonged through her mother's blood. Thunderbird had promised that once she took part in some unknown ritual, her heritage would be explained.

Tension knotted her stomach and she pressed her hands to her abdomen, kneading in an attempt to ease the discomfort. What was the nature of her people? How could ignorance of her cultural heritage have caused her mother's demise? What was this ritual Thunderbird had alluded to? For that matter, who or what was Thunderbird?

Dr. Gottschein seemed to think he was simply a manifestation of her own psyche, but Amelia didn't see how that could be. She'd felt a distinctly different personality calm her, soothe her, perhaps even save her, during that fateful hypnosis session. And after all, how could another aspect of her own psyche provide them with a distinct plan based on knowledge she had no way of ascertaining?

The bell sounded, informing her she was free to leave her berth, and she did so readily. Pondering unanswerable questions simply made her queasy.

She joined her father on the observation deck where they marveled at the miracle of flight.

CHAPTER 5

Two days later the Penfields joined Captain Markham on the bridge of the *Laura Lee*. They had reached the estuary where the Columbia River emptied into the Pacific Ocean. Salt water mixed with fresh in a dance of blue-green eddies, weaving in and out of shifting sand bars. It was an intoxicating and mesmerizing sight from the air.

"Where will we land?" Amelia asked the room at large.

"We won't," answered Captain Markham. "The *Laura Lee* doesn't settle to earth except in extreme emergencies. No, we must find an outcropping high enough to give her safe moorage."

"Of course," Amelia murmured, her cheeks heating.

"Shall we sail north or south to seek our moorage?" asked the Captain.

Professor Penfield shook his head. "I have no definite knowledge," he said, "but I seem to recall Masters Lewis and Clark mentioning a monolithic rock some miles to the south. If memory serves, it rises from the ocean, but at low tide can be accessed from land. Would that do?"

"Admirably, and it should be easily sighted. Mr. Jenkins, bring us about and head south. Keep a sharp eye out for this monolith."

As it happened, they found several such rocks, finally choosing one that was very close to its beach and mounded like a giant haystack. Captain Markham had two of his men lowered to the top of the rock with mooring lines. The process took Amelia's breath away as she watched the men dangle hundreds of feet above the ocean on ropes that seemed no more substantial than threads, but the crew seemed to take no notice of their fellows' precarious situation.

"Amelia, my dear," said Father once the moorage was well under way, "we shall be disembarking soon, and as there will be no gangplank or lift to convey us to the beach, I believe you should don the trousers I insisted you pack."

Amelia flushed, but lifted her chin and straightened her shoulders. "Of course, Father. Skirts and petticoats will definitely not lend themselves to rock climbing. I shall change at once."

When she returned, dressed in durable denim trousers, white button-front shirt, and sturdy walking boots, Amelia found a rope ladder descending from the hatch in the floor of the bridge and anchored to the surface of the rock. The ladder swayed in the wind, despite its firm attachments.

Her hand sought her heart as she closed her eyes and steeled her will. If those men could dangle at the ends of ropes to make her landing possible, she could climb down a rope ladder.

Pulling leather gloves from where she had tucked them under her belt, she prepared to make her descent.

"I'll go first," said Captain Markham. "I'm accustomed to making these climbs. Miss Penfield, you follow me. If you lose your footing, I'll be able to help you find it again. Professor, please follow your daughter. Mr. Jenkins, you have the bridge."

Amelia and her father nodded, while Mr. Jenkins called, "Aye, sir."

With her fear tightly reined, Amelia followed Captain Markham onto the ladder. The moment she left the security of the gondola, the wind whipped around her as though determined to tear her from her life-line. She clung tightly to the ropes, too frightened to move. Salt spray stung her face and the smell of dead fish assaulted her. What was she doing here? Why wasn't she at home surrounded by books and warmth and the smell of rose water?

And then her father leaned down from the hatch, touched her gloved hand, and called, "You can do this, my dear. I'll be right behind you."

She raised her eyes, met his gaze, and thought of all he had done, all he had risked to insure her safety. All she had to do was climb down a simple ladder.

Conviction warmed her soul and loosened fear's grip. She could do this. Carefully, with full attention and intent, she moved one foot down a rung, then a hand, then the other foot. Rhythm established, she continued until she felt Captain Markham's hand on her leg.

"Just two more rungs and you'll be on solid rock."

Relief sang through her soul as she stepped off the ladder. Not caring about the proprieties, she stepped close to the captain and allowed him to wrap his arms around her.

"Thank you," she said, reveling in the warmth and safety of his embrace.

"You did well, Miss Penfield. Very well." With a final squeeze, he released her. "I think your father could also use a hug."

She smiled and set action to words.

CHAPTER 6

A few hours later, Captain Markham, Professor Penfield, and Amelia were joined on the beach by a group of native men. Amelia studied them, noting the similarities between their long, straight black hair, copper skin, and high cheek-boned faces to her own. They were dressed in beaded buckskin tunics and leggings, their hair held back from their faces by bands of red fabric.

The eldest, with graying hair and deep wrinkles seaming his face, stepped forward. "You came, Lost Daughter."

Amelia glanced at her father. At his nod, she said, "We did, as quickly as we could. You speak English?"

The man grunted. "Some do. I don't. Thunderbird has granted me words so I can speak to you."

"I…I…uhm…I see," Amelia stammered. She bit her lip, but as neither of her companions seemed inclined to take up the conversation, continued. "How did you find us?"

"Thunderbird said you would come. When we saw the bloated whale in the sky, we followed."

Captain Markham snorted at the man's description of the *Laura Lee*, but held his tongue.

"I am called Eagle's Master. I am shaman of the People Who Soar. I speak for Thunderbird. It is good you have come, Lost Daughter. Come. Our people prepare for your ritual. You are old for this, it will not be pleasant."

He gestured for her to follow and turned toward the scrubby trees at the edge of the beach. One of his fellows whistled and another stepped onto the sand leading horses.

"Wait," called Amelia. "What about my father, my things?"

Eagle's Master turned. "You have no need of things. Your father is not of the people. He should go."

"I say, old chap," her father said, stepping forward, "I'm not just turning my only child over to you. I'm coming too."

The old man grunted and closed his eyes. No one moved. After a moment he opened them and nodded. "Thunderbird says you may come. You obeyed. You are not of the People, but you are Lost Daughter's close kin. You may come, but you must continue to obey."

Father nodded. "I won't interfere. I only want what's best for Amelia." Turning, he shook hands with Captain Markham. "Thank you, Captain. I don't know what to say now."

"I've never been this far west. My crew and I will sail the *Laura Lee* south for a few days. We'll moor here again in a week. If you're here, we'll be glad to take you back to Denver. If you're not, well, we wish you the best."

"Yes. That's a good plan. Thank you. I hope to see you in a week."

Captain Markham turned to Amelia and took her hand. "Take care, Miss Penfield. These natives seem well disposed toward you, but... well, take care."

"Thank you, sir. For everything." She gave his hand a squeeze before releasing it. "Safe journeys, Captain."

She and her father hurried to catch up with Eagle's Master. When the party was mounted, they gave a final wave to the captain and then followed her people away from the last tie to her former world.

The village of the People Who Soar surprised Amelia, accustomed as she was to the skin teepees of the plains peoples. The People Who Soar lived in wood huts. Not log cabins, more like huts built of cedar shakes that she might have expected to see on roofs. The people greeted her warmly, and while she didn't understand their words, their smiles were unmistakable.

They all dressed similarly to Eagle's Master, women and children as well as men. She and her father were led into one of the snug dwellings and offered food and drink. Before they finished, Eagle's Master joined them.

"Lost Daughter, the women of the people will prepare you for the ritual. You will go to the sweat lodge for purification. When the time is right, you will be given the water of life. You must drink it. All of it. After that, you will undergo the ritual with all the people as witness."

He turned his attention to her father. "You may observe, father of our lost daughter, but you must not interfere. You are not of our blood. You will not understand. Accept this and you will witness a wonder. Attempt to stop the rite, and you will be removed. Do you understand?"

Professor Penfield nodded. "I understand."

Hours later, Amelia emerged from the sweat lodge, wrapped in an odd blanket woven of multicolored feathers. She held it tightly to her body since she was naked beneath. The women led her to the center of the village where a huge totem pole, topped with a bird with outstretched wings, claimed pride of place. The whole village stood silent watch around that pole.

Amelia saw her father, standing well back from the circle of onlookers, flanked by two young men. She tried to smile, but it wavered so that she thought she might cry.

Onward the women led her, to the base of the totem pole. A drum began to beat, like a giant heart, muffled by the sighing of the wind. Eagle's Master approached, his footsteps synchronized to the drumbeats. He carried a large wooden cup, carved with intricate symbols. Raising the cup above his head, he chanted in a language she didn't comprehend. When he lowered the cup, he held it out to her.

"Drink the water of life, Lost Daughter. Do not waste a drop. This is your heritage. This is your right. Be one with Thunderbird."

She accepted the cup, lifted it to her lips. The liquid stung her tongue, tasted acrid and musty, gagged her. She mastered herself and swallowed. The next mouthful slid over her tongue like silk, tasted of rain and wildflowers. The dregs tasted of salt and fish, cool and warm knotted together and made one.

She handed the cup back to Eagle's Master. He grunted and returned to the circle.

Amelia stood there, unsure what was expected of her. No one had explained the ritual. Eagle's Master had left her alone, the only person with whom she could communicate. What had he said? She would drink the water of life and then complete the ritual. Well, she'd drunk what he'd given her. What next?

Stomach cramps! The pain bloomed so quickly, it took her breath away. The potion she'd ingested cramped her stomach and knotted her intestines. Something with claws tried to dig its way from her core. She fell to the ground, writhed in agony, and screamed for her father. Her muscles bunched and cramped, bulged and jerked, she was being pulled apart from the inside.

She straightened, panting, sweating. She had to stand. If she didn't get upright, she'd suffocate. She lunged up, the feather blanket forgotten. What did modesty matter in the face of agonizing death?

More! Standing wasn't enough. She needed to be straighter still. She threw her arms over her head, spearing them to the sky.

The drumbeat heightened, roared in her mind, commanded her obedience. Her arms fell to shoulder height and then in synch with the drum, she beat them up and down as she leapt to the sky.

The world fell away below her. She circled, observed with heightened sight as her people danced and whooped with joy. She circled higher, found her father. He'd fallen, was staring up at her with dazed amazement etched on his dear face. One more circuit of her people's village, and she arrowed toward the sea.

Welcome home, my lost daughter. Welcome to the People Who Soar.

Thunderbird, she thought. *Now I understand. We are one. I am of your blood.*

You are, my daughter. Now that you have attained your heritage, you are truly free. Only the first transformation requires the water of life. Now, you control your bodies. The choice of form is yours.

Thank you! And she lifted her beak and sang her praise to the setting sun.

PART XII
SORCHA'S HEART

DEBBIE MUMFORD

SORCHA'S
HEART

SORCHA'S CHILDREN PREQUEL

THE HEART OF FIRE

Sorcha knotted her fists so tightly her knuckles whitened. She glared at her mother across the rough oak worktable. "When are you going to acknowledge me as a fully capable wizard? I'm not an apprentice anymore. I don't need your permission to seek the Heart of Fire."

"Fine," Elspeth shot back, "but I'm warning you this is a mistake. The Heart of Fire is dangerous." The small, compact woman stretched to reach the braid of garlic hanging from the beam above her head, yanked a bulb loose and tossed it to her daughter.

"So is this war!" Sorcha caught the bulb by reflex, slammed it on the table and separated out three cloves for the strengthening potion. Her gaze never left her mother. "Don't you realize how powerful dragons are? If Leofric continues on his present course, he'll push them too far. They'll wipe us off the face of the earth."

Fear flashed across Elspeth's face, and Sorcha knew that her mother agreed; the King's recent aggressive actions could have serious repercussions.

471

Sorcha's mood softened. She picked up her paring knife and began to chop the cloves, pondering the enigma of the woman who had given her not only life, but a heritage of magic. Because of that heritage, strangers often assumed they were sisters rather than mother and child. Elspeth's long, dark hair sported only an occasional strand of gray. Trim, active, healthy. These words described both her and her mother. Neither of them possessed the lush curves so desired by other women at court, but neither really noted the lack, being too concerned with the practice of magic to worry about attracting the opposite sex.

Elspeth's bright green eyes glowed with fervent belief and wily intelligence. Sorcha shared her mother's fervency and intelligence, but not her eyes. She had inherited her unknown father's eyes; deep blue, with an exotic slant that engendered frequent comparisons to cats' eyes.

"Yes. I do understand," Elspeth said with calm assurance, "and I'm trying to convince Leofric how dangerous his present policy is."

Sorcha opened her mouth to push home her advantage, but Elspeth held up a slim hand to stem the flow of words.

"But that doesn't mean I'm willing to sacrifice my only child." She leaned forward, eyes wide, pleading and vulnerable. "Leave the Heart of Fire alone. It might end this war, but at what cost? Sorcha, you have no idea what that amulet will require as payment for its power."

A shiver ran down Sorcha's spine and she made a reflexive warding sign as she wiped her hands on the tattered hem of her potion-making apron.

———

THE QUIET WATERS of the isolated lagoon unnerved Sorcha. She knew a distant barrier reef protected the soft sand from the harsh pounding of the tide's ebb and flow, but she longed for the accustomed roar of surf—and home. The skirt of her simple shift and tunic tugged damply at her ankles as she prowled the water's edge. Her eyes darted warily from the aspen thickets that climbed the hill to the north, to the open path winding southward among the dunes covered in beach grass. She might have been the only living creature on the earth.

As much to reassure herself of her own existence as for something to do, she bent to stare into the unnaturally still water. A cool breeze tickled her nose with the scent of seaweed, and tugged a few wayward hairs from her tightly woven braid as she gazed at her reflection in the sparse predawn light.

Tension mounted as she waited for the perfect moment. Unable to remain still, she straightened, searching the sky's melting darkness. Only fading stars and dawn's awakening color met her restless gaze.

She must complete her quest, must recover the Heart of Fire. Humanity's existence depended on her success.

The warning, when it came, took the form of tingling skin as all the tiny hairs from neck to wrists rose in unison. The dragon soared into sight above the aspen covered hill, and Sorcha fought the instinct to run. Instead, she stood her ground and watched him land at the edge of the lagoon. Gods and goddesses, he was longer than the house she shared with her mother! He had to measure thirty feet from his deadly looking teeth to the triangular tail-tip that splashed the lagoon's still water. He folded leathery wings flat against glistening black scales, and turned his massive head, piercing her with a fiery gaze.

"Greetings, little wizard," he said, his rough voice conjuring windswept crags and the barren isolation of frozen wastes. "It seems the Heart of Fire requires more than one witness to its rebirth."

"Y-you know about the Heart of Fire?" she stammered. Her heart thundered, causing the pulse in her temple to throb and her ears to ring. She fought to calm herself, to retain the razor- edge of her intellect as she confronted her hereditary enemy. Human versus dragon; their skirmishes consumed her homeland, and now that King Leofric had initiated a more aggressive policy for his knights, she feared humanity's annihilation.

The dragon's huge maw twisted in what she hoped was a smile. "Of course, little wizard. Who do you think forged the medallion? Human wizards could not bend the stone's power to their will long enough to contain it in a prison of gold." He snorted at the thought and ejected a thin finger of flame. "Only a flight of dragons could create the Heart of Fire."

"If wizards are so weak," she said, standing tall, chin high in defiance, "why has it called *me* to bring it to light?" Understanding dawned, and she continued recklessly, ignoring the lingering smell of sulfur, "You are here to *witness* what I've been called to *do!*"

The dragon lowered his head and studied her closely. "Well spoken, little wizard." He paused, blinked, lower lid rising to cover his slit-pupiled, red eye. "What is your name?"

Sorcha swallowed hard and tried to ignore the fear that knotted her stomach. "I will not trade names with a dragon. Now stand aside. I have work to complete."

He jerked his head back and unfurled his wings. The brightening sky vanished behind a curtain of shadow.

"You dare insult me? Order me like a common dog?" His words thundered, rending the morning's soft peace. "I could devour you in a single bite!"

Though her legs wobbled and threatened to collapse, Sorcha stood her ground. She clenched her jaw to keep her teeth from chattering, and prayed she wouldn't squeak when she found her voice.

"But you won't," she said, amazed at the coolness of her tone. "The stone called me to find it. You need me. If you didn't, I'd already be dragon fodder."

The massive beast refolded his wings and the returning light warmed Sorcha's taut face. He shuffled his four huge clawed feet and settled himself on the lagoon's sandy beach.

"Very well," he said. "Call the stone. I'll not hinder your efforts." He laid his huge head upon his front feet, reminding Sorcha of her mother's sleek black tomcat.

She clung to her mother's image; Elspeth wouldn't let a dragon destroy her hard-earned competence. Sorcha's heart rate slowed and the pounding in her temple subsided as she focused on her mother's teaching. Concentrating on the runes she'd recently discovered and taken such pains to memorize, she turned to face a large rock that broke the water's surface a short distance from shore. She removed her leather boots, tossed them into the stiff beach grass, and stepped forward into the water, placing her bare feet in firm contact with the threshold between land and sea.

She lifted her hands in supplication and chanted the runes, giving voice to long dead syllables of an incantation ancient before her kingdom sprang to life. Behind her, she felt, as much as heard, the dragon's low rumble as he hummed a counterpoint to her invocation.

The runes of summoning wove the triune threshold (not sea—not land; not day—not night; not dragon—not human) into a knife with which to rend the fabric of time and space. The water surrounding the rock sizzled and vaporized as the granite glowed red, turned to lava and flowed away to congeal on the lagoon's floor. A blue-green sphere remained, hovered above the steaming mass for a moment, and then flew to Sorcha's outstretched hands.

A cool mist of salt water kissed her fingers before the sphere evaporated and the medallion fell into her palm. Gold filigree encircled a fire opal the size of her fist. The whole dangled from an extremely long, finely wrought, gold-link chain.

Elation overwhelmed her and she whooped with joy, squeezing the medallion to her chest. The Heart of Fire pulsed in her hand. She felt the raw power straining to be free, to escape the control of the sigil-worked gold filigree setting. She had done it! Despite her mother's dire warnings...

"Well done, little wizard," growled a whirlwind of sound. "Now give the stone to me."

Gods and goddesses, she'd forgotten the dragon! Sorcha whirled to face her adversary, agile mind searching for avenues of escape.

"The stone? Oh, well," she said, desperate to buy time. She'd think of something. She had to think of something! "I don't think so. I mean, I can't just hand over this much power." Her voice rose to an undignified pitch. "You could decimate my people!"

His laughter, a landslide of pebbles skittering down a slope of shale, jeered at her. "You don't have a choice. I needed you to bring the medallion out of hiding, but now that task is finished."

He rose above her, a mountain of muscle, black and menacing. In sheer defiance, Sorcha lifted the Heart of Fire and dropped its chain around her neck. The medallion thudded against her left thigh—and she knew she'd solved nothing. The dragon would slice her in two with one swipe of his claw and pull the opal from her quivering flesh.

"No!" The cry thundered across the lagoon, lashing Sorcha's mind with echoes of utter wretchedness. Her vision darkened and she wondered who had screamed; it had sounded more human than draconic.

Waves of pain rolled over her, tumbling her body against an unaccountably hard surface. She couldn't breathe, couldn't think, didn't understand what was happening. Air. Her lungs seared with a desperate need for air. She clawed her way to rational thought, forced her chest to expand, and gasped lungfuls of sweet, moist air into her tortured body.

She lay heaving and panting on the beach. The familiar scents of salt and seaweed, far from comforting her, inspired a violent urge to retch. She concentrated on quelling her unhappy stomach and attempted to lift her head. Pain swamped her mind and she desisted. Keeping her eyes tightly shut, she dug her claws into the damp sand, and willed her body to relax.

"Rest, little one. I am here." The dragon's voice, a soft rumble of distant thunder, comforted her. She wondered why, but before she could think of an answer, exhaustion conquered her anguished body and she slept.

TRANSFORMATION

*P*ain accompanied Sorcha's return to consciousness. Muscles she didn't know she possessed screamed their displeasure. Sand grated against the soft skin of cheek and neck, urging her to rise, but lethargy kept her grounded. The slightest movement caused a cascade of agony throughout her system. She'd never been beaten, but she couldn't imagine that a victim of mob violence would ache more than she did. She should open her eyes and orient herself in time and space, but the task felt too strenuous to attempt. She'd find a less active way to gather information.

Allowing her eyes to remain safely closed, Sorcha turned her attention from her body's tortured protests to the world surrounding her. She heard the roar of distant breakers and the soft susurrus of the breeze on the lagoon's sheltered beach. Yes, the lagoon, the beach. That explained the sand under her cheek. Above those soothing natural sounds, she heard an insistent thrumming, the deepened and magnified purring of a thousand cats. The dragon maintained his vigil.

Gods and goddesses, the dragon!

She focused her attention on her enemy's terrifying presence and discovered a strand of unknown power brushing the edge of her mind. Cat-like, it twisted and slipped away when she tried to grab it, but came willingly when she quieted her mind and ignored it. The connection it formed expanded her mind, altering its landscape forever.

Dragons whispered through this tunnel. She heard them—and understood. What's more, she felt their pain and embarrassment as her thoughts exploded into the conversational stream.

"Softly, little one," Caedyrn whispered. "Restrain yourself."

Sorcha pulled back, away from the vile, alien presence. She huddled on the sand, feeling violated beyond her ability to endure. Her body ached in a thousand places, and her mind... The sanctity of her mind had been breached. Her thoughts were no longer her own. An alien species, hostile and unknown, prowled in the depths. She couldn't live this way.

She *wouldn't* live this way!

With grim determination, Sorcha put aside her fear and confusion and searched her memory for an appropriate spell. An incantation bubbled to the surface of her mind and she tested its suitability for ousting the alien presence. She'd never attempted a working of this magnitude on herself before. Yes, she'd healed minor cuts and abrasions, but this problem required an application of magic she'd never studied. No matter; she had no choice.

"Perhaps you were right, Mother," she thought, examining each element of the spell one more time. "The price may have been too high, especially if I don't live to use the Heart of Fire." She sought her well of magic, always so comforting in its accessibility.

"No!" Caedyrn cried, distress tingeing his thoughts. "You must not use human magic against the flight." His thoughts echoed through every recess of her mind. "You'll destroy yourself and the Heart of Fire with you!"

She struggled to shield her thoughts from this unwelcome intruder, but a new terror sapped her remaining strength and caused her to ignore the dragon's presence—she couldn't touch her reserve of power! She could feel it, resting languidly just below the surface of her mind, but she couldn't reach it. Never before had her magic failed her, not since its awakening in early childhood. She retreated to a corner of her mind to search for nonexistent options.

The dragon called to her, quietly, soothingly. "You've nothing to fear," he crooned, directing her attention to the bright, pulsing strand that warmed the edges of her mind. "You're linked to the flight now. Push right *there* to broadcast to our species as a whole. Pull back *here* and touch an individual, or blank out all intrusions like *this*, for privacy and peaceful meditation."

When he finished, he nudged her toward the strand. "Try, little one," he cajoled. "I'll withdraw. Call me back."

Sorcha, bereft of her gift and unable to think of another option, gingerly checked the limits of her mind. The connection pulsed with eager vibration, but it awaited her touch. She exhaled a long groaning sigh, savored the privacy she'd always assumed inviolate, and remembered the overtone of concern she'd detected in Caedyrn's thoughts.

Could the dragon be worried about her? Ridiculous. If she'd detected concern, it had been for the Heart of Fire, not for her. Still, he offered assistance that she sorely needed.

"Caedyrn?"

The link responded to her tentative touch. His presence bloomed in her mind; calm, reassuring, protective.

"I am here, little one."

"How do I know your name?" Her mind-voice felt brittle, fragile as the sea-mist bubble that had surrounded the Heart of Fire.

"I sang it into the link as you slept. Your courage demanded my respect."

"Courage? I don't understand."

His mind-voice rang through her very soul. "Open your eyes, little one. Raise your head and accept your destiny."

Caedyrn's words bewildered and annoyed Sorcha. What did this dragon know about her, or her destiny? She tried to push her annoyance away; clear thinking was required. Everything had changed. Her adversary seemed to admire her and now offered support. She needed to throw off her lassitude, face the physical pain and discover what had transformed her enemy into a would- be guardian.

Consciously holding her pain in check, Sorcha opened her eyes. The world looked wrong. Details too distant for human sight snapped into focus, while items close by dissolved in red haze. She lifted her head and swung it around, searching for Caedyrn. Her first glimpse of him wavered in that bloody fog, then her head came into alignment and his features snapped into precise focus. She wanted to shake her head. Instead, she blinked several times in rapid succession. Halfway through pushing herself up—hands planted in the sand, head oriented on Caedyrn — she froze. Information assailed her: focused sight required her snout be pointed forward; her lower lid flew up when she blinked; claws flexed in the sand at the end of her arms...

She opened her maw and screamed at Caedyrn, "What am I?"

Her words rumbled in an avalanche whose overtones assaulted her sensitive ears. Worst of all, the act of speaking agitated a strange little lump on the roof of her mouth and flame scorched the air as her scream hiccupped into silence. Cautiously, she explored the bump with her tongue, amazed that the flame hadn't burned her mouth. A slightly acrid taste remained, but seemed to be the only after-effect.

She sniffed delicately, and detected a faint sulfur odor. Her human intellect catalogued the smell, but her dragon senses found it comforting rather than frightening.

A thought intruded on her inner confusion. "Speak to me here, little one. Human speech, as we produce it, pains our ears, and as you've seen, it can trigger fire if not carefully controlled." Caedyrn's words poured across her fear in soothing waves. "But to answer your question, you are a dragon. The Heart of Fire transformed you."

His words snapped her attention back to the larger issue. "That's impossible," she cried, forcing herself to use the link instead of her voice. "I can't be a dragon!"

"Rise, little one. Unfurl your wings. Feel the power at your command."

Sorcha stood. Four sturdy legs held her gargantuan body above the sun-warmed sand. She swiveled her head and felt the Heart of Fire thump against her breastbone. Pink ridges undulated down her back, ending an incredible distance away in an arrow-tip of tail. The length of beach she covered told her she had to be at least twenty-five feet long, snout to tail.

The pale pink color disturbed her. She turned back to Caedyrn and asked, "Am I ill? This color looks sickly."

His laughter bubbled through her thoughts. "You are no ordinary dragon. Your color reflects your essence; the pink of human flesh combined with the opal's milky fire." Sound thrummed from his body, and Sorcha realized it indicated happiness. "I find your color exotic — and attractive."

Confusion besieged her. She didn't have the experience necessary to decide if the innuendo implicit in his last comment was intentional. Dragons obviously didn't blush, or her strange color would have deepened to scarlet across her entire bulk. Lord, she was bigger than many of the huts in the village where she'd grown up! So much for feminine vanity, at least of the human variety. Were female dragons vain?

"I don't understand your question," came his immediate response. "If you mean, 'are they prideful,' then the answer is often yes. If you mean, 'are they concerned with their appearance,' then I'd have to say no. Dragon color cannot be changed, and dragon physique cannot run to fat. Our magical fires burn too brightly. If we do not control those fires, they consume our flesh."

His red-eyed gaze scrutinized Sorcha and the intensity of his study heightened her awareness of a growing ball of agony in her enormous mid-section. Pain flared and smoldered in an insistent pulse.

"Come," Caedyrn said. "Your transformation cost you dearly. You must eat."

He spread his vast wings, and with a single downward stroke, leapt to the sky. He didn't turn to see if she followed, but his voice rang through her mind. "Don't think about it, little one," he sang, "just follow me."

Sorcha stared after him, terror constricting her airways at the thought of being abandoned. Alone. Trapped in an alien body. What should she do? What *could* she do? She couldn't return to court, the king's knights would kill her on sight. She wouldn't be allowed to live long enough to explain, and if she somehow survived, she might roast someone when she tried to ask for her mother. Gods and goddesses! What if she flamed her mother? She had no other option. She had to stay with Caedyrn, at least until she learned to control this new body.

She focused on his lazily circling form, imagined herself catching hold of his triangular tail- tip, and threw herself into the sky. Unaccustomed muscles screamed as her wings yanked at the air currents. She gasped, closed her eyes in terror, and then forced them open to check her position. She flew! The muscle strain eased as she ceased to worry about what her wings were doing and focused on following Caedyrn.

Wind whipped past her face, and nictitating membranes rose, shielding the precious moisture of her eyes. She flew, high and fast. Soul-searing awe threatened to explode her heart. She flew! Elation swept through her system in a wave of exuberant delight.

A childish giggle rose from her human side, and she remembered a long-ago day when Elspeth had taken her to the cliffs near the sea to study the raptors that made their nests there.

"See how efficient they are?" Elspeth had said. "They use an economy of movement to reach the air currents and then they ride those streams, watching for prey."

As they'd observed the mighty birds, one had dived suddenly and disappeared from sight around the side of the hill.

Elspeth had nodded. "His prey won't have a chance. He's been resting in the arms of the wind, conserving his energy. You must learn the same restraint in your use of magic. Don't waste energy fighting your spells. Let the flow of power support you; rest in the assurance that it is in your blood, that it will be there when you need it."

With this memory to support her, Sorcha stretched her wingtips, caressed the heavens and raced to catch Caedyrn. "We had no idea, Mother," she whispered. "Flight is so much more than we could have possibly imagined." She laughed aloud, unconcerned about triggering a jet of flame here among the clouds. "But it is very much like magic!"

At that thought, a shadow marred her joy. She'd lost her magic — something had blocked her from her reservoir. The innate ability had defined her existence for so long that its loss eclipsed her recent transformation and first flight. Melancholy stole over her heart and her wing strokes slowed. She lost the steady rhythm and began to fall.

"No!" she screamed, and fought to pull herself back to an uplifting air current. Caedyrn turned to check on her, but she warned him off. "I can do this," she cried. The unaccustomed muscles in her back ached, and each stroke felt as if it would tear her wings from her body. She concentrated on forcing them to keep beating despite growing pain.

Caedyrn's voice intruded on her intense effort. "Stop thinking like a wizard. You humans worry too much. You think you control the world, when it would function just as well without you. Let go, little sister. Your body knows what to do." A silvery cascade of laughter highlighted his words.

Indignation replaced determination, and Sorcha glared at the rapidly disappearing dragon. So humans worried too much and tried to control everything, did they? She'd teach that arrogant lizard a thing or two about humanity!

A moment or two later, realization filtered through her irritation. Nothing hurt. She swooped across the sky, executed a tumbling aerial somersault, rose back to her previous level and hastened to catch up.

Exhilaration sizzled through her system as she pulled level with her mentor.

"I did it!"

She screamed the words into the cloudless sky, where the wind carried them away before the strange harmonics could abuse delicate dragon ears. On a whim of delight, she switched to their private link and crowed, "I am Sorcha and I can fly!"

She saw his smile and wondered how she could ever have found it threatening.

"Thank you, Sorcha," he said. "I am honored by your trust."

A wave of nausea swept her gut. She'd given her name to a dragon; she'd put her life in his keeping. A magic user could bind a being with their true name, and dragons were powerful magical beings. What if she'd made a mistake? Had she allowed the elation of flight to cloud her judgment?

But Caedyrn had trusted her with his name, how could she do less? She flicked her tongue against the lump on her palate and spat a gout of flame. Too late to worry now. The words couldn't be unsaid. She'd discover soon enough if Caedyrn was worthy of her trust.

No sooner had she soothed her qualms than her belly erupted in an onslaught of pain so intense she almost fell from the sky. Caedyrn arrowed beneath her and supported her until she found the rhythm of her strokes again.

"We must get you fed," he said. "Follow me and observe what I do."

Caedyrn streaked across the sky with Sorcha close behind. They swooped over thickly forested lands, where tree canopies made green waves of restless movement in the afternoon wind, and washed ashore on a far-reaching prairie. The golden undulation of the grassland fascinated Sorcha — until she saw their bovine prey.

The power of the longing, the white-hot need of dragon instinct shook Sorcha to her core. She tried to maintain distance, to watch and learn in a rational manner. She wanted the brutal immediacy of slaughter to horrify her. She wanted the lack of proper gratitude and respect to offend. But those human niceties failed to materialize. Her focus narrowed and her dragon side took over; she lost the thread of any thought not directly connected to the hunt.

Peripherally, she observed Caedyrn's technique, but was too focused on her chosen prey to emulate his precision. She arrowed toward her kill even as Caedyrn plucked his victim from the herd. The sheer physical pleasure that burst through her system as her claws ripped into the bull's hide strengthened her wing beats, and she shot back to the sky's embrace, dinner dangling from her front feet.

"Do we eat in the air?" she called as she rushed to Caedyrn's side.

His laughter roared aloud before he answered through their link. "No, little one, we will feast in a glen just past that outcropping rock."

The thrill of the hunt evaporated as they flew, so that when they landed Sorcha faced her kill with human sensibilities. She dropped the bull in the glade, and circled back to the sky. Caedyrn's massive black bulk filled the northern portion of the clearing among the trees. Two broken bodies of cattle lay in the center, their mangled limbs flung in impossible angles. Shame flooded Sorcha's soul, and she averted her eyes. Not only had she killed without proper ritual, without praise for the animal's life, she had stolen from the village folk. She shot higher still, seeking solace in the clean serenity of sun and wind.

But her wings grew heavy and she angled toward the glade with its alluring aroma of food. Twice more she circled the clearing, human mores fighting dragon hunger. At length she landed, stifled her ingrained scruples, and allowed new instincts to govern her actions. A cat-like pounce landed her on the broken body of the white-faced black bull. Powerful jaws ripped through tough hide and tore muscle mass from bone and sinew. Purposefully not thinking, she devoured the meat, slaked her thirst in blood, and felt the agony in her belly extinguish under the nourishing onslaught.

Hunger assuaged, she raised her head and watched Caedyrn demolish his meal. Efficient, like those long-ago raptors — not a sliver of flesh remained on the skeleton when he sat back and crunched a single bone he'd selected with care. Compared to Caedyrn's carefully piled stack of bones, the remains of her meal were a disaster. She looked away, preferring not to revisit the scene of carnage. The devastated carcass with its twisted mass of bone and sinew opened the way for too many disturbing thoughts.

Caedyrn seemed to sense the burgeoning attack of scruples, for he chose a bone from his own stash and pushed it toward her with his snout. "Relax. Chew a bone," he said. "It's good for your teeth, and it makes a nice finish to a feast."

Sorcha's heart skipped a beat as his flaming red gaze met her own. A new hunger sparked, one that had nothing to do with the needs of her stomach. Human dignity fought for control, but this new hunger spread like a wildfire, and with soul-scorching intensity. She stared at the virile black dragon and her over-full belly threatened to rebel. No, absolutely not. She refused to desire a dragon.

Masculine scent tempted her nostrils; she turned away, concentrated on the bone he'd given her to chew. Her tongue wrapped its length, and her loins clenched, provoking a wave of fire to race through her extremities. She closed her eyes, but images of the massive red-eyed demon haunted her.

She couldn't mate with her enemy. She wouldn't lust after a nonhuman male, no matter how attractive, how strong, how muscular, how...perfect he was.

Gods and goddesses, she didn't seem to care about his species, or her own! She burned to join with him, to absorb his thrusts in her own cushioning softness. Enemy — mentor — lover. Transformation, indeed! She needed divine assistance to resist this beautiful male.

A sudden, urgent need to fly seized her, and Sorcha withdrew from their link and threw herself into the cool evening sky.

As her strong strokes carried her higher, she felt an insistent barrage of thoughts hammering against the barrier she'd erected. A bellow ripped the evening calm as Caedyrn launched himself into the wind. The intimacy they'd established allowed her to hear the overtones of confused impatience in his roar. Human shame and draconic desire fought for dominance as he caught up with her frantic flight.

"Land!"

He didn't wait for agreement, but shot above her and used his mass to force her to ground. She plummeted the last few feet and absorbed the impact with quivering joints. Caedyrn managed to land close beside rather than on top of her, but the distinction didn't matter. Sorcha's lust ripped open the mind-link and lashed Caedyrn with the full force of her desire.

The black dragon turned his head and observed her through partially closed eyes. He stroked her back with the tip of his wing, a soothing hum issuing from his throat. After a quiet moment he crooned, "Breathe easy, little wizard. There will be time for that when you've adjusted to your new form. Dragon mating is strenuous and not for the faint of heart."

Shame won its battle and flooded her soul with disgust. She'd always detested spilling her emotions, and this had been a torrential flood. Elspeth would be appalled. Her mother had given up so much to bring her into the world. She'd refused to give her up, as wizards who had children were expected to do, had suffered ostracism and stigma to raise her in the craft. Elspeth had held her own desires in constant check to allow her daughter to reach for her destiny. She had never thrown herself at any male.

And yet, I exist, said a small voice from a deeply recessed corner of Sorcha's mind. *I exist, though no one has ever admitted to having known my father. Not even Mother.*

This unexpected thought quenched her shame like the bull's blood had slaked her fiery thirst. She couldn't undo the embarrassing emotional lapse, but her wounded pride would heal. She concentrated on drawing deep, cleansing breaths until the red haze retreated.

This new body's reaction startled her. As quickly as the lust had consumed her, it fled, leaving a bone-deep weariness in its wake. Her eyes closed, lower lids rising hesitantly.

Caedyrn's voice resonated through her mind with quiet conviction. "Rest, my Sorcha. When you awake, we'll journey to the ice aerie."

THE ICE AERIE

The ice aerie housed all the dragons that remained on earth. Sorcha cowered in Caedyrn's shadow as they wandered the maze of caves and rough-cut passageways. Dragons of every shape and size gazed at her with curious, bold-eyed stares. From hatchlings to grizzled elders, the inhabitants of the aerie pushed against the barrier of her mind.

"It is your choice, or course," Caedyrn said as one daring hatchling brushed a wingtip against the pearly pink scales of Sorcha's hide, "but their curiosity will abate faster if you open your mind and let them know your essence."

"They'll overrun my mind," she complained. "I won't be able to protect myself."

He nudged her neck with his snout. "Dragons know their boundaries. There are rules of etiquette for such things, rules ancient before the eldest among us was hatched. You will not be harmed."

They continued their shuffling pace toward the center of the community, and Sorcha felt a great horde of bodies crowd the passageway behind them. No going back, no going forward without a guide in this maze. The Heart of Fire felt cool where its chain banded her neck, reminding her of what she had already dared. Raising her head, Sorcha gathered her courage and opened the floodgates to the flight of dragons...

...and was swept away on the swell of their excited greeting.

"What an odd color," exclaimed one.

"Where did you find her?" asked another.

"I've never seen her like," growled an honored elder, "and I've watched every dragonet hatch."

Sorcha discovered that she could read the speaker's age, color, sex and character in their communications. She gasped under the weight of knowledge that crashed into her consciousness with each new comment. Just as she thought she must drown in detail, the torrent eddied away as the dragons withdrew to give her time to assimilate.

She listened from a quiet pool as the flight turned their questions on Caedyrn. He answered calmly, if nonspecifically, until a majestic voice stated what could not be denied.

"Her essence is human, Caedyrn," the awesome voice proclaimed. "Tell me what you have done."

"He didn't do it, Sire," Sorcha said. "I did."

Her dragon-sense informed her that the gigantic, red-brown male at the center of the aerie was the monarch, the rex of the flight. The oldest and wisest of dragon-kind.

The Rex turned his attention on her, and she felt like a butterfly pinned to one of her mother's displays; every nuance of her personality lay bared to his gaze. Then his focus broadened, softened, and he said, "Tell us of your adventures, little wizard."

She told the flight everything that had happened since she discovered the runes and followed them to the Heart of Fire. She faltered over her attraction to Caedyrn, but even that was confessed to the Rex and the community as a whole. The dragons listened with patience and consideration. Not a single hatchling interrupted with a stray thought.

"And what have you learned?" asked the Rex. "You alone, among the inhabitants of this earth, have seen the conflict from both sides. What have you learned?"

"Well, I've learned that things are not as simple as either side thinks they are," she said. "Dragons are certainly not the unreasoning monsters that human children are taught to fear, but neither are most humans callous butchers."

The aerie thrummed with agitated exhalations, but the Rex willed his dragons to silence. He nodded his great head at Sorcha. "Continue."

"If both species are to survive," she said, concentrating on the Rex, "then we must communicate. I realize, now, that human speech is a..." she hesitated, searching for the proper word, "challenge. I didn't understand these things before my transformation. Humans think dragons are unconcerned, unwilling to compromise. Some humans think you are little more than unintelligent beasts."

A barrage of indignant comments erupted from the flight at this affront to dragon wisdom, and Sorcha thanked the gods and goddesses that dragons couldn't blush as she picked out isolated grumblings about the many failings of the human race. She pulled back from the link, deciding she'd said enough for one day, and observed until the mutterings died away.

"Your thoughts are quiet, young wizard, yet I believe you have more to share."

A trace of a dare colored the Rex's tone. She cast Caedyrn a sidelong glance, looked around at the rest of the dragons crowded around them, and decided she might as well finish what she'd started.

"Well, there is the matter of humanity's flocks and herds."

Immediately, the angry comments began again, but this time the Rex quelled his flight. "Enough," he growled. "We will hear what the Heart of Fire has sent this human to tell us." Mention of the legendary stone, which now dangled from Sorcha's neck, silenced the dragons, and placed their focus firmly back on her. She thought of her mother's battle to convince King Leofric not to antagonize the dragons, and considered her phrasing carefully.

"Dragon depredation has brought many villages to the edge of starvation. Yet humanity's wanton destruction of habitat cost dragons their natural prey. These issues divide us, yet I'm sure they can be solved with time and diplomacy."

"And who will be our diplomats?" asked the Rex. "Who will go among the humans to plead our cause? How are we to communicate with creatures who think us monsters and whose speech is painful to our ears?"

The mind-link went silent, and so did the aerie. Not a thought sang through the flight's group mind; not a sound thrummed through the ice cave's hollow core.

Sorcha held her breath, and then expelled a fiery blip as she declared her conviction to the flight. "I will go, Sire. Perhaps the Heart of Fire transformed me for this purpose."

Again the flight clamored for the Rex's attention.

"You cannot trust her, Sire. She's a human at heart!"

"No. She knows nothing of our kind."

"And if I accompany her?" Caedyrn boomed into the link. "The Heart of Fire called me to witness her transformation. I will guard her when she returns to the humans. They will be hard pressed to recognize her now."

The Rex closed his eyes and breathed a benediction into the flight's mind. "Peace, my friends. We have no need to make such a weighty decision now. Sorcha has much to learn about being a dragon, and we must learn from her alien thoughts."

He turned his fiery eyes on Sorcha and spoke directly to her, though he eschewed a private link. "You are in no danger from us, little wizard. I guarantee your safety." He swept his head around to view his flight, "and we are in no danger from one untrained dragon, though she be a wizard in human form. It is my judgment that we live together in peace while Sorcha learns our ways. An envoy to the humans will wait until the flight is satisfied as to the character of the messengers."

With that, the tight focus of the flight collapsed and Sorcha endured chaos as a mob of exuberant voices exploded in her skull.

———

CAEDYRN HELPED Sorcha settle into her lair. He insisted she be allowed a private space among the un-bonded females.

"She's still adjusting to our communication strand. Remember, in her species each member is isolated within his or her own mind. She requires a little space."

The other young females thought this very odd, but agreed to give Sorcha the necessary privacy. Her first night in the lair, she regretted this decision.

Bereft of Caedyrn's companionship, she slipped into melancholy and mourned for Elspeth and her friends. What must they think? She'd never been gone so long before. After her argument with her mother, Sorcha had simply slipped away to retrieve the Heart of Fire without telling anyone where she'd gone. Elspeth must be out of her mind with worry.

Carefully, Sorcha tried to draw on the magic she'd practiced since childhood. She sought the familiar pool of strength, but couldn't push past the inexplicable barrier. In desperation, she touched the link with Caedyrn instead.

"What is it, my Sorcha," he said.

The feel of his voice in her mind soothed her agitation. "It's nothing," she replied. "I wanted to tell my mother I'm safe, but I can't seem to reach my magic."

"I asked the elders about that" he said. "It seems you cannot draw upon your human magic in this form, little wizard. I'm sorry. I wish humans could connect as we do; then you could ease your pain, and your mother's as well."

"Thank you, Caedyrn. Sleep well." Sorcha closed the link and withdrew to her private space, but it was long before she slept.

PREPARATION

*B*right and early the next morning, a prolonged susurrus of slithering near the entrance of her lair awakened Sorcha. She tried to rub the sleep from her eyes before she remembered her hands were now clawed feet. Everything felt wrong. She'd slept crooked, and unaccustomed muscles ached in strange places. Before settling in tonight, she'd make sure to ask someone to demonstrate a comfortable sleeping position.

How did a dragon begin her day? There'd be no tooth brushing without hands, no working tangles from non-existent long hair, no washing of face or selection of apparel. Bereft and bewildered, she realized that one aspect of her morning routine remained; dragon or human, she still needed to relieve herself first thing in the morning.

Feeling about as graceful as a horse on ice, Sorcha clambered out of her nest and made her way to her lair's opening. An unbonded female approached, and Sorcha cautiously touched her link.

"Greetings," she said cautiously. "Can you help me?"

The emerald green female gazed at her with open curiosity. "I'll try. What do you need?" Sorcha realized she had no idea what dragons would call that particular bodily function, so she simply allowed her need to color her thought.

"Oh," came the amused response, "of course. Follow me, and the place you're looking for is the urinal, though of course we use it for both functions."

"Thank you," Sorcha said, joining the young green in the corridor and following her lead.

"I'm Sorcha, and you are..."

"Morna, and you don't need to introduce yourself. Everyone knows who you are. Here's the urinal. If you like, I'll wait and show you the way to the great gallery."

"Thank you, Morna," she said, blessing the young dragon for neatly forestalling the need to make a solitary entrance to the great gallery. "I'd appreciate that."

When Sorcha rejoined Morna in the passageway, she found a cluster of excited females waiting for her.

"These are my lair mates," Morna explained. "They wanted to meet the human dragon. This is Oona. That's Nuala, Keeva, and Sabia."

As she said their names, Morna pointed her snout first at a blue, then an orange, a mauve, and finally an aqua dragon. Sorcha gazed at each young female in turn and sorted through the enormous amount of information that had assaulted her mind the evening before.

"Ah," she said. "I think I understand; tell me if I'm right. You are lair mates because you are all unbonded and you all learned to fly at about the same time."

Keeva nodded and the group began to meander toward the center of the aerie. "Very good! Yes, we all left hatchling status at about the same time, so we've trained together with the elders ever since."

"And the threshold between hatchling and dragonet is flight, correct?"

"Yes," said Nuala, her orange skin glowing against the white of the ice passage, "but we're not dragonets any longer."

Sorcha's mind whirled with the unfamiliar distinctions. Her confusion must have shown, because Oona picked up the thread of conversation.

"It's really very simple," the young blue said. "Hatchlings live with and are tended by their parents until they learn to fly, usually around five years of age. Once they can fly, they're known as dragonets and they train with the elders in maturation groups."

That's right," interrupted Sabia. "It doesn't matter how old they are. What matters is when they learned to fly. So all the first year dragonets train together, and so on."

"Yes," agreed Morna, taking the lead as the group crossed an intersecting passage, "we've been together since we learned to fly, along with the males. Of course, they don't stay in our lair!"

Bubbles of feminine humor peeled through Sorcha's brain, and she realized that these youngsters weren't so different from human maidens.

"So you've been lair mates since you learned to fly?" she asked.

"Oh, no!" said several voices at once.

"Dragonets train with the elders, but they still live with their parents." The sky blue scales around her eye ridges crinkled good-naturedly as Oona explained. "We don't move into unbonded lairs until we reach sexual maturity."

"Fortunately, we all changed station at about the same time," said Keeva. "I know I'd've felt just awful if I'd been left behind."

"That happens, sometimes," Nuala added, a dark overtone coloring her words. "The whole group will get to move to an unbonded lair except for one poor straggler!" She shuddered as if unable to contemplate a worse fate.

"And you stay together in the lair until you bond with a male," Sorcha said, cataloging the information for future reference.

"Right," chorused her new friends.

"I certainly hope the elders don't make you join a group of dragonets," Keeva blurted. The others immediately shushed her, but she turned wide eyes on her friends and said, "But that would be so mortifying!"

Morna nudged Sorcha to one side as Sabia and Nuala pushed Keeva into the aerie's great gallery. "Don't mind Keeva," Morna said. "Tact isn't her best aspect. I'm sure the elders will treat you with respect, Sorcha. It's not your fault you haven't been properly trained." With that pronouncement, she led Sorcha into the great gallery.

Dragons of all colors and sizes milled through the room. At first their movement appeared random, but gradually Sorcha detected patterns. Groups formed before her eyes and moved purposefully away. The young females she'd accompanied to the hall dispersed and new groups of small dragons formed around them. She couldn't tell if the youngsters were dragonets or hatchlings, but decided it didn't matter.

The groups swelled and eddied around a core that seemed as solid as the cliffs near her home. The sea of dragons parted and Sorcha saw that the cliff was composed of the red-brown Rex, Caedyrn's ebony black, and a deep purple male. She searched her memory and found his name— Lorcan, bond-mate to Etna, and an honored elder. As she stood pressed against the soothing comfort of the ice wall, Caedyrn turned his red-eyed gaze upon her and her pulse gave a quick staccato of delight.

"Welcome, Sorcha," he said. "Come and join us. We are discussing your education."

She relaxed, sure of Caedyrn's welcome, and approached the three males.

"Sire," she said, inclining her head to the Rex. "Lorcan, Caedyrn, I wish you good morning."

"Well done," said the Rex. "Caedyrn and I had a wager on whether or not you'd know Lorcan's name." His red eyes twinkled with humor. "Caedyrn won."

"I'm pleased to meet you, Sorcha," said Lorcan. "The Rex has given me the pleasant duty of explaining dragon history and lore to you."

She imagined herself sitting in a group of diminutive dragons, and Lorcan laughed aloud.

"No, little wizard," he said. "You are unique and you will be treated so. We will hold our lessons privately. My bond-mate, Etna, will train you in the specifics of female etiquette, and Caedyrn will see that you continue to increase your flight skills."

"And I," said the Rex, "will discuss politics and the governance of dragons with you."

"Oh, my," Sorcha said. "I am honored, Sire. I never expected that you would take an interest in my training."

His eye-ridge lifted in surprise. "Did you not? When you are the most unusual dragon ever to tread this ice? I will see to it that you understand our species before you attempt to explain us to your human relatives." He closed his eyes in dismissal. "Be gone, all of you. I must consider my first hearing of the day."

Lorcan guided Sorcha away from the Rex with Caedyrn close behind. As they passed, Sorcha heard a disembodied voice comment, "Her color's not so bad. I wouldn't mind having a go when she makes her first flight."

Before she could question what the speaker referred to, Caedyrn whipped around to stare down a small group of unbonded males. A charcoal male gazed at her appraisingly, while a scarlet male scooted to one side. The malachite stood his ground, but lowered his eyes in the wake of Caedyrn's reproachful glare.

"Keep your link controlled in this public space," he snarled. "Another uncouth comment like that, and you'll be flying 'til your wings drop off."

The younger males dropped their heads in submission, but Sorcha caught another sly glance, this time from the malachite male. She didn't understand their reference to her first flight — after all, she had flown to get to the aerie — but knew from Caedyrn's tautly controlled anger that she'd been insulted, and probably in a very crude manner.

"Get going," Caedyrn ordered, "before I find your elder and lodge a formal complaint." The trio disappeared down a nearby passageway.

"What was that all about?" she asked, as Caedyrn rejoined them.

"Do not concern yourself, my dear," said Lorcan. "The young are often thoughtless. Let us continue to my lair. Etna awaits."

Sorcha's days passed in flurries of dragon lore and flight, but her solitary nights dragged.

Often she wished she could move in with Morna and her friends, but when daylight arrived and she found herself besieged by their bright, but constant chatter, she longed for solitude. Her two natures warred. Alone, she longed for the comfort of dragon community. Swarmed by scaly bodies and alien thinking, she longed for hands and feet and sanctity of mind.

On one such restless night, Sorcha climbed to the heights where dragons sunned during the day. She curled into the tightest ball she could manage and gazed at the distant moon. That same moon watched over her mother's home as she slept, secure in the king's stronghold.

"I'm fine, Mother," she said aloud, ignoring the painful overtones for the sake of hearing a spoken word. "Really, I am." The words drifted away on the still night air, and she knew that if she still possessed human eyes, she'd be crying. She switched to her mind-voice, though she held it strictly confined. "The Heart of Fire's price was high, but not unbearable. I'm still me, still Sorcha at my core."

The loss of her magic pained her more than the loss of hands or hair or body, but there were compensations. Dragon magic functioned very differently, just as dragon logic often defied her understanding, but it was magic nonetheless, and its presence comforted her. And there was Caedyrn. The huge black remained her stalwart champion. Whether he was with her physically or not, she relied on the knowledge that the comfort of his mind-voice was only a thought away.

The moon, a slender curve of light, rose to its apex and began to decline before Sorcha stirred from her solitary vigil on the heights. She made her way back to her lair in a trance of melancholy sleepiness. Passing the great gallery, she came within range of a heated discussion. Caedyrn and the Rex, not expecting any listeners at this dark hour, raged at each other without bothering to keep their link private.

"You must back away from this female, Caedyrn," said the Rex, his words rife with command. "A rex cannot bond. You have waited this long. Let this infatuation pass."

"I haven't bonded, not out of desire to be rex," came Caedyrn's reply, "but because no female has tempted me. You have no right to deny me a bond-mate if I choose to seek one."

Caedyrn wanted to bond? The thought cut Sorcha's heart, and she stumbled back the way she'd come, pulling her thoughts away from the vibrant thread of communication. Blindly, she wandered the corridors until fate brought her back to her own empty nest. If she lost Caedyrn, if he bonded with a female... She didn't know if she could bear the loneliness. Dry eyed and silent, her heart cried her to sleep.

The next morning, she watched the unbonded females with predatory interest. Which had caught his eye? The golden beauty two maturation groups above Morna? Perhaps the sleek, doe- eyed green that chatted with Etna. No, more likely the terra cotta lovely who instructed Sabia in healing. Yes, that one had a regal bearing that would attract a virile male like Caedyrn.

Sorcha's soul shriveled as she imagined Caedyrn's glistening black scales curled around her red-brown glow in the privacy of a bonded pair's nest.

"You're very intent, this morning." Caedyrn's voice sounded in her mind as his snout nudged her shoulder. "Are you thinking of joining Sabia for healing lessons?"

Gods and goddesses! She'd been so lost in murderous thoughts she hadn't heard him coming. Thankfully, her thoughts had been firmly lodged in the most private portion of her mind.

"No," she said truthfully, "though I practiced healing as a wizard." Without giving herself time to think about it, she plunged into the subject that obsessed her thoughts. "No one has explained the bonding process to me," she said bluntly. "How do dragons choose their mates?"

He looked startled, even took a step backward before he stopped himself. "Well, when a couple is attracted, they spend time together, get to know each other, and then, well, they bond." He turned and headed for the passage that led to the flight cliff. "Aren't you supposed to be with Lorcan? My flight group should be assembled by now."

"That was a non-answer," she said, following him out of the great gallery. "How do dragons bond?"

He picked up his pace and pulled ahead of her. "I'm late, Sorcha. My students are expecting me. Besides," he cast a glance over his shoulder as he reached a turn in the corridor, "that is a question for Etna, not me." He disappeared around the bend and his words faded as well.

"Coward," she thought after him.

Later, Etna refused to expand on Caedyrn's answer, so Sorcha sought out a sure source of information, if not knowledge.

"May I join you?" she asked as she peered into the entrance of Morna's lair.

"Of course," said Morna.

"Definitely," chorused Oona, Nuala and Sabia.

"We thought you'd never ask," said Keeva.

She stepped inside the round room carved long ago by dragon magic. The nests of the young females lined the walls, and were satisfyingly scrunchy masses of limbs, river rocks and the occasional precious stone. The center of the chamber, where the females gathered to groom and chat, was bare, polished ice.

Keeva and Sabia reclined on their nests while Oona and Morna burnished Nuala's scales with alternating puffs of steam and fingers of fire. Nuala basked in the attention.

"My mentors have been avoiding my questions today," Sorcha said. "I wondered if you could answer them for me."

The three in the center froze, while the two on their nests quickly sat up.

Morna recovered first. "You asked a question they wouldn't answer?"

Sorcha nodded and the others encouraged her into the center of the room.

"Ooooo," said Keeva. "It must have been really bad! Elders are bound to answer our questions."

Oona nudged Keeva aside. "Don't mind her," she said, her voice dripping smug superiority. "Keeva just loves juicy gossip."

"As if you don't," cried Keeva.

Sabia pushed between the snorting blue and mauve. "Peace, friends. Let's hear the question!"

"Yes," said Nuala, the usually shy dragon's eyes shone with excitement. "What did you ask?"

"Well, I didn't think it was forbidden or anything," said Sorcha, beginning to worry that she might offend the young females. "I just asked how dragons bond. Um, I mean, how you choose your bond-mate. Though, I must admit, I'm curious about the actual mating, too."

"And they wouldn't tell you?" Morna looked appalled. "There's nothing secret or offensive about that."

Sorcha looked around the circle and saw multicolored expressions droop with disappointment. All but one, Oona looked thoughtful.

"What is it, Oona?" she asked.

"Well, it's probably nothing, but..." She stopped and her lair mates butted her with noses and triangular tails. "Okay. I heard the Rex telling Lorcan and Etna that Sorcha isn't to be allowed to rise."

"No!"

"You must have misunderstood."

"They wouldn't do that."

Oona nodded wisely. "It's because she's human," she said, giving Sorcha an apologetic glance. "The Rex doesn't want her joining the flight, because he isn't sure what she is."

A cold lump formed in the pit of Sorcha's stomach. If she couldn't be a human, and the dragons didn't want her, what would she do? She pushed the thought away and concentrated on a more tangible question.

"What do you mean, I'm not to be allowed to rise? Does he mean politically?"

Five pairs of eyes stared at her blankly. Finally Morna blinked. "Politically?" she asked.

Sabia laughed. "No, Sorcha. He means he doesn't want you to mate. Once a year, all the eligible females rise for their mating flight. Those of us who fly high enough have the opportunity to bond during that flight."

Varied pieces of information suddenly formed a recognizable picture. Caedyrn saying her odd color was exotic and attractive — his angry reaction to the young males' comments — the Rex arguing with him about bonding. Realization hit Sorcha like a breaker pounding the beach. If she'd still had a human body, the psychic blow might have knocked her off her feet. Caedyrn and the Rex had been arguing about her. Caedyrn wanted to mate with her, a human wizard turned to dragon by a magical talisman. Joy filled her soul and tingled down to her toes and tail. Maybe spending the rest of her life as a dragon wouldn't be so bad after all. If only she could bond with Caedyrn...

"Sorcha? Are you alright?" Sabia sounded worried, and when Sorcha glanced up, she found all five of the young females watching her closely.

She shook herself, a massive, body-wide shiver, and said, "Yes, I'm fine. It's okay. The Rex probably thinks I'm too inexperienced for such things. And he's right. I've still got so much to learn about being a dragon."

This statement eased the tension in the room. The lair-mates burst into excited speculation about which males might make good bond-mates, and Sorcha relaxed to listen and think.

A mating flight. Suddenly the comments she'd overheard from the group of males had meaning. Her first flight. They hadn't meant the first time she flew; they'd meant the first time she would participate in the mating ritual. Her mind whirled with the implications. She had suitors. Charcoal Goban, scarlet Toal and malachite Heber had been making seemingly good- natured comments to her about practicing her flying and improving her wind ever since that first encounter. Her human side groaned as she remembered the many times she'd answered that she loved to fly! Gods and goddesses, she'd been making sexually suggestive remarks without even knowing it. Those young males probably thought she was interested in them.

Another question lit her mind, and Sorcha blurted out, "Do dragons ever engage in sex without bonding?"

All chatter stopped. The group's attention centered on Sorcha and silence reigned.

At last, Morna answered. "Humans must be very strange creatures," she said. "We females rise once a year, and if we mate and bear a clutch, we don't feel the urge to rise again until the hatchlings have graduated to dragonets. Why would we squander such a precious moment on males unworthy of forming a lifelong bond?"

"No, Sorcha," Sabia said quietly. "As young unbondeds, we participate in the flight and try to fly high enough to qualify for a bond-mate. But there's more to it than flying. Once we're mature enough to reach mating height, we've already chosen the males we'll allow to catch us."

"It's a race," said Oona, "and it's exhilarating, but it's not random."

"Yeah," said Keeva, her eyes glowing with excitement, "and if an unbonded male gets excited and tries to catch a female who hasn't consented, she's allowed to attack him!"

"Only if her rightful male doesn't scorch him first," added Nuala, thumping her tail in emphasis.

"So, there aren't ever any bonding mistakes? No rogue males ravish unwilling females? No female says 'yes' to one male and then changes her mind mid-flight and allows another to catch her?"

The atmosphere in the room grew heavy, and the lair mates shifted positions uneasily. "Well, yes," said Morna. "We've heard whispers of such things."

"But they're not common," said Sabia.

"And dragons that commit such crimes are banished from the flight," said Oona with a prim little sniff. "We don't tolerate such misbehavior."

"Of course," added Nuala, "a female is free to change her mind until she bonds, as are the males."

"But I've never heard of anyone changing their choice during the mating flight," said Morna.

"Like Sabia said, there's more to it than the excitement of the moment."

"I'm sorry," Sorcha said, wishing to dispel the serious mood. "I hope I didn't offend."

"Don't worry," Sabia said. "You can't learn if you don't ask questions. I can't believe the elders wouldn't discuss these things with you."

"Yeah!"

"Tsk."

"Completely irresponsible."

And the group slid into a rousing chat about how they'd be more responsive to the needs of the young when they became elders. In the midst of covering laughter and unflattering comments about their teachers, Sorcha made her way to the corridor. She needed peace and quiet to sort through the evening's information.

"Good night, Sorcha." Morna's voice sounded quietly in her mind. "Come and join us anytime."

She smiled to herself and continued toward her solitary lair. "Good night, ladies."

THE BONDING

*S*orcha loved the crisp cleanliness of the ice aerie on bright summer mornings. The brilliant sun sparkled against bone-white ice and thrilled her soul with diamonds of reflected light. The sky, which welcomed her eager flight, shone a clear, cold blue not possible in the softer, hazier atmosphere of her human homelands. The aerie itself, formed by dragon magic from an ancient glacier, soothed her with its cold, slick surfaces; nothing to catch on scale or claw, only the glassy smooth luxury of ice. And the cold! What a blissful antidote to the fiery magic that raged within.

But magic wasn't the only fire that burned dragonkind. Not long after Morna and her friends instructed Sorcha in the ways of bonding, she became aware of an increasingly intense interest in the males of the aerie. Suddenly, their presence overwhelmed her whenever she entered the great gallery. Not only could she distinguish each by color and size, but heightened senses categorized each eligible male by smell, and the very sound of their claws and scales upon the icy corridors.

Four males loomed in Sorcha's imagination. Caedyrn, of course— black, massive, a born leader. He smelled of sulfur, salt, and masculine virility. And the sound of his scales sliding toward her as he approached for a training flight nearly drove her mad with fiery longing. But Caedyrn had company in her increasingly frenzied dreams. Goban, whose charcoal scales shone almost as darkly as Caedyrn's, often drew her gaze as he passed through the great gallery. And her conversations with malachite Heber had taken a more intimate tone of late. Finally, there was Toal; fun-loving, unpretentious, and utterly charming Toal. The scarlet male, with his comforting smell of burning leaves and rich, raw earth, came closest to dislodging Caedyrn from her thoughts. Close, but never quite close enough. Even when she flirted outrageously with one of the other males, Caedyrn dominated her thoughts.

She'd noticed that he'd become more aloof, the more at ease she'd become with the rest of the flight. Perhaps she'd flown to the wrong conclusion. Perhaps he didn't want to bond with her after all. He certainly didn't lavish her with attention the way her other three suitors did.

Toal had introduced her to the ice slide. Gods and goddesses! What fun she'd had sliding down that incredibly steep slope only to be launched into heart-pounding flight at the end. They'd snuck away from training and spent an exhilarating afternoon playing just last week.

She relished the philosophical discussions she had with Heber — the malachite's intelligence rivaled the deepest human thinker she'd ever met. And, oh my, could his agile mind find its way around an innuendo. When she failed to react to some of his more subtle verbal wooing, he always chuckled and explained where the barb lay hidden in his thoughts. He was a dragon who could keep her guessing for a lifetime.

Goban. She sighed, thinking of powerful Goban. The charcoal held none of Heber's subtlety, and lacked Toal's sense of fun, but exuded a powerful attraction with his dark strength. Yum.

Sorcha closed her eyes and pretended she couldn't smell and hear the various males in her vicinity. Her human side resented this heightened awareness. She'd managed to remain free of human sexual entanglements her entire life. Why should this dragon body be able to derail her mental control in such a short period of time? She shook her head and decided she needed space and privacy to meditate, to rid herself of unwanted desire.

But before she could seek solitude, her senses alerted her to Caedyrn's approach. Against her will, she breathed in a deep, lung-expanding gulp of his delicious scent. Tingles of delight raced through her system and she exhaled a sensuous sigh. She might not be his choice for bond-mate, but she knew he would always be hers. The other three males paled to mere dalliance beside her Caedyrn.

"Are you well, Sorcha?" he asked when he reached her side. "You look disoriented."

"I'm fine," she said, relishing his nearness. "Do we have a lesson scheduled this morning?"

"No, but I thought if you were free, we might chat while we sun on the ridge."

Her blood bubbled with delight and she fought an urge to rub her head against his neck. "I'd like that."

Caedyrn led the way, while Sorcha savored the sound of his progress as well as the sight of his sleekly folded wings and heavily muscled hips and tail. He'd told her once that dragon mating was strenuous exercise; she wondered exactly how it occurred. When the time came, would he cover her like a stallion on a mare? Her tail twitched to one side and her desire burned hotter still. Gods and goddesses, she'd melt the glacier if she followed that train of thought!

Etna interrupted Sorcha's ruminations with an impatient call. "Where are you, Sorcha?"

"I'm on my way to the heights with Caedyrn," she said, forcing her mind into ordered calmness. "Did I forget a lesson?"

"No, nothing like that." The elder female's mind-voice sounded agitated. "Everything is fine, but keep me apprised of your location today. We may need to go on an errand for the Rex."

"Certainly, Etna."

Sorcha glanced at Caedyrn as they settled into well-worn wallows on the sunny ridge and switched to their private link. "That was odd. Etna said she and I might need to do an errand for the Rex," she told him, stretching her wings for maximum exposure to the sun's blissful heat. Ah, this was heaven. Fire and ice—glacial cold on one side, sun-baked warmth on the other — the opposing sensations almost drove Caedyrn's presence from her mind. Almost.

"An errand for the Rex?" he said. "Hmmm."

They sunned in silence for a time before Sorcha's curiosity forced a question. "Did you have something you wanted to discuss?"

He folded one wing and rolled to one side to face her. "Yes. You seem to be making a place for yourself in the flight. Are you content?"

"Content? Why, yes. I suppose so. Why do you ask?"

He studied her for a moment before responding. "I suppose I'm really asking if you're content to remain a dragon? Do you wish to return to human form?"

Sorcha's heart thumped painfully and her breath came in ragged gasps. "Are you offering me a choice?" she asked. "Do you know how to reverse the transformation?"

He blinked rapidly and bumped her neck with his snout. "No," he whispered. "I'm sorry. I didn't mean to imply... I'm doing this badly."

Sorcha held her silence and allowed her heart to resume its normal pace. How strange. Relief, not disappointment, flooded her soul.

Relief that she wouldn't be required to choose between Caedyrn and her real life.

"You seem to enjoy spending time with Toal and Heber," Caedyrn said, pulling her thoughts back to their conversation.

"Yes, they're very entertaining."

"Do you prefer one over the other?"

She turned her head and gazed directly into his red eyes. Something glittered in their depths that she couldn't quite name. "These aren't idle questions. What are you getting at?"

He held her gaze without blinking. "I'm asking if you're prepared to bond with one of the males you've been spending time with?"

Her heartbeat quickened and she sat up, preparing herself for flight. "I don't see that that's any of your business."

He rose as well and placed himself between Sorcha and the ledge, blocking easy escape. "It is my business," he said, his words a dangerous rumble in the depths of her mind. "Dragons mate for life. An understanding must be reached before the female rises."

"What? I don't..."

"Sorcha!" Etna's voice rang through several layers of Sorcha's awareness. Caedyrn winced as he caught the echoes of her call.

Sorcha grimaced at Caedyrn and answered, "Yes?"

"Come to me now, Sorcha. I am in my lair."

"But I'm talking to..."

"Now, Sorcha!" Agitation tinged the elder female's command.

"Yes, honored one."

Sorcha sighed and moved toward the entrance that led to the warren of corridors. "I'm sorry, Caedyrn. We'll finish this later."

"Yes," he growled. "We will."

As Sorcha snaked through the seemingly endless passageways from the heights to Etna's lair, she noted an odd sensation in the pit of her stomach. At first she thought she was hungry, but that didn't make sense. She and Morna and the others had flown down the mountain and gorged on a herd of mountain goats just last week. Perhaps it was nerves. Maybe the possibility of an errand for the Rex had her on edge.

By the time she reached the great gallery, the sensation had moved from annoying to urgent.

"Where are you, Sorcha?" Even Etna sounded upset.

"I'm just passing the great gallery," Sorcha said.

"Hurry, child. Don't stop to talk. Don't linger. You must come quickly."

Etna's words added another layer to the urgency beating at Sorcha's heart, but the two pulled in opposite directions. Etna demanded that Sorcha go deeper into the caverns of ice, while the persistent need in her belly urged her toward the landing field.

"Oh, Sorcha! It's time! Are you coming?" Morna asked, excitement glittering in her eyes. Oona and Nuala looked at her over their shoulders as they moved toward the landing field. "What are you waiting for?" Oona called. "It's time!"

"Time for what?"

The three young females gave her nearly identical looks of exasperation. "It's time to rise," said Morna. "Can't you feel the pull?"

"Yes, but Etna has called me to her lair."

All three lair mates stopped and exchanged uneasy glances. Oona broke the silence. "Remember what I told you? The Rex doesn't want you to rise."

"It's your choice, Sorcha," said Morna. "Obey Etna and the Rex, or come with us and see if you can rise to mating height."

Anger at Etna boiled up, adding a further level of discomfort. Sorcha turned and galloped to join her friends. "What if I can't fly high enough?"

Nuala laughed. "Don't worry," she said. "This is our third rising. None of us has made it to the required height yet. Just think of it as a practice run."

The painful urgency expanded into a bubble of joy as Sorcha reached the field. All around her, females of every egg-bearing age crowded the ground. She glanced up and her heart leapt to her throat. Every eligible male, as well as every bonded male whose mate stood on the field, perched on the rim heights. Her eyes sought and found Caedyrn as the desire to rise peaked — and she launched herself into the air.

Wind flowed across her body and the sun dazzled her vision. Her nerves, afire with desire, fed on each individual, delicious sensation. She forgot about the horde of females surrounding her as she pushed for greater and greater height. At some remote level, she heard Goban, Toal, and Heber call to her as she arrowed into a bank of clouds, but she couldn't be bothered with them. Not when her blood fizzed with the need to rise as high as dragon wings could lift her.

At last her mind cleared and she saw that this portion of sky was hers alone. She screamed her triumph to the wind and soared higher still. In the back of her mind, three males urged her on, while throwing veiled insults at each other. When the fourth voice entered the fray, her wingstrokes faltered. Caedyrn!

"Leave her!" he roared. "She has not consented; she doesn't understand."

"I do understand," she screamed. "I am not a child!"

Caedyrn's attention locked on their intimate link. "You consent?" he said, each word clipped and tense. He widened the link to include the other males. "Who do you choose?"

The fire in her blood overruled human reason. "If you can catch me, you'll find out!"

All four males roared and a frenzy of intoxication shot her higher still. One by one, Toal, then Heber, and finally Goban dropped away, but Caedyrn pursued her into thin, rarified air.

"Do you accept me?" he screamed. "Will you bond with me for eternity?"

"Yes! Gladly, but you haven't caught me yet!" Inexpressible joy filled her. She feared she would burst into a glorious inferno if Caedyrn didn't catch her and carry her to the ice.

She glanced over her shoulder and saw Caedyrn racing toward her. He opened his mouth, and though the wind whipped past her ears in a deafening rush, she heard him roar. The ferocity of that sound goaded her higher and faster even as it filled her with an ecstatic, spine-tingling anticipation. She turned her attention skyward and sought to lead her would-be bond-mate beyond the earth's embrace.

Just as she thought her heart must burst from exhilaration and exertion, he overtook her. The slipstream of wind rushing over his wings threatened to flip her. She corrected for the new conditions and strove to get above him. He countered, forcing her beneath his great wings. She glanced up, struggling to draw sufficient oxygen from the thinning air, and faltered. His eyes burned with unrestrained passion, and the rawness of his lust robbed her of the will to resist.

She opened her mind to him and the shock of recognition made it hard to remember to keep flying. He loved her! How could she have ever doubted his interest and desire? She remembered the moment she sang her name to him, remembered the fear she'd felt, and knew that even then it had been groundless. He existed to love her. How had she not known? She laughed as he answered her question.

"Human reason clouded your dragon instinct," he said, his red eyes burning into her soul. "I've been waiting for this moment since I witnessed your transformation. You are my destiny, Sorcha, as I am yours."

He nudged her neck with his muzzle and that same, wonderful dragon instinct took control. She flipped over, grabbed his flanks with her talons and folded her wings.

He screamed his triumph, gripped her firmly in his claws, wrapped his wings around her and penetrated her trembling flesh as they tumbled through the atmosphere.

The purely human portion of Sorcha's mind whimpered in terror, but her dragon instinct laughed at the foolish fears and exalted in the exquisite sensations that ripped through her body.

Caedyrn pumped his seed into her and she responded by pulling him closer, seeking to merge — body, mind, and soul.

Still hurtling toward the earth, Caedyrn wrenched his wings away from her and began to beat the wind. Dazed, Sorcha dangled upside down beneath him and watched as his powerful wing muscles slowed their plummeting descent, to deposit her gently on a remote section of the aerie's glacial ice.

He released her and her own grip fell slack. Landing beside her, he collapsed in an untidy heap.

"I warned you," he said, his voice a lazy river, soothing the remnants of terror from her mind. "Dragon mating is strenuous exercise."

She acknowledged his self-satisfied expression with a possessive nudge of her snout, whispered, "I am Sorcha, and I am your bond-mate," and fell into blissful sleep.

When she woke, Caedyrn insisted that they fly south to feed. "You will require full strength when we face the Rex."

"It's true, then," she said. "He didn't want me to rise. Have we...have *I* done something wrong?"

Caedyrn nudged her toward the edge and took off, his answer floating toward her on the updraft. "No, little wizard. You did everything perfectly!"

Sorcha leapt into the air and raced to catch him. His smug laughter tantalized and drew her forward. She opened their mind-link and called to him, "Caedyrn, answer me. Why must we face the Rex?"

She watched as he circled back to her, stroked her side with one delicate wingtip and then arrowed toward the green slopes of the mountain's lower shoulder.

"Because the flight must accept our bond — and the Rex will not be happy, for more reasons than you know."

———

True to his word, Caedyrn sought out the Rex as soon as they returned from their hunt.

Sorcha discovered a strange lassitude creeping into her limbs as she settled again on the glacial ice. She desired nothing more than to rest on the aerie's cool floor. Her human mind fought to decipher the alien clues her body supplied. Yes, her belly was full, but she didn't remember feeling this soul-deep laziness after her other kills. Besides, she felt swollen, engorged beyond the limits of her meal.

"Caedyrn!" the Rex's roar pulled Sorcha's thoughts from her uncomfortable body to the present situation. "What have you done?"

"We have mated, Sire," Caedyrn replied, his mind-voice triumphant. "We come to be bonded in the presence of the flight, as is our custom."

Anger boiled beneath the surface of the Rex's reply. "She doesn't understand," he said, dark emotion leaking through his tight control. "More than that, her essence remains human. We don't know what will come of this. You had no right."

Possessive outrage flared in Caedyrn's link and he stepped closer to Sorcha as she lolled on the comforting ice. "She is mine. You cannot undo our choice; we are bonded whether you acknowledge our union or not. The clutch will be strong. She gave a magnificent mating flight."

"Be that as it may," growled the Rex, "you have betrayed my trust. You had no right to mate, Caedyrn."

"I had every right," Caedyrn answered, his words dangerously quiet. "I am not rex. I am free to take a mate if I choose."

"No, you are not rex, and now you never will be." The Rex turned his troubled gaze on Sorcha. "Do you accept Caedyrn as your bond-mate?" he asked.

Sorcha returned his stare, inclining her head slightly. "I have known him to be my destiny since I first awoke in dragon form." She turned to look at Caedyrn and their eyes locked. A thrill of excitement tingled all the way from nose to tail — and she understood part of the Rex's concern. "I accept Caedyrn," she said, her gaze never leaving her mate's, "and I accept the clutch that will soon arrive."

With great effort, Sorcha raised herself from the ice and faced the Rex, summoning all the dignity her years at court could provide. "I am no longer human. I am dragon; a member of your flight, bond-mate to Caedyrn and mother to the clutch I will soon lay. Will you accept me, Sire?"

The Rex sighed. "I accept you, Sorcha, Caedyrn's mate." His eyes locked with Caedyrn's. "Though I mourn the rex he would have been."

He turned his thoughts to the flight and widened their link. "Caedyrn and Sorcha have chosen each other, and Sorcha has chosen the flight.

Will you accept them? Will you accept their clutch and all future clutches?"

A tidal wave of excitement washed over Sorcha's mind, and she relaxed into the well wishes and congratulations of her flight. Only later, in the privacy of the lair she now shared with Caedyrn, did she realize that the Rex had chosen not to resolve her status as ambassador for the flight, despite her new status as accepted member.

THE CLUTCH

"*B*reathe deeply, Sorcha. Relax and let the eggs drop"

Drysta's encouragement filled the corner of Sorcha's mind not absorbed in ending the uncomfortable distention of her mid-section.

"My human nature keeps messing with me," Sorcha said with a rueful laugh. "Human females are anything but relaxed during childbirth." Her thoughts turned to Elspeth. Had her mother suffered giving her life? She wished her mother could be here, not just for Elspeth's calm, imperturbable presence, but because it would mean she knew of and shared in Sorcha's new life.

Instead, Keeva's mother, Drysta, murmured encouragement across their private link. Etna had claimed her right as Sorcha's teacher to attend the clutching, but Sorcha, still irritated by Etna's attempt to keep her from rising, had denied her request.

Well, then," said Drysta, "rejoice that you are a dragon now."

"Oh, believe me, I do!" Visions of her beloved Caedyrn flashed through her mind. She would always miss her human life and form, but life as a dragon held excellent compensations.

"You're doing fine. Soon this awkwardness will be behind you and you'll have the joy of a healthy clutch."

"Oh!" Sorcha cried aloud, making Drysta wince. "Oh, I think one's coming!"

"Quietly, little sister," Drysta said with a laugh, "use the link. Now, stand up straight. That's right, elongate your body and let the egg drop."

Gods and goddesses! Sorcha's first egg plopped into Drysta's waiting claws.

"Perfect," sighed Drysta, laying the egg carefully in the prepared depression beside Caedyrn and Sorcha's nest.

"Thank you for being here," Sorcha said as she curled back onto the ice. Caedyrn had wanted to stay while Sorcha laid their clutch, but she had turned on him and driven him from their lair with feminine volatility. Only another female, preferably an experienced mother, could guide her through this process.

Her mind turned again to her own mother. How had Elspeth managed? Deserted by Sorcha's father, abandoned by her mentor because she refused to give Sorcha up as wizard tradition demanded, shunned by her village because she had neither husband nor master; Sorcha had never fully appreciated her mother's sacrifice until this moment, when she could gaze upon the promise of her first child. A moment's melancholy seized her as she realized that, for all Elspeth knew, Sorcha, too, had abandoned her. She resolved to find a way to visit her mother as soon as this clutch was safely hatched.

The need to drop another egg drove all thought from her mind. She rose up onto her hind legs, blessing the ancient dragon who had carved this spacious lair, and expelled one egg, and then another.

"Excellent, little sister," Drysta crooned. "Three are safely out. A large clutch rarely exceeds seven, and since this is your first, you're probably nearly finished."

"I don't feel nearly finished," Sorcha panted. "I still feel bloated."

A bright thread of amusement shimmered across Sorcha's mind. "I remember. I thought I'd never be done dropping Keeva and her sibs, and yet here I am. You're doing fine, Sorcha."

Sorcha rose, elongated, and felt a fourth egg slide from her body. Relief and exhilaration swept over her. She rode the crest of that wonderful sensation, and wished her human friends could experience such satisfying deliveries.

Keeva slipped into the lair and approached Drysta. "Can I help?"

"Oh, Keeva," Sorcha sighed. "Thanks so much for loaning me your mom!"

The young female's eyes widened as she caught sight of the four gleaming eggs. Pride surged through Sorcha as she stretched high and expelled a fifth into Drysta's waiting claws. "Very nice," crooned the matron, placing the new arrival with its sibs. She turned to her daughter. "Inform Caedyrn that he has five eggs so far, and ask his permission to attend the clutch. If he agrees, you can guard her children while Sorcha rests."

Sorcha smiled at Keeva's eager expression as she slithered from the chamber.

"I hope you don't mind," Drysta said. "She'd hoped to bond and have a clutch of her own — being near your eggs will soothe her."

"Really? I would expect her to want to avoid my eggs. The reminder would be painful for a human."

Drysta looked shocked. "Well! How odd. Trust me; every unbonded female in the aerie would consider it an honor to help with your clutch. Keeva will be envied."

"Oh, goddess," Sorcha breathed as the sixth and final egg slid into Drysta's protective embrace. "I'm finished. I didn't realize I'd be able to tell!" Euphoria swept her body and she settled full length on the ice, a pleasant lethargy enfolding her mind. *Congratulations, Mother,* she thought. *You'll soon have six grandchildren, and I'm going to make sure you know it.*

"Well done, Sorcha. Six eggs is an excellent first clutch. May you produce many more."

"Thank you." She arranged her strangely empty body around her eggs and, satisfied that no one could approach her clutch without treading on her, she allowed herself to slip into blissful slumber. A dim recess of her mind acknowledged Caedyrn as he entered their lair, inspected his mate and their eggs, and then curled himself protectively around his family.

The next few weeks melted away in happy contentment. Drysta explained that the clutch would hatch approximately two months after being laid. Keeva spent a good portion of each day helping Sorcha care for the clutch. The dragons bathed the eggs in fiery breath every few hours before turning each one, carefully exposing a different section of shell to the cooling ice.

Fire and ice. Even before hatching, dragons lived in the precarious balance between those extremes. Occasionally Sorcha worried about that other knife-edge her children would face. Just how much would her human essence affect these soon-to-be hatchlings?

Time would tell, but she knew that she and Caedyrn would protect these precious lives with their own if necessary. Each night, just before falling into their own much-needed slumber, Caedyrn and Sorcha lovingly fired their eggs, turned them tenderly, and then curled around them to maintain their balance through the midnight hours.

DESTINY

That same delicate balance between extremes ruled the lives of the adult dragons. Living in the frozen wastes allowed the dragons to control their magical fires, which in turn allowed them to feed infrequently. Their energy reserves amazed Sorcha, and the glacial cold reduced their need to slake their power in blood.

But, inevitably, the need to feed drew Sorcha from the comfort of the aerie and the care of her clutch. Not her own need, but Keeva's. Her nursemaid, unwilling to leave the clutch, had nearly depleted her energy reserves. Because she'd waited too long, desperation had driven Keeva to take an unwise risk. She had attempted to snatch a ewe from a flock sheltered securely near the village that nestled at the base of their mountain.

Sorcha raced to the aerie entrance and leapt to the sky when she heard Keeva's scream of pain and terror. She arrowed toward the land of men, with Caedyrn bellowing in her wake.

"Sorcha," he screamed, both vocally and through their private link. "Wait. The flight will deal with this. You can't save her alone!"

"I can," she said without a pause in her furious wing strokes. "I must! If I can't, why did the Heart of Fire force this transformation upon me? Ask the Rex to let me try before his warriors interfere."

"You'll die with Keeva," he whispered into her mind, "and my life will end as well. Who, then, will care for our offspring?"

The entire flight saw the scene through Keeva's eyes, and Sorcha felt the Rex's reluctant restraint upon his dragons. The villagers had been ready for the young female. While she sat on the ground, claws slicing the ewe's white wool, men had catapulted a huge fishing net over her. She'd twisted at the mechanism's sound and the net had missed her head, but her wings were fouled and she couldn't get off the ground. While she fumbled against the restraints, armored knights staked the net into the ground. Keeva lay in her captor's power; unable to escape, unable to feed. The mauve female was doomed, whether the men knew how to slay her or not.

Sorcha sang soothing words into Keeva's link. "Rest, my friend," she crooned. "Don't let fear steal the last of your energy. Caedyrn and I will deal with the men. You shall have your feast. Close your eyes. Conserve your energy."

The pair of bond-mates cast a deep shadow over the glade when they arrived. Sorcha watched the villagers scatter and fought her desire to flame their homes out of existence. She reached deep within and found her human soul cowering behind her dragon indignation. Remember, she thought. Remember their fear, the terror of dragons on the wing. Remember what it is to be small and unscaled, with only your wits to save you.

"Stay aloft," she commanded Caedyrn as she landed beside Keeva and yanked stakes from the net. When the young female was free, Sorcha ordered her to take her ewe and escape. "Live well, my sister," she called to the mauve. "Guard my eggs."

Keeva obeyed, and Sorcha turned her bulky body toward the pair of knights on horseback who rode at her with lances set. Caedyrn screamed his rage and frustration from the air above, but Sorcha gave a small downbeat of wings and hopped over the mounted men. While they turned, she cried in a voice rusty with disuse, "Bring me Elspeth. I would treat with the King's Wizard."

The knights pulled up and kept their prancing horses at a safe distance. The one on the bay horse lifted his faceplate and asked, "How do you know that name?"

Sorcha's eyelids lifted closed as she remembered her mother—the warmth of her love, the smell of herbs that clung to her robes and hair, the joy in her smile when Sorcha succeeded in a simple charm. Elspeth. A woman of such intelligence and determination that she had risen to King's Wizard despite all the stigma and prejudice arrayed against her. Grief that Elspeth would never understand her mate or their offspring assailed Sorcha as she replied, "She is my mother."

Before the knights could react or Caedyrn recognize her peril, the transformation began. Pain wracked Sorcha's immense body. She burned from the tip of her pearly pink snout to the point of her thrashing tail. Her claws gouged the soft earth as she fought to keep from turning inside out. Waves of agony forced her to the ground. More intense than any sensation she'd ever endured, the pain twisted her gut, leaving her writhing and misshapen. The musty, moist smell of fresh- turned dirt assaulted her nostrils, and she knew she dug her own grave.

Through a tunnel, far away, she felt Caedyrn land, heard him bellow for men to bring blankets, hot drinks, and the King's Wizard. In her mind, through their private link, his voice cascaded over the fires searing her soul. "Be strong, my Sorcha. Don't let go, my love. You must live. I need you. Our clutch needs you. You are the hope of the world."

She didn't feel like the hope of the world. She didn't feel like anyone's hope. She succumbed to excruciating pain and consciousness fled.

———

Cold. Why was the lair so cold? Were her eggs safe? Sorcha couldn't remember ever being this cold. The ice aerie felt refreshing, but never cold. She tried to open her eyes, to check on the safety of her clutch, but her muscles refused to respond. She lay still and fought to assess her ills. Grass tickled her body and the loamy scent of tilled earth tugged at her memory. A scratchy, rough wool blanket weighed on her limbs, but did nothing to ease the bone-chilling cold. She searched her mind for the bright, pulsing thread that connected her to the flight, and panicked when she couldn't catch it.

"No!" Sorcha screamed and threw her body upright against her muscles' protests. Her eyes flew open and she fought to focus her eyes.

The massive black dragon lowered his head and stared into her eyes. Caedyrn had inflated monstrously. They had been nearly of a size. Now he dwarfed her. She clutched the blanket to her breasts and stared in disbelief.

"Be at ease, my love," he said. His words lit the darkness in her mind and tamed the elusive connecting thread. "You are human once more." She felt as well as heard the overtone of misery in his words. "But our bond remains strong. You will always be my bond-mate."

Careless of modesty, Sorcha struggled to her feet and threw herself at Caedyrn's neck. She clung to the black dragon and sobbed, stricken by their loss.

Caedyrn wrapped a wing around her, sheltering her from the villagers' curious stares. The whole community stood at the edge of the field and whispered over the spectacle of a dragon shielding a human woman.

"Sorcha?"

Elspeth called her daughter's name, and Caedyrn withdrew his curtaining wing. Elspeth stepped forward and offered a robe for

Sorcha's use. Sorcha accepted the covering and collapsed in her mother's arms.

"I don't understand what's happening," Elspeth said to Caedyrn, "but I thank you for protecting my daughter." She hugged Sorcha tightly, inclining her head to the massive beast.

"Your daughter will explain all," Caedyrn growled. "I will return when she calls." The mighty dragon lifted from the earth and circled the soft blue sky.

Sorcha raised her head and watched with swollen eyes as her heart and soul streaked toward the ice aerie — and home.

———

ELSPETH STROKED Sorcha's hair as they sat in the village elder's cottage. The townsfolk had retreated; allowing mother and daughter a measure of privacy, but Sorcha could hear their excited chatter just outside the thin wooden walls.

"Drink your tea, my love," Elspeth said.

Even without a mind link, Sorcha could hear the fear and concern in her mother's voice, but grief and loss clogged her throat and kept her silent. She took a tentative sip of tea and immediately spat it out. She'd forgotten that humans had to think about trivial things like the temperature of liquids. Rueful laughter followed the tea from her lips. She, who had expelled fire from her maw, couldn't deal with a mouthful of hot tea.

"Tell me, Sorcha," Elspeth murmured. "Tell me what happened. What did that dragon do to you?"

The cup clattered to the floor as Sorcha jumped to her feet and began to pace the kitchen. The elder's wife's best dress tangled around her legs, adding to Sorcha's agitation. She stopped abruptly as she caught sight of herself in an ancient mirror that hung beside the elder's desk.

Between her rigid posture, blazing eyes and richly embroidered dress, she looked like a noblewoman. The thought grounded her. Time to put aside her disorientation and take up the destiny laid on her by the amulet, which weighed more heavily upon her psyche than its double-looped chain did upon her neck.

"Caedyrn did nothing to me that I did not wish. This was my doing. Mine...and the Heart of Fire's." She yanked the medallion from around her neck and slammed it onto the table. "I found it. I summoned it from the lagoon, and yes, you were right about the cost. It transformed me into a dragon. It thrust me from one life into another, with no warning and no way to turn back."

As suddenly as it had begun, Sorcha's indignation deserted her and she crumpled onto the hard wooden bench beside her mother. "And now it has pulled me back, and I don't want to be here."

"What do you mean? Why don't you want to be here?"

"Because..." She drew a shuddering breath and lifted tear-filled eyes to meet her mother's. "I found my soul-mate. I bonded with Caedyrn. He is my life." She buried her head in her hands and sobbed with soul-deep misery.

"Sorcha, darling, think! You're confused. You don't know what you're saying. That was a dragon, our mortal enemy. He has bewitched you."

Sorcha dried her eyes and stared at her mother with all the glacial ice of her distant home. Fear bloomed in Elspeth's eyes.

Illumination seared Sorcha's soul, and she plucked the Heart of Fire from the table's solid surface. Her ambassadorship had never been the flight's to grant. The Heart of Fire intended her to represent humanity, but from a perspective of never-before-possible understanding.

"Take me to the king," she commanded. "I must fulfill the destiny the Heart of Fire has laid upon me."

AMBASSADOR OF PEACE

*K*ing Leofric regarded Sorcha with distrust and distaste. "You expect me to believe that necklace transformed you into a dragon?"

"I do, Sire," she replied. The icy calm that had gripped her soul since Caedyrn returned to their clutch allowed her to bear the King's obvious disbelief with equanimity. "I have witnesses to my transformation. Your own knights will verify my tale."

She saw his eyes flick to the other side of the hall where armored men stood in uneasy silence.

"Yes, very well." He sighed and rubbed his stubbled chin. "Assuming I accept your statement, what is it that you expect of me?"

"I expect you to listen to me as I explain the peculiarities of a dragon's hearing. I expect you to appoint me ambassador and allow me to help you negotiate with their representative when I invite him to return. I expect you to forbid your knights and subjects to harm a single scale of a dragon's hide while we hammer out a truce."

Leofric stilled, his expression cold and stiff. Grumbling erupted from the men behind her, and she ignored them with effort. Her ears no longer retained dragon sensitivity, but she had grown disused to physical sound. The echoes in this stone hall worried her nerves. Even the tapestries lining the walls couldn't provide the dampening effect she longed for. When Caedyrn returned, negotiations would need to be held in an open meadow. Someplace where sound could dissipate and not bounce around to assault his delicate hearing over and over again.

"Be careful, young woman," Leofric growled. "I think you forget to whom you speak."

She doused the flames of anger and retreated behind a mask worthy of the aerie's ice. Bowing her head, she said, "Forgive me, Sire. This has been a very stressful time for me." Taking a deep breath, she tried again. "Sire, I remain in contact with the flight of dragons. If you will guarantee his safety, I will request that my, uh, my colleague join us for negotiations."

"And who will guarantee *my* safety?"

"I will, Sire." Her pulse raced with the magnitude of the lie she was about to utter. But alien or not, she trusted dragonkind far more than she trusted humans. Her time with the flight had shown her little in the way of deceit or treachery. Traits she knew well on the human side of the equation. "The Heart of Fire has magnified my powers. I am fully capable of protecting you from human and dragon alike." She paused and turned to face the king's knights. "I am also capable of exacting a terrible price from any who breaks the king's peace."

Leofric remained silent for a moment and then said, "So be it. You will act as my ambassador. You will be present at all negotiations to augment my understanding and guide my decisions, but make no mistake. They will be *my* decisions."

He clapped his hands and cried to the room at large, "Let the dragon ambassador return under my personal protection."

He paused, narrowed his eyes and stared directly at Sorcha. "Be warned, Wizard. If this dragon breaks my peace, your life will be forfeit."

Sorcha bowed and murmured, "As you wish, Sire," before turning to leave the room.

Upon reaching the safety of her assigned chamber, Sorcha barred the heavy wooden door and collapsed on the bed. She took several calming breaths before touching the link to Caedyrn's mind. The golden thread sizzled and sparked, and she felt the familiar warmth of his presence.

"Welcome, my love," he murmured. "Are you well?"

She laughed, giddy with relief at the concern in his thoughts. "I am well. The King is suspicious of my request to allow a dragon at court, but I am in no danger. How are our children?"

"Keeva dedicates herself to their care. She blames herself for your loss. The Rex himself has vowed to guard them if I am called to return to the south. Will you call me, my love?"

"Yes. King Leofric has placed you under his personal protection. Come when the Rex allows and we will negotiate the peace as the Heart of Fire intended."

"I'm not sure what the Heart of Fire intended," he growled, "but I am grateful for our time together."

She felt his emotion light her soul, and shivered with a cruel mixture of delight and despair. "As am I. I'm not happy with this turn of events, but I am grateful. Give Keeva my love and my thanks. She is not to blame."

"I will tell her you said so. Be well, my love. I will join you tomorrow."

———

UNABLE TO SLEEP, Sorcha climbed to the battlements to greet the dawn. She carried herself with dignity though she could feel the suspicious glances of the guards who paced the wide stone walkway. Stepping into the shadow of a deep crenellation, she turned in time to see one warrior sketch a protective sigil between him and where she stood. As deep purple turned to rosy orange, she surveyed the brightening fields with tear-misted eyes. Once, this castle and its bustling town had been her home. She'd been happy here, practicing her craft and avoiding messy entanglements with men who found a young woman of power a compelling aphrodisiac. But then she'd chosen to call the Heart of Fire, and the price had indeed been great.

She blinked back her tears and studied her homeland. The sheltered valley rose in the southern distance to foothills and majestic crags, but at the north, a lake winked in the sun's first rays. The forest behind the lake remained dark, but the meadow before it gleamed with green-gold promise.

There, she thought. We will hold our council there before the lake. She raced down from the battlement, ignoring the whispered comments of the servants going about their morning tasks.

"You there, squire," she called to a youth standing near the castle gate.

He turned and approached with obvious reluctance. "My lady?"

"Run and fetch the castle steward. Ask him to join me there." She turned and pointed up to the top of the gate. "A gold piece will be yours if you have him back within ten minutes." The young man's face brightened and he ran to do her bidding.

He returned well within the allotted time, urging a panting older man in his wake. Sorcha laughed and pulled the promised coin from her pocket. The youth hesitated for only a moment before taking it, but avoided touching her fingers. Her smile hardened and she turned to face the steward.

"Thank you for coming, Sir Dougal. Please, join me."

The dignified, gray-haired man moved to stand beside her on the battlement. "How may I be of service?"

"I've decided that our negotiations with the dragon should take place beside the lake." She directed his attention to the meadow she'd chosen. "Please arrange for a pavilion for the king's comfort."

They spent a few moments discussing details about what the meeting would require, and then the steward bowed over her hand and left to make the preparations.

With that duty performed, Sorcha set out to walk to the lake. She strolled down the main street of the village, pretending she neither knew nor cared that the folk stared and made protective signs. Once beyond the gate, she relaxed and enjoyed her solitary stroll. The sun was well up by now and the sky a soft, hazy blue. Buttercups bloomed in profusion and red clover dotted the meadow. Before her sojourn in the ice aerie, she would have been watching for medicinal herbs as she walked, but now the sky called her. Gods and goddesses! It would be a glorious day for a flight!

She stopped, closed her eyes, and grounded herself in the here and now. She was what she had been born to be — a human woman with magical gifts. The breeze whispered through the tall grass, wafting sweet scents of blossoms and good earth to her nose. Birds warbled in bushes at the water's edge, and she detected the scurrying pace of a small creature in the undergrowth at her feet. The sun felt warm on her face and she could access her power once again.

Give it time, she thought. *Life will be good again.* But she knew she would never be completely happy, not without Caedyrn.

With a heavy sigh, she opened her eyes and continued to the lake's edge. Once there, she found a good sized rock, sat down and called Caedyrn to the chosen place. She barely touched his mind before she saw him soaring toward her, at first no larger than an eagle.

Her heart skipped a beat as he landed gracefully beside the lake. She jumped from her rock perch, ran forward and launched herself at him. Even widespread, her arms couldn't span his chest.

He stroked her back with a single claw. "You are so tiny, my love," he crooned into their link. "I must be careful not to crush you, or burn you with a flame."

Tears filled her eyes. "If you did, I would die happy. I've missed you so!"

"Your fragility concerns me," he said. "Climb onto my back where I'll know you're safe." She stepped carefully up on his knee and then pulled herself onto his shoulder. She nestled comfortably at the joint where his folded wing met his broad back, and caressed his leathery scales.

"What will become of us, Caedyrn?" she asked, leaning her cheek against his shoulder and reveling in his smoky smell.

"We will love from afar," he said. "We are bonded for eternity. I do not know about your human heart, but there can be no other for me."

"Nor for me," she agreed. "When they are old enough, you will bring the children to meet me?" A painful bubble threatened to steal her breath, making her glad she didn't have to speak aloud to be understood.

"Of course," he said. "They will be proud to know you, as is the entire aerie. Keeva and her lair mates sing your praises to our children already, though they are still in the shell."

The lovers rested quietly in the idyllic setting, content for the moment to be reunited in their thoughts, despite the bustle of the steward and his assistants, who came to ready the site for the king's comfort.

When the King and his entourage arrived, Sorcha scrambled down and smoothed her rumpled skirts. She pulled the Heart of Fire from her pocket and double-looped the chain around her neck. The amulet dangled at her breast, an indisputable badge of office.

"King Leofric." She made a low curtsey before rising to make introductions. "Sire, I am proud to present Caedyrn, ambassador of the dragons."

Leofric nodded to the dragon without relinquishing eye contact.

"Caedyrn, this is King Leofric. I will act as his advisor as the two of you negotiate our treaty."

"An honor, Sire. My Rex will be monitoring our conversations. If I agree to terms, you may be sure the flight, as a whole, agrees as well."

Sorcha reveled in the musicality of Caedyrn's speech, but glancing around she saw that the rest of the king's entourage found his voice unpleasant. She sighed. She took so much for granted these days, forgetting that her experience was unique.

The negotiations devoured the daylight hours. Caedyrn, and through him, the Rex, drove a hard bargain with Leofric. Sorcha restrained her desire to protect the flight and argued tirelessly for humanity's rights. By the end of the day, peace flickered on the edge of reality.

"With your permission, Sire," she said, bowing to Leofric, her voice hoarse from overuse, "King Leofric agrees to maintain a hunting preserve at the northern fringe of the kingdom for the sole use of the flight of dragons. The preserve will be kept stocked at all times and armed knights will patrol the borders to keep poachers at bay."

King Leofric nodded, his jaw clenched and mouth grim. Sorcha breathed a sigh of relief. This concession would cost the King dearly, forcing him to demand cattle and sheep from each village to build the self-sustaining herds, and then there was the matter of recruiting knights to guard dragon fodder. Sorcha smiled wearily, she would be working hard to help disgruntled people recognize the benefits of this treaty.

Caedyrn cleared his throat. "In return, the flight of dragons agrees to hunt only in the designated preserve, so long as sufficient stock is maintained," he added with a growl. "Further, the flight agrees to come to the aid of Leofric's people in the event of natural disaster, such as flood or fire. Hatchlings will be trained in the safe transportation of people and goods from one village to another, and Leofric will instruct his people in respect for dragons and proper etiquette for requesting the flight's assistance."

"The court scribe will draw up the papers, to be signed tomorrow afternoon," Leofric said. "Let these negotiations be at an end."

An hour later, Sorcha stood at the edge of the lake with King Leofric in the last rays of the evening sun.

"I don't pretend to understand how you brought this about, Sorcha," he said, "but you have served your people well. I have never treated directly with dragons before. I had no idea they possessed such intelligence and even honor. Thank you, my lady. I hope you will remain as one of my councilors, continuing to expand my understanding of dragons."

"I would be honored, Sire. And I hope that you will be willing to allow dragons to visit court on occasion."

He started to protest, but Sorcha cut him off. "It will set a good precedent. If the King is willing to receive dragons, his people will be as well."

Leofric eyed her narrowly, but then his gaze lightened and he nodded. "As you wish, my lady." He laughed gruffly. "Your mother is always pointing out that advisors are worthless if I refuse to heed them."

She smiled wearily and glanced over his shoulder to where her bond-mate waited. "Thank you, Sire. Elspeth will be pleased to hear that you remember her counsel." A sigh escaped her lips, and she experienced a moment's loss at the lack of flames. "If you will excuse me, Sire, I'd like a word with Caedyrn before he returns to the flight."

The King nodded, and she curtsied low before turning to walk with impatient dignity to Caedyrn's side.

"Will you trust me, my love," Caedyrn's voice whispered in Sorcha's mind.

"Always," she replied along their link.

"Then I have a surprise."

And before she could utter a word of warning to Leofric or his courtiers, Caedyrn scooped her gently in his taloned forefoot and sprang into the sky.

TRANSFORMING DESTINY

*C*aedyrn landed lightly on the lagoon's white sands and deposited Sorcha carefully on her feet. The last light of the dying sun stained the water blood red. She gazed at the pink-tinged waves breaking over the distant reef and sighed. So much had happened since she last stood upon these sands.

"You've grown on me since I first saw you standing there, my little wizard." Caedyrn nudged her with his muzzle and she stretched high to scratch his eye ridge.

"Indeed," she said. "When I put that chain around my neck, I acted in defiance. I expected to die. Instead I discovered the reason for my life."

"Have you ever wondered what would have happened if I had worn the Heart of Fire instead of you? Clearly, from the size of the chain, it was intended for a dragon's neck, not a human's."

She turned and stared at him, astonishment tingling along her spine. "No! I mean, I only knew it fit me fine in dragon form. But if you were to wear it, why should I be the one to summon it?"

"Perhaps we were destined to work together. Perhaps it made no difference who wore it, as long as the other was there to act as a guide."

Sorcha pulled the medallion from around her neck. The heavy opal glistened in its golden filigree setting. "You've certainly changed my life," she whispered to the stone, her eyes misting with tears.

"Sorcha, put it around my neck. Right here, where it all began — put it on me."

Her hand convulsed on the opal and she stared wide-eyed at Caedyrn. "What? Why?"

"Humor me, my love," he whispered. "If the magic has run its course, there can be no harm, but if..." His thought trailed off as if he were unwilling to share so fragile a hope.

Keeping his eyes locked on hers, Caedyrn lowered his majestic head. Sorcha hesitated an instant and then stretched high to lower the loop of gold across his neck. The blast of pain that seared her mind was not her own, but all the worse because it belonged to her beloved — and her hand had allowed it. She staggered away from the writhing dragon, all the while thrusting love and encouragement through their link, willing him to live, to thrive, to survive this transformation he had willingly sought.

When the seizure ended, a dark-skinned, well-muscled man lay naked and crumpled on the beach, as if thrown ashore by a violent storm. The Heart of Fire lay beside him on the sand, lapped by the quiet water. Sorcha watched in fascinated horror as the medallion gathered the threshold magic of sea/land, day/night, dragon/human into a blue-green sphere and vanished into the lagoon.

Caedyrn moaned and Sorcha raced to his side. Turning him gently, she cradled his head in her lap and brushed sand from his cheek and brow, all the while whispering words of reassurance both verbally and into their private link. Slowly, his muscles relaxed and he slept.

Sorcha rocked her now human mate and prayed he would never regret this irremediable choice.

"He will not regret it, Sorcha."

She turned her head to find the Rex resting on the sand a few hundred feet away. He inclined his head to her, and a bubble of happy contentment swelled her chest.

"You were too preoccupied to notice my arrival. To repeat, he will not regret his choice."

She glanced down at the handsome, powerfully built man who slept in her embrace. "How can you be sure?"

"Because his essence will always be dragon, and deprived of our bond-mates, we wither and die. Caedyrn could not live without you by his side. You will be together now. He will learn to function in your world, just as you learned to live in ours. Come, little wizard, let me return you to your home."

Very gently, the Rex lifted Caedyrn from her lap and cradled him in his right forefoot. Sorcha settled herself into his left forefoot and clung tightly to his leg. Emotionally exhausted as she was, the journey seemed interminable, but at last it ended with the Rex landing lightly on the road just beyond the castle gate. Guards ran out to meet them, but stopped well back, awed by the mighty dragon.

"Come quickly," Sorcha called, struggling to find her balance as the Rex released her. "Help me get this man to my chambers in the castle."

The guards exchanged puzzled looks, but did as directed. Sorcha smiled; being the king's councilor had its advantages.

"Thank you, Sire," she said, turning back to the Rex. A thought trembled on the edge of their link, but she refused to give it life.

"You are welcome, Sorcha. Keep him safe." He lowered his head so that his eye twinkled on a level with her own. "And have no fear for your clutch. They will be raised as my own and will be brought to visit as soon as they are old enough to fly."

He raised his head, and with a mighty swipe of his wings leapt to the sky. "Be well, Sorcha of the humans. May the peace you have wrought last for a thousand years!"

———

Sorcha slept deeply, comforted by Caedyrn's solid presence in her bed. When she woke, she found her beloved bond-mate examining his new body. She smiled and slipped beneath his arm, snuggling her own soft curves neatly against the lean plane of his side. She rested her head in the hollow of his shoulder and threw one leg possessively across his upper thighs.

He responded by stroking her back with one long-fingered hand, while his other traced the outline of her fingers where they splayed across his chest.

Sorcha touched their private link and shared his pleasure as he recognized the essentially male tensions of desire his new body exhibited. He raised his head and gazed down at the erection prominently displayed against the delicate pink skin of her leg.

He grinned broadly, and Sorcha shivered with delight at the thought of learning the ways of human sexuality together.

"Good morning, beloved," she said, her voice husky with desire. "Human mating doesn't involve flight, but I'm told it can be strenuous. Would you like to eat before we explore our new union?"

He rested his head back on the pillow and gazed into her eyes. His stomach rumbled loudly, but a wicked smile played across his lips. "Teach me, my love," he said, eager anticipation burning through their link. "I am yours to command, and my strength is legendary."

Sorcha smiled and kept her eyes locked on his as she slid her hand down his body to stroke his first erection. "This will be a new experience for both of us," she said. "I've never made love as a human, either." She leaned close and kissed him lightly. "But I do understand the theory. We'll perfect our craft together."

Caedyrn pulled her close and kissed her again. "I like this dance of tongues," he whispered, practicing his verbal speech, "but I think I'd like to explore other parts of this new form you're in."

And with that, all formal communication ceased as the reunited lovers explored every inch of skin each possessed. Caedyrn delighted in finding places that made Sorcha writhe and pant, and Sorcha took equal joy in producing a glassy-eyed, completely mindless expression on her bond-mate's face.

At last, Sorcha moved to straddle his hips as he lay on his back, watching her with growing appreciation. "We have a lifetime to explore all our possibilities," she murmured. "This morning let's try a simple position."

She leaned forward, brushed his lips with her own, and then straightened, shifted back a few inches, and took him fully into herself. His eyes widened and dilated, and she knew her own expression must mirror his. She shuddered convulsively at the unexpected overload of sensations. Trying to adjust to his shaft, she moved up and down. Gods and goddesses! The sensations just kept coming! She increased the pace of her rhythm — exquisite sensations filling, receding, pushing, expanding.

"Touch me!" she cried, her words terse, but their link filled with inexpressible joy.

His hands flew to her breasts, her sides, her belly. Everywhere his fingers touched, her skin burned. Dragon flame! Exhilarating dragon flame lived in his passionate caresses.

Caedyrn's culmination came quickly. He jerked upright, clenched her hips to his loins, and experienced his first shuddering release. Sorcha contracted around him, accepting his offering with wild abandon, until she cried out and fell forward onto his chest, well satisfied and content.

After a few moments, she slid bonelessly from atop him and snuggled against his side. Touching their link with a sudden shyness, she found him enraptured.

"It's not necessary to produce eggs with each mating?" he asked, absorbing knowledge from her mind. "We can do this often?"

She smiled, her eyelids drowsing closed. "As often as you are able," she murmured.

He hugged her tightly. "Then I shall work to increase my stamina. This new body may not be able to fly, but it has definite advantages."

EPILOGUE

Sorcha raced into the king's study and grabbed Caedyrn's hand.

"Excuse me, Sire." She bobbed a sketchy curtsey to the King and pulled Caedyrn away from the chessboard. "You've closed your link again," she scolded as she pushed, pulled and shoved him into the corridor. "It's time! Our clutch is hatching."

Caedyrn roared with delight, picked up his wife and swung her in a wide circle, much to the amusement of passing courtiers.

"Not here," she cried, trying and failing to suppress a giggle. "We've got to get to our chamber!"

The pair fairly flew along the hall, up the stairs and into their private chamber where they collapsed in a frantic heap on the bed.

Caedyrn pulled her securely into his arms and they opened their link as wide as possible to the flight of dragons.

Keeva summoned the flight, her excitement palpable. "It's time! They're hatching! Caedyrn and Sorcha's clutch, they're hatching!"

Even the Rex forgot his dignity in his rush to be present at the momentous event. Every dragon who could squeezed into the lair to witness the emergence of the legendary couple's hatchlings. Sorcha recognized Morna pressed tightly beside Goban. Oona pushed to the front with scarlet Toal close behind. Nuala, Sabia, Heber, Drysta, Etna. All her friends crowded the lair and passageways to greet her children. Keeva and the Rex curled close to the eggs, ready to breathe warm fires of welcome upon their tiny, damp inhabitants.

Sorcha held her breath and squeezed Caedyrn's arm. Gods and goddesses! What she wouldn't give to be there to greet her children! Thankfully, the dragon link gave her instant information.

Shells cracked and a blue female emerged, followed by two black males, a red female, a green female, and finally, a small, opalescent male.

The flight breathed a sigh of relief, and tears flowed down Sorcha's cheeks. All six hatchlings appeared healthy and whole. Those in the lair relayed images to the rest of the flight and the aerie rang with celebration.

Pop!

Sorcha held her breath as the Rex straightened upright so fast he cracked his skull on the lair's ceiling. Keeva drew back in surprise.

Pop. Pop; pop-pop-pop!

Silence blanketed the ice aerie as the flight of dragons received their first view of six naked human infants. Before Sorcha could say 'gods and goddesses', all six babies *popped* back to dragonets.

Keeva recovered first. "Well, Sire," she sighed. "No one said parenthood would be easy."

At the Rex's hearty guffaw, the entire flight dissolved in laughter, while Sorcha and Caedyrn stared at each other, too shocked for words.

———

WANT to know what happens next? Don't miss *Dragons' Choice*!

ALSO BY DEB LOGAN

Children's Stories and Chapter Books:

Cinnamon Chou Files:

- The Case of the Missing Inarian
- The Case of the Glittering Hoard
- The Case of the Recreational Thief
- The Case of the Vanishing Puppy
- The Case of the Missing Merchandise

Prentiss Twins Novels:

- Thunderbird
- Coyote
- White Buffalo
- The Twelve Days of Tricksters (Short Story)
- A Trickster Halloween (Short Story)

"Read-to-Me" Stories:

- Chattermaster
- Deirdre's Dragon
- The Fox and the Fleas
- Mom's Helper
- Read-to-Me Stories (Collection)

Short Story Collections:

- Galactic Cadets: Kids in Space
- Read-to-Me Stories

Short Stories:

- ANGELIC VOICES
- LILAH'S GHOST

Young Adult Stories and Novels:

Dani Erickson Stories:

- DEMON DAZE
- SCHOOL DAZE
- FAMILY DAZE
- CHALLENGING DAZE
- DANGEROUS DAZE
- DANI'S DEMONS (COLLECTION)

Faery Chronicles:

- FAERY UNEXPECTED (NOVEL)
- FAERY BEAUTIFUL (SHORT STORY)
- FAERY UNPREDICTABLE (NOVELETTE)
- LEXIE'S CHOICE (SHORT STORY)
- OF DRAGONS AND CENTAURS (SHORT STORY)
- FAERY COLLECTIBLE (COLLECTION)

Feyland Tie-Ins:

- EMMA: A FEYLAND DRYAD
- ON GUARD: A FEYLAND STORY

Seer Chronicles:

- THE SEER CHRONICLES: VOLUME 1 (COLLECTION)
- TERRORS (SHORT STORY)
- TO HAVE...AND TO HOLD (SHORT STORY)
- SELKIES IN PARADISE (SHORT STORY)

- The Journal (short story)
- Paladin Shield (short story)

Siren Tales:

- Salt Water
- Siren Surf

Short Story Collections:

- Ghosts and Ghoulies
- More Ghosts and Ghoulies

Short Fiction:

- Amelia Fox: Spy in Training
- Beauty or Butterface?
- Flutterbies and French Toast
- Rush!
- That Lake House Summer

"WDM Presents" Anthologies:

- Spun Yarns Unwound, Vol. 1
- Spun Yarns Unwound: Vol. 2
- Tales of Mystery & Mayhem
- 2016: A Year of Short Fiction
- 2017: A Year of Short Fiction
- WDM Presents: Short Fiction from 2018
- WDM Presents: Short Fiction from 2019
- WDM Presents: Short Fiction from 2020
- WDM Presents: Short Fiction from 2021

ABOUT DEB LOGAN

Deb Logan specializes in tales for the young – and the young at heart! Author of the popular Faery Chronicles series, Deb loves the unknown, whether it's the lure of space or earthbound mythology. She writes about demon hunters, thunderbirds, and everyday life on a space station for tweens, teens, and anyone who enjoys young adult fiction. Her work has been published in multiple volumes of *Fiction River*, as well as in *2017 Young Explorer's Adventure Guide*, *Feyland Tales*, and other popular anthologies.

Sign up for Deb's newsletter and receive a FREE story!

To learn more, visit Deb at:
debloganwrites.com
Or send her an email at:
debloganwrites@gmail.com

ALSO BY DEBBIE MUMFORD

Kristi Lundrigan Mysteries:

- DELECTABLE MOUNTAIN QUILTING (NOVEL)
- IN A PICKLE (NOVEL)
- FOOL'S PUZZLE (SHORT STORY)
- WILDFIRE! (SHORT STORY)

Gus and Ghost Short Story Series:

- SEVENTH
- SEVENTH: FIRST FRUITS
- DEATH OF AN ALCHEMIST (UNCOLLECTED ANTHOLOGY)
- SEVENTH: THE SAMHAIN DILEMMA
- DARK OF THE MOON (UNCOLLECTED ANTHOLOGY)

Logans of Lastalrig Series:

- HER HIGHLAND LAIRD (NOVELLA)
- HER HIGHLAND YULE (SHORT STORY)

Red's Series:

- RED'S MAGICK (SHORT STORY COLLECTION)
- SEEING RED (SHORT STORY)

Signs of the Prophecy Novels:

- YOUNGEST
- SEEKER
- CHOSEN (COMING SOON!)

Sorcha's Children Series:

- Sorcha's Children (Omnibus Edition)
- Sorcha's Heart (Novella)
- Dragons' Choice (Novel)
- Dragons' Flight (Novel)
- Dragons' Desire (Novel)
- Dragons' Destiny (Novel)

Supernatural Yellowstone Short Story Series:

- Reality Bites
- The Cat Lady of Yellowstone

Uncollected Anthology Short Stories:

- Death of an Alchemist (UA Alchemy)
- The Wedding Cake (UA Magical Arts)
- Dark of the Moon (UA Paranormal Pirates)
- In the Banyan Copse (UA Unexpected Histories)
- Old One (UA Magical Quests)

Universal Star League Short Story Series:

- Voyages Into The Black (Collection)
- The Warbirds of Absaroka
- Awakening the Warrior
- Incident on the Odyssey
- The Queen's Captive
- The Lost Colony
- Freighter Families in Space

Witchling Short Story Series:

- Witchling

- THE SOLITARY SORCERESS
- TO PROTECT A PRINCESS

Stand Alone Novels:

- SECOND SIGHT

Historical Fiction:

- HER HIGHLAND LAIRD (NOVELLA)
- HER HIGHLAND YULE
- INCIDENT ON THE HIGH LINE
- MISS BAINBRIDGE'S SUMMER ADVENTURE
- MISS BAINBRIDGE'S CHRISTMAS PARTY
- SISTERS IN SUFFRAGE
- THE TRAIL WHERE WE CRIED
- THE WHITE DRAGON AND THE RED

Short Story Collections:

- LOVE IN A FLASH
- TALES OF BYGONE DAYS
- TALES OF LOVE & MAGICK
- TALES OF THE UNEXPECTED
- TALES OF TOMORROW
- TALES OF DISASTROUS DEEDS

Short Fiction:

- A GROVE OF MOUNTAIN ASH
- A WALK WITH GEORGIA
- AN ALIEN ADVENTURE
- ASTROMANCER
- BECAUSE OF THE CHRISTMAS STROLL
- BENEATH AND BEYOND

- DEEP DREAMING
- DELIA'S DECISION
- EGG THIEF
- ICE STORM
- INCIDENT ON THE HIGH LINE
- IN SEARCH OF A VALENTINIAN
- JOLLY WELL DONE
- MISS BAINBRIDGE'S CHRISTMAS PARTY
- MISS BAINBRIDGE'S SUMMER ADVENTURE
- NEEDLE-GREEN
- NEW YEAR
- OPENING HER EYES
- REMEMBRANCE
- SILVER-TIPPED DEATH
- SIMON SAYS
- SISTERS IN SUFFRAGE
- SKYE DREAMS
- SPINNING
- THE TIE THAT BINDS
- THE TRAIL WHERE WE CRIED
- THE WHITE DRAGON AND THE RED
- TO DREAM OF FLYING
- TREASURES
- TRIAL ON THE TRAIL
- WAKINYAN'S VALLEY

"WDM Presents" Anthologies:

- SPUN YARNS UNWOUND, VOL. 1
- SPUN YARNS UNWOUND: VOL. 2
- TALES OF MYSTERY & MAYHEM
- 2016: A YEAR OF SHORT FICTION
- 2017: A YEAR OF SHORT FICTION
- WDM PRESENTS: SHORT FICTION FROM 2018
- WDM PRESENTS: SHORT FICTION FROM 2019

www.ingramcontent.com/pod-product-compliance
Lightning Source LLC
Chambersburg PA
CBHW060209030726
47499CB00004B/979